HERITAGE

THE SKY JEWEL LEGACY

GREGORY HEAL

ACKNOWLEDGEMENTS

To my family. Thank you for your support and patiently listening to me ramble on about this book during so many family dinners.

To my friends who have read over parts of this book in its many different iterations. You've pushed me to become a better writer.

To my editor. I enjoyed our journey and I hope to embark on more with you.

To you, the reader. It makes me feel so special that you are reading a story that has taken over my imagination since 2017. I hope it captures your imagination too.

HERITAGE

Book One of The Sky Jewel Legacy

By Gregory Heal

PROLOGUE

England
   Almost 1,500 years ago

With her last ounce of effort, Genevieve Lancaster reached deep into her nexus, casting every spell she had learned, deploying every tactic she had used in past duels, and relying on every instinct that had kept her alive for the past ten years as a mystra, the highest mantle given to a sorcerer or sorceress.

She could tell her life force was weakening as the continuous attacks of dark magic rammed into her protection spell. Every other sorcerer lay dead or dying around her—she was the only one of her kind left on Earth.

How did this happen? Genevieve thought.

Under the bright light of a full moon, Genevieve sent out a beacon spell calling for reinforcements, but she knew they would not get there in time. Gale-force winds buffeted her body, threatening to break her concentration. Her cloak flapped straight behind her, tugging at her throat. Yet still she focused on weakening Lord Ferox, funneling all of her power through the rings that glistened on her fingers.

Lord Ferox . . . the most sinister of all dark sorcerers.

Gritting her teeth, Genevieve planted her feet more firmly on the charred grass and pushed harder than she had ever pushed before, sending out spells to attack Ferox from every side.

He's just too strong!

The dark sorcerer was growing more powerful by the minute with the help of the combined powers of the five MystiCrystals and the ShadowCrystal, which were orbiting him like miniature moons. Her spells crashed into his own, ricocheting off with flashes of light that blinded Genevieve's vision.

I have to do something!

From out of the corner of her eye, Genevieve caught a glimpse of her younger sister, Gwendolyn, lying on the ground not twenty feet from her. For a moment she feared the worst, but then she saw Gwendolyn's chest rise and fall almost imperceptibly. They were shallow breaths, but thankfully she was still alive.

Gwendolyn awoke in that moment, as if she could sense her sister's eyes on her, and their eyes met. From where she lay, she faintly smiled through the pain and took out a small, oval stone from her ruffled cloak which shimmered with the most iridescent of purples. Her sister had treasured that stone for as long as Genevieve could remember. She still recalled the fond childhood memory of the day they were playing in the Sherwood Forest and Gwendolyn stumbled upon that very stone in a cave. Since then, she had always carried it with her, calling it her "Halostone" because it had a large, natural ring of gold inlaid in its polished surface, reminding Gwendolyn of an angel's halo. *My Halostone,* she'd said, and Genevieve could hear its proper title in her sister's voice as she stared long and hard at her keepsake.

Lord Ferox's voice brought Genevieve back to the present. Booming, he spewed, "How could you, of all people, expect to defeat *me*? I can feel your energy waning, Genevieve. No spell can hide that fact."

Taking her eyes off her sister, Genevieve shot a loathsome look at the dark lord. He was trying to get under her skin, she knew, but he wasn't lying: she only had a limited amount of time left before he would overtake her.

"Imagine what a fine apprentice young Philip would be . . . all of the things I could teach him . . ." He smirked, and all while his attacks bombarded her mercilessly.

Philip! Fear crept into her heart when she thought about what would happen to her infant son—Philip Lancaster II—if Ferox defeated her. Genevieve would do anything to keep him out of harm's way, and that meant keeping him out of the reach of Ferox and his infectious dark magic.

With that final bolstering thought, she nodded at Gwendolyn while Ferox was cackling away. With all her strength, Gwendolyn tossed the Halostone; it soared in a graceful arc between Genevieve and Ferox. When the stone reached the perfect center of the dueling sorcerers, Genevieve stopped attacking with her left hand and, with tears in her eyes, focused on the stone.

* * *

Gwendolyn watched helplessly as a beam of blue light shot forth from her sister's rings and hit her cherished Halostone. The whipping winds were so raucous that she couldn't hear what Genevieve yelled as a blinding light exploded from the stone and quickly enveloped the two sorcerers.

With surprise in his bedeviled eyes, Ferox let out a blood-curdling yell that faded into oblivion.

Gwendolyn pulled her hand away from her eyes in time to see the MystiCrystals and the ShadowCrystal shoot off in every direction, propelled by the shockwave of her sister's last spell. Turning her attention back to the aftermath, she found no sign of either Genevieve or Lord Ferox. The only items left on the eerily quiet, smoldering battlefield were the Halostone and Genevieve's signet ring, the Ring of Lancaster, both now lying harmlessly on the scorched grass.

Whimpering with effort, Gwendolyn crawled to the center of the battlefield and, before fainting from exhaustion, hugged the Halostone and her brave sister's ring to her chest.

For a brief moment, the full moon over England shone purple.

3

CHAPTER ONE

"Haaappy birrrthdayyy tooo youuu!"

The congregation of friends and family were slightly out of tune, but it was still heartwarming. They were all huddled around the kitchenette counter of a small studio apartment—just big enough for a college student who was attending New York University.

With happiness in her violet eyes and a big smile on her face, Jennifer Smith made a wish and blew out the twenty-one candles on her Danish layer cake. Once all the candles were extinguished, Jen leaned back into her chair while everyone clapped. She felt the ring on her necklace shift beneath her shirt, its metal cold against her collarbone.

Jen was considered attractive by many: a slender girl with wavy black hair. But her most striking feature was that of her enchanting eyes. Admiration seemed to come from everyone she met, and they would invariably comment on her eyes' rare coloring—deep violet irises flecked with gold. Her parents affectionately called her Jenny Jasmine, after one of the most beautiful purple flowers in the world. She loved her parents more than anything; they were supportive, encouraging, and loving to both her and her twelve-year-old brother, Tyler.

This year, her birthday was shaping up to be the best one yet—everyone she cared about was able to attend, including her boyfriend, Alex. He had been such a great addition to her life; in the three months since they had met, Jen already knew that Alex was different than every other guy she'd dated in the past, to the point where, sometimes, Jen thought he was too good to be true. What's more, her parents approved of him—which, according to their high standards, had seemed impossible.

Her dad started to sing: *"How ooold are youuu?"*

Before anyone else could chime in, Tyler interrupted, "Oh, come on, Dad! Can I have some cake now? I've been staring at it all day. I'm gonna die!"

Laughter broke out. With a smirk, Jen nodded. "Yeah, Dad. Ty's death would put a damper on my birthday, so we'd better feed him some cake," she joked.

As their mom cut the first slice of cake, Tyler pumped his fist in the air and stage-whispered, "Yes!"

* * *

In a quick fifteen minutes, the cake was thoroughly demolished, leaving only crumbs on the platter; wrapping paper lay strewn about the honorary chair where the birthday girl had opened her presents.

As the festivities died down, Jen walked outside and sat on the balcony of her apartment, absentmindedly playing with the ring on her necklace. She stared at the sunset, a lovely mix of yellow, orange, and red with wisps of pink and purple.

Alex snuck up behind her and, leaning in, kissed her on the cheek. "What are you doing out here all alone, babe?" he asked. "Everyone's inside."

Coming out of deep thought, she looked up into his eyes and smiled. "Hey. I know, I'm sorry. It's strange—I just have this . . .

feeling. I don't know how to explain it, but it feels like something's missing. Like I forgot to invite somebody or something . . ." She trailed off.

"Okay, look," Alex started, sitting down next to her and pointing at the group inside. "There are your parents, your brother Tyler"—his finger jumped from person to person—"your best friend Courtney. Am I forgetting anyone?" After scratching his head, his finger jabbed the center of his chest. "Oh, right—your amazing, good-looking boyfriend!" He showed that million-dollar smile before taking her free hand; her other was still grasping the ring. Alex looked at her necklace, then up into her eyes. "Who else could you have forgotten?"

She smiled again. "You're right. Thanks for reminding me. Something came over me right after I opened up my presents." In fact, Jen had noticed that the clock had struck her birth minute right after she had torn into her last present.

Alex paused as if in thought, then, only half jokingly, asked, "Mine was the best present, wasn't it?"

Jen did love the tennis bracelet he'd gifted her, but the diary from her parents meant the most to her. "Of course," she said, not wanting to hurt his feelings. She let go of the ring and squeezed his knee.

The ring glistened as the sun's low rays bounced off of its brushed silver and Jen noticed Alex intently staring at it. She looked down to admire its design as well. Top to bottom, the ring was only an inch long, but it held an intricate design: the writhing body of a ferocious yet svelte dragon, wrapped around two clashing swords. It all fit seamlessly inside an ornate shield. The ring's band was a deep obsidian black with mesmerizing purple flecks—vaguely reminiscent of Jen's beautiful eyes—all of which was inside two thin borders of brushed silver. None in her family knew its true age, but it looked to Jen as if it came straight from Arthurian legend.

Alex broke his gaze from the ring and looked at his girlfriend again. "That ring must mean a lot to you, huh?"

Jen cradled the ring. "Quite a lot. I've had it for as long as I can remember. My parents said it was given to me by a close family friend when I was born. I've never met them, but I've heard stories about how nice they were." She'd told all of this to him before, of course, but repeated the words now more out of comfort.

"How come you don't wear it on your finger?"

Jen was surprised at Alex's sudden interest in the ring. "I used to, but whenever I put it on, I wouldn't feel like myself. It felt too . . . regal. It means a lot to me, though, so I wear it on my necklace." She chuckled and looked at the ring. "Now I feel naked without it." She sighed, tucking the ring back beneath her shirt. "I'm just so glad you could make it." She put her head on his shoulder.

"I wouldn't miss it for the world."

The two of them stared off into the sunset in silence.

* * *

As the partygoers were filing out of the apartment, her parents gave Jen a big hug. "Happy birthday, Jenny Jasmine," her dad said with a smile.

"You're twenty-one!" exclaimed her mom, adding with a wink, "Don't party too late."

"That'll be easy once the Life of the Party is gone," Jen said, gesturing to Tyler. "Gimme a hug, you lug." She managed to grab his arm and pull him close.

"Eww, cooties . . . COOTIES!" Tyler squirmed as Jen enveloped him in a tight hug.

"Love you too, Ty," Jen said, letting him go.

"Good luck with all your finals, sweetie," her mom said, shrugging on her jacket.

"Thanks, Mom. I'll let you know how they go when I see you all this weekend!"

Jen waved as they walked down the hallway to the elevator. It chimed and its stainless-steel doors slid open. Jen watched as the three of them disappeared into the elevator. Time always seemed to pass too quickly whenever she was with her family, and she always couldn't wait to see them again.

Back inside her apartment, Alex and Courtney were the last remaining members of the cleanup crew. Courtney was finishing the dishes while Alex began picking up the shredded pieces of wrapping paper from the floor.

"How could this much wrapping paper come from five presents?" Alex said, wiping his forehead in exaggeration. "It just doesn't make sense."

"You should see the mess Tyler made during dessert!" Courtney countered. "He had three slices of cake, but it looks like the majority of it didn't even make it into his mouth."

They all laughed.

Jen walked over to help Alex with his task. "Ty sometimes eats so fast his mouth doesn't open in time for the next bite! That kid . . ." Jen laughed, shaking her head.

Courtney shut off the faucet and dried her hands. "Well, the kitchen is spotless, thanks to the dish-fairy." She curtsied, then walked over to the counter, picked up her purse, and yawned. "I'm beat."

Jen walked her to the door.

Courtney winked and whispered, "Have fun."

Jen blushed. "Thanks for coming, Court."

"Of course! I expect you to throw me a crazier party for *my* twenty-first."

"I'm already planning it. You're gonna love it, bestie."

"I'd better, or we're through," Courtney joked. "Ta!" She flipped her hair and walked to the elevator.

"Thanks—no pressure or anything!" Jen yelled after her. She locked the door and turned to Alex, who was hunched over, picking up the last, smallest paper pieces stuck to the carpeting.

"Hey, *Alllex* . . ."

He looked up just in time to drop the trash bag, catching her in his arms.

"Happy birthday, Jen."

His lips softly touched hers. The full moon peeked through the

9

windows as he put her on the couch and sat down beside her. Jen leaned in for another kiss, but he pulled away slightly and started to talk.

"You know, your eyes are so beautiful. They remind me of the Halostone." His thumb lightly brushed the outline of her cheekbone.

Jen rested her shoulder on the couch cushion and said, " 'The Halostone'? I've never heard of that kind of stone before. Is there such a thing?"

"Don't play coy with me, babe," Alex said. "Surely you know of the Halostone. It's the only one of its kind."

"And my eyes remind you of it?" Jen smiled. "That's very sweet. What does it look like?"

"Ha-ha, I think you know." Even though he gave a quick chuckle, Jen could see a different look in his eyes. He wasn't joking.

"No, I don't, *sweetie*," Jen responded, becoming slightly irritated. "How about you tell me about it?"

Alex let out another chuckle as he reached into his pocket and pulled out two rings. "Well, it's an oval, purple stone as big as your palm . . ." He slowly slid the rings onto his fingers as he spoke. "And it holds the world's most powerful dark sorcerer and his magic." He looked up, straight into Jen's eyes. All joking and flirting were gone.

Jen had never seen Alex act this way before. It was as if he'd become a different person. An uneasy feeling began to coil in the pit of her stomach. Feeling she should keep up the conversation, she commented, "A dark sorcerer, huh? That's pretty scary."

"Oh, you have no idea. He's the most powerful sorcerer the world has ever seen, but he's trapped in the Halostone." Alex grabbed ahold of her wrist, none too gently. "And now, Jen, I want you to tell me where it is."

A jolt of panic rushed through Jen. She tried to tug her wrist free, but his grasp only tightened. "Alex, what are you doing? I have no idea what you're talking about."

What's gotten into him?

"Come on, Jenny." He tugged harder. "You're a Lancaster. I *know* you know."

The evening had taken a quick turn, and now she was desperately thinking of how to get away from Alex. "A Lancaster?" Jen raised her voice. "You're hurting me!"

"Maybe I'll ease up if you're more cooperative." He squeezed harder.

With her free hand, Jen slapped Alex hard across the face. Not expecting the hit, he released his grip. Jen shot up off the couch and ran toward her balcony. Panicking, she tugged at its sliding door, but realized it was locked as cold sweat erupted from her skin.

"Come on, come on, *come on!*" Jen pleaded as she fumbled with the lock.

Alex felt his jaw, moving it from side to side as he stood up. He scoffed, incredulous, and clenched his fists. His rings began to glow a sickly orange, and suddenly Jen couldn't move. It was as if she were gripped with paralysis. Alex lifted his hands and Jen started to rise off the ground, all while invisible chords tightened around her body.

"Tell me where the Halostone is!" he yelled.

Jen could not speak. She could barely breathe. She was so frightened beyond belief that she couldn't even find the breath to scream for help. She felt a warmth on her chest and managed to look down to see her ring start to glow a soft purple.

Alex noticed it, too, and twisted his hands like he was turning doorknobs. Jen felt the pressure slowly crushing her.

"You can tell me." He was eerily calm now. "I'll give you a biiig kiss." A hideous smile spread his lips as he walked over to Jen, who was now levitating four feet off the ground.

The ring on her necklace shone more brightly. As the invisible chords constricted further, Jen began to lose consciousness.

Suddenly, she felt a warm burst of energy expel from her chest and slam into Alex. Caught unaware, he was thrown back fifteen feet, hitting the small of his back on the edge of the coffee table. With the wind knocked out of him, he lay there groaning in pain.

Almost immediately, the constricting pressure on her body dissipated and Jen fell to the ground in a heap, too weak to get up and run. No longer under Alex's spell—for that's what it was, she realized, a *spell*, some kind of magic—she breathed deeply before doubling over, clutching the right side of her chest. Swaying, the ring lightly tapped her on the chin, dangling just below her eyeline. Weakly grabbing it, Jen's surprise compounded as she noticed it was pulsing, from light to dark purple and back again.

What the hell is happening?

Sloughing off his daze with a quick shake of the head, Alex picked himself up and walked closer to Jen. "No one can save you or the world from Lord Ferox," he snarled.

He clenched his fist and Jen could see the two rings start to illuminate again. She crawled backward until her back bumped up against the closed balcony door.

"Help . . ." she whispered weakly.

Alex laughed. "No one can hear you, Jen."

He took one step closer to her but stopped when a figure walked through the door . . . without opening it.

Did he just walk through *my door? The one I had closed, locked, and dead-bolted shut?*

Clenching his jaw in mild frustration, Alex paused to look back at the intruder. A middle-aged man stood at the opposite end of the apartment. He was wearing a thick, deep navy cloak, and grasped a long silver staff almost as tall as him.

"Well, look who it is! Welcome, *Victor*," Alex spat, dripping sarcasm.

"Let her go, Malcolm," the man—Victor—demanded.

"Now she knows my real name," Alex said. "Thanks a lot."

Alex's real name is Malcolm? Jen thought, too shocked to move. *What is going on?* She could feel herself hyperventilating. She became light-headed as the room spun all around her.

"Let her go," the man repeated, this time more forcefully, as he stepped farther into the room.

Alex—*Malcolm*—pretended to think. "Hmm, I don't think so.

She has something I need." He turned back to Jen, pinning her to the floor with his gaze.

"She doesn't know anything about this," Victor said. The staff silently switched to his opposite hand.

"Then why does she have the Ring of Lancaster?" Malcolm shot back.

That was the last thing Jen heard. Tunnel vision swept over her and her hearing first became muffled then completely muted. The last thing she saw, incredibly, was Malcolm shooting Victor with a bolt of lightning. The blast seemed to sprout directly from his fingertips, or maybe his rings, and hit the older man straight in the chest, sending him crashing through the door and out into the hall.

And then, only black.

* * *

Malcolm turned back and noticed that Jen had lost consciousness. He smiled and walked toward the front entrance. Looking out into the hall, he stepped onto the splintered doorway, making sure Victor was not underneath.

"I have always been quicker than you, *Mystra*," taunted Malcolm.

"Always the first to initiate a fight," came the reply, seeming to echo from all around.

"Don't talk down to me!" Malcolm yelled. "I'm not your tenderfoot anymore!"

A sudden arctic breeze hit Malcolm, sending him stumbling back inside the apartment and into the sofa. His muscles spasmed from the subzero spell.

"R-r-really?" Malcolm stammered, visibly shaking. "A bit of a chilly breeze? That's the best you can d-do?" He slowly stood up.

In the blink of an eye, Victor appeared ten feet away, facing his former tenderfoot. "The colder you are, the slower your body reacts."

Victor's next three spells came in quick succession. He pointed his staff at his former student and a bright flash of light exploded in front of Malcolm's eyes, blinding him; a jolt traveled through his body, electrifying all of his nerves; and a darkness swallowed his senses, disorienting him. Malcolm's cold muscles were still too stiff and slow to allow him adequate time to block and counter with his own attacks. Panicking, he threw an escape spell and vanished in the blink of an eye.

* * *

Victor stepped to where Malcolm had stood, finding only wisps of smoke.

"Coward."

He turned to the sleeping form of Jennifer Smith. She looked to be in a peaceful slumber, but Victor could sense that her mind was in torment. At only twenty-one years of age, she was about to embark on her most harrowing journey—a journey that would not only test her, but also those she loved.

He swirled his silver staff high above his head and Jen's apartment returned to its tidy setting. Crouching down, he gingerly picked her up and vanished into thin air.

* * *

That night, for only a few brief seconds and for the first time in over a millennia, the full moon shone purple.

CHAPTER TWO

Jen awoke with a throbbing headache on a soft bed. The room was dark and the only light came from its one door, which was slightly ajar. Her first thought was that she was in her bedroom; she let out a sigh and whispered, "It was only a dream . . . thank goodness."

Jen had the sudden feeling that she wasn't alone. Squinting, she barely made out a figure standing just inside the doorway. Jen blinked, trying to clear her eyes and her head.

"Dad? Is that you? You won't *believe* the nightmare I had."

The figure walked closer to the bedside and said, in a voice that most certainly wasn't her father's, "Rallumé."

A soft light filled the room, slowly brightening, to show the man who had walked through her apartment door. He was still draped in the same flowing cloak and holding his gleaming silver staff. What had his name been? Malcolm? No—that was Alex's real name. Her boyfriend . . .

I guess we're broken up now, though.

"How are you feeling, Jennifer?" he asked.

Startled, her fight-or-flight instincts kicked in, causing Jen to throw off her covers and spring off the bed. She set her sights on the open door, which was behind the man.

What's his name?

But once she stood up, her right side split in hot agony. Yelling in pain, she crumpled to the floor and crawled back until she bumped into the back wall.

"Whoa, little lady, settle down. I'm not going to hurt you." The man set his staff aside and raised his hands in a peaceful gesture.

"Who . . . who are you?" Jen stammered, still reeling from her blasting headache.

"My name is Victor Huxley. I was the one who stopped Malcolm from hurting you." His smile was friendly and soothing, framed by a thick salt-and-pepper beard. He looked to be in his mid-fifties, but his crystal-blue eyes seemed to dance with youth. His hair was parted down the center, falling in thick waves to just below his ears but above his square jawline.

Still grabbing her side and watching Victor like a hawk, Jen tried to calm her breathing, tried not to break into sobs. Balancing on the wall for support, she slowly stood up.

"Wait—it wasn't a nightmare?" Jen asked, growing more concerned. She inhaled sharply and said, "I think my ribs are broken."

"May I see? I've broken many bones in my lifetime." Victor offered his hand, but waited for her approval.

Jen looked deep into Victor's blue eyes, searching for any signs of malevolence. When she sensed none and felt another stabbing pain shoot through her chest, Jen dropped her hands to her sides and nodded.

"Here, sit back down." He led her back to the bed and picked up his staff. Once Jen was situated, Victor said, "Take a deep breath. You're going to feel very warm." With his staff hovering a few inches over her broken ribs, Victor closed his eyes and faintly hummed.

The orb on top of his staff softly glowed as Jen began to feel her chest comfortably heat up. She inhaled again, slower this time, at first feeling stiffness from her bruised ribs; but as she continued to fill her lungs, the pressure alleviated and she somehow felt better. Entranced with what Victor was doing, Jen continued to stare at him until he opened his eyes and dropped his hands.

"*Now* how does it feel?" he asked.

Jen gingerly felt the areas of her ribs that had shown the most pain, but she felt not even the slightest discomfort. She stared up at him incredulously. "How did you *do* that?"

Victor grinned. "This might come as a shock, but I need you to keep an open mind, okay, Jennifer?" When she didn't respond, he continued, saying softly, "I am a practitioner of one of the five mystical planes, called 'Mancy planes,' that surround us all." He stood up and walked to a small counter she hadn't noticed before.

"So . . . you're a wizard?" Jen asked, half skeptical because she'd always thought they were fictitious, but half impressed because, well, he *did* just heal her broken bones.

"Sorcerer," Victor corrected. Putting down his staff once more, he took a goblet from a shelf and began making some sort of drink. "Many people mistake wizards and sorcerers as being one and the same when, in reality, we are very different." He put the utensils away and walked back toward Jen, offering a bubbly drink. "This will help with your headache."

She took the goblet and swirled the liquid around. "A potion?"

"Advil," he said matter-of-factly. "Sometimes modern medicine is just as good as potions . . . and more convenient." He winked. "Potions usually have a long list of ingredients that typically aren't just lying around." He turned back to the counter to clean up. "Eye of newt, dragon's blood, goblin hair, pollywog tail . . . the list goes on and on. Advil's only a quick stop at the nearest pharmacy." He looked back to find Jen cautiously staring at the contents of the goblet.

Picking up on some wariness, Victor went to Jen and gestured to the goblet. "Here." Jen handed it to him and he took a sip. "I wouldn't dream of harming you." With a kind smile, Victor gave Jen back the goblet.

"Thank you." Jen started to feel more relieved. She cupped the goblet with both hands and and took a sip. Afterward, she asked, "Do you have a wand?"

Victor chuckled. "Again, strictly a wizard thing. Sorcerers are born with a nexus, an innate power that lets us access one of the five Mancy planes. Wizards, on the other hand, aren't born with any powers, but learn to cast spells using wands. We sorcerers do use totems to help concentrate our powers, though. Many of us forge rings—like the one on your necklace."

Jen touched the ring on her chest as Victor continued to explain.

"Others choose different totems like swords, bows, knives, whips"—he picked up his staff, which was leaning next to the front door—"staffs. The item a sorcerer chooses usually has a special meaning to him or her."

"So girls can be sorcerers, too?"

Victor chuckled. "Of course!"

Jen drank a few more sips. "Why did you choose a staff?"

Victor was silent for a moment. "This particular one belonged to someone very close to me." He became somber, but for only a split second before cheering up and adding, "And it helps me walk. Crickety knees." He wobbled his legs for emphasis.

Jen returned the smile Victor gave her. Finishing off the contents in the goblet, her head already feeling better, she changed the subject. "So how did you know I was in trouble, Victor?"

"Call me Vic, please," he said with another smile.

"And I go by Jen. Only my grandparents call me Jennifer." She winked, tucking a few curls behind an ear.

"You're making me feel so old," Victor joked, clutching his heart with his hands. "To preserve my youth: Jen it is."

Jen giggled. "Deal."

His cleaning done, Victor turned back around and looked directly at her. "We've been keeping an eye on you for some time, Jen."

"Who's 'we'? There are more like you?"

"There are many. We call ourselves Light Seekers, and together we form the League of Light."

"So you're a part of a . . ." Jen hesitated. "A magical society?"

"It's a secret society of sorts. The religions we practice do

18

include sorcery and alchemy. Some label us a cult because of this," Victor said, "but I promise you they are mistaken."

"Oh!" Jen perked up. "Don't alchemists turn lead and other metals into gold?"

"Someone knows her history." Victor raised an eyebrow, impressed.

"I do pay attention in class every now and then." Jen smiled again, then wondered out loud, "Vic . . . you said that you've been watching over me for a while. Why?"

He took the empty goblet from Jen and placed it back on the counter. Victor was silent for a few minutes, seeming to gather his thoughts. Finally, he spoke.

"You come from a long line of powerful sorcerers, Jen . . . and the League of Light has vowed to protect you."

Jen laughed. "You can't be serious! My family is the most normal family that has ever walked the Earth. I mean, my last name is *Smith*. If that's not ordinary, I don't know what is."

"You are everything but ordinary, my dear."

He looked at her in a familiar way that made Jen ask herself if she had met him before. She blushed and averted her eyes, looking at the blanket that was covering her. She smoothed the creases out when she remembered something that her boyfriend had said to her.

"Alex—um, sorry, *Malcolm*—said that I'm a Lancaster . . . ?" She trailed off, hoping that Victor would explain that puzzling piece of knowledge.

Victor opened his mouth to speak, then closed it. As Jen looked at him pleadingly, he leaned on the kitchen counter, slightly rocking, his fingernails softly *tap, tap, tapping* against its granite top.

Jen guessed he knew why Malcolm had said that to her, but it seemed like he was carefully planning what to say next. Maybe she had been too trusting so far.

He finally replied, "Your last name is actually Lancaster. Smith is your adopted family name." Victor looked over his shoulder at Jen, watching her face shift to a look of disbelief.

Jen's eyes dropped to the floor. She furrowed her brow and looked back up at Victor. A flurry of questions zipped through her mind.

I'm not really a Smith?

What else have they been keeping from me?

Is Tyler really my brother? What about Mom and Dad?

What's happened to my perfect life?!

"I'm so terribly sorry that you had to learn your true heritage under such poor circumstances, Jen."

Jen finally found the breath to spit out some of the questions swirling in her head. "I'm adopted? Who are my biological parents?"

Victor let out a long sigh. "It's been a trying past couple of days for you, Jen. I think you'd better have this talk with your parents. Get some sleep, and then I'll take you home."

Jen felt tears forming. "How am I supposed to sleep now? My whole life's been turned upside down."

Victor said nothing, only looked at her with sorrowful understanding.

Finally, after gathering her wits and calming down again, she said firmly, "I would like to see them now."

Victor nodded, not taking his eyes from the floor. "If that's what you wish." Victor pushed himself from the counter, grabbed his silver staff, and waved for Jen to follow him through the doorway.

Opening the door farther revealed a circular cottage built of stone. Jen admired the archaic tapestries hanging from the walls. Sconces bearing lit torches framed each of the windows.

Victor tapped his staff twice on the ground, commanding in a booming voice, "Venere!"

"CEEEE-*AAAAWWW!*" came a shriek from outside.

Startled, Jen looked around to see a large creature land just outside the window closest to her, flapping its wings as it dropped from the sky. It was like nothing Jen had witnessed before: the head, talons, and wings of an eagle, but the body, hind legs, and tail of a lion. Its muscles rippled underneath its tawny lion hide and its large brown and white eagle feathers shone in the diminishing sunlight.

"What is that?!" Jen exclaimed.

Victor smiled and looked proudly at the noble creature outside. "That, Jen, is a griffin . . . the king of all beasts."

"Is it your pet?" Jen asked, still entranced by the griffin.

"He's more of a friend to me than a pet. His name is Skarmor. Would you like to meet him?"

"Sure! I've never met a griffin before," Jen said, not fully believing what she had just agreed to as she followed Victor outside.

As they walked around the cottage's perimeter, Jen saw a beautiful sunset just above lush, rolling hills. The shadows of the trees and other cottages were slowly stretching across the land. Jen couldn't put her finger on it, but the place she found herself in was as familiar as it was foreign . . . as if she were still on Earth, but in the far distant past.

At first sight of Victor, Skarmor's bushy lion tail thumped on the ground. He stood an immense eight feet tall on his front eagle talons, with a wingspan upward of twenty feet. Jen had no doubt that this griffin could fly with ease for hours.

Victor muttered something that Jen couldn't pick up as he gently touched his forehead to Skarmor's. The griffin made a soothing sound deep in his throat, and after a few seconds, he brought his head back up to his full height as he noticed Jen.

Turning toward her, Victor started, "Skarmor has been by my side for twenty-five years." A nostalgic smile flashed across his face as he recalled their first meeting. "I rescued him from a rather cruel group of Hyperborean Giants just north of Thrace. They were going to kill him because he was sickly and weak." He paused, recounting the memory. "Let's just say I convinced them otherwise and I took him in. I nursed him back to health, and he's been my trusty guardian ever since."

"Wow . . ." Jen breathed, transfixed.

"Would you like to pet him? He won't bite," Victor reassured, motioning her to get closer.

Clutching the ring around her neck, Jen cautiously side-stepped her way closer to Skarmor. His eyes, towering above, followed her without blinking.

"That's it," Victor said calmly as she came closer, inch by inch. "Don't make any sudden movements or sounds. He needs to know he can trust you. His most acute senses are sight and hearing, much like every other type of avian. He'll observe you, just as he is now, to determine if you're friend or foe. If he deems you trustworthy, he'll spread his wings." Victor stepped out of Jen's way so there was nothing between her and Skarmor. "Stand strong, Jennifer."

Skarmor slightly twitched his neck downward and cocked his head to one side. Silently, he paced around Jen, who kept herself frozen like a statue. After he made a full circle around her, Skarmor released a piercing cry and spread his wings wide, standing only on his hind legs.

Staying as silent as she could, she craned her head up to look at him. The enormous silhouette of the griffin enveloped Jen in shadow as the bright sun was setting. The mighty creature dropped to his front talons and slowly brought his head to Jen's until their foreheads touched.

"Ha," she let out a nervous chuckle. "He likes me?"

"He likes you," Victor confirmed, off to the side.

Skarmor backed up and sat down. After Victor's nod of approval, Jen reached out and gingerly put her right hand atop Skarmor's head. He welcomed it as Jen brought her hand down the back of his head and onto his neck. The feathers felt soft and silky.

"Hey, there," Jen said with increasing ease.

"Looks like you two will be good friends," chuckled Victor. "Which is good, since we'll be riding him out of here."

Jen stopped petting and, mouth agape, looked at the sorcerer. "Sorry . . . *ride* him?"

"Of course! Otherwise it'll take us days to reach the gateway portal," Victor said, walking toward Skarmor.

"Where in the world is that?" Jen asked.

"Not on Earth, that's for sure. We are on a planet we call Azumar," Victor responded, taking in everything around him as if it were the most natural thing in the world—or *worlds*—to be on a different planet.

Jen snickered, clapping at his joke. "Okay, Vic, good one. Ya got me. Where are we really?" She surveyed the landscape one more time. "This place does *not* remind me of New York, so I'll guess New Zealand . . . even though I find it hard to believe that we could've traveled there so quickly." She crossed her arms.

Victor straightened and looked around in every direction, as if this were his first time here as well. "Now that you mention it, it does kind of look like New Zealand." He chuckled as he spun his staff in his hand. "But my answer is still the same: we're on Azumar."

He's serious.

"Time out," Jen said, trying to wrap her mind around what she was experiencing. This was getting to be too much for her. Hours after her twenty-first birthday, her boyfriend had turned out to be a complete stranger, a mysterious man had saved her from him and had miraculously healed her broken bones, she was told that she was adopted and was related to powerful sorcerers, and now she was supposed to believe that she was not on Earth, but a completely different planet.

How is this not a dream?

Jen could feel the beginnings of another headache in the back of her skull. Rubbing her temples with her fingers, she looked at the ground beneath her feet, focusing on a few rather long blades of grass as strands of her wavy hair cascaded into her vision. Jen closed her eyes and said, "This is . . . impossible."

"I know this is a lot to take in, especially after what you've just been through. But you need to believe me." Victor held out a hand, smiling sympathetically. "Do you need to sit down?"

"No . . ." Jen ran her fingers through her hair, brushing it from her face. "I think I'll be fine, thanks." Rolling a new-found stiffness from her neck, she cleared her throat and took a few breaths before asking, "Is Azumar even in our solar system?"

"Not in our solar system, nor our galaxy—nor even our universe."

"What? So, like, a different dimension?"

"Yes, I suppose that's technically what it is, though we call it a *realm*," Victor replied. "Over countless centuries, sorcerers have discovered hotspots on Earth which channel energy from other realms—the Bermuda Triangle, Easter Island, and Stonehenge, for example. Magic has helped us understand these mystical doorways and travel through them at our whim."

Skarmor was patiently waiting, preening his feathers, as if he'd heard Victor's explanations before.

"Unreal." Jen stared at her surroundings with renewed admiration. "Why not choose to live on Earth?"

"Azumar is our safe haven to practice sorcery and magic without the judgmental eyes of human society," Victor explained, his voice now serious. "We learned quickly that non-believers fear what they don't understand, and they've proven unable to take the time to open their minds to the capabilities of magic. So as a result, we were forced to find another home so our religion would no longer be in danger of dying off."

"I've never really thought about it that way . . ." Jen was reminded of the Salem witch trials and the atrocities committed there—and that had been when the witchcraft hadn't even been real. Surely that only fanned the flame of fear of sorcery. "Though why would I? I never believed magic was actually *real* until yesterday."

"Magic is all around us—we just have to choose to see it." Victor winked and, with a quick running start, leapt onto Skarmor's back, extending his hand down to her. "Ready, Jen?"

"Sure . . ." she said hesitantly. She accepted Victor's outstretched hand and swung into a sitting position behind him. She saw no seatbelt or something to cling to. "Do I—"

"Wrap your hands around my waist and hold tight. Flying on a griffin takes some getting used to." Turning forward, Victor commanded Skarmor to take flight.

Jen put her arms around Victor and felt the large feathers

beneath her move as the griffin spread his wings and stood up. Jen wobbled a bit as Skarmor turned to an open path, screeched, and began to bound toward the nearest hillcrest. His strides were long as he built up speed, and when he reached the top of the hill he jumped high into the air.

Instinctively, Jen bunched her eyes shut and tightened her hold around Victor's waist as her breath involuntarily caught in her throat. After hearing a faint chuckle from Victor and not feeling the tickling sensation of falling, she slowly opened up one eye to see them completely free from the ground, the verdant landscape far beneath her feet.

Easing her grip, Jen smiled and deeply inhaled the fresh Azumarian air. She was surprised to hear herself whoop in pure elation as Victor's cottage receded in the shadow-filled distance.

Two strong flaps of Skarmor's wings steadied them in the air and they soared smoothly into Azumar's sunset.

CHAPTER THREE

Malcolm screamed in frustration. He toppled the table in front of him, sending his books, candles, and potions to the ground with a loud crash. His cavernous chamber made the cacophony of falling books, splintering wood, and tinkling glass sound like an avalanche.

Since he fled from the battle with Victor, Malcolm had been furious—furious that he'd spent months getting close to Jen Lancaster, only to have her slip through his fingers at the last possible moment; furious that he hadn't beat his former master to a pulp. He was stronger than Victor—he knew it—but Victor had surprise and luck on his side that night.

Next time you won't be so lucky, Victor, thought the irate dark sorcerer. He had something up his sleeve that would make their paths cross again. And when the time came . . .

Heavy footfalls echoed through the corridor outside until a mass of stone walked through the doorway. Malcolm looked up to see a hulking golem crouch through the doorframe.

"I didn't call for you, you dimwit!" he yelled, hurling the nearest object at the door. "Leave me alone!"

The stone giant silently stared at him for a few moments with black, soulless eyes before turning around and walking back out of the chamber. It nicked the side of the doorframe with one of its chiseled shoulders, causing the centuries-old wooden frame to splinter. Malcolm was too angry, too *tired*, to reprimand the clumsy beast; he just clenched his jaw until the ringing in his ears became too loud to continue.

Sniffling from a cold he had caught from Victor's subzero spell, Malcolm shuffled over to the mess on the ground and picked up a time-worn book. Righting the now slightly bent table, he lit a candle and opened the book to where he'd left off.

"The time is coming, My Lord," whispered Malcolm as he flipped through the pages, searching for clues as to where the Halostone might rest. With an evil grin, he fantasized about the day he would bring his true master back to the land of the living.

CHAPTER FOUR

The night brought a cool nip to the air, which kept Jen awake, though she wasn't that cold with Victor blocking most of the wind. It was hard to imagine that they had been flying for over an hour, as Jen found herself in utter rapture as they glided through the air hundreds of feet above the rolling hills. Trees, valleys, rivers, and other cottages whizzed by, leaving Jen to only guess at how fast they were traveling.

Looking over Victor's shoulder, Jen started to make out faint lights glimmering in the distance. As they flew closer, the lights formed a large oval the size of a tennis court. Around it were cheering spectators. There seemed to be a contest of some sort involving two men. One looked to be Jen's age, the other as old as Victor.

Jen pointed toward the activity. "What's happening down there?"

Victor looked to where Jen was pointing. "That's the last part of the Sorcerer Trials, where a tenderfoot must duel his or her mystra. For this specific duel, if that boy scores enough points, he will pass and be bestowed the rank of paladin."

Jen was perplexed. "Tenderfoot? What's that?"

"A tenderfoot is what we call an apprentice of sorcery."

"And mystra?"

Victor chuckled at Jen's boundless questions. "A master."

"How many ranks are there?" Jen asked, not missing a beat.

Over the wind, Victor said, "There are four. You start as a tenderfoot, then, through training and the successful completion of the Sorcery Trials, you rise to become a paladin, an advanced level of sorcery. Mystra is the next rank. There have been many mystras throughout the millennia, but few ever reach the fourth and final rank of grand mystra, Those who earn the privilege of attaining grand mystra status have reached true harmony with their nexus and are given a spot on the Elder Synod, the presiding ministry of the Sorcery Guild." Victor turned back to look her in the eye. "Some of your ancestors were grand mystras, Jen."

Jen smiled, then quickly looked away, feeling conflicted. She was proud of her supposed heritage, making her feel as if she should follow in her ancestors' footsteps; but at the same time, she also felt devoted to her life back home in New York. For as long as she could remember, Jen had wanted to become a doctor so she could help people in their time of need. Now, she needed to reevaluate her future. She couldn't explain it, but she felt an irresistible calling to this new world—a world she hadn't even known existed a day before.

Her thoughts slowly lifted away like leaves in a breeze as her eyes locked back on the spectacle in the distance. They were getting closer to the dancing lights, making it possible for Jen to see the individuals instead of only their black silhouettes. A duel was underway, and Jen saw colorful lights shoot out from both of the sorcerers' hands almost simultaneously.

As they passed, Jen let go of Victor to get a better look and slipped. Victor's hand shot out and grabbed Jen's arm, right before she slid off of Skarmor. There was no time to scream and before Jen knew it, Victor had pulled her back onto Skarmor and firmly, but nicely, said, "Hold on tightly . . . and do not let go."

"Right." Jen nodded, eyes wide open and heart thumping.

Twenty more minutes passed as they flew through the night. Jen hoped that the tenderfoot won his match. Something inside her awakened, making her wish that she would be given that opportunity in the future, the thought of which gave her a mix of excitement and dread to be embarking on this new life, filled with new possibilities . . . and dangers.

* * *

Jen's eyelids were becoming heavy as Skarmor gently settled to the ground. After another hour of flying, they were finally at their destination.

The Gate of Eternal Flame.

Victor masterfully dismounted his loyal griffin and offered his hand to Jen, which she accepted appreciatively.

Dropping to the ground, Jen scratched the underside of Skarmor's neck and said, "Thanks, boy."

Skarmor made a sound deep within his throat, enjoying Jen's affection. Patting the griffin on the side of his neck, she turned her attention to the large, dark cave that seemed to beckon her inside. It looked ominous, its only light a yellow-orange flame from deep within its maw.

"Welcome to the Gate of Eternal Flame," Victor announced. "This is one of the many gateways from Azumar to Earth. It is named after the flame on its Earth side, which keeps this portal open. If it should ever be extinguished, this portal will be forever lost."

"How many gates are there?"

"At least fifteen, but some of them don't lead to Azumar. There are other more foreign—and more treacherous—realms that you can stumble into," Victor warned.

"Not all realms are good. Got it."

Skarmor cawed as if in agreement.

Victor patted Skarmor as he looked at Jen. "Trust me." Taking a deep breath, he said, "We should continue. There's a deep river that runs through the middle of this cave, so follow my steps closely." The sorcerer manifested an orb of bright light to help Jen see the terrain of the craggy landscape of the cave.

In awe, she brought a hand to her mouth to stifle a surprised laugh. "Okay. Can you please teach me that trick so the next time my apartment's electricity shorts out, I can still do the dishes?"

Victor glanced at her out of the corner of his eye. "All in due time, my dear." His voice bounced all around them as they stepped farther into the cave.

Jen immediately noticed the river Victor had mentioned. The water looked to be rushing, but it made no sound to indicate a fast-moving stream. They walked alongside it, Victor leading Jen and Skarmor.

Drip . . . drip . . . drip . . .

Every so often Jen could hear drops of water from the stalactites all around them, echoing through the interminable cave. As they proceeded deeper and deeper, she felt a sense of calmness envelop her, despite her claustrophobic nature. Jen felt safe with Victor, even though she barely knew the man. That sense of familiarity she had felt when she first awakened in Victor's cottage resurfaced as she followed him step by step, not wanting to fall into the river, which she imagined was icy cold.

In no time they reached the flame, which floated about three feet off the damp, cold floor. Once they were near it, Victor extinguished his own light, leaving them with only the flame's soothing glow. About the size of a basketball, the spherical flame gave off no heat, which seemed strange to Jen.

"Do as I do," instructed Victor. As Skarmor walked up beside his master, Victor brought his hand closer and closer to the flame until it was fully engulfed. He didn't seem to get burned. He turned to Jen and smiled, then muttered, "Ad Gaia."

Immediately Victor and Skarmor's bodies atomized as they turned into hundreds of specks of colored light and floated into the flame. Unable to fully comprehend what had just happened, Jen rubbed her eyes and tried to blink away her confusion.

"Vic?" Concern filled her voice as she waited for her echo to fade before saying, "Skarmor?" Finding herself completely alone in the cold, damp cave, she felt the claws of claustrophobia scratch at her throat. Stepping closer to the flame, she began to shake as a memory surfaced of when she was burned as a child. Not wanting to stay in this cave for much longer, Jen closed her eyes and took a deep breath. After letting it out slowly, she cautiously reached out to the flame.

Wincing, she put her right hand into the fire and . . . felt no horrible sensation of burning. There were only slight tingles in her hand where the tips of the flame licked her palm, but other than that, nothing.

Remembering what Victor dictated before he vanished, Jen repeated, "Ad Gaia," and she felt a pulse of energy travel across her skin as her vision turned white. In a heartbeat she was in another cave, except the entrance was on the opposite side, behind the waiting form of Victor. She could hear the steady roar of a waterfall in the distance.

"Whoa!" Jen stumbled, raising a hand to her forehead as nausea took over her senses.

"Easy does it." Victor was there to steady her. "Inter-realm travel makes you a little dizzy, especially when you haven't done it before."

"Yeah, you can say that again." After blinking a few times and getting her breathing under control, she looked around and said, "Hey, where's Skarmor?"

A high-pitched caw echoed throughout the cave, reverberating off the rock walls. Jen looked up to see a small, colorful bird flying in a circle above her head. It dove to land on Victor's outstretched arm.

"Wait . . ." Jen said unbelievably. "Is that . . . *Skarmor*?"

Skarmor chirped and fluttered in the air for a few seconds before hopping on his master's shoulder. Victor laughed and tickled beneath Skarmor's substantially smaller chin. "Indeed! To help conceal his true form, Skarmor takes the form of a halcyon whenever he and I travel to Earth."

Jen walked up to Victor and little Skarmor. "He's so *cute*! I love all of his colors." She looked at the silver sheen of his breast feathers, which blended into the black and azure blue of his tiny wings. His beak was the brightest magenta. This time she petted him only with her index finger.

"He's much less conspicuous as this common bird than a giant, supposedly *mythical* creature," Victor joked.

"Yeah, I bet." Jen smiled at Skarmor and stepped back. "So where are we now?"

"Eternal Flame Falls, New York."

"Oh, really? That's not too far from my parents," Jen said.

Victor nodded. "We have to be careful. You're more vulnerable than ever now, since the spell is wearing off."

Alarmed at what Victor had just said, Jen grabbed his arm before he could start leading the way out of the cave. "What spell?"

CHAPTER FIVE

A soft light pulsed from a crystal ball in a corner of Malcolm's lonely chamber. He noticed it almost immediately and closed the withered book, standing to his full height. A snapshot of the United States materialized in the crystal ball, as if taken from outer space, and a faint, blinking dot surfaced over a spot in the state of New York.

"The prodigal daughter returns," he said aloud.

Before Malcolm fled from his confrontation with Victor, he'd placed a locator spell on Jen. Even though the ring's presence gave off a reading, it was too faint to track unless a sorcerer knew exactly where to look. With this type of location spell, he could only track her if she was on Earth—and it looked as though she had finally returned.

With a flick of his cloak, Malcolm ran out of his room, sliding his rings on as he went.

CHAPTER SIX

Victor's words echoed in Jen's ears.

The spell is wearing off . . .

"What spell?" she repeated.

Victor sighed. "We can't talk about this right now, Jen. Malcolm is probably tracking us." He took her arm to lead her out of the cave.

"No," she said forcefully. "I'm not going anywhere until you explain." Jen hugged her arms to her chest, but Victor still didn't let go.

He ignored her comment, now pulling her as he made his way into the crisp New York night.

Skarmor chirped, frantically flapping his little wings to keep up.

"Let go of me, Victor!" Jen couldn't help but be reminded of when Malcolm—her *Alex*—had grabbed her on her birthday. Trying to find a handhold in the curved cave wall with her free hand, she said, "For me to trust you, I need you to tell me everything!"

A flash of lightning briefly lit up the sky, shortly followed by a roar of thunder. Its echo was still reverberating throughout the cave when a few raindrops fell. In no time, the slight drizzle turned into a downpour.

At the mouth of the cave, just before the rushing waterfall, Victor let go of her, exasperated. "Fine. I'm getting too old for this anyway." He spun around on his heels to face her.

Jen took two steps back, holding the spot where Victor had grabbed. She looked him square in the eyes and said, "Don't ever touch me like that again." She could feel the warm buildup of tears. It took everything for her to not break down and cry.

A loud thunderclap roared in the distance, reverberating throughout the cave.

Realizing what he had inadvertently done, Victor closed his eyes in shame. After pursing his lips, he said, "I'm sorry, Jen. I didn't mean to hurt you . . . it won't happen again." It looked as if he was fighting back tears as well. "Unfortunately, we don't have the luxury of time."

"Then tell me what this spell is and who put it on me." Jen crossed her arms again and started tapping her right foot, waiting for an explanation. When none came, she repeated again: "What spell?"

"Okay," Victor said, realizing he had to make up for his treatment of Jen. "To protect your identity, your birth parents cast a temporary warding spell around you so none of their enemies could track you down and harm you."

"A warding spell?" she asked.

He nodded. "Good until your twenty-first birthday. Now that warding spell is finally wearing off. The power of that ring around your neck"—he pointed at the Ring of Lancaster—"isn't helping either. I can feel its power getting stronger each day."

Jen looked down at the ring and clasped it in her hand.

Warding spell?

Why did my birth parents put it on me?

Where did this ring even come from?

Finally, she found her voice and asked a new question that had just popped into her mind. "Who would possibly want to hurt me? I've done nothing wrong."

"It's not what you've *done*, Jen. It's who you are—your heritage. Almost fifteen hundred years ago, your ancestor

Genevieve was the sorceress responsible for locking away the most powerful dark sorcerer, Lord Ferox, during what is known as the Great Battle. Afterward, there were factions of brainwashed sorcerers that still pledged allegiance to Lord Ferox and his new world order. These warped followers—Dark Watchers, we call them—have been waiting for the resurrection of their dark lord for centuries, and they have vowed to find and release him with the Ring of Lancaster, the totem that was used to lock Ferox away —and thus the only one that can resurrect him—which now hangs on your necklace." Victor had to shout to be heard over the rushing waterfall.

Jen stood there silently for a few seconds with her arms still crossed. That was the first time she'd heard the name of one of her ancestors, and she was startled when she realized how closely it resembled her own.

Maybe this isn't too impossible to believe . . .

Finally, she asked, "You won't let them take my ring, will you?" She clutched her necklace so tightly that she felt the ring's edges digging into her palm.

Victor hesitantly put a hand on her shoulder. "I promise."

Jen wiped a stray tear from her cheek, feeling a little better. "Is Malcolm one of these . . . Dark Watchers?" Jen still had feelings for Malcolm—or at least for the version of him she'd grown to know, Alex—but she kept telling herself that he'd only acted like he cared about her to get close to the ring.

It was all an act. And I was falling for him. Why is it so hard for me to let go?

Malcolm's betrayal continued to devastate Jen; when they were together, it had felt so real, so right. His smile, his humor, his tender touch . . .

Victor looked to the ground, crestfallen. "Yes, Malcolm is a Dark Watcher. His lust, his greed, to become the most powerful sorcerer has driven him to darkness. He believes the only way to obtain true mastery is to learn from Lord Ferox himself. I . . . I have failed him." His last words were barely audible over the waterfall. After a moment of silence, he cleared his throat and, remembering his task, said with more urgency, "It's only a matter of time before more Dark Watchers latch onto your location. We have to get to your parents *now*."

"Fine," Jen said, somewhat satisfied with Victor's explanation. Her many other questions would have to wait, but for now, she still trusted him.

Victor started to turn, then caught himself. "Jen, I'm ashamed of my actions earlier. Can you forgive me?"

Jen dropped her hands to her sides and nodded, giving him a reassuring smile. "Apology accepted, Vic. I'm beginning to realize how close your past is to my situation."

"Thank you." He cleared his throat and rocked his staff back and forth.

"And that makes me appreciate your help even more." She rubbed his arm consolingly.

"I'll do my best to keep you safe. But for that to happen, we must keep moving."

"Right."

Victor turned toward the cave's exit. It seemed as if he were looking *through* the waterfall. "Here. Grab my hand and say your parents' address," Victor said.

Thunder rolled around them. Jen reached out and wrapped her fingers around his large hand. It felt strong . . . safe. She knew, in that moment, standing with him behind a waterfall that led to a portal to another world, that this man would not let anything happen to her.

After taking a deep breath, she spoke the street address, and in the blink of an eye they were gone, leaving the Eternal Flame to silently burn through the dreary night.

CHAPTER SEVEN

Dinggg-donggggg!

The doorbell rang inside the Smiths' cozy Wanakah home overlooking Lake Erie. The rainstorm had already blown through, leaving a cold wetness that seemed to suck the heat right out of you.

Richard Smith made his way down the carpeted stairs of his two-story home and peered into his front door's peephole. His eyes lit up and he immediately unlocked his front door. Making sure he wouldn't wake up his wife, Richard hugged his daughter tightly and stage-whispered, "Jenny Jasmine! What are you doing here?"

Jen squeezed him back. "Hi, Dad! Did we wake you?"

"Oh, not at all!" He released her from the hug. "I was up reading." His smile faded when he looked at the man who was with her, and a flicker of recognition flashed across his eyes. "Victor . . . ?"

Victor greeted him with a nod. "Richard."

Jen searched her father's face and cast a confused look behind her at Victor, raising a finger. "Wait . . . you two *know* each other?"

Jen's father pursed his lips, still looking at Victor. "It's time, isn't it?"

Jen found herself in her father's study, waiting with Victor on her favorite couch as Richard went upstairs to wake up her mother. She waved at Skarmor, who, at the request of her father, was perched on a low-hanging branch outside. He raised a wing—his version of waving back—as he hopped up and down on the branch. Giggling, Jen turned her attention back inside to see Victor trying to get comfortable. He had set his staff down in the foyer, so he was awkwardly trying to find something to do with his hands as he waited, but he only succeeded in making Jen laugh.

"So how do you know my parents, Vic?"

Victor finally clasped his hands together and rested them in his lap. "Let's wait for your parents to come, if you don't mind."

Silently nodding, Jen anxiously bounced her legs up and down. She looked away and found herself recounting so many fond memories that she had made in this very room, whether it was from family game nights, weekend coffee talks with her mother, or rainy days curled up with a good book. Her heart was filled with such nostalgia that she couldn't help but smile as she looked around at the Norman Rockwell paintings hanging on the hunter-green walls and the classic models of boats and cars accenting each bookshelf.

A faint shuffling of footsteps issued from the ceiling, forcing Jen out of her thoughts. She knew without a doubt that they were from her mother. Now Jen could hear the footsteps quickly descend the staircase, which was just out of sight. Before her mother entered the study, Jen heard her call in a sing-songy voice:

"My Jenny Jaaaaasminnnnnne!"

"Hey, Mom," Jen greeted as she stood up to hug Beth Smith. "Sorry for waking you."

"Oh, stop it." Beth brushed Jen's comment off with a wave of her hands. "I wouldn't want to miss a surprise visit by my daughter." She did a double-take when she saw Victor stand up. "Vic?

My goodness, how are you?" Beth wrapped her arms around him before he could respond.

"I'm doing okay, Beth."

"What brings you here?" Beth asked, but she seemed to answer her own question as she looked from Victor to Jen then back again. "Something's wrong."

Richard entered from behind and said, "I just put up some coffee, it should be done soon. Any takers?"

"I think I'm going to need some." Beth rubbed her husband's arm. "Thanks, hon."

Richard winked. "Why don't you all sit down?" he offered; then, to his wife: "I'll pour you a cup."

As he walked out of sight and into the kitchen, Beth joined Jen where she had been sitting on the couch while Vic found a spot on a corner loveseat.

"Mom, there's something I need to ask you," Jen said, hoping her voice wouldn't break.

"Anything, Jenny." Her mother smiled as she caressed Jen's cheek.

"Here it is, one scalding-hot cup of joe for the lady!" Richard said as he came back in and sat down next to his wife after carefully handing the steaming cup to her.

Jen took a deep breath and rubbed her thighs nervously as she mustered up the courage to ask the single most important question that she had ever asked. "Mom . . . Dad . . . am I adopted?"

Both of her parents seemed to sag their shoulders simultaneously and exchanged sympathetic looks with each other. Beth placed her cup on a coaster after she took a sip, and waited for Richard to start.

"Jen . . . you are our daughter and a part of our family, and that will never change, but . . ." He trailed off as he looked at his wife for support.

"But yes, you are adopted," Beth finished.

Jen felt the air get sucked out of her lungs as she let the truth finally sink in. "Why . . . why haven't you told me this before?"

Richard glanced at Victor before reaching out and taking her

41

shaky hand. "We wanted to—so badly—but we promised your birth parents and Victor that we would protect you. For that to happen, we had to keep you as far away as possible from the world that you were born into."

Jen sniffled, taking her hand back. "Then you know who my birth parents are?" She couldn't bear to look her parents in the eye; she knew if she did, she wouldn't be able to hold in her emotions. So instead, she played with her fingernail cuticles. After Jen counted to ten, she looked up to see her mother weakly holding her head in her hands and her father consoling her by rubbing her back.

Finally Richard spoke. "We met your parents, Charles and Jocelyn Lancaster, a year before you were born, when your mother and I were living in Arizona. As luck would have it, they were at the table next to us at this nice restaurant in Grand Canyon Village called . . ." He snapped his fingers, momentarily forgetting the name.

"El Tovar Dining Room," Beth said, pulling a tissue from her pocket.

"Ah, yes! El Tovar . . . thanks, sweetheart." He put his hand in hers and squeezed. "They have the best sautéed duck breast." Richard licked his lips. "But anyway, I spilled my water and ran out of napkins, so I asked Charles if he could spare one from his table. He agreed, and next thing we knew, he and his wife had joined our table. Instant connection, wasn't it, Beth?"

"Yes, it was great," she said, wiping away tears with a tissue. "As dinner was winding down, they asked if we knew of any good hotels for the night and, well, Rick and I felt comfortable in offering them our guest room. So we got to know them better over a glass of wine before we all were so tired we reluctantly called it a night." Beth somberly smiled at the memory.

It was Richard's turn to chime in. "Now, our neighborhood was very safe back then—still is—but that night, around two in the morning, we had a break-in."

Jen furrowed her brow, worried about what would happen next.

"I discovered the burglar walking up the stairs and I tried to head him off, but was lifted off the ground by some invisible force and thrown across the hallway." Her father's eyes went wide and he raised his arms incredulously.

Jen felt the cold sensation of goosebumps rolling down her arms, thinking back to how Malcolm had lifted her off the ground with a spell just two days before.

Richard continued, "The noise must've alerted Charles, because he came out of the guest room and started fighting with the intruder, who shot him with a . . ." He paused, trying to think of the right words. "A ball of light? That's the best way I can describe it. It slammed him into the stairs railing, but before anything else could happen, Jocelyn ran out to see what was going on." Richard squinted, as if still not quite believing what he was saying after all these years. "Her earrings were glowing, and she pointed at the intruder, who immediately disappeared, leaving only dust in his place."

"That night your birth parents told us that they were sorcerers and that magic is real," Beth said to Jen. She picked up her full cup of coffee and took another sip.

"And that intruder was a Dark Watcher or something." Richard looked to Victor for confirmation, who nodded, remaining silent. "They left a few hours later, after realizing that they had put us in harm's way."

"We didn't see them again until two years later, when they showed up at our front door," Beth said, putting down her cup and stroking Jen's cheek. "With a beautiful baby girl."

Jen put her hand over her mother's, closing her eyes. "Why did they give me up?" If there was a chance for her to find her birth parents, Jen wouldn't hesitate, but she needed to know why they left in the first place.

"They told us it was safer that we didn't know, just that they trusted us to look after you until it was safe for them to return," Richard replied.

"You remember how you got that ring on your necklace?" Beth

smiled, quickly glancing at her husband before looking back at her daughter. "It was actually from Charles."

Jen slowly nodded and took the Ring of Lancaster out from beneath her shirt collar. It seemed heavier as she stared intently at its grooves and patterns, trying to imagine what her birth parents had looked like all those years ago.

"Both Charles and Jocelyn were grateful, and they promised to return as soon as they could," Richard said.

"But days turned into weeks, and weeks into months," Beth recounted. "Almost a year later . . ." She was beside herself with grief, finding it hard to finish her thought. "Victor knocked on the door and . . . and explained that Charles and Jocelyn had . . . had died."

Jen's heart shattered. Her birth parents . . . gone?

"Charles and Jocelyn were the bravest sorcerers I've ever had the privilege of knowing," Victor said. "And I vowed to help look after you—from a distance—as Richard and Beth raised you."

In an instant, Jen's newfound hopes in finding her birth parents were dashed like a ship on jagged rocks. "What . . . ?" she breathed. Tears began to sting her eyes, but Jen didn't care any longer.

"I'm so sorry, honey," Beth consoled, offering a clean tissue.

"I'll never get to meet them." Taking the tissue, Jen dabbed her eyes, then looked at her parents. "Or even talk with them."

Victor said firmly, "They live through you and your family ring."

She was trying immensely to process what she was being told, but Jen couldn't think straight. She managed to say, "I don't remember ever living in Arizona."

"That's because Victor suggested we move to a more heavily populated area, so it would be next to impossible for any Dark Watcher to find you," Richard said.

"That's why we moved to New York," Jen whispered. She closed her eyes to steady her whirling mind. Jen felt as if her world had been turned upside down. As if her strength had been sucked out of her. Jen weakly put her hands on her knees. It was unbearable to think that she would never be able to meet her birth parents. Not knowing what to say next, she stayed quiet as tears streaked down her cheeks and left dark stains on her jeans.

She sniffled, looking at Victor through puffy eyelids. "Since I have the ring, that means I'm a target, right?"

Victor responded, "Your warding spell was only good until your twenty-first birthday, when your birth parents believed that you'd be strong enough as a sorceress to protect yourself. They had no idea that they'd never see you again and not be able to instruct you themselves." He took a deep breath. "I can still pick up some of the spell's traces on you, but it's bound to vanish any day now. At this point, you have two options: run . . . or face this threat and fight it."

Jen looked up at him through a veil of tears.

"You have a strong nexus, Jen," he continued. "I can feel it. If you'd like to fight, I would be honored to train you."

Jen turned her head when she heard her father's voice: "Born or thrust."

She smiled. That was her dad's way of paraphrasing the old adage by William Shakespeare: *Some are born great, some achieve greatness, and some have greatness thrust upon them.* He would say that to Jen when she was faced with a tough decision—and today was no different. Perhaps the toughest decision of them all.

"Born," Jen said quietly.

Richard smiled at his daughter, pride shining from his eyes, then turned to Victor. "Can I speak with you privately, Victor?"

Victor silently gestured, letting Richard lead the way.

Her father rose, squeezing her shoulder as he passed. "Be right back, Jenny Jasmine." He walked into the adjoining room with Victor close in tow, and Jen could just faintly hear her father start, "Have you told her—"

"Well, my coffee is too cold. Would you like some fresh coffee too, hon?" her mom said over her father's muffled voice. She was trying to sound chipper, but her body language said otherwise: her hands were shaking, nearly causing the cold coffee in her cup to spill.

"My appetite is next to nothing, but thanks," Jen said, standing up and taking the coffee cup. "Let me get more coffee for you, though. Cream and sugar?"

Her mother nodded and smiled sadly, touching Jen's right cheek again with her hand.

Jen was about to enter the kitchen when a high-pitched sound pierced the window. Something from outside . . .

Skarmor! she realized. *A warning call!*

A few seconds later, a bright orange light burst through the study's windows and a distant blast rocked the house. A few drops of cold coffee splattered on the ground as the door flew straight back and hit the stair railing, splintering it into sharp pieces.

Jen heard a scream and dropped the cup, which shattered on the hardwood floor, spilling coffee everywhere as she ran back into the study to see her mom completely frozen in horror. Around the staircase, Jen caught a glimpse of her father, also frozen in place, and Victor, unconscious and sprawled in a corner of the family room, laying in a wreck of wood that was once a vintage radio cabinet.

In the destroyed foyer stood Malcolm, his evil smile stretching the width of his face. When he noticed Jen rush into the study, his malicious smile vanished and his body slightly relaxed.

A jolt of confused sadness hit Jen as she saw Malcolm. She still thought of him as Alex—*her* Alex. She shook the thought from her head—"Alex" was nothing but a mask that Malcolm had worn to get the ring from her.

Malcolm broke her gaze and shook his head himself, as if the same thought had crossed his mind.

Wait . . . could my Alex still be in there somewhere?

Jen froze as she saw the hazel eyes into which she had once looked so deeply turn wicked as Malcolm brushed debris off his shoulders.

As Jen wrestled with her emotions, Skarmor swooped inside and started pecking at Malcolm's eyes. He swatted at the halcyon until he got so irritated that he shot a gust of wind that brought

Skarmor crashing into the wall next to Victor. Lightning then began to crackle around his left hand, which was now pointed at his former master, still prone and unconscious. Before he could release his high-voltage spell, his focus was shattered—much like the vase that had just hit him across the head.

Malcolm wailed and staggered back a few steps. "Nice throw, Jenny." He wiped a trail of blood out of his eyes, which was running down the right side of his head.

Hearing his voice reminded her of all the good times they'd had together. All she wanted to do was clean up the cut on his temple, but it took every ounce of concentration to remain poised and focus on saving her parents, Victor, and Skarmor instead.

Alex is gone. It's only Malcolm, she reminded herself as her heart broke all over again.

"Ever thought of going pro?" Malcolm asked, sneering at her. "I heard the Washington Wizards are looking for a point guard!"

Just then, a trail of white lightning streaked toward Jen, barely missing her as she dove behind the couch. Unhurt, she looked at the wall and saw a smoking crater the size of a basketball, and she smelled burnt drywall. As she heard Malcolm's cackling laughter, the ring around her neck started to glow for the second time in as many days. The pale purple light pulsated as her emotions swirled.

"Come out, come out, wherever you are . . ." Malcolm said in a sing-song voice.

Huddled behind the couch, Jen peered over the armrest to see Malcolm looking back over his shoulder, making sure Victor wouldn't blindside him if he were to regain consciousness. She quickly ducked down before he turned toward her, but she heard broken glass and masonry crunching beneath Malcolm's boots as he stepped closer. Her heart was racing as she held the ring up to eye level and looked deep into it, desperate to find an answer inside.

I don't know what to do!

She made a split decision, and it took every ounce of courage for Jen to stand up to face her ex-boyfriend. "Malcolm, stop . . .

please!" She was clenching her fists so tightly that her knuckles were turning white.

"I won't let down my dark lord again," he said, fully ignoring Jen's plea.

Frustrated and scared, Jen tried to focus on Malcolm's chest, and suddenly she felt a surge of cold energy shoot out from her own. He was expecting some sort of attack, so he deftly blocked the weak spell, letting it ricochet into the ground. Not knowing what she actually did, Jen felt the coldness leave as quickly as it had come. She felt her chest; her shirt was as cold as if she had just pulled it out of a freezer.

What did I just do?

"Wow, your first spell—without even one lesson! You're a natural." Malcolm lunged toward Jen in an attempt to grab her, but as soon as he took his first step forward, he immediately slipped on something on the hardwood floor and came crashing down.

Seizing this opportunity to get to Victor, Jen sprinted out of the study. As she passed the prostrate Malcolm, she found the reason for his fall: a frozen puddle of the coffee she had spilled earlier, turned to ice by her spell that Malcolm had deflected.

Kneeling down next to Victor, she picked up Skarmor and panted, "Vic—wake up!" She frantically looked behind her shoulder, expecting to see Malcolm whip around the corner at any moment. "Vic!" She rocked him from side to side, trying to wake him up; she had no clue how to break the spell that her parents were under.

Malcolm groaned, still in the study.

Victor's eyes fluttered open and Jen started breathing again. He shook his head and the cloudiness in his eyes vanished. With all of his senses reawakened and heightened, he put a large hand on Jen's forearm. "Get behind me."

Victor stood to his full height as Malcolm staggered around the corner, warm blood staining his right temple. Jen held Skarmor tight to her chest.

"Well, well," Malcolm chuckled, trying to hide his defeat. "If I can't capture you or your ring, Jen, I guess I'll have to settle for a consolation prize." He snapped his fingers and he and Jen's parents, still under Malcolm's mannequin spell, vanished.

"No!" Jen screamed. Victor tried to hold her back as she reached for her parents, but she pushed past him.

It was too late. They were gone.

CHAPTER EIGHT

"Jen, they're gone," Victor said, rubbing a tender bump on the back of his head that he had sustained from Malcolm's surprise attack.

"Then let's go after them!" Jen yelled, fresh tears rolling down her cheeks.

Victor seemed dazed and confused. "How did he know we were here?" he said, mostly to himself. Stiffening, as if he had just realized something, he picked up his staff and held it over Jen.

"What are you doing, Vic?" Jen sniffled, staring up at the staff, which was now glowing and making a humming noise. Feeling a tingle, Jen looked down to see goosebumps prickling her forearms. Seconds later, she felt an invisible veil lift off her.

Tapping his staff on the ground, Victor said, "Malcolm placed a location spell on you sometime in the past couple days." He shook his head. "I should have known."

Jen looked around where she stood, expecting to see the spell like shed skin. "Is it gone?" she said, worried.

Victor nodded. "Yes, you're free from it. That type of location spell is easy enough to break, now that I knew what to look for."

"Well, now that it's gone, he won't be expecting us. Let's go after them!" Jen repeated.

Victor took Skarmor from Jen's cradled hands, which were

shaking. "Malcolm probably took them back to the Dark Watcher lair, Feralot. It's too dangerous to break in without a foolproof strategy. Plus, no one knows where it could be. It's a nomadic fortress."

"But . . . then . . . how are we going to rescue Mom and Dad?" Jen pleaded. She didn't know what to think now; her mind was spinning.

"If there's one thing for certain, Malcolm *will* return. If anything, now he has more bargaining chips to get what he wants from you."

"They're not 'bargaining chips,' they're my *parents!*"

"Shh . . . I know, Jennifer."

"But *I* don't know—I don't know anything!" Jen crumpled to the ground; it felt as if the life had been drained from her body.

Alex—my Alex—would never have done something like this . . . he really was just pretending when we were dating. He's not Alex . . . he's Malcolm, and he's a monster.

Victor stood over her solemnly. "He's toying with you, Jen, to get you to turn over the ring." He knelt down beside her. "I know you feel like the world is against you right now, but I need you to never forget that when life throws you obstacles, as unfair as they might seem, you and only you have the power to let them define you."

Jen met his gaze with her own, but said nothing.

"Question is: Will you let each obstacle break you apart, or make you stronger so you can overcome them?"

Jen sighed as he brushed a stray curl behind her ear.

"Just know that I'll be here with you every step of the way, never leaving your side . . . until you're absolutely sick of me, of course," Victor said, hugging her close.

They both were silent for a moment, until Jen's eyes widened suddenly, and she remembered. "Tyler!" She shot up and ran upstairs to her younger brother's room.

It was empty.

Oh no! Did Malcolm kidnap Tyler too?!

A cell phone alarm trilled from the kitchen. Still shaking from the adrenaline, she grasped the hand railing and sped down the stairs, taking two steps at a time. She made it to the butler's pantry and knelt down by her dad's briefcase. Lifting his cell phone from the front compartment, she turned off his bedtime alarm, then scrolled down to see an unread text from Tyler.

Relief washed over Jen as she quickly read his message, standing up:

We r back @ Sam's house! Just picked up the pizza. Thx for letting me sleep over tonite :) Luv u

Victor was hovering in the background like a shadow, giving Jen some space. Skarmor's eyes began to flit open and he softly chirped. Victor looked down and said, "Welcome back, old friend."

"Okay," Jen said finally, turning to Victor. "Tyler's at a friend's house. I need to see him to make sure he's safe."

"Of course. Whatever you need."

Victor grimaced. Skarmor flapped his tiny wings and fluttered above his head.

"Thank you," Jen said. Her body was tense as she looked around, trying to focus. She turned on her phone, which was marvelously unscathed, and dialed her aunt's number.

Luckily, her aunt was still awake and took her call. After answering all of the questions she had as to why Tyler needed to stay with her after his sleepover, she agreed.

It was time to see Tyler one last time before she went back to Azumar.

Making their way through the destroyed foyer, Victor repaired what he could with a wave of his staff, but Jen, unlike her child-hood home, still felt completely shattered, unable to pick up the pieces of her former life. She silently vowed that she would find her parents and take Malcolm down any way she could.

* * *

Jen and Victor made a stop at Sam's house to see Tyler. He was glad to see her, but put on an indifferent air since Sam was just around the corner. "'Sup?" Tyler said as he stepped outside and closed the front door.

Jen softly smiled and said with a wink, "The door's closed now. No one can see or hear us."

Tyler sucked in his cheeks and quickly looked from side to side and behind him before quickly giving his big sister a hug. Jen tried her hardest to keep tears at bay as she pulled away and looked into Tyler's eyes.

"Mom and Dad needed to visit Grandma and Grandpa, so they'll be down in Arizona for a bit."

Excited, Tyler stood on tippy-toes. "Does that mean I get the house all to myself?"

Jen tried her best to conceal her heartache by giving him a sweet smile. "No, you'll be staying with Aunt Karen until they come back."

"Man." Tyler sighed and stuffed his hands in his pockets. He nodded. "She does make really good chocolate-chip pancakes . . ."

"Oh, the best," Jen agreed. It killed Jen to lie to Tyler, but she couldn't bring herself to tell him what had truly happened to their parents.

After wishing him a fun sleepover, she and Victor stood outside of the house underneath a street lamp. The wind started to pick up and the branches were silently swaying in a nightly dance. Crossing her arms to stay warm, Jen looked straight into Victor's steel blue eyes.

"Teach me."

CHAPTER NINE

Malcolm returned to Feralot, the Dark Watcher lair named in honor of Lord Ferox, with a blasting headache and an undelivered promise. Powered by dark magic, this nomadic fortress chewed up the barren landscape of the planet Ocuul, far away from the prying eyes of the League of Light.

Donning a prison guard helmet, Malcolm brought his two newest trophies—Richard and Beth Smith, his former fake girl-friend's adoptive parents—into Feralot's cold and impossibly dark prison bay. Activating the helmet's night vision sensors, he found an open cell next to one occupied by a dingy, gaunt pris-oner. Disgust clear on his face, Malcolm opened the rusty door and tossed them inside.

Richard and Beth, still completely paralyzed, bounced around like stiff plastic toys until they settled on the damp prison floor. The hinges creaked like nails on a chalkboard as Malcolm slammed the cell door shut behind them.

Malcolm dropped his hands to his sides as his rings' lights faded. He groaned from frustration and fatigue as he haphazardly threw the prison guard helmet back on its hanger.

What is wrong with me? I wasn't expecting to let Jen affect me this much. I—

As Malcolm left the prison bay and stepped into a dimly lit

corridor, he was jerked out of his thoughts when he heard a deep voice echo from all around him, vibrating deep into his bone marrow.

"I see that you've returned with a different catch than promised."

"It's all part of my plan, don't worry," Malcolm said testily.

"You promised you could bring the Lancaster girl to us quicker than any other Watcher. What made me believe you and grant you this task, I will never understand."

"Don't worry," Malcolm said again, more forcefully, through clenched teeth, letting frustration slip into his tone. "I have her right where I want her."

"I want her *here*, in front of *me*. That's the only place that matters, boy." The voice rose in volume, emanating from a sunken face that materialized from the shadows.

Malcolm swallowed as he saw the full shrouded form of Lord Draconex tower over him. Draped in a flowing dark maroon cloak, Lord Draconex stood close to seven feet tall and filled the air—and anyone unlucky enough to be in the same room as him—with fear. Malcolm could only see the tip of Draconex's nose, the only part of his face that was not enveloped in a shadow-filled abyss from the hood resting upon his head.

Malcolm tried to maintain eye contact, but couldn't, and sheepishly looked away. His heart rate skyrocketed as if he had just ran a marathon.

"And do not talk back to me"—Draconex leaned down, getting uncomfortably closer to Malcolm's face—"*boy*."

"Y-yes, sir," he stammered, his mouth now cotton-dry.

A hand shot forth from the thick robes like lightning and bony fingers clamped around Malcolm's throat like steel vices. "Did I tell you to speak? You are impetuous in both your words and actions." He finally released Malcolm, dropping him to the floor. Without knowing it, Draconex had lifted him two feet off the ground.

The boy grabbed his throat, hoarsely gulping in air. Tears

made his vision shimmer as he looked up at Draconex, who looked even more menacing through tear-stained eyes.

Standing as still as a statue, but as commanding as a ruthless warrior, the dark sorcerer continued, "The next time you cross paths with your old lover, make sure you capture her alive . . . or your fate will be far worse than that of a prisoner behind these cell walls." Draconex pointed into the cold darkness of the prison bay.

Malcolm nodded silently, feeling cold sweat erupt from every pore on his body. The skin around his throat was tender, burned from Draconex's touch.

"Get out of my sight," Draconex commanded.

Malcolm didn't wait another second before picking himself up off the ground and speeding off to his chamber, head down all the while. Once inside, he closed the door, locked it, and stood in the dark, stifling sobs that only grew in frequency and volume as his adrenaline wore off, leaving him with frayed nerves that were on the brink of collapse.

CHAPTER TEN

For Jen, it was a solemn but determined journey back to Eternal Flame Falls and the gateway portal that led back to Azumar. There was nothing in her life that she wanted more than to rescue her parents, but she began to come to the realization that first, she would need Victor to train her.

Train her in sorcery.

She, Victor, and Skarmor entered the dark cave nestled deep in Chestnut Ridge Park and exited the opposite side in Azumar almost immediately, staying silent for the duration of the short trip. Daylight had come once again, the sun beaming high in the azure sky. A soft wind played across Jen's curly black hair, but she didn't notice it; she was too focused on what needed to be done.

Reading her body language, Victor hazarded a question to Jen before they took off on Skarmor, who was now back to normal as a griffin: "How are you doing, Jen?"

She massaged her neck with her hand. "I'll be fine once we start training."

Victor gave her a long look and exhaled. "I know that you want to do everything possible to rescue your parents, but what lies ahead is as treacherous as it is difficult. I want to make sure you're ready for anything that might come your way."

"All the doubts I had died when I helplessly watched Malcolm take my parents." Jen bit her cheek as that painful memory resurfaced. Looking Victor squarely in the eye, she said, "I understand and am more ready than ever."

Accepting her answer and how she felt, he nodded while patting Skarmor on the neck. "We need to get you enrolled as a tenderfoot of the Sorcery Guild, then." He deftly mounted his griffin and reached out to Jen with an open palm. "Hop on," he said.

"Where do we need to go for that?" She took his outstretched hand and jumped onto Skarmor.

"The institution where I spent my formative years: Watercress Castle."

Despite her tired and frail state, Jen's spirits brightened a touch when she heard the word *castle*. "I guess we can go there," Jen said, playing down her excitement as she propped her head on Victor's shoulder and looked back into the cave at the floating flame.

"Trust me . . . you'll love it." He turned Skarmor to the west and commanded him to take off.

With ten bounding steps and two flaps of his mighty wings, they were soon airborne, gliding above the rolling, lush hills of a faraway land. Victor was scanning the landscape ahead when he noticed Jen's arms had become loose around his waist. He peered over his right shoulder and felt Jen's head resting on his back, her eyelids closed in sleep.

She clearly needed to rest, so Victor commanded Skarmor to change course to his cottage; they would embark on their journey to Watercress Castle, the school of sorcery, the following day.

Partly relieved, Victor decided he would take this extra time to better prepare himself for a return to the place that had banished him ten years before.

CHAPTER ELEVEN

Help! HELP! yelled Jen—

But no sound came from her lips. She felt her veins pulsing in her neck, but she still didn't make a peep. Horror-stricken, she saw her parents imprisoned in a dark, dingy cell. She tried to move, but it was as if she were made of stone. Her eyes strained in the darkness, trying to find a way to reach her family.

A dark figure concealed in a hooded cloak floated into the room and snapped his bony fingers. Her parents disappeared in a plume of smoke and she was left feeling like her heart had been ripped out with those same bony fingers. The figure whipped his head around to look at Jen, revealing his face.

A long, jagged scar ran through his glazed-white left eye. The pupil of his other eye was so contracted that it looked to be as small as the tip of a finely-sharpened pencil. His grin spoke of unspeakable evil as he let out a hoarse yet powerful laugh that chilled Jen to her core.

Finally, she broke her gaze with him and noticed a third presence, immediately feeling more at ease. She couldn't explain it, but she was suddenly filled with trust that everything would be all right.

That was when the tall, evil figure rushed Jen, swallowing her in his cape like a black hole.

* * *

The next thing Jen knew she was back in Victor's cottage.

She shot up from the bed she was laying on, drenched in sweat. Breathing heavily, she put her hands to her cold forehead. The ring on her necklace was glowing a bright purple. As she calmed down, the glowing faded until it was completely gone.

Mom . . . Dad . . .

She laid back down, staring at the fan above her. She followed one of its blades as it made its lazy revolution around and around, calming her as she became lost in her thoughts. She couldn't fall back asleep; her mind was too active.

When will I begin my training?

How long will it take before I'm ready?

Where did Malcolm take my parents?

Every permutation of those questions and a thousand others floated around in her head until she finally drifted off into a dreamless sleep—a sleep that wasn't broken until a ray of morning sunshine hit her face.

Not wanting to get out of bed, Jen reluctantly sat up. There— something familiar on the nightstand. Upon further inspection, Jen realized that it was the diary her parents had given her as a birthday present two days before. Smiling, Jen picked it up and held it to her chest. That diary was the only tangible thing that connected Jen to her parents in this realm. Not her biological parents—her *real* parents. Richard and Beth Smith.

But how did my diary get here?

After praying for their safety, Jen put the diary back on the nightstand, took a deep breath, and walked to the bedroom door. She turned the knob slowly and pushed the door open as quietly as she could.

The first thing she saw was a stack of freshly-made pancakes and a pot of oatmeal. The smells reminded her of waking up on a sunny Sunday morning, the sounds of her mom making breakfast in the kitchen. That memory, paired with these current smells, made her happier—and instantly hungry.

Victor turned from the stove, hearing her, and said: "Looks like someone picked the perfect time to wake up. Just finished making breakfast—I hope you're hungry." He waved her over as he picked up a frying pan and flipped another pancake onto the stack.

With everything that had happened in Jen's life over the past couple days, she had nearly forgotten to eat. Now her hunger was finally at a level that she could no longer ignore. Victor handed her a plate on which she slid three pancakes.

"Thank you," Jen said.

"You need your strength for today." Victor handed her a cup of juice.

Jen took the closest seat at the kitchen table. "Thank you for bringing my diary here."

"My pleasure," Victor said as he stirred the simmering oatmeal. "I wanted you to feel at home while you're with me."

"My parents gave it to me as a gift. For my twenty-first. You have no idea how much it means to me . . . especially now." Jen felt tears form in her eyes, so she stared out the nearest window to collect herself and saw the profile of Skarmor bathing in the sunlight.

"All the more reason why I did it."

Jen sniffled, looking back inside. "I can't wait until I have time to write in it. Some of the things that have happened to me so far . . ." She shook her head.

"There will be more. Trust me." Victor poured some oatmeal into a bowl.

"I don't doubt it," Jen agreed, then suddenly wished to change the subject. "I'm glad you and Skarmor are all right." She began eating her breakfast.

"You and me both." Victor sat down with his bowl of oatmeal and cup of orange juice. "I'm impressed that you were able to hold off Malcolm as long as you did, Jen." He saluted her with a raise of his cup.

She took another sip before stabbing another piece of pancake with her fork. "You never told me why Malcolm left the Guild."

He stopped eating and swirled his cup around, staring at it for what seemed like ages before he cleared his throat and said solemnly, "There's still good in him . . . I can feel it. I first met him when he was eight years old. He was being sent to face the Elder Synod for his rebellious behavior and attitude toward his former mystras, of which he'd already had three by the time I met him." Victor played with his oatmeal, folding it over on itself in his bowl. "My tenderfoot at the time had just passed the Sorcery Trials, so I was searching for another student to instruct. Malcolm seemed like he could excel if put on the right path, so I accepted the challenge." He smiled sadly. "I quickly realized why he had bounced around to so many mystras: his powers were acutely strong for his age, but his temper and need for control made him insubordinate. Lucky for him, I had time. I worked with him day and night, never giving up. As the years passed, he started to mature and develop his powers and skills in a more constructive manner, but it seemed that he was attracted to anything that was forbidden. I would often catch him in underground duels at a place called the Pit."

"What's the Pit?" Jen asked.

"It's an underground dueling club. Sorcery is only allowed on school grounds as an instrument for instruction, which makes the duels in the Pit illegal. As a result, the magic used down there was unchecked and far too dangerous. Many students who dueled in the Pit either left mortally wounded or didn't make it out at all. One night I found Malcolm in the Pit."

Victor placed his left middle finger on the orb atop his silver staff and began to methodically rub it counter-clockwise. A cloud materialized in front of them and in it was a younger Victor. Jen realized he was playing a memory for her, like a home video. She stopped eating and intently watched.

In the memory, Victor was walking quickly down a dimly lit tunnel. His lips were pursed and brow furrowed as he passed flaming torches fastened to the tunnel's walls. Flames flickered as he rushed past them and his footsteps echoed off stone walls, which alerted the sentries standing guard by the Pit's door.

With leveled spears, the guards tried to scare Victor, but he didn't slow down. He simply pointed his gleaming staff at the guard on the left, then the one on the right. Both slammed against the wall, knocked unconscious and slumping to the floor. Without slowing, Victor pointed his staff at the door, busting it open with a powerful gust of wind.

The door's deadbolt shattered as it forcefully flung open into the Pit. Inside, Victor found Malcolm battling another student in the center of a caged ring. Victor was just in time to see his tenderfoot throw a spell that picked up his opponent and tossed him across the ring into a wall of smudged Plexiglas, which cracked but did not break.

The ring was in the shape of a crude hexagon, reaching thirty-five feet in diameter. A dense crowd formed around its edges, stopping only in front of the Plexiglas barriers. Spectators around the perimeter were pounding on it, shouting different spells at Malcolm, hoping he would use one of their suggestions to finish off his defeated opponent.

Those closest to Victor immediately recognized him and parted until there was a clear path straight to the ring. He walked to the railing, ashamed at what he was witnessing.

Watching this, Jen was reminded of ancient Roman Colosseum battles. Back then, gladiators would be pitted against each other to fight to the death for sport. The warrior who gained the upper hand would gauge the crowd's desire for either mercy—shown by a thumbs-down—or death—a thumbs-up. The ruling emperor would make the final decision; except in this case, the Pit's mob-like crowd would just yell their desires, followed by more pounding on the Plexiglas walls.

Victor watched in horror as the defenseless boy, battered and bruised, raised his hands to protect his face from Malcolm's finishing blow. Fire roared in Malcolm's eyes and an eager smile flicked across his face—a smile Victor had seen often—and he raised his hand, which wore his totem ring. It pulsated with orange flares as he started walking toward the other boy.

The crowd's cheering and jeering rose to an unbearable

volume just as Victor slammed the butt-end of his staff on the floor and bellowed, "MALCOLM!" A ripple of energy emanated from his staff, cracking the Plexiglas walls and shaking the solid ground in the deep depths of the Pit.

The mob's raucous noise abruptly stopped. Malcolm lost his balance and fell to the ground. The Pit became eerily quiet. Malcolm turned to flash Victor a look full of surprise that quickly morphed into disdain.

"I thought I taught you better," Victor said, stepping into the ring. " 'Never attack the defenseless,' and 'Only use sorcery for noble purposes.' I'm disappointed."

"Don't judge me, Mystra," Malcolm shot back, still sprawled on the ground. "He told me you're holding me back from my true potential."

Victor stared in confusion as his tenderfoot stood back up. "Who is this 'he'?"

Malcolm dusted off his robes and chuckled. "You know."

Victor paused. "Say his name."

"Lord Draconex."

Victor's eyes went wide with shock. "Malcolm, you cannot trust that man."

"He's already shown me things that you refuse to teach me. That's why I'm here: to practice what he's taught me."

As this unintended conversation unfolded, Malcolm's opponent scrambled for the ring's exit. Malcolm saw him move out of the corner of his eye.

Victor reached out. "Let him go, Malcolm. This is between you and me now."

The boy fumbled with the iron latch. After finally lifting it off, he was swallowed up by the crowd, which had stayed quiet and unmoving, riveted at what might soon take place in the Pit.

"Oh, so you want to see what I've learned? No thanks to you?" Sarcasm dripped from his voice as Malcolm began to circle his master.

"Draconex is manipulating you, like all of the other Dark Watchers! There's a reason why he was expelled from the Guild!"

"Because he had more ambition! He understands my frustration with the Guild . . . and with you! He isn't afraid to push the boundaries."

"There are reasons why the Guild has those rules. We've been over this."

"And that's why we are still stuck in the past," Malcolm spat, "exiled to Azumar instead of taking our rightful place on Earth as rulers!"

Victor could see that Malcolm's temper was starting to boil. He knew him well enough to expect a fight; he could smell it coming in the air.

"Malcolm, it's not too late. Come with me. Forget Draconex and his false promises. You have no idea what you've gotten yourself into. I'll help you get through this. It will be okay . . . if you just follow me."

But Victor knew that Malcolm had made up his mind.

"You've had your chance, *Mystra*." Malcolm shook his head. "I've been limited under your thumb for the past eight years."

Without warning, a blue beam shot forth from one of Malcolm's rings, straight for Victor. He twirled his staff and deflected the attack, sending it to the ground. A hiss erupted from the blast and after the steam evaporated, a deep crater gaped in the Pit's sandy floor.

The commotion in the ring stirred the crowd and once more they were cheering, but for who it was anyone's guess. Victor adopted a fighting stance, holding his staff behind his back so the tip pointed diagonally toward the ceiling.

Malcolm flung another volley of spells Victor's way, which were either deflected or masterfully evaded by the veteran sorcerer. Malcolm was beginning to feel true irritation as he saw Victor start to move. He cursed as his spells missed their mark one after another; Victor deftly maneuvered closer and closer to Malcolm until he was within reach for a sweeping staff blow.

Sensing his master's tactic—a tactic he had once been taught by this very sorcerer—Malcolm pushed off the ground and flipped gracefully over Victor, landing softly on the opposite side of the ring.

Sweat started to bead down Victor's forehead as he looked at the distance Malcolm had put between them with just one leap.

I'm getting too old for this, he thought.

Just as Malcolm and Victor were powering up their rings and staff respectively for another bout, a nauseating wave slammed into both of them, seeming to slow down time. Victor had trouble swallowing as his eyes searched for the new threat. The silver staff slipped from his grasp, slowly falling to the ground, and once it did, a crash loud enough to burst eardrums shocked the ring and everything else in the Pit. Malcolm looked dazed as he fought to remain upright.

Gliding down from the rafters was a dark figure, hands stretched to his sides and rings glowing blood red and sickly green. The yellow ceiling lights shrouded the newcomer in a silhouette. His tall, lanky body was covered in a thick cloak which came to a point on each shoulder, like talons of a killer hawk. With ease, the tips of his boots kissed the ground, and in two steps he stood between Victor and Malcolm. He turned his head and looked straight at Victor, who couldn't believe what he was seeing. Eyes like lava met his and all Victor could think of was his old friend—but much time had passed since he could call this creature a friend.

Immediately the nausea lifted, but Victor's legs still felt like they were made of lead. Blinking, in a haze, he said to the dark figure: "Orin—"

"Ah-ah-ahhhh," the figure chided, shaking a finger. "I don't go by that name anymore, Victor. Say my proper name." He inclined his head, waiting for Victor to respond. When nothing came, he shot Victor a death glare, which looked more menacing with those red eyes. He turned to his new apprentice instead. "Malcolm. Say my name."

"Lord Draconex," Malcolm said haughtily.

Draconex slowly inhaled, like he was drinking in his name. "Yesssss."

He reached outward and clenched his fist. Immediately, a bystander came hurtling from the crowd and into the ring, bringing shattered Plexiglas along with him. It was the same boy who had been dueling Malcolm before. He grimaced in pain, as if trapped in an invisible coil.

"It's not nice to interrupt a duel, Victor. We should let them finish." Draconex's fist was still closed as he looked across the ring, a malicious smile plastered on his face.

Victor tried to move, but he stumbled. He fell to the ground, his hands braced for impact. Right next to him was his staff, having apparently been dropped from senseless fingers.

Draconex laughed and slowly shook his head. "Your time away from dueling has made you weak, Victor. I can sense you've gone soft in your old age."

"The Pit is a place for no one. Let both Malcolm and the boy go." Victor labored between breaths, ignoring Draconex's last verbal jab.

"What's the fun in that?" Draconex asked. The young boy began to levitate while Draconex walked over to Malcolm. "Finish him."

"Malcolm, don't do this!" Victor yelled.

Draconex twisted his fist and the boy let out a piercing scream —his rib cage was being crushed.

"Let the boy go! He's innocent." Victor said to Draconex. "Your issue is with me, not him."

"Oh, but you see, the boy *is* a part of this, whether you like it or not. Whatever happens next will rest on your shoulders," Draconex shot back. "What's your name, boy?"

Draconex loosened his invisible grip on the boy so he could speak clearer. "Gavin," the boy wheezed out.

"Gavin," Draconex repeated, "you do understand that you deserve to be punished, right?"

The boy didn't respond; he met Draconex's gaze with his own and spat on his boots.

Draconex glanced down at his sullied boots. "Seems we have a little fighter in our midst. Too bad he won't be here for much longer."

"Malcolm . . ." Victor looked at his tenderfoot with imploring eyes.

Malcolm's body was stiff with indecision. Clenching his teeth, he looked down at his totem ring, back up at Victor, then to Gavin, then at Draconex.

"You beat him without contest," Draconex whispered. "He deserves to feel your dominance."

With a quick exhale, Malcolm took a step forward and raised his hand toward the boy, willing his ring to illuminate. There was complete stillness in the Pit; no one dared to speak or even breathe.

The captured boy shook with fear. "Please . . . d-d-don't," he stammered.

Sweat poured into Malcolm's eyes and his outstretched hand began to waver. Seconds seemed to stretch into infinity and the whole world stopped.

Then it all happened in the blink of an eye.

"Fine, I'll just do it myself," Draconex said matter-of-factly. Malcolm looked at Draconex with surprise and right before the dark sorcerer was about to crush the boy's ribcage, Victor grabbed his staff and cast an air spell that flung sand into Draconex's eyes, causing him to drop his hold on the boy.

The spell also blew back his hood, revealing a deformed face that told a story of immense pain. Draconex had a shock of black hair that was pulled back into a ponytail, which was held together by a hollow dragon tooth. His face had more scar tissue than healthy skin, including his lips, which were charred, badly burned in some past accident. His left eye, which was intersected by a sharp scar, was a milky white.

Outside of the memory frame, Jen's breath caught in her throat.

With renewed energy, the Victor from the memory ran to the now-unconscious boy, guarding him from a counterattack that never came. Instead, Draconex smiled, pulling back his cracked lips until filed, pointy teeth glinted in the Pit's dim light.

It was then that Victor realized Draconex's true plan. And he'd fallen for it. There was no stopping it now.

"So that's what spurred you into action, Victor?" Draconex yelled. "You would save a random boy over your own tenderfoot!"

Draconex's words hit Malcolm like a hammer to the chest. His eyes welled up with tears, and he screamed at Victor.

"*I hate you!*"

And with that, Draconex snapped his fingers and both were gone, leaving Victor and Gavin in the center of the Pit, surrounded by a crowd that dared not to breathe, let alone move.

* * *

Victor closed the memory frame as quickly as he had manifested it and looked down at his oatmeal, barely touched and now cold and congealed. He looked up to see Jen's ashen complexion. "Jen?"

Jen stared at him silently for a while, then said, "I've seen Draconex before."

Victor raised his eyebrows in alarm. "How?"

"I had a nightmare last night. He was in it."

Victor pursed his lips, hesitant to answer. "It was no nightmare, my dear . . . you had a vision. Your nexus is trying to tell you something."

"He looked a little different in my vision. Who exactly is this Draconex?"

"He was a . . . *is* the commander of the Dark Watcher tribe."

"So he's the one who converted Malcolm?" Jen asked, no longer hungry.

"Yes. What you saw happened ten years ago. The Elder Synod convened a trial after hearing of my involvement in the Pit the night before—a place forbidden for any sorcerer. After deliberation, they banished me from the Guild and stripped away my rank of mystra." He got up and walked to the window by Skarmor.

"But . . . it wasn't your fault. You were there to try and save Malcolm."

"The Elders didn't see it that way," Victor said as he opened up the window and gave his griffin what was left of his breakfast. "Their decision was only strengthened by the fact that there was a comatose boy in the infirmary. In a matter of twenty-four hours, I had lost my tenderfoot and put a stain on my reputation." He grimaced, still living the pain from all those years ago. When Skarmor finished the oatmeal, Victor took the bowl to the sink to wash it off.

Jen walked to Victor and placed her hand on his arm. "You did the best you could, Victor . . . and you saved that boy. Just like you saved me."

Victor looked at her and smiled grimly. "I don't have a lot of regrets in my life, Jennifer, but the one that plagues me the most is losing Malcolm. I should have seen the signs, but I thought I'd prepared him well enough . . . enough, at least, to not be swayed by Draconex and his hold. Now, ten years later, I'm faced with my worst demon: the only student I have ever failed."

Jen could see how tortured Victor was, and it broke her heart. She wished she could reach out to the Victor of ten years ago. Instead she squeezed this Victor's arm. "You're not to blame for the path Malcolm chose."

"Thank you," Victor said, "but it still hurts. Back then, it made me realize that the Dark Watchers were growing in size. I pleaded with the Elder Synod to listen to me, saying that they had infil-trated the Guild. If they could get to Malcolm, there were sure to be others who had been or were currently in the process of being turned. The Elders scoffed at my claim, defending that the Guild could never be compromised in such a way and that they had their sentinels, called the Shepherds of Watercress, in charge of hunting down any Dark Watchers and keeping the Guild pure. Right away, I knew that they were ineffective and that Dark Watchers had slipped through the cracks. This realization led me to form the League of Light, an anti–dark magic unit independent of and unknown to the Guild. Our members are called Light Seekers and our ranks have swelled to over two hundred, which has helped in successfully forcing Draconex and his Dark Watchers deep into hiding, all the while keeping an eye on their movements."

"That's how you knew that I was in trouble on my birthday," Jen realized aloud.

"Yes, though I shouldn't take all the credit. One of my best Light Seekers was responsible for giving me the intel. His name is Gavin Kingsland." Victor put the plate on the drying rack and looked at Jen. "The boy I saved in the Pit."

CHAPTER TWELVE

After breakfast, Jen followed Victor outside to prepare Skarmor for the flight to Watercress Castle. "So, what happened to Gavin?"

"After that night in the Pit, Gavin fell into a coma that lasted four months," Victor said as they worked. "Once he awakened, he searched for me. Through perseverance, Gavin found me here, living on the outskirts of the Great Highlands. Since then, he's become a loyal friend and a trusted Light Seeker." Pride momentarily flashed across his face.

"Where's Gavin now?" Jen asked, feeling the need to thank him.

"Gavin studied with Mystra Mangstrom for years as a Light Seeker. He has since become quite the adept paladin, strong in astromancy." Victor began strapping the riding saddle onto Skarmor's back.

"Astromancy? What's that?" Jen asked.

Victor brushed Skarmor's feathers with his right hand and chuckled. "Never run out of questions, do you, Jen? A sorcerer's nexus can manipulate one of five Mancy planes." He counted them off on his hand. "Astromancy, terramancy, chronomancy, animancy, or telemancy."

Jen focused, committing them to memory.

"Gavin is an astromancer, giving him the ability to tap into the astral plane and connect with cosmic forces. I, on the other hand, am a terramancer and can control natural elements like air, earth, water, and fire."

"Whoa! There's a lot more to sorcery than I realized." Jen scratched her head. "Where do you think I fit in?"

Victor mounted Skarmor, then said with a smile: "You, Jennifer Lancaster, are an omnimancer."

Jen cocked her head slightly to the side. "Omnimancer? That's not one of the five Mancy planes you mentioned, though."

"You're right. Omnimancers have the rare ability to tap into all five planes." Victor looked down at her proudly. "Let's go. We don't want to be late."

* * *

As Skarmor carried Victor and Jen through the skies toward Watercress Castle, Jen listened in rapture as Victor told her more about her heritage.

"There have been hundreds of thousands of sorcerers over the millennia, living across multiple realms." He sat facing Jen so he could be heard above the rushing wind. "But there were only five omnimancer clans: the Goldammers, the Dwins, the Scymarths, the Castleberrys . . ." Victor put a hand on Jen's shoulder ". . . and the Lancasters. They were known as the First Five. For generations, the First Five were the entrusted guardians of the five known MystiCrystals: the ChronoCrystal, TeleCrystal, AniCrystal, AstroCrystal, and TerraCrystal. They were formed from the Big Bang, and together they created life in the universe and the Mancy planes. At the same time, the ShadowCrystal was formed from the five MystiCrystals' residual energies. It remained lost in the universe for billions of years until Lord Ferox discovered it. Unlike the MystiCrystals, the ShadowCrystal is radioactive, making anyone who touches it turn insane."

Jen could see the palpable fear in Victor's eyes.

He continued, "Unleashing what he called the Dark Purge, Ferox used the volatile power of the ShadowCrystal to help him obtain the MystiCrystals by ruthlessly killing off each clan of the First Five, ending with the Lancasters. That was when Genevieve Lancaster sacrificed herself by using the Ring of Lancaster to trap Ferox in the Halostone, stopping his destruction. She left behind an only son, Philip, who would continue on the Lancaster heritage. Genevieve's stand would forever be remembered as the Great Battle, which ended Ferox's attempted coup that would have enslaved the eleven known realms and caused the disappearances of both the MystiCrystals and the ShadowCrystal—something with such dire consequences as the sorcerers could only guess. Since then, the Ring of Lancaster has been sought out by the Dark Watchers, which is the only thing powerful enough to release Ferox from the Halostone," Victor finished.

Jen looked down at the ring around her neck. "It's hard to believe that something as small as this ring holds so much power . . ."

"Jennifer, your family has done an honorable job in keeping it away from the Dark Watchers," Victor said, "but now they are more desperate than ever since Draconex usurped the throne from Gehennon the Wicked and became their undisputed commander." He paused, making sure Jen was looking at him. "That's why you shouldn't place your trust in anyone at Watercress. I'm convinced that more Dark Watchers have infiltrated the Guild than ever before, so we have to be careful when we arrive, even though the only one who knows what you look like is Malcolm."

"I will," Jen promised.

"It is inevitable that your true heritage will come to light, though. I was able to get counsel with the Elders without telling them your true name . . . but once they discover your powers, once they see that you are an omnimancer, they'll know."

Am I ready for this? Jen clutched the ring, pondering what Victor had just said as he twisted back around to face the front. She was surely awestruck, but her determination to save her parents and train to fight this war against Dark Watchers never once waned.

Jen lifted her eyes from the ring and stared at the back of

Victor's head, only able to imagine what he must be feeling, given that he was risking his reputation—or what was left of it—by bringing her to the place that had so diffidently banished him from the Guild all those years ago.

Unable to find the right words to express her gratitude, Jen slid her arms around Victor's waist and gave him a squeeze, hoping that would be sufficient enough to convey her sentiments. She smiled sweetly and rested her head on his shoulder when she felt his hand cover hers and squeeze back in return. As she followed the sun's reflection shimmering across the wind-kissed river, Jen promised herself that she would not let Victor down; she would not let anything stop her from becoming a recognized tenderfoot.

"Jen," Victor called over his shoulder.

Aroused out of her thoughts, Jen lifted her eyes from the lush greenery and sparkling river below to see the magnificent home of the Sorcery Guild.

Overlooking a steep bluff above Lac Cravath, Watercress Castle took up fifty thousand square feet of fertile Azumarian soil. Its design was decidedly unique, taking inspiration from many different cultures as each new headmaster added on to its pre-existing structure as a way to cement their legacy. Jen was impressed by the castle's immense exterior, which had clearly been influenced by architecture from the Gothic steeples of Medieval England and the noble arches of Ancient Rome to the colorful papyriform columns of Ancient Egypt and the romantic domed roofs of Renaissance Italy. The blending of those cultures worked in marvelous harmony, creating an everlasting hallmark from great civilizations.

Seeing movement along the eastern edge of the castle, Jen spotted two men on winged horses—*Pegasuses?* she thought in amazement—fly in their direction, one pegasus as white as freshly-fallen snow and the other black as night.

"Don't be alarmed," Victor called over his shoulder. "These are the Shepherds of Watercress."

Skarmor slowed to a third of his usual speed as the sentinels flew closer. Even though Victor seemed like he was expecting them, Jen's heart was still beating like a racehorse. She found herself holding her breath as the first one spoke, his voice ringing in the clear air.

"State your business!"

"We come to speak to the Elder Synod," Victor said loudly.

The inter-realm crest of the Sorcery Guild was emblazoned on their cuirasses, the breastplates worn by ancient Roman soldiers. It had four quadrants and each one contained a different design: a djinn's lamp with smoke emanating from its spout, a phoenix with wings raised outward like it was about to take flight, five stars that made an X, and a lone flower, which looked to be an elegant rose. Their arms were covered in chain mail and they wore Grecian-inspired helmets that sparkled in the sunlight and had long, flowing mohawks that matched the colors of their pegasuses. On their feet were traditional medieval sandals called sabatons.

Skarmor had completely stopped and hung in the air, beating his wings in strong strokes while Victor talked to the Shepherds.

"Under whose authority?" the other Shepherd asked.

"The Elder Synod," Victor answered.

The Shepherds were quiet for a moment and exchanged glances, until they finally turned their pegasuses around and called back, "Follow us."

Victor stroked his griffin's feathers and relaxed a bit. "Come on, Skar."

Skarmor obeyed and followed the two Shepherds toward Watercress Castle.

Their path of descent took them around a tall, pointed battlement on the castle's east wing, giving Jen a clear view of people walking along open corridors and on grass-covered courtyards below. The Shepherds directed them toward one of the inner courtyards. They peeled off and went back to their job of being on lookout for any unwanted—and potentially hostile—guests. All the while, Victor's words rung in her ear: *I'm convinced that more Dark Watchers have infiltrated the Guild than ever before.*

In total, the flight to Watercress took half an hour, and the sun was almost straight overhead as Skarmor gracefully landed in the central courtyard. Jen looked around the finely manicured area and noticed beautiful, blooming fruit trees. She breathed in and could smell the succulent aromas of honeycrisp apples, Asian pears, Georgia peaches, mandarin oranges, Indian gooseberries, and more, which dotted the courtyard's perimeter.

Victor inhaled long and deep. "I never thought I'd set foot here again," he said as he looked around.

A small coed crowd of tenderfeet were gathering around the southwest edge as children and teenagers alike began chattering and whispering and pointing at the unexpected visitors. An older sorceress who happened to walk by tried to break up the flock, but more were stopping to see what was causing the commotion than leaving, so she inevitably gave up and silently stared alongside them.

All this attention was making Skarmor jittery. Jen could feel his sinewy muscles tighten beneath his furry hide and his breathing become more shallow. Victor put both of his hands on the griffin's neck, calming him down. "Settle, boy. Everything's all right," Victor reassured.

Skarmor clicked his tongue and ruffled his feathers, reluctantly believing his friend. He dropped his massive lion legs to the ground and Victor slid off, followed by Jen. The group that had formed became a gathering, and soon that gathering became a dense crowd—not only of tenderfeet, but also paladins and mystras alike.

Victor and Jen stayed in the center of the courtyard until a sorceress stepped out onto the lawn and walked toward them. Her gait was feminine and authoritative as she made her way toward the center of the neatly manicured lawn. Her black hair was streaked with silver and pulled back into a high bun. Her cloak had a heavy hood, which hung in folds behind her neck, almost reaching her hands, which were clasped behind her back.

Jen picked up on Victor's body language, which had grown tense. A light wind moved leaves on the trees, giving off a slight rustling sound that reminded Jen of playing outside as a kid with her parents and brother.

"Simone," Victor said, giving a soft smile.

"That's Mystra Chen," she corrected, her tone as stiff as her demeanor. "The Elders are expecting you." She then turned her attention to Jen, her voice and expression lightening. "You must be the one we've been expecting."

Before Jen could respond, Victor said, "Yes. This is Jennifer—a true prodigy."

"We'll see about that," Mystra Chen rebutted. Looking around the courtyard, she said, "Well, come along now. Before every other sorcerer and sorceress comes out to stop and stare."

"After you," Victor said. Turning around, he patted Skarmor and told him to wait for them in the courtyard. The griffin ruffled his feathers in bemusement, but reluctantly obeyed and fully sat on the warm grass. He watched as both Victor and Jen followed Mystra Chen, disappearing under a large archway that led farther into Watercress Castle.

CHAPTER THIRTEEN

Jen was acutely aware of the many sets of eyes watching her as she walked down the center of the hallway. Diverting her gaze, she looked to the walls and ceiling.

It's just as beautiful on the inside! she thought.

The crowd of students and teachers stopped following her and just stared into the corridor, waiting to see what Jen would do next—like bystanders at a zoo looking into an animal enclosure.

Jen was so caught up in marveling at all of the wonderful tapestries, painted frames, and eloquent furnishings that she almost lost track of Victor and Chen. Polished marble busts of men and women lined the hallway that they turned down, clearly sculpted by a master; as impressive as this was, it was also a bit unsettling because the busts looked to Jen as if they were alive, silently blinking as they stared straight ahead. One of them had long, curly hair and somehow reminded Jen of herself.

Victor spoke, to cut through the uncomfortable silence as they walked. "These are the founding members of the Sorcery Guild"—he pointed to the six busts on his left, going down the line—"Elwin Castleberry, Merek Scymarth, Meredith Dwin, Elvin Goldammer, and Genevieve Lancaster."

Jen's eyes widened as she recognized her ancestor's name—

but that was all she showed of her surprise; she didn't want to tip off any potential Dark Watcher agent as to who she really was.

"And over here"—he gestured to another five busts to their right—"are the current council members of the Elder Synod. The busts are sculpted to replicate the likeness of each Elder. As they age, so does their bust. Finally, when they pass onto a higher plane of existence, the bust reverts back to how they looked during their prime."

Jen just nodded as she passed the busts, doing her best to soak up all this information. Victor put his hand on her shoulder and gave it a reassuring squeeze this time, telling her that everything would be all right.

Chen didn't say anything or turn around; she just continued to lead them to the Elder Synod's chamber door. It was enormous and gouged out of centuries-old wood. The ceiling soared above them, and the top of the doors matched that height, perhaps thirty-five feet. Jen surmised that ten people abreast could easily walk through the doorway and wondered why it needed to be that tall and wide in the first place. Then again, this *was* a castle . . .

As if the door noticed the three approaching, it silently swung inward on strong, gold-plated hinges to show a great chamber with five vacant chairs, each with matching golden cushions. The giant door closed as quietly and quickly as it had opened, leaving the group alone in the immense chamber.

Walking in, Jen felt the true immensity of the room. Large marble pillars graced the left and right sides of the chairs, which were situated in a hemisphere; the floor of the council chamber was also smooth marble, cut from the same stone as the pillars, and looked to be recently waxed; a deep red rug with golden fringes began under the entrance doors and rolled all the way up to stairs that led to the dais of chairs; a breathtaking chandelier hung high in the center of the chamber, glistening from the sun's rays, which were streaming through the glass dome at the peak of the ceiling; a large mural the size of a school bus towered behind the line of regal chairs, depicting the founding of Watercress Castle.

Jen looked around the cavernous chamber, searching for the five Elders. She had been expecting to see them, all cloaked and distinguished, sitting in each of the five comfortable chairs, but instead she only saw an empty room.

Victor and Chen seemed to think this was normal, for they continued to walk toward the stairs. There was an intricately sculpted font at its base—one that would be seen in a church, used for baptisms—with five crystal bottles, each with a different color, adorning its rim.

Jen tapped Victor's shoulder. "Vic . . . there's no one here."

Without breaking his straight expression, he simply said, "We must request a formal audience with them."

Before Jen could wonder how, Chen walked to the water-filled font. She took each crystal bottle and poured a drop of its contents into the water, which began to glow the colors of the rainbow. As the water continued to shimmer, Chen stepped back in line with Victor and waited.

Jen looked forward just as a bright light shone from the far left chair. Even though it looked bright, it didn't hurt Jen's eyes to stare directly at it. The light's color turned from white to blue while forming the outline of a person. As the light faded, she gazed in astonishment at a middle-aged woman sitting on one of the five chairs like she had been there all along.

A few seconds later there was a second shaft of white light, this time coming from the opposite side of the semicircle of thrones. This light shaft began red before it coalesced into a gentleman slightly older than the woman. He silently nodded at Victor and Chen just as another light appeared, followed by two others that filled the remaining empty chairs. Each light changed from white to the color in one of the crystal bottles before turning into the remaining members of the Elder Synod. In total, there were three men and two women—and Jen recognized all of their faces from the life-like busts Victor showed her back out in the hallway.

For the first time since seeing Beyoncé in concert, Jen was starstruck. She was standing in front of the oldest and quite possibly most powerful sorcerers alive. Without warning, her legs nearly buckled, but she remained upright. Just in case she needed to sit, Jen glanced around for chairs on her level, but couldn't find any.

What I wouldn't give to have Skarmor by my side, she thought, imagining herself collapsing onto his soft fur instead of the hard marble floor.

Jen looked down the row of Elders and stopped when she locked gazes with the sorcerer sitting in the middle chair. He wore a deep purple, velvet robe that cascaded over his shoulders and draped to the floor in heavy waves. Flecks of silver dotted his robes like stars twinkling in a clear night sky. Even though he was sitting, Jen could tell this sorcerer was tall and muscular, though his age bordered seventy years. His strong jaw shaped his silver beard quite nicely on his face, and his eyes never parted from hers, like he was discovering who she really was just by looking into her eyes. He was the first to speak.

"Simone . . . Victor," he said in a dignified deep voice.

Both Chen and Victor bowed their heads and said in unison: "Grand Mystra Cindergray."

Cindergray continued, "We debated on whether or not we should convene under such vague intentions as testing an unknown potential tenderfoot, but this recommendation—coming from a trusted and esteemed sorceress like Simone—could not be denied."

Victor nodded his approval at Chen, who quickly responded, "I can assure you, sir, that this meeting is paramount."

"Victor . . . I never imagined seeing you back on the Guild's grounds," Cindergray said, "but it's good to see that you're well."

"Thank you, sir." Victor bowed again. "Even though I have no right to be here in front of you, I still feel that it is my duty to help strengthen our ranks by bringing in candidates if I come across any."

Still two full steps behind Victor, Jen grimaced as she felt her heart pull. She didn't like how gracious Victor was to the very sorcerers who had vilified him ten years ago for going after Malcolm and ultimately saving Gavin. Even if they were the sagacious Elder Synod, she expected more of a fair trial.

Victor stepped to the side and presented Jen, who froze in surprise. Her mouth went cotton-dry and she found it hard to talk —even breathe—but then she looked at Victor and his presence calmed her enough to move her feet and step forward.

"Good tidings, my dear," Cindergray said, though his face was still grave. "Welcome to Watercress. I am Aldred Cindergray, the Grand Mystra of the Sorcery Guild."

Before Jen could say her name, the Elder on the far left began talking. "I am Merek Stonebridge, Mystra Terramancer. Welcome." Stonebridge looked to be in his mid-forties, with no hair on his perfectly spherical head aside from salt-and-pepper eyebrows that curled up near the ends, making them look like bat wings. He wore an old gray cloak that was clasped around his neck with a golden chain. He had a stolid demeanor, even in his introduction.

"I am Ellwyn Skycap but you can call me Elle, Mystra Animancer." The woman sitting to the right of Stonebridge winked down at Jen. She wore a shiny mink-fur coat and knee-high leather boots. She looked to be around fifty years old, with wisps of gray in her deep brown, wavy hair. Skycap reminded Jen of a movie star from the 1940s.

Next in line was Cindergray, who had started the introductions, so he let the fellow on his right speak. "Étoilier. Jayden Étoilier. Mystra of the Astromancy Plane. Enchanté." The way Étoilier introduced himself made Jen immediately think of the fictitious debonair spy, James Bond. He said his name like *Shay-duh A-twol-ee-ay*, with the help of his slight French accent. His square jaw ended in a cleft chin. Jen assumed he once had dirty-blond hair, but now it was lighter as white hair started to emerge with age.

And finally, the last Mystra said, "Good afternoon, young lady. I'm Ingrede Childahorn. Mystra Telemancer." Her spectacles were rose-gold and had round, thick lenses that made her eyes look comically large, like she was looking at you through magnifying glasses. Her red bangs just touched her thinly trimmed eyebrows, making her look younger than the rest of the Elders.

"And I'm the chronomancer of this council," Cindergray said.

Once it was clear they had finished their introductions, Jen said in a shy voice, "I'm Jennifer, but you can call me Jen if you'd like. Very nice to meet you all."

"Likewise, my dear," said Cindergray. "And where are you from?"

"Uh . . . New York, sir." She still had her hands clasped in front of her, like she was wringing out a wet towel.

"Ah, the Big Apple. It's been a while since I visited that metropolis," the Grand Mystra mused, then warmly asked, "How was your trip to Watercress?"

Swallowing a few times and hoping that she could find her voice, she looked up and said, "Good, sir."

"Good?" Cindergray laughed. "Don't be shy, my dear. We were all in your position at one point." He motioned to his left and right, sweeping over all of the Elders.

Jen took a deep breath and said, "It was . . . *extraordinary*, sir. I rode a griffin here, which sure beats flying in a plane. And this castle is breathtaking." As she began letting down her guard, she dropped her hands to her sides, feeling a bit more comfortable.

"It is truly a marvel, yes. How about I give you a tour after our discussion?" Cindergray proposed with a twinkle in his eye.

"If you could spare the time, sir." Smiling, Jen had enough presence of mind to slightly bow in gratitude.

"It will be my most humble of pleasures." Cindergray's smile grew. "You'll get to see all of the wonderful decorations for the upcoming Sesquimillennial Jubilee."

Jen's smile broadened with his. "A jubilee?"

The Grand Mystra chuckled. "Yes, indeed. It's to celebrate the fifteen hundredth anniversary of the Great Battle, when darkness was vanquished from the known realms."

Wow! Fifteen hundred years? Jen tried to hold in her surprise.

"Victor told me about that on the way here. I'm even more excited and honored to be here for it."

Cindergray nodded and looked at Victor. "If her nexus's power is half as impressive as the way she presents herself, she should make a wonderful tenderfoot."

"I'm glad you think so, sir," he said to Cindergray, then took in the rest of the Elders. "I can guarantee that her nexus is very strong."

"Let's find out," Cindergray replied, "shall we?"

CHAPTER FOURTEEN

In the hours that had passed since his confrontation with Lord Draconex, Malcolm stayed locked in his room, embarrassed and obsessed. Embarrassed to show his face again and obsessed to find Jen's whereabouts. Still feeling the aftereffects of his master's stifling chokehold, Malcolm winced as he stretched his neck to the left and right.

As he racked his brain, Malcolm thought, *If I'm not the one to bring Jen in, Draconex will still think me stupid and weak, effectively ruining my plans. I need to show him I can capture her! That'll put me in perfect position to find the Halostone and free Lord Ferox. He'll be so thankful he'll give me everything I could ever desire.*

He was flipping through the pages of one of his old books too quickly; one page ripped completely out. Rage filled his vision as he slammed the book shut and threw it at his chamber door. In the instant the book left his hand, his door swung open to reveal Lord Draconex, who caught the book before it could slam into his face.

A cold chill ran through Malcolm's body. The quick movement had shaken the dark hood from his lord's head to reveal the vertical scar on his face, along with an expression of disapproval.

"Now what did this inanimate, millennia-old book do to you to make you so furious?" Draconex asked, condescension dripping in his voice.

Malcolm held the ripped piece of paper up in explanation. "I ripped a page and—"

"You have been a thorn in my side for too long," Draconex cut him off. He dropped the book on the ground, sending dust up into the air as he entered the chamber.

Malcolm didn't know what to think except that Draconex was here to kill him. But how? A quick snap of the neck, breaking his vertebrae? A dark spell, stopping his heart, perhaps? A heel strike to the throat, crushing his windpipe?

Malcolm glanced at his fists for his rings, but remembered with a cold panic that he'd taken them off. With regret, he saw them on their holders near the door, which was on the other side of Draconex.

Draconex noticed Malcolm eyeing his rings. "A worthy sorcerer can conjure spells without his totem, even if it is difficult to do. Are you so weak that you need your precious rings to do battle?" He stepped closer to Malcolm, feeling the boy's fear escalate. His faded scar began to flare a dull, mauve color and faintly throb as he tried to control his temper.

"I-I-I . . . I can prove to you I'm a strong sorcerer," the boy stammered. "Let me go out one more time and capture Jen!" Malcolm was on the edge of hysteria. He backpedaled, tripped on the edge of his table, and clumsily crashed to the ground. He quickly whipped his head around so he could see Draconex, potentially for the last time.

"Stow it, boy," Draconex demanded. "I've heard the last of your useless promises." He stopped to pick up another book that had fallen from the table Malcolm had tripped over. Flipping through the pages, not caring what was on them, he continued, "I wouldn't let you try again even if I thought you could capture her and the ring. My source at Watercress tells me that Victor has already arrived with her." Draconex closed the book so hard that dust erupted from its yellowed pages.

SLAM!

"That is why I have been forced to set a stealthier plan into motion."

Malcolm felt a twinge of resentment as he realized what Draconex must mean.

"Dark Watcher Blake will make the next move." Draconex shot an icy glare of contempt at Malcolm, who hadn't moved from the ground. He placed the book back on the table and loomed above the cowering sorcerer. "You have so many limitations of which you need to break free, boy."

The Dark Watcher commander took a few more steps closer, then stopped again. Malcolm couldn't think straight; his body froze in fear as he bumped up against his bookshelf, fearing what Draconex would say or do to him.

* * *

Watching him sweat, Draconex stood over Malcolm, imposing his will and reminding the boy of who was in charge.

After a few minutes of heart-stopping silence, he replaced his hood on his head and said, "If you're going to remain here, you need proper training so I don't kill you myself."

It was painful for him to get the sentence out, as he was fighting against his better judgment; but he allowed Malcolm to relax a bit . . . just enough so the boy wouldn't have a stroke.

"Come up to my den tomorrow morning. Don't be tardy."

Lord Draconex opened the door and left Malcolm's chamber, partly to prepare Malcolm's first instruction, partly to calm his nerves before he snapped and killed the boy. Malcolm had been a thorn in his side ever since that night at the Pit. At first Malcolm had shown promise, but his impatience and volatile temper proved him a difficult tenderfoot.

Draconex had chuckled at how easy it was to steal Malcolm away from Victor, but his perception quickly changed to one of regret and loathing. He couldn't kill the boy because Malcolm wasn't completely useless . . . *some* of the time.

He had to acknowledge the boy's persistence when it came to Jennifer Lancaster, though. Draconex had never seen Malcolm so passionate about anything in the decade he had known him. In fact, surprisingly enough, Malcolm was the first to discover Jen and realize that her warding spell was wearing off. But his poor execution had tipped off the League of Light and had given himself and the whole Dark Watcher tribe more embarrassment and frustration than respect.

If Malcolm wasn't going to give up, Draconex had to instruct him properly so that when the time was ripe, he could trust that Malcolm would finally, *successfully* return with Lancaster . . . and that blasted ring.

Until then, he could trust that his sleeper agents in Watercress would keep an eye on Lancaster and her movements; that put the lord's mind at ease as he strode down the empty, dimly lit corridor. His scar had finally stopped throbbing, and when he glanced in a mirror he was pleased to see that it was returning to its normal color of dead scar tissue.

Malcolm was the only person in all the realms to make his scar flare up so quickly; he was not looking forward to instructing the boy, but it was a means to an end. It had become a necessary part of Draconex's plan—a plan that would shake the realms to their cores and reveal their true, destined ruler.

CHAPTER FIFTEEN

Cindergray waved her over. "Come up, young lady."

Before she moved, Jen glanced at Victor. He flashed her a reassuring smile and mouthed, *You'll do great.*

Jen smirked, but still felt a knot of anxiety over what the Elders were going to have her do. She poised herself, took a deep breath, and walked up the glistening marble stairs.

As she ascended, Cindergray twirled his fingers and a chalice formed out of thin air. It was lined with rubies, sapphires, and emeralds, immediately catching Jen's eye. Still suspended in midair, it smoothly levitated into one of Cindergray's outstretched hands. With his free hand, he pointed into the chalice and a glowing liquid filled it almost to the rim.

Jen had already reached the top, but she was so mesmerized at the spectacle that she didn't notice she had reached the top of the stairs. When she brought her leg up, her foot found only thin air and slammed to the ground, loudly echoing throughout the chamber.

All of the Elders were jolted at the unexpected noise, but not so much as Cindergray; he nearly spilled the contents of the chalice. Victor couldn't suppress a small chuckle as he saw the Grand Mystra break composure, even if it was only for a second.

Jen blushed furiously, forcing out an awkward laugh and clasping her hands once more in front of her.

After taking hold of the chalice firmly with both hands, Cindergray cleared his throat and said, "We need to discover just how powerful your nexus is, Jennifer. This elixir"—he slightly raised the chalice—"will briefly augment your power so we can identify which Mancy plane you can connect with."

Jen was so nervous that her hands began to shake as she took the chalice from Cindergray, causing an almost imperceptible ripple across the surface of its contents. It was comfortably warm as she cupped the bejeweled chalice; she noticed steam rising from the elixir. She blew softly over the surface to cool it down and tentatively took a first sip. The flavors she experienced could not be explained in any other way except to say that it was absolutely *intoxicating*. As the warm liquid filled her, she closed her eyes in delight and took the liberty of finishing every drop. Jen felt warm and cozy inside, and she was suddenly reminded of a New York memory: enjoying a hot cup of coffee on a cold, rainy morning.

Holding the now-empty chalice, Jen noticed that the ring on her necklace had begun to glow purple yet again. Her sense of dread multiplied; the only other times the ring had glowed was when Malcolm—and danger—were nearby. To her relief, he didn't pop out from behind any of the pillars or chairs, or break down the immense door behind her, and she attempted to calm down.

Cindergray's eyes widened as he and the rest of the Elders noticed the faint purple glow beneath Jen's shirt, but none asked about it, instead continuing on with the testing process.

"Do you feel any different, my dear?" Cindergray asked.

"I feel . . . at peace. Content," Jen said honestly.

Mystras Stonebridge and Childahorn, the Elders farthest away from the center, leaned in to make sure their eyes weren't playing tricks on them and that there was in fact something glowing on Jen's chest.

"Good," the Grand Mystra said, for now choosing to ignore

the glowing ring. "The more relaxed you are, the easier it is for your nexus's power to surface."

"Here's your chalice." Jen lifted her hands, but noticed that the chalice was no longer in her grasp. She glanced toward her feet to make sure it hadn't dropped from her hands and was lying dented on the marble floor, but she could see no sign of the ornately encrusted chalice anywhere. Before she could say anything, all of the Elders began to talk—not in English, but a language Jen had never heard before.

Jen couldn't understand a single word, but the more she listened the more she inexplicably began to intuit that each Elder was speaking in a different, alien tongue. She tightly closed her eyes and tried to focus on each; some were harsh and short while others were smooth and sing-songy. Each dialect became more and more noticeable and less alien until, shockingly, she realized she could clearly hear each Elder and understand what they were saying. Jen's eyes popped wide open and she looked at each Elder, amazed; it was like a light switch had flipped inside her brain, giving her knowledge and fluency of several new languages at once.

She looked from one mystra to another, beginning with Mystra Childahorn, who was sitting as straight as a board, eyes closed, and holding a finger to her temple. Her mouth was closed, but Jen could hear her in her mind as clear as day.

—*the mindpower bestowed upon humans hath separated us from other animals. We are wielders of influence and concept, determined to forge our own destiny . . .*

Jen then focused on Mystra Skycap, who was chanting and rhythmically pounding on the arms of her chair. "—it is our duty as animancers to maintain a harmonious union with our brethren, the animals. They give us strength and powers akin to their own . . ."

Mystra Étoilier's voice suddenly captivated Jen's attention: "—we are all made from stardust that spans each quadrant of the known universe, giving us an unbreakable connection to the cosmos . . ."

"—the four elements give balance to life: air . . . water . . . fire . . . earth. For that we are more connected to the soul of Terra Firma than any other species . . ." recited Mystra Stonebridge.

Finally, Jen looked at Cindergray.

"—time is a concept," he was saying, "a concept that can be manipulated. The only thing that time gives us is age. Age is merely an illusion when looking into the hourglass of existence . . ."

It became too much for Jen. She closed her eyes again and held out her hands. "My head's starting to hurt. Could you all take turns, please?"

All of the Elders stopped talking almost simultaneously, their faces showing the same look of surprise and awe. Cindergray was the first to start speaking again, this time in English.

"You understand . . . *all* of us?"

She opened her eyes hesitantly. "Eventually. At first it was just noise, but I picked up on what each of you were saying once I focused. It sounded like you all were reciting oaths of some kind . . . ?"

All of the Elders exchanged looks, but said nothing.

"Very astute of you, Jen," Cindergray finally acknowledged. "Each Mancy clan has its own dialect of the ancient language, Sorcier. The first part of the placement test is to see which dialect you can understand when they are simultaneously spoken. Usually untrained tenderfeet can only focus on one dialect with the help of the elixir, but you seem to understand them all—a great feat."

Étoilier was leaning on the edge of his chair with a slack-jawed expression. A tiny smirk began to crawl up his face. He laughed and clapped his hands together. "*Mon Dieu*, could this be true?!"

The remaining Elders seemed equally stunned. Some of them were softly whispering to each other until Cindergray held up a hand, calling for silence.

"We will see if it holds true in the second part of the test." He stood up to his full height and motioned for Jen to follow. "Come this way, my dear."

* * *

The ring was still glowing around her neck as Jen followed Cindergray out of the council chamber and into an open, rectangular courtyard which seemed to be only accessible from the Elders' chamber. The sun shone brilliantly over its expert landscaping and the greenest grass Jen had ever laid her eyes on. In the center of the courtyard were two parallel rows of crisp hedges, which spanned the entire length of the courtyard. There was a pool of tranquil water a third of the way into the path and, Jen noticed as she looked farther behind it, a pedestal at the opposite end of the courtyard. It looked to be about chest-high and was cut from the same marble as the magnificent columns found in the chamber of the Elder Synod. Resting on the altar was a slightly irregular but spherical orb that glistened the color of polished gunmetal.

Jen felt a tug on her neck and looked down to see that the ring was being drawn to the orb, like a powerful magnet. She quickly put her hand over it, which seemed to do the trick as it fell back onto her collarbone, still glowing.

Cindergray stopped at the beginning of the hedged area and Jen followed suit. He waited for the rest of the Elders, Victor, and finally Chen to file out of the castle before he spoke.

"Now that you have passed the mental half of the placement test—with flying colors, I might add—it is now time for the physical portion: the Chimera Course." Cindergray pointed at the row of hedges. "You seem to have a connection to all of the planes, but this course gauges the actual outward strength of your powers. Much like the powerful chimera—an immortal creature with the combined look and abilities of a lion, goat, dragon, and snake—this obstacle course has four parts. Your goal is to make it through each part and retrieve that orb on the altar." He pointed to the pedestal in the distance. "The only rule is that you must stay between the two rows of hedges . . . otherwise, you will be disqualified."

Jen stared at the pedestal, her lips pressed into a determined line.

"You are older than the average age of a fledgling tenderfoot, my dear, which is nine years old. Having said that, we have made a few adjustments to this course, but I assure you it is just as safe." Cindergray put his large hand on Jen's shoulder. "You may start whenever you wish."

"Before I start, may I speak with Mystra Huxley?"

Cindergray said, "As you wish." He stepped aside so Jen could walk over to the man who had only walked into her life a few short days ago, but who was now the only person she implicitly trusted.

Before Jen could ask her question, Victor started speaking. "Jen, I can't tell you anything about this part of the test, only that you must never let your guard down."

As he spoke, Jen's eyes floated from Victor to the course. It looked too easy to be true. The hedges bordered an open lane of grass with a pool, and all that was between Jen and the altar was empty air.

Victor noticed that Jen wasn't looking at him. "*Jenny*—pay attention." He deliberately stepped in front of her, blocking her view of the course. "They already know that you are an omnimancer, so don't be afraid to hold back. Your reflexes will be tested as well as your powers. This course isn't as straightforward as it looks."

"That's what I'm afraid of." Jen's voice became desperate. "What if I don't make it to the altar, Vic? How am I supposed to save my parents if I can't even complete a lousy obstacle course?" She felt her composure beginning to break.

Victor placed both hands on her shoulders. "You were able to stop Malcolm from capturing you at your parents' house—and save me and Skarmor in the process. You have more courage and strength than you realize, Jen. Just focus on getting that orb, okay?"

Jen was biting her lower lip and her left leg shook slightly—nervous ticks she'd developed as a young girl. "Okay."

"You can do this," he said, wrapping her in his arms.

This was the first time Victor had hugged Jen, and she was thankful for his embrace. That hug embodied her mentor's confidence in her, and it gave her renewed vigor to face the Chimera Course.

"Okay . . . I'm ready."

At her pronouncement, Jen watched Cindergray and the rest of the Elders line the length of the hedges. With hands clasped in front or behind them, they waited for her to start.

As she quickly pulled her hair into a ponytail, Jen looked down at her feet and stepped to the course's starting line.

At Cindergray's pronouncement, the clock began counting up . . . but nothing happened.

Well, that was anticlimactic, she thought.

She cautiously walked toward the edge of the pool, making her way well into the course. As she approached the moat, she realized that it was too long for her to jump across. As she considered jumping in and swimming to the other side, the ring began to pulse again and she saw movement out of the corner of her eye.

Mystra Stonebridge, the Elder terramancer, fell into an L-stance and extended his right hand, which carried a ring on each finger. Scorching flames erupted from his clenched fist and roared toward her.

Jen's life flashed before her eyes, and she was unable to move as fear paralyzed her body. Time seemed to slow down as the fire flicked toward her, triggering her most traumatic memory—getting badly burned as a child—and a recurring nightmare . . . being burned alive.

Without thinking, she managed to dive into the cold water just as a wall of flames passed over where she had just stood. Her body seized up from the shock of the frigid water, but at that moment Jen felt the safest in the freezing water. Stubbornly, she tried staying underwater for as long as possible, all the while being bombarded with traumatic memories of when she was horribly burned by an out-of-control bonfire. She could still remember feeling the scorching flames wrap around her, hearing her parents scream in horror, smelling the stench of burnt hair and skin . . . but eventually she had to resurface or risk drowning. Frantically, she swam upward and gulped in air once she broke the surface of the water, sputtering.

She was only able to take in one deep breath as another spurt of searing-hot fire was launched at her. Shaking, she dove back down into the water to escape the onslaught. This time, her worst nightmare took control over her mind and body—the nightmare in which she was trapped in a small room with no doors or windows and a floor of fire that kept growing and getting hotter. In the nightmare, she couldn't move or yell for help as she was slowly burned to death.

Wanting to never leave the eerily serene waters of the Chimera Course, Jen floated motionless as her body went catatonic. Eventually, she reverted into the fetal position, wishing Victor would rescue her from this real-life nightmare at any moment.

When Jen thought she had used up all of her oxygen, a pulse from her ring sent a shock wave through the water. Astonished, Jen involuntarily inhaled and began to breathe . . . *underwater*. Looking around in shock, Jen hesitantly took in another breath and experienced the same strange paradox of feeling water flow through her nose but also breathing as easily as if she were on dry land.

Her vision focused and she could see as clearly as if she were above the water. Relaxing her muscles, she looked toward the surface to see orange light filtering through the water, telling her that Mystra Stonebridge was keeping up his barrage of fire.

Focus, Jen. Go forward, never backward. She imagined Victor by her side, saying those words.

And focus she did.

The water was crystal-clear, making it easy for Jen to get ahold of her bearings. She looked below to see how deep the pool was, but only saw it extend down into endlessness. Not interested in seeing how far down it went, she looked forward and could see the other side, which was about twelve meters in front of her. Jen had swam in college, so she equated the distance to about half of a regulation-size lap pool.

Kicking off of the wall like a trained swimmer, Jen fell into a streamlined post and dolphin-kicked for the first several meters before transitioning into a breaststroke. She didn't want to risk resurfacing only to get burned, so she gladly stayed fully immersed in the water.

In to time, Jen had made it to the other side. A quick glance upward revealed no orange refractions on the surface, only sky blue, so she swallowed her fear and slowly swam toward the light.

Breaking the water's surface, she was relieved to see that Stonebridge didn't shoot any more fireballs at her . . . but the ground in front of her was crackling with fire.

Great. Thanks, Stonebridge.

She looked behind her to see the same result on the other end. She was effectively trapped.

She was at a loss for what to do next, until she felt a power surge through her. The ring warmed her numbing arms and feet as she looked at the wall of fire, feeling the heat on her cheeks. With just her sopping-wet head above the water, she opened her hands and felt water swirl around her buoyant body. Instinctively, Jen pointed her palms away from her, and suddenly it felt as if she was standing on something solid. Her body elevated out into the hot air until it looked as if she were standing on the surface of the water.

She clenched her fists. Water on each side of her spewed forth at the blazing fire. The water immediately turned into steam when it made contact with the fire, but still she willed the water forward. In a matter of seconds, the blazing flames were completely extinguished and it was safe for Jen to run to the edge of the moat.

Standing on solid ground again and amazed at what she had just done, Jen dropped her hands to her sides and inhaled deeply; a brisk wind picked up and dried her off.

* * *

From behind the course's starting line, Victor looked on in amazement. At first, he was worried by how long Jen had managed to stay underwater, but his worst thoughts dissipated when he saw her emerge unharmed on the other side of the pond.

He couldn't believe it was coming this easily to Jen. She was able to control the water like an adept terramancer. Victor glanced at Stonebridge and saw amazement reflecting back at him, and pride swelled in his chest.

* * *

Feeling the power die down momentarily, Jen looked ahead and saw an open path of grass that led straight to the altar.

As soon as she began to run, she heard a deep, muffled groan. A large stone slab the width of the course rose up in front of her, blocking her view of the finish line and altar. She looked across the hedges to see Mystra Étoilier motioning with his hands.

He's using astromancy to create another obstacle!

When the slab stopped rising, Jen looked up and guessed it was about forty feet high—something she could not jump. It looked smooth and didn't seem to have any foot- or handholds, so climbing it was out of the question as well. Jen also dismissed going around the hedges—that would disqualify her.

Stepping back, she closed her eyes and breathed in slowly. Trying to mimic Étoilier's hand movements, she twirled her hands in front of her . . . but nothing came of it; the black, shiny slab was just as solid and imposing as before.

Okay . . . different tactic, then, thought Jen.

She walked to the slab and ran her hands across its surface, which was smooth and slightly warm. A few seconds later, with her hands still touching the gargantuan wall, Jen's eyes widened in surprise when she could sense the molecules that made up the slab. Its bonds were symmetrical and strong, much like her own.

The answer came to her suddenly: it was made of carbon.

Over the years, Jen had taken a lot of chemistry classes to prepare for medical school, so she knew the periodic table of elements like the ABCs. Jen chuckled. That was why Étoilier was able to make the barrier: his powers of astromancy could tap into not only his knowledge of the cosmos, but also the elements from which the cosmos were constructed.

Jen backed away from the wall.

What is the most powerful force in the universe?

Jen said aloud with a slight smirk: "Gravity."

The Ring of Lancaster's purple glow reflected in the polished slab in front of her, but now that glow was joined by—

My eyes . . . my eyes are glowing, too!

Jen reached out and clenched her fists. As if she had been doing this her entire life, the carbon barrier cracked under the immense pressure of gravity until it started to crumble. Before long, the once-great wall was nothing but a pile of jagged, broken shards of debris.

Jen carefully jumped over the rubble, getting closer to the atlar step by step.

* * *

Étoilier laughed and clapped his hands together, calling, "*Bon travail, ma chérie!*"

"Well done, indeed," Victor repeated, mostly to himself.

He looked over at Chen, who was still standing next to him. She at first looked indifferent, but a glimmer of her old self broke through as she looked into his eyes. Fleetingly, Victor felt as if they were young again—before they both became mystras and before he was banished from the Guild.

With sorrow creeping into his heart, he was the first to look away and again focus on Jen, who was about to encounter the next obstacle.

* * *

Having now completed over half the course, Jen clipped along as quickly as a track star running in a race until the ground began to rumble beneath her. She slowed down and glanced across the hedges to see Mystra Skycap stomping on the ground like an angry elephant. The Elder let out a loud bellow akin to a pachyderm's trumpeting call and raised her head to the sky. Jen would have laughed at the strangeness of it if the rumbling wasn't increasing in magnitude. Focusing back on the task at hand, Jen tried to remain upright, but the tremors threw her balance off so badly that she fell to the ground.

She could see the altar straight ahead, even though it was blurry from the ground's seismic shaking. Jen tried getting up, but soon found herself back on the ground, unable to steady herself.

Jen could feel the ring softly bounce on her chest as the ground continued to shake, and when she looked down at it she wasn't surprised that it was still glowing. Preparing for another display of power from her nexus, Jen's eyes locked onto the pedestal, making her vision clear and crisp as she felt her chest swell with a warm energy.

She jumped—

I'm levitating!

Sure enough, she hadn't come down from her leap, instead floating ten feet off the ground, safe from the effects of Skycap's earthquake.

"All right! Let's go forward," Jen said to herself.

Testing out her newfound ability of flight, she started to drift backward when she slightly shifted her weight and twirled her arms.

"Okay, okay, okay, no," Jen said. "*Forward*, not back."

She tilted her arms in the opposite direction and began to hover toward the finish line.

Is this for real?!

She flew forward about ten yards until her arms were too exhausted to keep her airborne. Mystra Skycap was evidently pleased with Jen's solution to her earthquake; she'd stopped stomping, and the ground settled just as Jen landed. She exhaled and wiped beads of sweat from her forehead as she stretched out her tired arms.

Even though her surprise flying lesson had sapped a lot of energy out of her, Jen could see the altar just twenty-five yards away.

Nothing was going to stop her—not now.

She broke into a run again and was surprised to see that no other obstacles appeared before her, nor were any of the mystras casting spells.

Maybe the earthquake was the last test?

Jen ran faster, and in a few quick bounds, she was only five yards away from the altar. Her heart raced with excitement as she counted the steps to the finish line, but her smile faded when she realized she was going . . . *backward*. Looking down, Jen at first couldn't comprehend what she was seeing.

One step forward . . . was actually one step backward.

What the . . . ?

She looked back up and saw Cindergray standing to the right of the altar, holding a large pocket-watch which was glowing a bright white.

Jen realized what must be happening.

He's manipulating time to reverse my progress through chronomancy!

With this knowledge, she tried walking backward in hopes she would move forward, but she still moved farther away from the altar. Side to side was the same result.

Jen was stuck.

She looked down at her ring. "Come on, wake up."

The tighter Jen clenched the ring around her neck, the more powerful she felt. She opened her hand and saw the familiar purple glow emanating from her palm. Clenching her eyes shut, Jen pictured an hourglass, its sand traveling upward against gravity instead of cascading down to its base.

Focusing so hard that she felt her neck muscles strain, Jen imagined the sand slowly reversing its trajectory and beginning to fall downward with the friendly help of gravity. Time then seemed to slow down as she felt direction right itself.

Jen put her left foot in front of her and moved forward; she felt as though she were moving through thick molasses—but at least she was moving in the right direction. She continued to put one foot in front of the other, more determined to reach the altar with every step.

* * *

Victor, Chen, Cindergray, and the rest of the Elder Synod looked on as Jen seemed to jump from five yards behind the finish line to a yard over it in the blink of an eye.

Jennifer Lancaster had passed the Chimera Course, and in record time.

* * *

Cindergray flashed a tight smile as he tucked his totem pocket-watch deep within the folds of his robes. The smirk was barely visible under his heavy beard, but Jen caught it in time. Smiling back without stopping, Jen walked to the altar to pick up the shiny, metallic orb she'd earned.

Her hand stopped a few inches from it as a vision overtook her senses. It was hazy around the edges, but she could make out the courtyard of the Elders and—and . . . *herself*? And as if she were looking through a stranger's eyes, she saw an arm thrust a spear directly toward her.

The vision immediately dissipated and Jen heard the piercing call of Skarmor high overhead. Jen instinctively ducked and felt the *whoosh!* of a spear shooting over her head. It stuck deep in the ground a few yards from her. She stared at the projectile in astonishment, then looked to the top of the courtyard's highest wall just in time to see Skarmor attack a hooded figure with his razor-sharp claws.

Victor and Cindergray were immediately by Jen's side, standing protectively over her as they too watched the battle between human and griffin unfold. The black cloak was so thick that it made Jen unable to distinguish if the assailant was male or female.

The figure attempted to cast one more spell, but was instead slammed into a stone railing by Skarmor. The railing cracked like dry wood, spilling the figure over the wall's edge. The assailant fell thirty-five feet onto the courtyard's lawn.

Skarmor unleashed a victory cry as he swooped down and landed next to Jen, covering her with his wing in case any other attempts at her life were made.

The intruder was surrounded by the rest of the Elders before a move was made. Mystras Étoilier and Childahorn were already powering up their totems as Victor went over to inspect the spear. He waved his staff over the weapon, careful not to touch it. His staff glowed and faintly hummed for just a few seconds, then fell still. With a worried look on his face, Victor walked over to Cindergray and whispered in his ear.

Cindergray's eyes widened with surprise before he thanked Victor and marched over to the intruder, who was still motionless on the ground.

Victor went back to where Jen sat and patted Skarmor fondly on his side. "Good job, Skar."

Jen looked up at Victor. She was still shaking from the adrenaline in her system. "What did you find out?"

Victor didn't say a word, nor did he take his eyes off Cindergray as he idly patted his griffin.

Jen moved toward the Elders, but Victor caught her arm. "No, Jen."

Jen pulled her arm out of his grasp, flashing him a look of irritation "This person tried to *kill* me, Vic. I deserve to know."

Skarmor quietly offered his agreement, but before Victor could respond Jen was already on her way to where her would-be assassin lay. A few yards away, she saw Cindergray enter the circle of Elders right before she arrived. He then knelt down and pulled the hood back to reveal a face Jen didn't recognize; but, judging by the gasps around the circle, everyone else did.

Who is it? she wanted to shout.

"Paladin Blake!"

Cindergray was astonished as he looked down at one of the Guild's most promising sorcerers.

Blake tried to laugh, but instead he coughed up blood. It was thick and dark-red, telling Cindergray that the injury was deep and potentially fatal if left untreated. "You have no idea how long we've waited for a Lancaster to show up here," Blake said through winces of pain.

Lancaster? Cindergray thought. *But how does he . . . ?*

"Why are you doing this?" It was Chen this time, who peeked over Mystra Skycap's shoulder to look him in the eye.

"*He . . .* shall rise again . . ." Blake trailed off. His face was contorted in pain as he wheezed out his last breath. His eyes glazed over and his body went limp.

Cindergray's head slumped to his chest as silence spread over the courtyard. He softly laid Blake's head back on the grass and touched one of his rings to the young man's forehead, muttering a chant that would send him to his final resting place.

* * *

The would-be assassin's body glowed and began to disappear in front of Jen's eyes. All that was left was his black hooded cape and totem spear, still piercing the ground a few yards away.

Cindergray stood to his full height and turned to Jen. "You're safe now. He can't hurt you anymore, but we should get you indoors in case there are others."

Over Cindergray's shoulder, Jen saw Mystra Skycap roll up Blake's cape.

"Thank you . . ." Still in a daze, Jen lazily looked at Cindergray. Never had she been the target of an assassination attempt, and she could feel her body beginning to shut down from residual fear. Her hands went clammy, her eyes narrowed to tunnel vision, her hearing became muffled, and her legs felt like lead. Trying her hardest to remain upright, she scuffled over to Skarmor and put a shaky hand on his neck for balance.

By now, everyone was looking at her, which only heightened her level of anxiety.

Keep it together. You're safe now . . . safe . . .

Feeling tears start to form, Jen bit the inside of her cheek and petted Skarmor. "Thank you too, boy. You saved my life."

Skarmor let out a high-pitched whine and gently pressed his forehead to hers, ruffling his feathers. The affection she felt from the griffin calmed her down a little, but she still didn't feel like herself.

"Let's get you inside, Jen," Victor said from behind her, touching her shoulder.

Jen nearly jumped out of her skin, her nerves frayed to their limits. Shaking her head to clear the haze, she said, "What did . . . Blake . . . say?" She was trying desperately to convince herself more than anyone else that she was okay, but inside she knew she was everything but.

After waiting a few seconds, Cindergray politely repeated, "We should get you inside, my dear. It's still dangerous to be exposed like this."

Jen's muscles were so taut that they were beginning to feel sore, but as Victor tried placing his hands on her shoulders again, she instinctively relaxed and let him turn her toward the Elder's chamber. Out of the corner of her eye, she saw Skycap pull Blake's spear from the ground, wrapping it into the Dark Watcher's cape after retracting it like an old handheld telescope.

"Skarmor," Victor whispered back at his trusty griffin, "let us know if any activity crops up out here while we're inside."

At first, Skarmor was jealous that he couldn't follow them inside, but he must have realized that keeping guard outside meant protecting Jen, because he stood to his full height and started scanning the skies.

Victor patted him on the neck and led Jen inside, followed by everyone else.

CHAPTER SIXTEEN

Malcolm's ears still rang from the loud slam of his door. Lord Draconex had left, allowing him time to get prepared for his first instruction on the following day.

After his perceived near-death experience at the hands of his master, Malcolm could feel his strength returning little by little. After some time he slowly stood up, dusted off his robes, and steadied himself on the bookshelf.

Malcolm hadn't felt this kind of rejection before; not only had Draconex benched him from pursuing Jen, but he'd also assigned other Dark Watchers to the mission—*his* mission. Fear suddenly struck Malcolm as he realized that the other Watchers could potentially outshine him, sealing his fate as an incompetent, ineffective sorcerer.

Draconex wants to instruct me, he reminded himself. *He wants me to grow stronger. That must mean something promising, right?*

His dark master had never been so adamant that he instruct him before. He would always push off Malcolm's requests, eventually getting around to showing him something new; but more often than not, he would simply not even bother.

Malcolm should have seen this coming, though. He *did* return empty-handed—*twice*—all the while promising an easy capture of the heir of Lancaster.

Jen . . . She bubbled up in his thoughts again, and he couldn't suppress the way she made him feel.

He knew she was just a target—a means to an end—but something inside him stirred every time he thought of Jen. He berated himself for feeling something that had grown stronger within him for the three months he was pretending to be her boyfriend. He begged it to leave—but, like an old injury, it lingered. Every time Malcolm felt this way toward Jen, he would stuff it deep inside him and try to forget about it.

He did so now. He couldn't afford to let it resurface, especially now since Draconex was making arrangements to instruct him. The stakes had just gotten higher, and Malcolm was even more determined to receive Draconex's approval. If not, he wouldn't be alive to witness the resurrection of Lord Ferox.

Feeling as if Atlas had just placed the weight of the world on his shoulders, Malcolm walked over to the door and inspected the lock that Draconex had broken, exhaling loudly.

I want to start training now! he thought.

But after contemplation, he realized that Draconex needed to take the night off too, probably to calm himself, before any spells were to be taught; Malcolm surely didn't want Draconex to maim him—intentionally or unintentionally—out of pure frustration. Maybe it was a good idea that they both took the night to regroup, even though Malcolm knew he would not be able to sleep a wink.

He kicked the door, frustrated at how quickly this had turned sour. Shuffling over to his cot, he kicked off his boots, let his cloak fall to the ground, and fell face first onto the prickly sheets, ready to accept that no sleep would come to him this night.

* * *

The following morning, after limited sleep, Malcolm walked Feralot's empty corridors, nervous like a kid on the first day at a new school, but determined nonetheless. He was about to embark on a new path; a path that would make him stronger and more respected.

The next time I see you, Jen . . . he thought with bated breath.

His hands, bedecked with his rings—one that he had forged as a tenderfoot of Victor Huxley's, the other under Draconex—held an old book filled with spells and the history of dark magic and a vial of fresh griffin blood. The latter was Draconex's favorite snack.

Malcolm had to win points with his instructor, after all.

Draconex's chambers were on the opposite end of the labyrinthine lair of Feralot on the highest and darkest level . . . even darker than the prison bay.

Malcolm made his way down the corridor that overlooked the prison bay, not bothering to look inside the cells or stop to hear the mournful wails echoing out of the dark abyss. Walking that route for years had desensitized him to the horrid conditions afforded to their prisoners.

He certainly didn't envy the Watchers who were stuck on guard duty, either; they did nothing except watch the inmates wither before their eyes, thanks to their night-vision guard helmets. Some guard who'd obviously had too much time on his hands had once affectionately dubbed the prison "The Lair of Despair," and it just stuck.

The prisoners, whom Malcolm was sure were mostly wrongfully condemned, had given up hope and relinquished themselves to the fate of dying cold, blind, and alone in the Stygian darkness. They were captured one of two ways: either by being at the wrong place at the wrong time—often by merely witnessing an atrocious act committed by a Dark Watcher, thus landing themselves a life sentence at Feralot—or by posing what Draconex deemed to be a true threat to the Dark Watchers. What made Draconex decide to keep them breathing, Malcolm didn't know.

All he did know was that Lord Draconex was judge, jury, and executioner. No one questioned his decisions—not even his mistress, Madame Diaema.

No prisoner had ever escaped; there were many attempts, but all who tried had met a grisly end. Every time the Watchers caught an escapee, Draconex had them dragged alive through the prison bay by their fingernails, with nothing covering their bodies except hordes of zombie leeches burning their skin and eating their way to their host's vital organs.

And the screams . . . in the Lair of Despair, prisoners and guards alike were used to hearing hopeless wails from current inmates, but the sound made by someone being eaten alive by zombie leeches hit an inhuman frequency, one that vibrated through your teeth and bones and stood your hair on edge.

There hadn't been thoughts of escape since the attempt by Old Man Percy Grumblebee. At sixty-five years old, Percy feigned a heart attack, and when a guard went in to check on him the old man knocked him unconscious with his food tray and stole the keys to his entire row of cells.

Percy unlocked his neighbor's cell, which held a friend he had made during his imprisonment, and once free, the two managed to evade capture and make their way to the surface before they were captured and beaten nearly to death. Per usual, Lord Draconex then paraded them through the prison bay, their skin nearly entirely eclipsed by hordes of zombie leeches.

The next day, the whole row of inmates was gone without a trace.

Draconex had warned everyone else, "Whosoever wishes to escape now will know that you will be responsible for the death of your entire row!"

Since then, no escapes were attempted . . . or even thought of.

Malcolm grimaced as he neared the end of the prison bay's corridor, thinking of Jen's adoptive parents languishing down there, probably scared out of their skulls.

He had only met Jen's parents twice while he was dating her. They were the kind of parents that Malcolm had wished he'd had while growing up . . . he wasn't particularly proud of kidnapping them, but he knew that if he had returned to Feralot without anything—or anyone—to show for himself, Draconex would have skewered him alive.

She'll come to save them. When that happens, I'll be ready, Malcolm promised himself as he turned down another long corridor.

By the time he reached its end, he became more anxious about his first lesson with Lord Draconex. What if he couldn't prove himself a worthy pupil? Would that be the end of Malcolm Powell? Surely Draconex would dispose of him if it came to that—and for the first time, Malcolm started to believe that his time might just run out.

Before he knew it, he had walked the remaining distance and was standing outside of Draconex's den. Malcolm shook his self-despair from his thoughts and looked down at the book and vial he carried. His ears pricked up as the door's latches unlocked, and his heart rate shot to a dangerous level. He looked back up to see a dark, tall figure propping the heavy door open.

"Well, look what we have here," said the figure. "And he brought us presents."

The figure stepped forward into the light cast by the corridor's torches just enough for Malcolm to see the beautiful but haunting face of Madame Diaema.

Her face was teardrop in shape, which accentuated her high cheekbones even further. The middle half of her slender frame was covered in a skin-tight leather dress the color of the blackest night. Contrarily, her hair was sterile-white, flowing over her bony shoulders like a waterfall. Her chalk-white skin looked even whiter as Malcolm watched her lick her blood-red lips as she saw —or did she smell?—his blood vial.

"It's fresh griffin's blood," Malcolm indicated.

"I assure you I could smell it a mile away," said Madame Diaema, reaching for the vial. "You have no idea how long it's been since I've had"—she took in a deep, shuddering breath —"*griffin* blood." Her piercing red eyes remained glued to the vial.

Malcolm took a step back, tightening his grip on the vial. "Lord Draconex is expecting me."

"Of course." Diaema winked and leaned closer to him, caressing the underside of Malcolm's chin with one of her long, pointy nails, and he suppressed a shudder. "He's expecting you, all right."

"Great."

Malcolm started to sweat as he tried to squeeze his way around the albino vampire, but she only playfully blocked his path.

"Is that blood only for Draconex?" She pouted her full lips and batted her eyes.

Malcolm swallowed hard. "Um . . . I'm sure he'll share with you?" He smiled uncomfortably as she got closer, so close that he could feel her cold breath upon his cheek.

"Di, as much as it pleases me to watch Malcolm sweat, you've tortured the boy long enough," said Draconex.

Malcolm couldn't see Draconex as he peered over Diaema's shoulder, but he was relieved that he had called off his insatiable mistress.

"Trust me, dear, this isn't torture." She whispered in Malcolm's ear, "Let me know if you change your mind."

Before Malcolm could even think of a response, she morphed into an albino vampire bat, plucked the blood vial from his hand with her teeth, and swooped deeper into Draconex's den, swallowed by the foreboding darkness.

With an audible gulp, Malcolm waited for Draconex's permission to enter. Seconds turned into minutes, and Malcolm began to wonder if he had been forgotten, but then he heard his lord say, "Enter."

On shaky legs, Malcolm slowly entered for the third time in the ten years he had lived in Feralot. The first was the night he betrayed Victor in the Pit, and the second was when he forged his Dark Watcher ring. He looked back on those memories with fondness—pivotal milestones in his journey. Now back for a third time, he was more full of dread than nostalgia as he continued to slowly shuffle toward Draconex.

As he tentatively stepped fully into the antechamber of Draconex's den, he felt a breeze hit the nape of his neck. Just as he looked behind his shoulder, the door slammed shut, cutting off the faint light from the corridor's torches. Immediately he shuffled farther inside, instinctively putting his hands out so he wouldn't run into anything. Without warning, small torches on the walls sparked to life, giving Malcolm enough light to see his path—and, eventually, Draconex—straight ahead. Malcolm's nostrils picked up a slight stench of something burning as he made his way closer and discovered the origin of the odor.

In his den, Lord Draconex was sitting upon the fabled Throne of Dragons, where he commanded his Dark Watcher army. Built on bloodshed, conquest, and subterfuge since the time of Lord Ferox, that throne was said to have mystical powers of its own. Its seat was sculpted from black volcanic rock that glistened in the den's torchlight. Its backrest was a pair of taxidermized dragon wings, which gave the illusion that Draconex had his own pair of leathery wings sprouting out of his back. The armrests were sculpted into heads of dragons with mouths agape as if preparing to shoot fire at any moment and scorch unexpected visitors.

Draconex's head was arched back as he emptied the vial of griffin blood into his mouth. Next to him was a brittle-looking, ashen tree on which hung Madame Diaema, who was still in bat form. She wriggled, watching with agonizing desperation as the blood disappeared drop by drop.

Draconex must have caught Diaema's attempt at attention, for after a while he stopped; he'd saved a few drops of the griffin blood, and held out the vial to her then.

Wings flapped, Diaema floated in midair to swallow the remaining drops as Draconex tipped the vial upside down. Once Diaema's thirst was quenched, she glided back to her branch and swung there, upside down, staring at Malcolm as he stopped a few yards before the Throne of Dragons.

Draconex threw the vial aside, letting it crash onto the cobblestone floor, and said, "You had a good donor, my boy. Where did you come across such rich blood?"

"Skarmor," Malcolm replied, affecting a mischievous smirk on his lips.

Draconex sat up straighter, suddenly more interested. He

squinted his blood-red eyes as he searched Malcolm's face for a bluff. "I should have savored each drop even more, then. But alas. You are off to a good start, boy."

Malcolm resented it whenever Draconex called him "boy." It was demeaning; he was twenty-six years old—a fully developed man! One day Draconex would stop insulting him like that—though Malcolm would never say that directly to his lord's face. Aside from the demeaning nickname, Malcolm did mentally pat himself on the back for deciding to bring the griffin blood.

"Let's hope it stays that way," Draconex continued, threading his comment with a hint of a threat.

Malcolm stiffly bowed his head. "Of course, My Lord."

Draconex made a nasal sound expressing agreement—or was it a scoff? Malcolm wasn't sure. He looked up in time to see the lord looking at the rings on Malcolm's fingers with a sneer. "After all these years, you still hang on to the ring you forged with Victor Huxley. Why?"

"I still use it to channel my terramancy, My Lord."

"I wonder if that ring—and its associated memories—are keeping you from reaching your full potential . . ." Draconex tapped his chin with a bony finger as if in deep thought. "Destroy it!" he yelled.

The leather-bound book in Malcolm's hand struck the ground with a *thud*. He was speechless. His master's command shocked him, but not as much as the way he felt about destroying his first totem ring. Up until then, he had believed that he had fully denounced Victor as his mystra; but now, when faced with destroying his only remaining connection to his past, he hesitated. With shallow breaths, Malcolm slid the ring off his finger and cupped it in his hands. He was hit by a sudden realization just then: no matter how hard he tried, he could not—would not—get rid of his first ring.

Draconex's eyes burned bright with hot anger. "You weakling!"

He pointed at Malcolm, and Diaema swooped down, plucked the ring from Malcolm's hands, and dropped it in Draconex's outstretched palm before shapeshifting back into a devastatingly seductive woman. Diaema leaned on one of Draconex's armrests and placed a hand on his shoulder.

He lifted Malcolm's ring to the light as if to inspect it, but then tossed it in the air. Draconex opened his slitted mouth, which spewed dripping flames that engulfed the ring. Malcolm covered his unprotected face with his arms to block the swell of heat that slammed into him. Through slits in his fingers, he watched as his most prized possession was melted down and burned to a crisp.

It was over in a second; the damage had been done. A part of Malcolm died when he saw his charred and melted ring shatter as it hit the hard, stone floor.

"Now you will not be rooted in the past," Draconex said.

Malcolm shot Draconex a furious look that could have melted his dead skin from his face.

In response, Draconex laughed and slowly clapped. "*There's that fire!* I was wondering if you still had it in you at all, after dating that Lancaster girl."

Malcolm did not find this the least bit funny, but he couldn't anger the dark sorcerer who sat in front of him any more. He just took a deep breath and swallowed the first response that came to his mind, instead saying, "If you think that is necessary."

"You do not realize the power that ring had over you. It tethered you to your past, to the Sorcery Guild, to *Victor*," the lord spat. "It was what failed you in capturing Jennifer Lancaster . . . twice."

Malcolm, with limp arms and legs, dropped to his knees on the unforgiving floor, but didn't look away from Draconex.

"That was the first act of my instruction. You will not find that it gets easier from here," Draconex said unmercifully.

"But how will you be able to teach me? You're an animancer and I'm a terramancer . . ."

Draconex rubbed his forehead. "I now realize my selfish mistake of not teaching you enough in your decade of serving me. Dark magic is a fickle mistress, but if properly honed, it can expand your powers—not only in one Mancy plane, but also in every other."

Malcolm's ears pricked up as chills ran down his spine.

"Yessssss . . . that's right . . ." Draconex played with Diaema's silky white hair. "Dark magic can give you the power to manipulate every Mancy plane, essentially making you an omnimancer. Years ago, when I realized this truth and approached the Elder Synod, they forbade me to even think about tapping into the dark magic necessary for such a glorious achievement. 'It's too volatile,' they said." He ground his teeth in repressed annoyance. "I quickly realized they were being cowards, scared of its potential—and *my* potential with it." Draconex brushed the vertical scar on his face with two bony fingers. "I had to escape their narrow focus and pathetic, fearsome mindset."

Diaema massaged Draconex's massive shoulders.

"And now," he continued, "don't you see all that I've accomplished since then? Ever since I took command of the Dark Watcher forces, I've led us to conquer realms, vanquish sorcerers, and reach closer to the promise we have made to resurrect our rightful ruler." Draconex was shaking with excitement and anticipation.

"Lord Ferox," Malcolm breathed. Every time he said that name, it scared him half to death yet sent a thrill through his body. But it wasn't until this moment that he realized how close they were to freeing the world's greatest evil.

"And I would be remiss if I didn't acknowledge your efforts in tracking down a Lancaster . . . a Lancaster we thought had died as an infant."

"Thank you, My Lord." Malcolm bowed deeply.

Diaema hissed, and Draconex said, "But you have nothing to show for it except a few bruises and Lancaster's useless foster parents! I would flay the skin off your bones right now if you hadn't courted her for as long as you did and gleaned important details of her. Pray that you show enough improvement so I don't have to go back on my word."

Malcolm had wondered when the threat on his life would

come. Admittedly, it came sooner than expected, but he was sure Draconex must have another Dark Watcher waiting in the wings to take his place if he failed once more.

Do or die.

Malcolm intended to do.

CHAPTER SEVENTEEN

The cold and decrepit cell bay of Feralot reeked of unwashed and malnourished prisoners. No one knew how deep it went. Darkness ate up all the light, making it seem either claustrophobically cramped . . . or interminably vast. Whimpers, incoherent babbling, and shallow breathing echoed throughout the abyss, making its true size one of conjecture.

On the cold and dingy floor, as Malcolm's paralysis spell slowly wore off, Richard Smith began to move. His body was stiff and sore, but he could move—even if it was only an inch at first. After some time, he had enough strength to call out his wife's name.

"Beth . . . ?" Richard croaked. His vocal chords were still tight, like taut guitar strings. When he heard nothing in reply, he cautiously put his hands out around him to feel for his wife. Even though he didn't hear her respond, Richard knew she was with him in the cell; she had to be. Just before he gave up, his left hand swept over a piece of fabric. It felt like his wife's sweater.

He followed the sweater up until he could feel her arm, then recoiled in horror; she was as stiff as a board. He slid over and enveloped her in his arms. He could feel that she was still under the spell, so he held her until her muscles contracted and she began to breathe normally again.

"Richard," Beth finally said to her husband.

Weakly, she hugged him back. He wanted more than anything to make her feel safe, but he knew that was impossible; he didn't even know where they were.

Nothing else was said; they just held one another, comforted by each other's presence until they heard a voice say: "Glad the spell is wearing off."

Richard felt Beth startle in his arms at the unexpected voice. He was already using his hearing to decipher where that voice was coming from in the black—and if it was in their cell. It sounded like a man's voice, raspy and no louder than a whisper.

"Don't be alarmed. I'm not going to hurt you," the voice said again, this time a little louder.

"Where are you?" Richard said. His voice was getting back to normal. He tried to hide the fear from his voice for his wife's sake.

"In the next cell. Been here for a while," the voice said, a tone of biting cynicism in his words. "Welcome to the neighborhood."

Richard didn't pay attention to the dry humor, but instead asked, "Who are you?"

Silence. Then: "Someone to talk to . . . a friend. There aren't many in here with whom you can converse . . . especially after what the monsters on the other side of these bars do to them."

"So you're saying we're the *lucky* ones?"

"Trust me, you could be worse off. Do you remember how you got here?"

Richard racked his brain, but it was useless. He looked down to where Beth was and softly squeezed her, even though he couldn't see anything. "Not one bit."

"I was the same way when I woke up in here, but then—"

"I don't really feel like talking now," Richard said, cutting the voice off. "I'm sorry." He cleared his throat, fighting back tears. Tears for the dread that replaced his confusion; tears for not being there for Jen and Tyler; tears for being powerless and trapped in this godforsaken place. Feeling the most vulnerable he had been in decades, Richard reached out for his wife. Once he found her, he hugged her tightly as his sorrow was temporarily alleviated by a dreamless sleep.

* * *

CLANG! CLANG! CLANG!

The sound of a guard's rod hitting thick metal cell bars echoed throughout the prison bay as its owner made his way down the row of cells—the monotonous role of keeping an eye on the worn-out, tortured enemies of the Dark Watcher tribe.

Richard Smith was jolted out of his sleep as the clanging got closer and louder. Ever since he'd found his wife in the pure darkness, they had never left each other's side; she seemed to still be fast asleep.

Good, thought Richard. His wife had been through enough. They both had.

He had no idea how long they had been down there, just that he had eaten four meals—or what was *supposed* to be "meals." The food was dense and rubbery, giving a taste of cardboard that sucked out all the moisture in his mouth. The water wasn't much better, leaving behind a metallic taste that seemed to line his throat as he swallowed it. He only drank the water to wash down the dry bites of food.

A raspy voice muttered, "Eat up, you slobs," right before a cheap tray slid into their cell.

He didn't move or thank the guard for the food; he just sat there, holding on to his love, thinking of ways to escape.

CHAPTER EIGHTEEN

Once back inside the Elder council chamber, Mystra Étoilier came up to Jen and said, "*Ma chérie,* I'm relieved that you weren't hurt. I hope the attack doesn't dissuade you from starting your training."

Jen sat in Grand Mystra Cindergray's chair as he talked with Victor near the courtyard door. As her emotions began to settle, she said, "If anything, it has convinced me that I need to start soon to protect myself and help you stop any more attacks."

Étoilier smiled and nodded. "If it's not too much trouble, I'd like to be your astromancer mystra when the time comes."

Jen blinked away her surprise and said, "I'd like that too. Thank you, Mystra Étoilier."

"*Avec plaisir,*" he said, bowing his head and retreating to his chair farther down the row.

Jen turned to see Cindergray ascend the stairs after ending his conversation with Victor. His hands were behind his back as he methodically stepped up to her. It looked like he was holding something.

"I'm glad to see that your complexion is returning, my dear," Cindergray said. "Are you feeling better? No scratches or lacerations from that spear?"

"I've been better." Jen let out a sigh, realizing just then how tired she had become. "But no. It just missed me."

"Your nexus protected you," Cindergray said, nodding. "I'm very glad you're uninjured."

"Thank you," Jen said, wondering what Cindergray had behind his back.

Cindergray brought his hands from behind his back and revealed the orb that Jen had earned. "With everything that occurred, you forgot to claim your prize."

Jen blinked twice, remembering why she had come to Watercress Castle in the first place. Taking the orb from Cindergray's outstretched hand, she held it out in front of her, surprised as how light it was.

"Congratulations, Jennifer. You have passed the Chimera Course, thus officially becoming a sorceress tenderfoot. What you now hold is the mineral you will use to forge your totem. It will help you better channel and control your nexus," Cindergray announced.

Jen rolled the orb around in her hands, feeling the cold metal slide over her palms. Beginning to understand the meaning of her trophy, thoughts of what she would make the orb into were cast aside when she noticed that every other Elder had taken their seats except for Cindergray.

Blushing with embarrassment, Jen stood up and bowed her head. "Thank you for the seat." She side-stepped away respectfully.

"My pleasure, dear child." Cindergray chuckled as he resumed his spot at the center of the chamber. Still holding her prize, Jen started making her way to the stairs, but Cindergray stopped her with a hand gesture. "Stay here for a moment."

Holding the orb firmly in both hands, Jen glanced down at Victor, who simply nodded as he stood in the center of the room below.

Cindergray was the first to address everyone. "In light of recent events, please excuse me while I congratulate Jennifer in private." He then looked to his left and right at the other Elders. "Thank you for witnessing an impressive completion of the Chimera Course by our newest tenderfoot. I'm sure she will be a

valuable addition here, but for now I'm sure you all have obliga-
tions to return to."

Each Elder transported from the chamber in the same fashion
as they had arrived, but not before congratulating Jen on a job
well done. Before Mystra Skycap left the chamber, Jen noticed that
she was no longer holding Blake's cape or spear.

"Please come forward, my dear," Cindergray said, beckoning.

Silently, Jen stepped forward until she was by his side.

"You too, Victor, since you're her guardian." As Jen and Victor
ascended the stairs, he looked at Chen, who was still standing by
the glass door that led out to the courtyard. "Mystra Chen, may
you stay behind to keep an eye on the courtyard for any further
suspicious activity?"

"Of course, Grand Mystra." Chen bowed with her hands
nestled in her flowing cloak.

When Jen and Victor reached Cindergray, he asked for their
hands. Standing up, he took them and looked to the ceiling. With
closed eyes he deeply inhaled . . . and the next thing Jen saw was
white.

* * *

Jen quite literally wasn't herself. She had no feet, no arms, nor
even a head; she was pure energy, along with Victor and
Cindergray. As she flew through time and space, all Jen could
think about was how alive she felt, and she let everything else
melt away. For a split second, she forgot about her many brushes
with death, the search for her parents, and the life she'd left
behind when she agreed to embark on this journey to become a
sorceress.

Jen had never felt so free. She wanted that feeling to last
forever, but as the light faded and she started to distinguish the
forms of Victor and Cindergray in front of her, she realized with
some chagrin that the ride was over.

Before she let reality sink back in, Jen looked around in awe at
the room to which she had been transported. It was hemispheri-

cal, ending with a domed point at the top of the ceiling. Ornate carvings spanned the circumference of its border. Wrought iron lanterns hung from the walls, giving off a soft, warm light. Beneath her feet, Jen saw the gleam of varnished hardwood flooring, which led up to a grand desk that looked to be made out of deep mahogany wood. Behind it rested a chair fit for the Grand Mystra of the Sorcery Guild.

Just then her nostrils caught a familiar scent of cinnamon and leather, one that was also associated with her father's home office. A wave of nostalgia hit Jen, which led her to think about her parents. Sadness invaded her heart and she swallowed, hoping it would go away, but she could feel it rising like the morning tide. What didn't help was that her adrenaline was also wearing off, causing her guard to drop even further. She tightly grasped her orb with both hands as her eyes started to water. Victor noticed her change, and he gently squeezed her shoulder. Too emotionally tired to hold her fear in for any longer, she turned around and hugged Victor, nestling her face in his shoulder and trying to compose herself as best she could.

"There, there," Victor consoled.

"You've been through quite a lot, Jennifer. It is completely appropriate to feel the way you do," Cindergray said, walking up to his chair.

Hello, emotions.

Jen was wondering when they would hit. She couldn't stop thinking about her parents and where they could be right now. So many things had happened in such a short timespan that her brain was finally beginning to fully process it. After a few more moments in Victor's embrace, Jen started feeling better.

"Thank you," she said.

"I'll always be here for you, Jenny," he said, still holding her.

After only knowing him for a few days, Jen was amazed at how much she trusted Victor. She couldn't explain it, but she knew he truly cared for her—and, on top of that, she felt the same way about him.

He rubbed her back once more before saying, "I'm just glad that you were able to dodge that spear."

Sniffling, Jen stepped out of Victor's arms. "I have to give that credit to my new-found powers, I think."

Victor raised an eyebrow. "What do you mean? Your nexus?"

"Well . . . it's hard to explain. Before I ducked, I guess I had a vision. I didn't know what to make of it at the time, but now I think that maybe I saw through the eyes of Blake." She looked into Victor's eyes. "I think he was a—"

"A Dark Watcher," Cindergray finished. "A Dark Watcher who was sent after you and the Ring of Lancaster. This is most disconcerting." He pulled at his beard, withdrawing into deep thought.

"Wait . . ." Jen said, then lowered her voice to a whisper. "Vic . . . he knows who I really am?" She tilted her head at the distinguished grand mystra.

"Yes," Victor responded. "He's known for a while."

"Please, sit," Cindergray said, coming out of his reverie.

At first, the only chair that Jen could see in the entire room was Cindergray's, but after a quick wave of his hand, two leather chairs appeared in front of his desk. Victor motioned for Jen to take one, waiting for her to sit down before following suit.

"What you are about to learn must never leave this room, my dear. Is that clear?" Cindergray waited for confirmation.

Jen nodded, still shocked that he knew her true identity. She could see visible strain on his body as well as hear it in his voice; his soothing tone became more curt and reserved.

Before she could stop herself, she asked, "You know who I really am?"

Cindergray leaned forward. "You are Jennifer Lancaster, the last surviving omnimancer."

Jen looked at Victor in complete bafflement.

"The League of Light has taken a blood oath to protect you," Cindergray went on.

Jen's mind started to whirl. "Wait . . . you're a part of the League of Light too? But you didn't believe Victor about Draconex or the Dark Watcher threat. You *banished* him."

"It needed to happen to keep his secret intact," Victor chimed in.

"Unfortunate, but true," Cindergray continued. "When Victor approached me the morning after the incident in the Pit, I was as concerned as he was, so I pledged my allegiance to the League of Light and agreed to go along with his plan, which, unfortunately, included his banishment."

"It was the only way for me to focus all my attention to tracking Dark Watchers down and watching over you, Jen," Victor said.

Jen was trying to process it all, so she had to focus when Cindergray spoke again. "For the last ten years Victor has kept the League cognizant of our enemy's movements and your safety. It took someone wholeheartedly devoted to our cause to sacrifice all that he did. I owe him more than I can say."

"Me too," Jen said truthfully, putting her hand on Victor's arm, reminded of how he came to her rescue on the night of her birthday—a night that already felt eons away. "So . . . are the other Elders *also* part of the League of Light?"

"No." Cindergray was stone serious. "We didn't know if they were turned. We still don't know, in fact. It's imperative that you keep this to yourself, Jennifer, especially now."

"I promise."

"Especially when someone so pure can be turned," Victor said. "You don't know who is working against you." He made meaningful eye contact with Cindergray.

The Grand Mystra looked down and let out a long breath.

"You mean Blake?" Jen asked, noticing Cindergray's change in attitude. "I take it he meant a lot to you."

Cindergray nodded gravely. "Archibald Blake was a gifted chronomancer. I teach beginning chronomancy to tenderfeet, and he was one of my star pupils years ago. Before he was old enough to start individual instruction with Mystra Cloque, I could tell he was destined to become one of the greatest chronomancers in the Sorcery Guild."

"He will be greatly missed," Victor said with his head down.

Jen straightened in her chair. "Do you think Mystra Cloque was the one who turned Blake?"

Cindergray raised his eyebrows. "Very impressive, Jennifer. I've sent Mystra Étoilier to investigate him." He was visibly torn apart, letting his shoulders drop once more. "I can't comprehend what would make Blake betray the Guild and side with the likes of Draconex."

Jen was reminded of when she saw Draconex both in her nightmare and Victor's memory frame. All Jen hoped was that she was ready by the time she crossed paths with him.

Preferably never.

"I noticed the ring that you have on your necklace." The Grand Mystra pointed at Jen's neck, taking her away from her thoughts. "At first I thought my old eyes were playing tricks on me, but after seeing the ring glow, I knew for certain that it had to be the Ring of Lancaster." Cindergray smiled at her, showing deep crow's feet at the edges of his eyes.

"So this ring must be more than just a family heirloom," Jen surmised. She was learning as much, but she wanted to hear it from one of the most knowledgeable sorcerers.

"It most definitely is, my dear. It is the legendary ring forged by your ancestor Genevieve." He paused before asking, "May I take a closer look at it?"

Cindergray's genuine interest made Jen's reluctance fade away, and she went to unclasp her necklace. Victor watched as Jen stood up and gave the Ring of Lancaster to the Grand Mystra.

With appreciation in his eyes, he took the ring and silently stared at it for several seconds. Before he gave it back to Jen, he tightly squeezed it in his palm and looked away, clearing his throat. "This is a legendary ring, and if an old man with poor eyesight like myself can detect it, I'm willing to bargain that the rest of the Elders have noticed it too." A grimace took over his face.

"We don't have any conclusive evidence to support that the Elder Synod aren't in some way involved with the Dark Watchers," Victor realized, picking up on Cindergray's insinuation.

Jen looked between the two sorcerers, trying to keep up.

"Thank you, Jennifer," he said. He put on a warm tone as he leaned over his desk and pressed the ring in her palm.

"You're welcome, sir." Jen accepted her heirloom back and replaced it on her neck.

After a few seconds of tense silence, Cindergray stood to his full height and addressed Victor. "She needs to train on Camelore."

Victor nodded. "I was about to suggest that. She will be the safest there."

Jen knotted her eyebrows and cocked her head to the side. "Camelore? Where's that, and what's wrong with training here?"

Victor was the first to respond. "Camelore is the home base for the League of Light. Completely guarded, and its location is untraceable, making it impossible for any Dark Watcher to discover it."

Cindergray pursed his lips before answering the second part of Jen's question. "Your safety is paramount. The Dark Watchers are more desperate than ever now that they know you're alive, and I won't risk you falling prey to another Dark Watcher while you're on Watercress grounds. They'll stop at nothing until they can use the ring to free Lord Ferox from the Halostone."

"Well, it's a good thing that the Halostone is safe, right?" Jen said. When Cindergray and Victor didn't reassure her, she shot up off the chair and asked, "Wait—is the Halostone *lost*?"

All along, she'd assumed that the Halostone was kept under lock and key, but deep in her gut she realized that had been a naïve fantasy. Jen desperately looked at Cindergray and Victor, waiting for them to deny it, but all they did was nod their heads.

"I'm not sure how much Victor has told you, but after your ancestor Mystra Genevieve sacrificed herself to trap Lord Ferox in the Halostone," Grand Mystra Cindergray explained, his expression somber, "her younger sister, Gwendolyn, vowed to protect it at any cost, making your family its sole guardian. Over the ensuing centuries, the Halostone was passed down from one Lancaster to another, all the while being tirelessly tracked by Dark

Watchers, eager to steal it. As time went on and the Halostone continued to change hands, it inexplicably disappeared. This was about five hundred years ago." Cindergray paused, choosing his words carefully. "Until about twenty years ago, when its location was ascertained by two very gifted sorcerers."

"Did they bring it back here to Watercress?" Jen asked eagerly.

"They kept the location to themselves, since it was too dangerous to risk leaking that information to the wrong person. Unfortunately, they disappeared on their way to retrieve it," Cindergray replied, "before putting their daughter in hiding."

Jen's throat tightened as she realized what Cindergray was saying.

"Jennifer, the sorcerers who found the whereabouts of the Halostone were your biological parents," he said. "It lived—and died—with them."

* * *

Like another puzzle piece falling into place, it suddenly became clear why Jen's biological parents had let another couple raise her. They had been on the verge of reclaiming the most sought-after and dangerous relic in the world—or in any realm, for that matter.

They had to, she realized, *for me . . . for everyone.*

Ever since her father had told her that she was adopted, Jen had wrestled with why she had been given up; now it became clear. Her real parents had loved her so much that they had risked valuable time to ensure that their daughter would be safe.

An important question suddenly occurred to her. "How . . . how did they die?"

"Protecting the one thing they valued most." Cindergray pointed at Jen, smiling sadly. "Once word of their disappearance reached the League of Light, we spent the next year tirelessly searching for them, until Victor followed a lead to Ocuul, a far-distant realm. There, he found a colony of Dark Watchers enslaving natives to search for the Halostone."

Jen gasped, horrified.

Victor picked up the story. "After a stakeout that lasted a couple of days, I sent for my strike team. What ensued was a violent skirmish, and as we pushed deeper into their base, I discovered your parents in a protected bunker. They were being tortured, forced to give any clues to the Halostone's location, but your parents were strong. They hadn't given the Watchers anything of value."

Jen could tell Victor truly admired her parents; it was clear in the way he spoke of them. She wished even more then to have known them.

"Between their ineffective torture methods and our surprise ambush, the Dark Watchers were running out of time . . ." Victor trailed off. He looked away from Jen and took a deep breath. "So Draconex gave the command to destroy the base."

Jen's heart sunk lower than ever before. She had an aching feeling that she knew how the story was going to end.

"One of my agents intercepted the call, so we knew how long we had. Instead of taking over the Dark Watchers' Ocuul base, our objective changed to rescuing your parents," Victor recalled, a far-off quality to his voice. "We made it to their bunker, but there were too many warding spells and not enough time to break them out before the base exploded."

Victor reached over and held her hand.

"They told me to run so I could fight another day . . . and that they loved you with all their hearts."

Victor's eyes had gone misty; Jen was already past that stage, and her flushed cheeks were streaked with tears.

"Our hearts ache telling you this, my dear," Cindergray said.

Victor let go of Jen's hand so she could wipe the tears away, still holding onto the orb with her other.

"No, uh . . . ahem." She cleared her throat. "Thank you for telling me. I needed to hear it."

"They live through you, Jennifer," Cindergray said warmly. "That's what they wanted more than anything."

Jen's spirits were slightly lifted, even if it didn't bring her birth parents back.

After she was sure her emotions were more stable, she asked, "How can we find the Halostone before the Dark Watchers?"

Cindergray exchanged a look with Victor, then said, "I need to show you something."

"Show me what?" Jen nervously juggled the orb in her hands.

It has to do with the Halostone . . . right? Or something else my birth parents left me?

After hearing that her parents were lost in an explosion on another planet, she knew they were gone forever . . . but a small part of her did not want to give up hope. If anything, their sacrifice motivated Jen to find the Halostone even more.

She walked to the front of the hand-carved desk while Cindergray, on the other side, turned one of his drawer's knobs twice. A soft rumble vibrated the floor, and Jen curiously craned her neck to look over the desk. To her amazement, a secret staircase had sunk into the floor, leading to a subterranean chamber.

"What I'm about to show you is extremely sensitive. Nary a word should be spoken about this place," Cindergray declared as he began to descend the staircase.

Victor motioned for Jen to follow the Grand Mystra. "This is only meant for you, Jen. I'll be back in the courtyard tending to Skarmor."

"Okay . . . I'll see you soon?" Jen waved at Victor as he left the office. Cupping her orb in her left hand, she turned around and followed Cindergray down into a surprisingly wide and tall corridor lined with lit candles on rusted iron sconces.

For the next several minutes, she walked in silence behind the distinguished sorcerer as they went deeper and deeper into the bowels of Watercress Castle, sometimes turning down a new corridor, sometimes descending another set of stairs. Jen was soon completely lost, knowing that she would be unable to confidently trace back her steps if she ever found herself alone, so she picked up the pace and made sure she would not lose sight of Cindergray.

The Grand Mystra still hadn't given Jen any hint as to what he was about to show her, just that it might help them find the

Halostone. Whatever it was, Jen feared that it was their last hope.

"Here we are," Cindergray said.

Jen was brought out of her thoughts as they stopped at a dead end in front of a brick wall. She peered over his shoulder to make sure he wasn't obstructing a small door or entrance, but found nothing except a sturdy brick wall.

"Did we take a wrong turn, or . . . ?"

Jen let her question trail off as she waited for Cindergray to say that they had, in fact, taken a wrong turn. Instead, the Grand Mystra simply glanced over his shoulder at her, then held out both of his hands like he was warming them over an invisible fire.

The ground shifted beneath their feet suddenly; it was ever so slight a shift, but just enough for Jen to notice. Looking around, senses alert, she saw a metal stand emerge from the brick wall. On top of it rested a circular wheel, similar to one aboard a pirate ship, but smaller. In the center of the wheel was a depression.

Cindergray didn't break his concentration as he made a fist with his right hand and pressed one of his rings into the depression.

His ring is like a key!

He looked down at Jen and said, "Always turn counter-clockwise . . . *never* clockwise."

Jen nodded, wondering what would happen if you turned it the wrong way, as Cindergray began to twist his hand counter-clockwise. The cobblestones both of them stood on and the wall in front of them began to tip forward.

It felt as if Jen was about to get launched head-first into the brick wall.

To prevent herself from careening into the unforgiving wall, Jen tucked her orb into her chest and grabbed Cindergray for support. It dawned on her that she was clutching him rather intensely, but she dared not let go as they passed through the wall like it was a mirage.

Looking around, Jen could tell that they were now in a secret chamber.

Amazingly, Jen and Cindergray were still standing on the tiles, which were now completely perpendicular to the ground. If the laws of gravity stayed true, Jen was expecting her and Cindergray to fall flat onto the new floor, but that didn't happen. Releasing her vice-like grip on Cindergray, Jen marveled at the fact that she was still standing on the tiles.

Like Spider-Man! she thought. She couldn't help but giggle as she tried to compose herself.

Cindergray, who acted like he had done this countless times, put his left foot square onto the floor in front of him and proceeded to do the same with his right foot. In one fluid motion, he'd changed his orientation a full ninety degrees. He turned around, waiting for Jen to do the same.

"Careful now, my dear. Take it slowly," Cindergray cautioned her.

Eager to follow the master sorcerer's lead, Jen said, "Here goes nothing."

She placed her right foot on the wall—which was the floor to Cindergray—quickly followed by her left. The reorientation happened so fast that dizziness hit her unexpectedly and she lost her balance, feeling as if she had just gotten off a spinning teacup ride.

"I guess my 'slow' wasn't slow enough," Jen said with embarrassment.

"The reorientation is a tough one to master if completed too quickly." He bent down to help her up, then said, "Welcome to the Sacrarium." He gestured with both hands, taking in the whole room.

"It really is beautiful." Jen saw pedestals holding treasures you'd only believe if you saw them with your own eyes. The room had a scent of old books, time-worn leather, and wood that had been varnished and revarnished many times over. She was instantly reminded of the smell of her grandparents' house.

Cindergray led her past bookcases and display cases filled with relics and weaponry of a bygone era. Half of the items Jen had never seen before, and she could only guess what they could have been used for. Countless questions formed in her mind as if she were a child on her first field trip to a museum.

Before she could verbalize them, Cindergray stopped before a glass room. It was completely empty, save for a lone podium whereupon rested an ancient book. A spotlight was directed on it, giving it a sense of importance. The book's front face had deep cracks spreading its length like crooked bolts of lightning. Two golden clasps held the book shut, those in turn bound together by leather straps.

"What you see before you is the lost journal of Merlin," Cindergray told Jen. "It is over fifteen hundred years old and contains a veritable collection of valuable secrets."

Merlin kept a journal? thought Jen. *How cool is that?!*

"What's all in it?" Jen decided to ask aloud, trying to keep her tone casual.

"His experiences and insights as he became a sorcerer . . . stories of him, King Arthur, and the Knights of the Round Table . . . and clues he successfully deciphered when looking for the lost MystiCrystals," Cindergray explained.

"He helped search for the MystiCrystals too?"

Cindergray nodded. "Merlin was the first sorcerer to take up the search. Genevieve was one of his most talented tenderfeet, and when he learned she had sacrificed herself to stop Ferox he vowed to find the MystiCrystals before they fell into the wrong hands again."

"Wow . . ." Jen breathed, studying the book. "Did he complete his search?"

"Merlin was only able to find one MystiCrystal before he left us. It is stowed in the wall behind his journal." Cindergray pointed above the book.

Jen followed his finger until she noticed a small alcove, which held six thin stands, five of which were empty. Leaning forward, inches from the glass wall of the museum-like display room, she spotted a breathtaking crystal floating over the first stand, immediately reminding her of a water opal. Looking to be about four inches long, it came to pointy tips on both of its ends. Blues, greens, and oranges swam underneath its near-translucent surface, giving off a wonderful, soothing light.

In all of her wildest dreams, Jen hadn't expected to be shown that.

An actual MystiCrystal!

"That is the ChronoCrystal, the MystiCrystal that gave the universe the dimension of time. This is what gives us chrono-mancers our powers." Cindergray stared deep into the crystal, getting lost in its effervescent gleam. "The other four remain lost . . . along with the ShadowCrystal, encapsulation of the residual dark energies of the five MystiCrystals."

"Where did he find the ChronoCrystal?" Jen asked.

"The concentrated impact of Genevieve's spell blasted all the MystiCrystals—including the ShadowCrystal—far and wide . . . but eventually Merlin found the ChronoCrystal in Southern England, deep beneath Stonehenge."

Jen's jaw almost dropped down to the floor. "Stonehenge? One of the world's most mysterious locations?"

"Yes, indeed. Ironic, almost. No one expected to look so close to the spot of the Great Battle. That's why it took Merlin so long to find it. Through the clues he had unearthed, he realized that the ChronoCrystal was hit at a low angle, causing it to only travel a few kilometers before burying itself deep into the ground."

Jen couldn't believe what she was hearing—but then, what was new?

She remembered a family trip to England where they toured Stonehenge when she was younger. It amazed her that, in just a few short years, she would be standing next to a grand sorcerer, looking at one of the most powerful objects in the entire universe, which had once been buried deep underneath that very tourist spot in Southern England.

Cindergray continued, "Shortly after he brought the Chrono-Crystal back to Watercress, Merlin fell ill. Some say he was so distraught after Genevieve's death that the only thing sustaining him was the search for the MystiCrystals . . . but even he realized that the other five would not be found in his lifetime."

Jen continued to stare, transfixed, as she listened.

"So, in hopes that someone would continue his quest after he was gone, Merlin preserved his findings and clues in this journal." Cindergray gestured to the book. "But at that time—much like the current climate now—tensions between the Sorcery Guild and Dark Watchers were extremely volatile, and double agents had infiltrated the Guild. Merlin didn't know who to trust with this information, so he cast a coding spell that could only be deciphered by the Light Bringer, the one he prophesied would bring balance to the realms."

"The Light Bringer," Jen repeated.

"Lord Draconex believes that he is the Light Bringer incarnate," Cindergray explained, "and that is why he is after the journal."

Jen began to realize the true complexity of this war. "I thought he was only after my ring?" She looked down at her chest, touching her family heirloom.

"The only thing that can free Lord Ferox from the Halostone is your ring, the totem that cast the incarceration spell. But Draconex can't find the Halostone without the lost journal . . . even if he cannot read it."

"He can't?"

"No." The Grand Mystra shook his head, frowning gravely. "But he thinks he can with the help of the ShadowCrystal and its dark magic."

"Do we know who the real Light Bringer is? Did Merlin leave us any clues?"

Cindergray turned toward Jen, facing her straight on and pulling her from her trance. "Unfortunately, no . . . it's rather enigmatic. He disappeared before anyone could ask. No one knows for sure how—or why—Merlin disappeared. Some say he went into hiding, waiting for his prophecy to come true. Others say he was trapped in a cave-in somewhere in the English countryside. Still others believe he was imprisoned in a giant tree, left to watch the world change around him for eternity."

Jen pursed her lips. "It looks like our work is cut out for us, huh?"

Cindergray chuckled. "Indeed . . . though there is another reason why I brought you down here, Jennifer." He clasped his hands behind him, as if waiting for something from her.

"Okay . . . what else do you have to show me?" Then she followed Cindergray's gaze. He was staring at her necklace; Jen touched the ring, not quite sure what to expect.

"I understand that you've had the ring ever since you were born, but we need to keep you safe. As long as you have the ring on your person, your life will continually be in jeopardy," Cindergray said. "For that reason, I am asking if you would allow me to store the ring here in the Sacrarium."

Jen had not expected him to ask her to give up one of the few things she had left to her name—the only thing that reminded her of her most cherished memories; the only thing that mattered to her.

"I wouldn't forgive myself if anything ever happened to you, Jennifer." He slowly reached out, opening his hand.

After gazing at the ring, taking in all of its fine craftsmanship, its brushed silver etchings, she slid it off her necklace and, with hesitation, gingerly placed it in the Grand Mystra's outstretched hand.

There was an empty display case to the left of the glass room, and she watched as Cindergay pushed the Ring of Lancaster into it and shut the lid. A cylinder of glass dropped from the ceiling to encase the ring.

Cindergray walked back to her and laid a strong hand on her shoulder. "Don't fret, my dear. No one else knows of this room, and that glass is tempered with the wild sands of Oxhualta, known for their strong bonding properties. The ring couldn't be under better guardianship."

"But I will be able to get it back . . ." She looked longingly up at Cindergray. "Right?"

Every second after Jen had handed her ring to the Grand Mystra, she felt like a another part had been ripped from her very being; she felt completely and utterly naked—depressed and alone. The ring was the last vestige that connected Jen to both her past life on Earth and her newfound connection to her true lineage. Her heart wanted her to grab that longsword hanging on the wall to her left and break the glass to retrieve it, but her brain convinced her that it needed to stay guarded in the Sacrarium.

"The Ring of Lancaster is your birthright. It is, and will always be, yours," Cindergray said, trying to soothe her pain. "But until then, you will need *another* totem."

Jen looked down at the orb she still held in her hand, running her thumbs across its smooth surface. "Another totem?"

"I know nothing can replace your family's ring, but you are going to need a new totem for your training," Cindergray said.

Jen let out a sigh and sheepishly smiled, looking away and blinking rapidly to fight back tears. It made sense—of course she'd need something else. Until she could get her ring back, of course.

Leading her back to the Sacrarium's entrance, the Grand Mystra said, "While you think about it, let me give you the rest of the tour, as promised."

CHAPTER NINETEEN

Beth Smith was startled from a sleep that left her drowsier than before when she heard the loud, reverberating clang of metal keys opening up a rusted cell door.

CRREEEEEEAAAAAAKK!

She opened her eyes, then quickly shut them against a sudden light; it was faint, but her eyes hadn't seen light for a few days, so they were extremely sensitive. She softly stirred Richard awake, and he instinctively ducked under her shoulder to protect his unprepared eyes from the same light.

Beth squinted to near blindness, but she was able to take in some of her surroundings. It looked worse than she had envisioned: columns of haphazardly stacked food trays along the sides of cells, gaunt prisoners scraping and clawing toward the light like delusional flies, and a motionless inmate—the friend who had talked to them—in the fetal position.

"Oh my . . ." Richard whispered—loud enough for the guards to hear.

"What's that?" said the taller of the two guards, and shone the light directly at Beth and Richard, who closed their eyes and pretended to sleep.

A few heart-racing seconds later, the light was directed back at their friend in the next cell over. They didn't know his name, just that he'd wanted to be their friend . . . whatever *that* meant in a place as hopeless and friendless as this.

"Come on, you rat. It's your time again," said tall guard, and the shorter one snickered.

The tall guard held the light while the other grabbed the inmate's emaciated arm. The short guard dragged their friend out of the cell and Beth cringed, hoping that his arm wouldn't snap. The light receded and the dragging sound got softer and softer until both were replaced by the hungry dark and overwhelming silence of the Lair of Despair.

Beth curled up and put her head on Richard's arm, wondering where they took him. Richard hugged her closer, trying to keep warm in the unlivable conditions and wondering the same thing.

"Let's hope they don't do that to us," he said.

"I'd hate to get separated from you," she replied.

Over the next few hours, Beth dozed in and out of sleep until she heard footsteps approaching, the noises deafening in the echoing abyss.

JINGLE-JANGLE!

CLANG!

SCREEEEEEEEKK!

The dim light returned as Beth, with blurred vision, saw a gray shape fall to the dense, wet floor and sit, unmoving.

"Next time be more cooperative," reprimanded the tall guard.

The short guard said, "Like he'll listen to you. He's been a pain in the ass for years."

The tall guard sniffed. "Yeah, I know, but maybe next time he'll finally give in and realize that this will never stop as long as he's alive."

"True, though prisoners who put up a fight keep it interesting," the short guard commented as they locked the rusty cell and walked away. Their words seemed calculated, meant for the prisoners' ears.

The first guard snickered and turned off the light. That was the last Beth and Richard heard of them until a few days later, when they returned to drag their friend away again.

CHAPTER TWENTY

Just kill me now, prayed Malcolm. Every time he moved a muscle, even just to breathe, an incendiary burst of sharp pain traveled through his body.

After Draconex had so considerately destroyed Malcolm's first totem, he hadn't wasted time in preparing him for his first true instruction, which felt more like a punishment. Draconex insisted on dueling Malcolm so he could identify areas of weakness and correct them. Malcolm quickly realized that Draconex didn't give advice through words, but spells that would, more often than not, land him on his back.

"You still default to the basic approaches Victor has drilled into you," Draconex reprimanded. "We're going to have to erase them from your memory, boy."

Boy. There was that word again.

As his temper rose, Malcolm pushed through the pain and threw a spell that would have sunken Draconex up to his kneecaps in the floor like quicksand—if it had hit its mark. Like a psychic seeing the future, Draconex swiftly jumped into the air as the spell fizzled through the ground; then, with blinding speed, he covered the space that separated the two sorcerers.

With a quick turn of his neck, his ponytail whipped around and the metal dragon's tooth on its end grazed Malcolm's cheek.

It was so subtle, so sharp was its tip, that he didn't even feel it until the poison kicked in.

Malcolm lost all strength in his legs and dropped to the ground, catatonic. Draconex didn't catch him to break his fall, instead letting him slam into the ground.

Just like that, Malcolm knew he'd lost the duel. Again.

Draconex laughed derisively. "Your strategy is ineffective, boy. You are still rooted in the Guild's teachings. That will get you killed in the real world."

He dropped to his haunches, slid Malcolm's only ring off his finger, and stared at it. "Remember this: you're only as good as your weakest trait." He stood back up, sliding Malcolm's ring onto a free finger. "Part one of your lesson is done. Let's commence with part two."

There came a faint hissing sound as Draconex straightened his right arm to let out an anaconda that had scales as black as night. It poured out of his long sleeve and slithered to the ground, sniffing the air for any food nearby. Its forked tongue intermittently flicked out as it searched for living prey with its eyes and nostrils.

"Your poison will wear off in ten minutes. By then, Quickfang here"—he gestured at the large snake—"will be on the brink of starvation. Your test is to kill it before it kills—and eats—you."

Malcolm started to sweat and tremble as his fear receptors went berserk.

Quickfang slowly slithered into Malcolm's field of vision, then started to slide over his prostrate body. He shut his eyes as he felt the heavy, slimy anaconda roll over him.

Draconex let out a deep chuckle. "Oh, and to make sure Quickfang doesn't escape, I'm going to lock this door. You'll find the key inside of him."

Malcolm would have whimpered if his vocal cords worked.

Draconex slammed the heavy door shut.

CLANG!

As the anaconda started to straighten itself out, preparing for its feast, sheer terror gripped Malcolm's body and mind.

Nine minutes to go.

* * *

Draconex is insane! thought Malcolm.

He couldn't speak—partially from the poison in his system, partially from pure fear—as he watched Quickfang stretch out in front of him. The snake had been doing that for the past eight minutes. Malcolm thought the anaconda was playing mind games with its prey.

But something switched inside the serpent just then. It turned still and glared at Malcolm.

A shiver shot up his spine as he realized what was about to happen.

The poison was still coursing through his veins, so Malcolm couldn't instinctively tense up as Quickfang coiled around his body, which apparently tricked the anaconda into thinking its prey was already dead; it only slightly tightened its hold for good measure, but that was enough to snap a few of Malcolm's ribs and collapse half of his left lung.

With sweat dripping down his face, he felt the anaconda release its hold. It was positioning itself right above his head. His ears twitched at a soft popping noise as Quickfang unhinged its jaw, preparing to eat Malcolm whole.

A rush of adrenaline cleared out the remaining effects of the poison and activated his fight-or-flight response. He forced himself to roll to the side as the anaconda bit through empty air where Malcolm's head had been moments before, hissing angrily after realizing its food was still alive.

Malcolm rolled all the way to the nearest wall and stood up, not feeling the pain from his badly injured chest thanks to the adrenaline rush. He drew his small but sharp ankle blade and twirled it in his hand, awaiting Quickfang's charge. He knew an anaconda's venom was one of the deadliest kinds—Draconex had taught him this himself—so he needed to take out its fangs.

Inversely, Quickfang got lower, glaring at its prey with slitted eyes full of insatiable hunger. Its forked tongue flicked silently in and out of its mouth as it waited for the opportune moment to strike.

Malcolm moved, feigning left, which was enough of a cue for the serpent to launch for a killing strike. He ducked right before Quickfang rushed at him, flying over his head and headbutting the stone wall.

Dazed, Quickfang slid to the ground, giving Malcolm an opening. He rushed to the anaconda's head, stabbed his blade into its eyes, and yanked its two front fangs out with his one good hand, flinging the snake across the room for good measure. He didn't want to worry about an unlucky bite as he was killing it.

The snake hissed in pain as its thick, muscly body writhed and whipped where it lay, trying desperately to strike Malcolm, but he had discarded the fangs and sprung back to the snake, straddling Quickfang and raising his blade for a final strike.

CRUNCH!

The blade penetrated the top of Quickfang's scaly head, digging deep into its brain. In its death throes, its body writhed before going straight . . . then limp.

Malcolm tried to yell in victory, but all that came out was a cry of pain. Giving in to his exhaustion, he slid off the snake and fell to the ground. He needed to get his breathing under control, but it was getting harder and harder as his adrenaline wore off, bringing with it the throbbing agony of a partially collapsed lung.

With increasing effort, he propped himself up and looked at his kill.

"Where's the key?" he wheezed in desperation.

He still held his ankle blade, so he gripped it and punctured the skin near the base of Quickfang's skull, pulling it down the length of the anaconda—all twenty feet of it.

The smell that affronted his nostrils stunk of stomach acid and bile buildup from the lack of food in its system. Nausea hit Malcolm like a bag full of bricks—but he needed to remain conscious so he could find the key.

With disgust, he wiped the blade on his cloak, slid it back into its holster, and dug his hands into the serpent's innards. Malcolm was so tired, he couldn't even gag as he pushed around hot, squishy muscle and fat. Finally, he felt something dense and hard, so he grabbed it and pulled the key out of Quickfang's intestines.

Covered in fresh snake juice, Malcolm limply moved his neck to view the locked door at the other end of the chamber. His heart was thumping in his chest as he tried to get up, but his legs felt like rubber.

Whimpering, he stayed on his right side and crawled with his right arm to the door; the left side of his rib cage was splintered and part of his left lung was collapsed—any attempt at moving his left arm was met with shooting pain that almost caused him to faint.

After what seemed like an eternity, Malcolm finally reached the door and slid the slimy key into the lock with a shaky hand. Letting out a breath of accomplishment, he turned the key, and the door opened to a blast of fresh air, giving Malcolm's brain fresh oxygen to stay awake.

Nothing moved on the other side of the door, so Malcolm dragged his broken body across the threshold—to the utter surprise of Lord Draconex.

* * *

In his mind's eye, all he could see was the anaconda wrapping itself around his motionless body, coiling, writhing, squeezing . . .

Malcolm opened his eyes, fighting the urge scream. There he was, still alive—but barely—and unable to fall asleep on his itchy cot.

He didn't even try putting his shirt over his bandaged chest; it hurt too much. Even breathing put him in a tremendous amount of pain—but that was what a half-collapsed lung and a few fractured ribs would do to a person. Malcolm was lucky it wasn't worse, but he still resented Draconex for refusing to heal him. Especially after he passed the stupid "lesson" and made it out of that torture chamber alive.

He'd never forget that moment, clawing his way out of the torture chamber and straight to his torturer's feet. With his eyes bleeding from Quickfang's bind and his body covered in snake guts, all Malcolm could do was force himself not to faint as Draconex had said, "Your next lesson is how to deal with physical pain. You may have escaped my anaconda, but you now have to function with the punishment your body sustained. Every duel in which you find yourself will have consequences that you have to push through to claim victory—no matter what."

"I can barely breathe . . ." Malcolm had slurred. He was on the brink of blacking out.

Draconex had knelt down and clamped the sides of his face in a vice-like grip. "Make no mistake, boy, my intention is to make you wish that you were dead. I need you to feel like you are dying so you realize how much you want to live. The lengths you must take to ensure your enemy is the one who will never breathe again . . . *those* are the costs of victory."

That was when Malcolm's body decided to shut down. His vision blurred and his face went numb. The next thing he remembered was waking up on the floor of his chamber in a pool of blood. He somehow managed to claw his way to his closet, slide out of his bloodstained clothes, and temporarily set his broken ribs in pieces of a torn-up blanket to keep them from piercing his bruised skin.

Now, Malcolm just lay there, blankly staring at the ceiling, ruing the morning when he had to face Draconex and his next potentially fatal lesson. He was in for another sleepless night, since every time he would let his eyelids droop down, Quickfang would appear, with its hungry eyes and sharp fangs dripping with venom.

The night kept ticking away as Malcolm filled his quiet room with sobs.

CHAPTER TWENTY-ONE

Back at Watercress, before Victor returned to Skarmor, he found Mystra Chen with the other Elders and took her aside. He thanked her for helping him get an audience with the Elder Synod. He believed it was Chen's persistence to the Elders that made it possible for him to return and bring in an unknown candidate for testing. He also expressed his thanks for her staying during the whole meeting, watching Jen undergo the Chimera Course, and helping during the violent ambush by Paladin Blake. Chen remained reserved throughout their entire exchange, telling him that it was only because of their history that she had decided to help him at all; she knew that he wouldn't contact her or the Guild if it wasn't important. Victor was slightly disappointed in her indifferent reaction, but expected as much; their falling out was hard on both of them.

He then returned to his faithful friend Skarmor, who was soaking up some rays of sunlight in the Elder's courtyard. He gave the griffin a quick physical, making sure he wasn't injured from his confrontation with Blake. Then, with a lot on his mind and time to kill while he waited for Jen and Cindergray to return, he decided to take Skarmor up for a quick flight.

As Skarmor took off into the clear afternoon skies, Victor tried to direct his thoughts elsewhere. But every thought he had managed to circle back to Simone Chen . . . his Simone. Then, tired of fighting his heart, he gave in.

Simone . . .

Victor had never wanted it to end the way it did, but times were different back then. Everyone warned them not to get involved personally; it would only lead to disastrous results, they said. And, as always, they were right—especially once Victor was accused of casting spells in the Pit.

No matter how hard he had fought to make Chen believe that his actions that night were to save Malcolm, she stood by the Sorcerer's Oath. Victor couldn't do anything but respect her stance. But then everything seemed to simultaneously crumble for him, like a domino effect of bad luck.

His relationship with Simone had disintegrated just after his fateful meeting with the Elder Synod. Even though it was his idea to sacrifice himself, he wasn't prepared for the way Simone had looked at him when she found out about his banishment. The loss he felt was real . . . but now that he had returned, his feelings had resurfaced. If she really did love him, how could she not feel the same way he did? Either she didn't see Victor like that anymore or she was very adept at hiding her true feelings. Victor had no clue.

Skarmor's sharp, piercing call echoed far and wide over the fertile hills of Azumar, jolting Victor out of his thoughts. They still soared high off the ground at a good clip. He patted Skarmor on his strong neck and glanced down at Watercress Castle. Despite the conflicting emotions, it felt good to be back.

Almost as if I never left.

"Maybe things do eventually work out, even if they seem unfair at the time," Victor said aloud, his words lost on the wind. Skarmor chirped his agreement as they circled Watercress.

During their third pass, Victor saw the tiny forms of Jen and Cindergray emerge from the castle. "Ho, boy!" He clicked his tongue and directed Skarmor back to the Elder's courtyard.

As Skarmor came in for a landing, Jen and Cindergray grew larger and larger, and Victor found himself anxious to hear what Jen thought about everything Cindergray had shown her.

Skarmor touched ground as lightly as a feather and took a few steps to further slow down his momentum before stopping just in front of the Grand Mystra and tenderfoot.

"So I see you made it back in one piece," Victor joked. He figured she needed some levity, given her witnessing an assassination attempt less than an hour ago.

Jen's face was flushed and her eyelids looked slightly puffy like she had been crying, but Victor did not get that sense from the way she spoke. "Victor! Cindergray gave me an *amazing* tour of Watercress after showing me the Sacrarium."

"Pretty cool where they hid it, huh?" Victor winked at her.

"Yeah, I mean, just getting there was hard enough."

Cindergray added, "We both decided to stow the Ring of Lancaster there to take the target off her back while she trains with her very own totem."

Victor noticed that Jen was still going through the emotional loss of her ring. He could see her bottom lip start to quiver, so he gave a nonverbal signal to Skarmor. The mighty griffin cocked his large eagle's head and walked over to Jen. She smiled when she saw him come closer and they touched foreheads.

"Hey, Skar," she said as she put a hand atop his head. That was all she needed to compose herself before facing Victor and saying, "Yep. I left it there, Vic. This is the first time I haven't worn the ring since I was a baby."

Victor put his hand on her shoulder. "I'm proud of you, Jenny. I know how much it must have hurt to part with it." He shot a glance over at Cindergray. "But it was for the best. At this time, you're much safer with your ring protected in the Sacrarium."

"That's what Cindergray told me, and I believe it." Jen turned her orb over in her hands a few times.

Victor noticed. "So have you decided on what totem you are going to make?"

Jen gripped the orb a little tighter. "I have a few ideas."

Victor smirked. The more he got to know Jen, the more she reminded him of a younger version of himself. She was full of inherent bravery, abundant creativity, and the willingness to do the right thing, no matter what. "I think I know who might be able to help you." He smiled at Cindergray and asked, "May I?"

"I think Jen has had enough of me for the day." Cindergray winked at Jen. "You may, Mystra Huxley."

Mystra Huxley . . .

Victor hadn't expected to hear his old title. Frankly, he hadn't been called that in so long that he had erased it from his mind— no one in the history of the Guild had been reinstated after being banished. Granted, Victor's crime wasn't as severe as others—if you could call what he did a "crime"—but he was still officially dismissed. But to hear it now, and from the Grand Mystra no less, made his heart swell with pride.

Happier than he had ever been, Victor bowed deeply to Cindergray and offered his elbow to Jen, gesturing to Skarmor with his other hand. "It would be my honor to escort you to the metallurgy, Jennifer Lancaster. I think it's time for you to get acquainted with Mystra Hephalon, the forger of totems."

Jen seemed relieved. "Oh, good!" She laughed. "I thought I had to make my own totem . . . *that* would have been disastrous."

She slid her arm around Victor's bent elbow and together they walked to Skarmor, who seemed excited to take them to the metallurgy. His lion tail thumped on the ground as he stretched his large eagle wings.

Jen asked, "What has gotten into Skarmor?"

Victor smiled knowingly. "Mystra Hephalon has a female griffin. Pernissa."

"Oh my . . ." Jen laughed.

Victor was about to help Jen get on Skarmor when she stopped him. "Thanks, Vic, but let me try it alone. Here." She handed him her orb.

She pulled herself up onto Skarmor, straddling him with both legs.

Victor was impressed. "Very nice, but it could use a bit of work," he joked. He deftly mounted Skarmor in front of Jen while still holding the orb.

Jen scoffed and took the orb back. "Show-off," she muttered.

"Hya!" yelled Victor, and Skarmor gained speed to take flight.

* * *

As the griffin took off from Watercress for the metallurgy, Cindergray watched them go. He was filled with so many thoughts, but once they were swallowed by the horizon and the setting sun, Cindergray then focused on what needed to be done.

* * *

Jen didn't realize how tired she was until Skarmor was airborne. The griffin's smooth flying rocked her to sleep, and by the time she opened her eyes again the sun had almost set over a massive and dense forest that went as far as Jen could see. Before the forest's tree line started, though, there stood a compound with a medieval-looking factory, pumping gray smoke from a lone chimney vent, and a modest stone cottage that gave off a warm light through its windows.

"Welcome to the metallurgy, situated at the base of the Amaranthine Forest." Victor gestured forward over the dense canopy of trees. "Now, Mystra Hephalon can get overly excited when meeting new people, so be prepared," Victor called over his shoulder.

The compound grew as Skarmor descended. Jen squinted through the dwindling sunlight as she caught sight of a large, burly man chopping wood outside. She guessed that he was Mystra Hephalon.

CRACK!

As Skarmor touched down, Hephalon brought his axe down with such force that the thick log in front of him split as easily as a toothpick. Seeing Skarmor, he kicked the log pieces to the ground, stuck his axe into the cutting stump, and turned to them.

Wiping his hands, he bellowed, "Well, poke my eyes, look who it is!" He lumbered over to Victor, who had already dismounted and was walking toward his friend.

"It's good to see you too, Heph," Victor said before all his air was pushed from his lungs by a bear hug.

Hephalon released Victor and laughed. "When I heard you had returned, I couldn't believe it! I thought some tenderfoot was pranking me when my carrier hawk returned from a grocery trip with a message tied on his leg, but lo and behold!"

Victor patted his friend's broad shoulders and led him toward Jen, who was still sitting atop Skarmor. "It's a long story, but there's someone who needs your ever-capable hands to forge her a totem."

"Oh, enough with your plaudits—you have already won me over, you nobbler!" Hephalon said, clearly still appreciating the compliment. "So who's the lucky tenderfoot?"

"Mystra Hephalon, I give you Jennifer," Victor started, and Hephalon dropped into a big, embellished bow. "Daughter of Charles and Jocelyn," Victor continued, despite Hephalon freezing mid-bow, "descendant of Genevieve Lancaster."

Hephalon gasped, quickly bringing himself up to his normal posture. "Merlin's beard!" exclaimed the metallurgist.

With a smirk, Victor introduced his old friend. "Jen, I give you Mystra Sterling Hephalon, son of Vulcus, the most renowned of totem metallurgists."

Hephalon was still in comical shock as Jen said with a giggle, "Very nice to meet you, Mystra Hephalon." She slid off of Skarmor and landed with soft feet.

"Lancast— So the stories are true . . ." Hephalon stumbled over his words as Jen made her way to shake his hand, which was three times the size of hers. She held her hand out until he shook off his amazement and brought both arms around her for a bear hug. Jen was lifted off the ground as Hephalon said, "I never thought I'd see the day!" He softly put her back onto the ground and bowed more eloquently this time. "I am at thee service, milady."

It took a couple of breaths for Jen to find her voice, then she replied, "Thank you, Mystra Hephalon."

"Oh, please call me Heph. Hephalon was my father." He

scratched his head. "And my uncles and grandfather, now that I mention it. It surely is a wonder how nobody got confused!"

Jen shot a glance at Victor and laughed.

Behind them, Skarmor patted the ground with his bushy lion tail and beat his wings in eagerness.

"Looks like Skarmor is interested in reuniting with a certain female griffin of yours," Victor said coyly.

"Ah, yes! Pernissa will enjoy seeing him as well," Hephalon said. He led the group to the stable behind his cottage. Upon opening the sliding door, Hephalon stood to the side to let Skarmor eagerly trot inside, trilling in delight.

Following Skarmor inside, Jen watched as he greeted another griffin—Pernissa, she assumed—by dropping to one of his front haunches and bowing his feathered head. Pernissa was first stunned to see Skarmor, then cawed in glee, standing up. She was smaller and trimmer than Skarmor, and had lighter coloring on both her lion hide and eagle feathers. Once Skarmor stood up, she touched his forehead and wrapped her neck around his.

"They haven't seen each other in ten years," Victor commented, leaning on the stable's doorframe.

"They're so cute together," Jen gushed, placing her hands over her heart. "I could just *die*."

"Let's let them catch up, while we do the same over a stein or two of Azumarian ale." Hephalon put a meaty hand on the back of Victor's neck and waved Jen to follow. "Come!"

"You still drink that stuff?" Victor laughed as they walked toward the cottage's front door.

Jen had a hard time tearing her eyes away from the griffins, catching herself yearning to feel that way toward someone —*anyone but Malcolm!*—but once she did, she saw the soft glow of a fire burning inside the cottage as the tired sun finally dipped beneath the horizon.

* * *

Azumarian ale turned out to be quite sour—so sour that Jen

found herself puckering as she wiped the foam mustache from her upper lip after cautiously accepting the first stein poured by Hephalon. Even though she didn't know the drinking age on Azumar, her conscious was clear since she had been twenty-one years old for four days at that time.

Hephalon guffawed and Victor chuckled as Jen swallowed hard and put on a polite face. She quietly slid the stein, which was as big and round as her head, closer to the center of the wooden table, indicating she'd had her fill.

"It's an acquired taste," Victor empathetically said to her, as though he'd had that same experience the first time he'd tried the ale.

"But you'll learn to love it," Hephalon added. "It's all I drink!"

Victor leaned closer to Jen. "And he's got the figure to prove it."

They all laughed as Hephalon posed like a bodybuilder before sitting down with two more full steins for himself and Victor. For the next hour, Jen was regaled with many of Victor and Hephalon's stories as they emptied a keg of ale, the majority of which found its way into Hephalon's belly.

". . . so we decided to make a bet on who would become a paladin first," Hephalon was saying about one of their shared memories. He animatedly stroked his chin in mock-thought. "Do you remember who did, Vic?"

Victor held up his hands and gave a dismissive smile. "Hey, let the record show that the only reason you made Paladin first was because you were obsessed with winning the bet! You failed twice before you got lucky and passed the day before I applied. I wanted to make sure I passed the Trials on my first try."

"Slow and steady didn't win the race that time, old friend! It was I who claimed the victory!" Hephalon raised his glass in triumph. Both laughed and clinked their steins before Victor and Hephalon took a sip and a gulp respectively.

As she sat there listening, Jen realized just how much Victor had sacrificed watching over her for the past nineteen years. She had never seen Victor laugh as much as he did with Hephalon—of course, she had only known him for a short time, but nevertheless Jen felt a mix of admiration and sorrow for what he'd parted with to ensure her protection. She felt a warmth in her heart, a thankfulness that Victor was her guardian.

They shared a couple more stories with Jen, one in particular about a girl they'd both had a massive crush on when they were tenderfeet—only to learn she was a telemancer and could read their minds.

Then the clock chimed the start of a new hour, and Hephalon decided to cork the keg. To Jen, he said, "I still cannot fathom that you are a Lancaster. The story was that you had disappeared with your parents when you were a wee babe. Where were you hiding this whole time?"

Jen sat up straighter. "I—uh . . . I'm actually still coming to grips with it too. Up until a few days ago, I was living in New York—New York City, it's on Earth?—when Vic saved me from a Dark Watcher." She glanced appreciatively at Victor, thinking again about Malcolm.

Hephalon patted his long-time friend on the back. "You're in the safest hands around."

Victor thanked him and said, "That's actually why we're here, Heph . . . now that the Dark Watchers are aware of Jen and her potential, we need to prepare her for training." He indicated the orb Jen had placed in the corner of the room when they entered.

She walked over, picked it up, and brought it back to the table.

"Yes," Hephalon agreed. "It would be an honor to forge your totem, milady."

"Thank you," Jen replied, silently grateful he hadn't made her ask for it.

"Have you given thought to what you would like?" Hephalon asked, eyeing the orb. "A ring? A staff? A dagger, perhaps?"

Victor folded his hands and rested his chin on his thumbs as he waited for Jen's response.

"I was actually thinking about a bracelet," Jen answered.

Victor raised his eyebrows in surprise as Hephalon swirled around the remaining drops of ale in his stein.

Jen continued, holding the orb in her hands. "Since I'm learning to be an omnimancer, I feel it would be fitting to have charms on the bracelet, one for each Mancy plane."

Victor nodded his approval. "Very creative."

"And elegant." The master blacksmith looked to the ceiling in deep thought.

"And to show your progress, every time you master a plane, Heph would forge you a new charm," Victor offered.

Jen liked that proposal; each charm would be a milestone in her journey.

"Yes! That would give me an excuse to see you two more often!" said Hephalon.

"But you would need one charm to start out with, Jen," Victor pointed out, "to act as a totem specifically for the first plane you decide to learn. Do you have a preference?"

Without hesitation, Jen said, "Terramancy. And I want you to instruct me, Vic."

Victor smiled, touched. "I wouldn't have it any other way."

"It's settled then," Hephalon interjected, slamming his empty stein on the table. He scratched his cleft chin, thinking. "Your orb has more than enough metal for a bracelet and several charms. If I start now, I can forge a terramancy charm and a few different bracelet designs that you can choose from in an hour."

"That sounds great!" Jen was beside herself with excitement. With both hands, she handed the orb over to him.

"Splendid!" Hephalon exclaimed, taking it carefully from her. He downed the dregs of his drink and slammed his stein on the table, shaking it slightly. "I'll throw some more coal on the fire!"

"You've had quite a few drinks," Jen pointed out.

"I appreciate your concern, milady, but I've built up quite a tolerance to the fine Azumarian ale. It's like water to me!"

He did seem sober enough, so Jen let it go, especially when Victor remained silent.

"Speaking of, would anyone care for more?" Hephalon patted the large wooden keg.

Both Jen and Victor shook their heads before Hephalon,

slightly tempted, agreed to leave the keg and invited them to tour his factory instead.

The night had turned very dark as the group walked across the yard to the metallurgy; Jen was constantly surprised at that, given she had grown up around and attended New York University, which had noticeable light pollution at night. She felt like she had stepped into one of her old history books and was actually experiencing the Middle Ages.

Skarmor called out in delight when he saw his friends come outside. Jen had never seen Skarmor this happy, lounging in front of the cottage with Pernissa. He jumped up and bounced over to her and Victor, making high-pitched noises as if he were trying to tell them everything he and Pernissa had talked about. Jen laughed while she petted him before Skarmor went to Victor.

"Oh really?" Victor played along. "That's so interesting, Skar." He petted the griffin's neck as he tried to calm him down. "We're heading into Heph's factory now, so why don't you go back to your conversation with Pernissa?"

Skarmor chirped and trotted back to where his friend was sitting preening herself.

By then, Hephalon had made it to the factory's door and now held it open for Victor and Jen.

* * *

After the trio had entered and the door was closed shut, Skarmor and Pernissa's eagle ears picked up a noise near the perimeter as they caught the tail-end of a small creature scampering behind a bush near the tree line.

Playfully, they both got up and stealthily began investigating.

* * *

Inside, the metallurgy looked much bigger than what Jen had expected.

Hephalon placed Jen's orb on the nearest workbench and

plucked a leather apron off a hanger near the door. Putting it on, he lumbered over to the central blast furnace to check on the fire. It was all but embers, so he slid on some welding gloves and picked up a large shovel, tossing in a heaping pile of coal, which turned the embers into a roaring fire almost instantly and sent heat outward in all directions. At first, the heat felt surprisingly good, but before Jen knew it she was sweating. Victor slid off his thick cloak and hung it on a free hanger.

"Welcome to where the true magic happens!" Hephalon raised his hands high as he gestured to his domain. The fire grew larger behind him, silhouetting his form and making him look like a movie villain who'd just explained his fool-proof plan for world domination.

"Toasty!" Jen had to yell to be heard over the fire and machinery, but she heard Victor snicker behind her.

As Jen wiped her forehead with the end of her sleeve, she looked around. There was a workbench pushed up against each wall which held smelting and casting tools along with pieces of metal that Jen assumed were current projects.

"Heph built this factory with his own hands—with the help of some terramancy—once he made Mystra," Victor said.

"This is my true home." Hephalon inhaled the smoky, hot air. "That other place?" He jutted a thumb at the cottage. "That's just where I sleep and entertain."

Hephalon led Jen and Victor around the blast furnace, showing off some casts he had made for new tools and weapons. Then, at the other end of the factory, he opened a door and invited them inside a darker and slightly cooler room.

Thank you, Jen thought as she wiped more sweat from her forehead and neck. Her hair, once curly and voluminous, had lost some of its life from the intense heat and lay limp on her head and shoulders.

Hephalon lit a lantern, casting light on the room's contents. "This is where I keep all of my most cherished pieces."

He walked over to the wall, whereupon rested many different weapons and types of armor, each ornate and beautiful, glistening from the lantern's light. He placed the lantern on a table in the center of the room and went to his trophy wall. Finding what he was looking for, he slid a band of brass knuckles off a rung. Putting them on his meaty fingers, he made a fist and lifted it to chin level. After playing with the grip a few times, he took the brass knuckles off and offered them to Jen.

"Behold . . . *my* totem."

Jen took it, surprised at how heavy the totem truly was. She looked up at Hephalon and, at his reassuring nod, slid it onto her fingers. Unsurprisingly, her ring size was quite a bit smaller than his, so it felt very awkward as some of the edges dug into her skin as it slid around on her hand.

Hephalon guffawed and motioned for it back. Gladly, Jen returned the knuckles to him as he said, "A totem should be an embodiment of the sorcerer—something so meaningful yet reliable that it feels like an extension of themselves." He looked at his totem again. "I couldn't think of anything other than brass knuckles for me! Quite the brawler, I am—always have been, always will be." He replaced the brass knuckles on the wall and turned to Jen. "Enough about me! Now that we let the fire build up, let's get started on your bracelet. Would you like to wait here or back in the cottage?"

Beginning to feel the heat again, Jen was in desperate need of some water. She looked at Victor and noticed that his hair was starting to droop over his eyes.

Simultaneously, they both said, "Cottage."

* * *

"Permit me an hour, then you'll have your choice of bracelets!"

Hephalon closed the door, cutting off the stifling heat from the factory.

Jen gasped delightedly as coldness surrounded her, feeling relief as she breathed in the brisk night air. She plucked at her sweaty shirt, which was sticking to her back as she waited for Victor to catch up.

"Hey, where's Skarmor?" she asked.

Victor stopped to look around as he put his cloak back on. Not seeing his griffin anywhere, he gave a short whistle and waited.

There was a reassuring call from behind the cottage, and without warning a cat emerged from that area, limping as Skarmor and Pernissa cautiously followed it into view.

"Looks like we have a surprise visitor," Victor commented.

The cat cautiously swayed up to him and Jen. The griffins still seemed a little unsure, for they cocked their heads to the left, then to the right, never taking their eyes off of the cat, which seemed to be nursing an injury to its right front leg.

"It looks hurt!" Jen put her hands to her heart, looking at Victor.

Victor exhaled, thinking. "Skar," he called out to his griffin.

Skarmor slowly came around to Victor.

So as not to scare off the cat, Victor whispered a command in Skarmor's ear and stepped back as his griffin lightly walked toward the injured feline.

Sitting on its hind legs, the cat stopped licking its right front leg and purred questioningly as Skarmor traced the injured limb with one of his eagle claws.

Dumfounded, Jen watched as the cat's leg started to glow white, and before long the cat was walking up to her without the slightest limp or sign of discomfort.

"How did . . . ?" Jen pointed at the miracle she had witnessed, speechless.

Victor grinned, walking over to pat Skarmor. "Griffins' claws have special healing abilities. Just one touch with their claws heals everything short of dying."

Smiling from ear to ear, Jen let the cat walk through and around her legs. "That is amazing." Kneeling down, she petted the cat. "Hey, you. Where did you come from?" It arched its back as she stroked it a few times. Its fur felt a little prickly and rough in some places; Jen picked a twig out from behind one of its ears.

"Looks like it's been rolling around in the forest." Victor took the twig and knelt down to get a better view of the cat, but it hissed and scampered into the cover of the forest.

"Vic, what did you do that for?" Jen pleaded, immediately seeing if she could find the cat near the tree line.

"It looked like a stray cat. Could've even been feral. You have to be careful with those, Jen. They have volatile tempers." Victor dismissed the encounter and started toward the cottage. He looked back at Jen and said, "You coming?"

Still scanning the tree line, Jen said distantly, "Yeah . . . right behind you." She slowly started walking toward the cottage and eventually gave up her search for the mysterious cat.

"Keep an eye out for that cat, Skarmor," Victor told the griffin.

Skarmor clicked his beak in affirmation and flew to the roof of the cottage, landing there to survey the surroundings. His majestic form was silhouetted in front of the brilliant full moon, giving the griffin a larger-than-life persona. Pernissa trilled and sat down, letting Skarmor play the guard dog.

Jen found it endearing how Skarmor took Victor's commands so seriously. She followed Victor inside to wait for Hephalon to return with her totem bracelet and charm.

CHAPTER TWENTY-TWO

The food was horrible, but the aftertaste was worse; it could gag even a maggot.

Richard and Beth Smith could feel themselves losing strength, as though their rations were engineered to barely keep their bodies functioning, teetering on the brink of starvation and death. After four days of eating the same filth, they began to wonder what was worse: the food or the constant darkness that filled every crack and crevice of the prison bay—if there even were cracks or crevices. They suspected that not even the cockroaches could escape this place.

Both Richard and Beth had started keeping their eyes closed, for opening them was worthless; they couldn't see anything anyways, and with their current lack of strength, it became difficult to even keep their eyelids open. So, with eyes shut, they relied on their hearing to figure out what was going on.

They had overheard some guards call the prison the "Lair of Despair," more in jest or annoyance for being stuck on guard duty. Richard didn't care what they called it; to him, it was Hell on Earth—or wherever they were.

They quickly came to dread the guards' treatment of their friend. Every other day, they would drag him off to some unknown place and, roughly two hours later, drag him back and ask him the same question: "Will you be more cooperative next time?"

Finally, Richard decided to talk to their neighbor, who had given them the only ounce of friendship since they'd woke up cold and confused in their cell. It often took a while for his friend to gain consciousness after he was brought back, so he waited for sounds of movement and unsteady breathing.

As he waited, Richard's mind began to wander. Whenever he fell asleep, he didn't dream—or at least he didn't remember any dreams. He had been a consistent dreamer back in his old life, which seemed like decades ago now. He couldn't put a finger on it, but it was as if the Lair of Despair had begun to take everything from him, including his dreams. Every night—or every time he was tired enough to contemplate falling asleep—he prayed for Beth to remain safe and by his side.

Even if he couldn't dream, he still awaited the chance to drift off to sleep, after he'd tried to drown out the wailing, scuffling, and mad jabbering all around him. Richard leaned on the bars of his cell, putting a hand on his wife's arm just so he knew she was by him, and waited . . . waited for his friend to awaken while he himself drifted off.

* * *

Richard awoke, rubbing his forehead. He felt a slight depression on the front of his right temple; he must have propped his head on one of his cell's bars and fallen asleep. Rolling his neck to stretch out the stiff muscles, he listened for any noise in the next cell.

With his eyes still shut, he tried to drown out all his other senses and focus solely on his hearing. Finally, his ears perked up when he heard movement. Richard almost opened his eyes to look at the source of the noise, but quickly realized that he wouldn't be able to see anything, so he kept his eyes closed.

"Hey . . . friend," Richard whispered.

Nothing.

He softly rubbed his wife's arm, hoping to relax her while he waited for another sound.

He waited a few heartbeats, then tried again.

"Pssst. Friend."

This time there was the sound of moving fabric, but no reply.

After clicking his jaw a few times—a nervous tick he had developed when he was a child—he waited a few more heartbeats.

Finally, he broke the cold silence once more.

"Are you okay?"

Nothing.

"I don't know where they take you, but it seems to really affect you."

A few more heartbeats passed, and just as Richard was about to give up, he heard, "I've gotten used to it."

"Where do they take you?" Richard repeated.

"I-I don't know for sure. They blindfold me before they take me out of the cell bay." Before Richard could ask another question, the man continued, "Every time, I'm brought before this . . . this *man*. His voice is scratchy and as hollow as a dead tree trunk, but for some reason I . . . I *recognize* it? He's called Lord Draconex, but that name doesn't ring a bell . . . it's killing me."

"Why is this Draconex doing this to you?"

"I-I . . . I can't remember," his friend stuttered. "Just that they tell me I have a secret and if I don't tell them what it is, they'll hurt me."

"Do you know what they're talking about?"

"No!" The voice echoed throughout the deep prison, bouncing off all the cell walls so it seemed as if a hundred prisoners were screaming, one after another, *No! no! no!*

Richard wasn't prepared for the loud volume of his friend's response; he instinctively flinched, accidentally nudging Beth and waking her up.

"Is everything okay, honey?" she asked groggily.

"Yes, everything is fine, dear. Try to go back to sleep," Richard said, stroking her hair.

Richard turned his ear toward his friend's cell and noticed his breathing was erratic, quick—what you'd hear from people who were freezing or terribly frightened.

"I'm sorry. I don't know what came over me." His friend sounded as if he had moved closer to the cell bars, the only things separating him from Richard.

"Well, maybe I can help you . . . but first I would appreciate it if you would talk with me." Richard was thinking on his feet, but if he could get some of his questions answered, he could help this man feel better. As a psychiatrist, he had dealt with clients who had extreme cases of trauma. Sure, he didn't know this person's background or mental history, let alone even his *name*, but he was determined to give it his best.

The next hour was spent trying to calm his friend down. It was very hard for Richard to know if it was working, talking in the dark like this, so he relied on hearing signs from his friend's breathing and tone of voice. Richard remembered how volatile the man had become when he felt he was being interrogated, so he tried to alter his tactics. Instead of asking him direct question after direct question, Richard planned on letting it surface naturally through conversation.

"This food sucks," Richard commented.

"Pure garbage, but you get used to it."

"Don't tell me you *like* this stuff?"

"Well, when you've been down here eating the same slog for countless years, your taste buds tend to get used to it, or just die off."

Richard forced a chuckle. "I can't imagine being down here for *years*, my friend."

A quick inhale came through the cell bars. "We're . . . friends?"

"Course. We gotta stick together here in . . ." Richard purposefully trailed off, hoping his friend would finish the sentence.

"The Lair of Despair? You know, that's not the actual name for this place, but it sums it up nicely."

"Oh? I thought it was." Richard tried to keep his eagerness at bay. This was the first time he was feeling like himself again, and even in the depths of despair, finding clues kept him from falling into severe depression.

Richard heard his friend scuffle closer to the bars and whisper, "They may *call* it the Lair of Despair . . . but we're in a prison on a nomadic city called the Feralot."

Progress!

"Feralot," Richard repeated. He tucked that name into his memory. "I've never heard of a nomadic *city* before."

"That's because it's the only one of its kind. Feralot roams around the planet by dark magic. It can even move between *realms*," his friend said, slightly louder and with a hint of awe in his voice.

Richard felt blindsided, as if he'd been hit by a bus.

Dark magic? Between realms?

Suddenly things started to make sense, and he began to piece together why he and his wife had been captured and dumped into this hellhole.

Dark Watchers must have discovered Jen's true identity.

Richard needed time to process his realization that Jen had been discovered, so he tapered off the conversation with his friend, reassuring him that they would talk again soon. For a couple of long minutes, he didn't move, just thought. He was consumed with grief at the safety of his children—Tyler was back home all alone and that he had no idea where Jen was. He began to get jittery and almost fall into a panic attack, but then he remembered how resourceful Tyler was—he prayed that he was safe either at one of his friends' houses or with his aunt—and that Victor was watching over Jen. Those thoughts gave him some reassurance, but the worry inside him didn't fade.

A slight chill ran through him, making Richard slide over to be by his wife, who was fast asleep. Curling up beside her, he was simultaneously glad and envious that she had fallen back asleep so quickly; for as long as he had been imprisoned here—however long that had actually been, he did not know—Richard could not seem to be able to fall back asleep even if his life had depended on it. Maybe because he couldn't turn his mind off, plagued by two questions: Why were he and his wife captured? And how could they escape?

Thanks to his friend, he now had a pretty good grip on why he was here, stuck in a decrepit prison cell aboard the roaming citadel, Feralot: because he'd sworn to protect and raise Jennifer Lancaster. Now he began to focus on the other question: How could they escape? Was such an escape even possible?

Whoever his friend was, he seemed to have once been a smart, able-bodied man, but his frequent visits to Lord Draconex for questioning had led him to become constantly weak and delirious. Questioning for what, Richard didn't know, but he did know that the information his friend had must be extremely important to Draconex.

But Richard needed rest. A fresh and alert mind would be better suited for thinking of escape plans than a tired one. He tried his best to focus on a way to fall asleep, and quickly. Finally deciding on the old trick of counting sheep, he imagined one, two, three sheep jumping over a wooden fence underneath a full moon. Reaching sheep number thirty proved he wasn't getting tired, but he pushed on, sending more sheep over that fence one after another.

Sheep number seventy-five was when Richard felt drowsy . . . when, all of a sudden, a cat jumped over the fence in place of sheep number seventy-six. There was something different about that cat, though . . . it exuded a calming effect on Richard's mind.

Being a psychologist, he knew that people tended to exhibit unrelated and sometimes even random sequences right before they fell asleep, so he professionally concluded he was experiencing a similar phenomenon. The last sheep he counted before falling into another dreamless sleep was not a cat, and it was number ninety-nine.

CHAPTER TWENTY-THREE

"Am I surrounded only by imbeciles?!" Draconex spewed rhetorically. He channeled the strength of a silverback gorilla as he splintered a table in two with his clenched fists that were glowing with his dragon rings.

Madame Diaema quickly morphed into a bat and flew away, making sure she was out of the dangerous vicinity of her lord's anger.

After he commanded one of his personal golems to take the injured Malcolm back to his chambers, Draconex's short fuse had been lit once again when Diaema brought him news from Watercress. Apparently Archibald Blake, the sleeper agent he had entrusted to capture the Lancaster girl, was discovered and had tried to kill his target in a desperate panic to escape. His former handler had sent the message, along with his cloak and totem spear.

With his scar turning a deep mauve color, he picked up Blake's collapsible spear, inspecting its metal head. Retracting it to its full length, he thrust it into a large mirror on the opposite side of his den.

CRASH!

The mirror broke into a thousand little shards that danced on the floor like frozen raindrops. Draconex then spun around and paced in front of his throne before sitting down and clenching the ends of his armrests so intensely that his bony knuckles turned snow-white.

Paralyzed with fear, Diaema remained quiet and gripped her branch until she thought it safe to offer him comfort.

Ever since Jennifer Lancaster was discovered, everything seemed to be going wrong for Draconex; every one of his well-formulated plans had fallen well short of their marks. Every Watcher he had dispatched either came back empty-handed or not at all. In all of the contingency plans he had made, Draconex would have never imagined that it would be this difficult to capture a naïve, ignorant college girl. Granted, she was a Lancaster; but, based on the intel gained during Malcolm's three-month mission, he knew that she had no prior knowledge of sorcery, nor of her true family heritage.

That left only one explanation: Victor Huxley.

Like a bad penny, Victor had turned up and ruined his master plan, and foolishly he had sent boys to do a man's job.

That will never happen again, thought Draconex.

The soft beating of wings made his pointy ears prick up. Madame Diaema turned back into her ghoulishly radiant female form and sauntered closer to him, carrying a goblet. Draconex could smell the fresh blood that had been poured for him, but he was too angry to stop and enjoy a glass.

"For My Liege," Diaema said seductively, bringing the goblet in front of him.

If there is one thing you must know about Lord Draconex, it is that he hates being interrupted and distracted.

Without warning, he smacked the cup out of his mistress's hand, sending the goblet clattering to the floor amid a pool of dark blood. He shot her a look so loathsome that it turned her cold blood even colder.

He didn't say anything, which made it worse. Diaema shied away, dreading what punishment he might inflict upon her; but instead of lashing out, Draconex looked back out in front of him and put his long-nailed fingertips to his temples. He tried desperately to calm down, but his temper only rose further as he thought about the embarrassing failures of Malcolm and Blake and how different it could have been if it were *he* who had went after Lancaster.

Just then, an idea popped into his mind, and without a word he pushed himself from his throne and headed for the dungeon level.

"Where are you going?" Diaema asked, disappointment in her voice.

"To pay Volcanor a visit."

Draconex didn't stop to wait for a reply.

CHAPTER TWENTY-FOUR

Jen was starting to catch a chill from the crisp night air, so Victor threw some wood into the cottage's fireplace. Before long, the entire first level warmed up and Jen could hear the wood starting to crackle as it grew into a pleasant fire.

Warming her hands, Jen finally spoke after a few minutes of silent contemplation. "Have you ever tried reading the lost journal of Merlin, Vic?"

Victor leaned forward and started stoking the fire. "Yes, back when I was a tenderfoot. After I had my totem forged, Grand Mystra Cindergray brought the journal into the ballroom for all of the new tenderfeet to read. At the time I didn't realize that it was Merlin's journal, but even if I had known, it still wouldn't have helped me. No one could decipher the scribbles and shapes on any page, and I felt like I failed my first test—right up until my mystra explained Merlin's prophecy of the Light Bringer."

"Yeah, Grand Mystra Cindergray also told me about the prophecy." She paused, thinking. "So . . . *every* tenderfoot is shown the journal?"

"It's a rite of passage, yes. Ever since Merlin's journal was discovered, every tenderfoot class gets a crack at reading it, but no one has been able to." Victor saw Jen's concerned look. "What's wrong, Jenny?"

Jen chewed on her lower lip and said, "It's just that I was right in front of the lost journal . . . but he didn't give me a chance to read it."

Victor moved his chair closer to hers. His tone was reassuring but firm. "The Grand Mystra has always respected the Guild's rules and traditions, and one of them is to present the lost journal of Merlin to the new tenderfeet—*after* their totems have been forged. I could tell that the Grand Mystra was fully aware he was breaching protocol by taking you down to the Sacrarium to deposit the Ring of Lancaster right after you passed the Chimera Course, but I think Blake's attack made him realize he needed to protect you. I'm sure you'll be given a chance once we return with your new totem."

Victor's rationale put her mind at ease. "Thanks, Vic." Jen leaned back into her chair and let the fire warm her core. She wondered if she'd be the same as every other tenderfoot and not be able to read it.

Victor stared at her for a bit, then asked, "Do you know who found the journal after Merlin disappeared?"

Jen's eyebrows shot up, suddenly intrigued. "No. Who found it?"

Victor smirked. "Philip Lancaster II, Genevieve's son—and another one of your ancestors."

Jen couldn't conceal the surprise on her face. "You've *got* to be kidding me! That's awesome!"

Victor's smirk turned into a grimace. "You'd think , . . but once he found it, Philip devoted his life to hunting down the rest of the MystiCrystals so he could avenge his parents' deaths and make sure that kind of power would never fall into the wrong hands again. It consumed his every waking thought—and his inability to read Merlin's journal nearly drove him insane." Victor took the fire poker and stoked the fire.

"What happened to Philip?"

"It's said that his obsessive desire to find the remaining Mysti-Crystals turned him into a paranoid recluse who shut out his family and friends. He spent the rest of his days in seclusion until he embarked on what would be his last quest. Nobody knew where he went, and he was never seen again."

Jen, sorrowful at Vic's tale, was surprised at how tragic Philip's life had turned out. She felt for his family, *her* family—only able to imagine how they would have felt. She just hoped that he died peacefully.

Victor stood up and gestured at the pile of wood by the fireplace. "More wood?"

Before Jen could answer, the front door of the cottage swung open to reveal a man almost as wide as the door. The fire flickered as a breeze entered with Hephalon, who side-stepped through the opening, shouldering a leather satchel.

"Salutations once again!" he shouted jovially after he closed the door.

Jen was so focused on her conversation with Victor that she had completely forgotten that Hephalon was forging her totem on the other side of the compound. To her surprise, an hour had already passed—that explained why the fire needed more wood.

"How did it go?" Victor asked.

"I've never been asked to forge a totem *bracelet* before, so I undertook this challenge with great zest!" The master blacksmith walked into the kitchen and slid a stein underneath the keg's spout. "I hope one of my designs will tickle your fancy, milady."

Jen got up from her chair and made her way to the kitchen table, eager to view his creations. Victor tossed three more pieces of wood into the fireplace and joined her.

Hephalon plopped into a chair next to Jen and started to sift through his satchel, but only after downing a full stein and refilling it. Finally finding what he desired, he produced the first of three bracelets, saying, "Aye, yes. This was the first design I cast." He held the shiny bracelet between his index fingers and thumbs. As he moved it from side to side, the fire's light played off its depressions and inlays, making it come alive. "I made the metal into two cords and twisted it around to give it a dimension of interlocking strength." He handed Jen the bracelet, then went back into his satchel to look for another.

It was a solid cuff, bent into an oval with a half-inch opening that was able to open wider so Jen could slide it on. The hard metal didn't conform to her wrist; it retained its oval shape, lifting itself an inch and a half off of her wrist when her arm rested on the table. It seemed too rigid, the sides of her wrist pinched by the cuff.

"This one here," Hephalon continued, "is more fluid in nature. More delicate also, but just as impressive." Lifting it up with two fingers, he showed them a bracelet formed by several interlocking oval links. It jingled and jangled as he laid it on Jen's open palm.

She took off the first bracelet and put the chained one on, letting it hang off her wrist. It was lighter than the first, but it didn't seem as durable. The chain also made constant noise whenever she moved her wrist.

"And last but not least," announced Hephalon. He pulled out one that was thicker than the others and had an intricate design between two metal borders that looked like thin ropes. This one had the durability of the first bracelet and the flexibility of the second. Jen knew before she even tried it on that she would choose this one, but ever eager to see how it would look on her, she unclasped it and slid it onto her wrist.

Jen let it fall into a normal resting position after she clasped it in place, and she immediately felt a connection. Beaming, she looked up at Hephalon.

"This one is absolutely beautiful."

"I had a feeling that one would enchant you," Hephalon agreed.

"I can't believe you made all three in just an hour," Jen said, still in awe.

"It's the least I could do for a Lancaster."

Victor, still tending the fire, put down the poker and stepped closer to see which bracelet Jen had chosen. With appreciation and amazement in her eyes, Jen got up and showed him her pick.

Victor nodded his approval. "It is very beautiful, Jen."

Jen ran back into the kitchen and wrapped her arms around Hephalon, who was still sitting. "Thank you so much, Heph!"

"Oh, my!" The metallurgist's cheeks flushed bright pink with surprise and humility. "You're most welcome, milady." Jen pulled away from Hephalon, who had to take a few seconds to compose himself before he remembered, "Oh! Let's not forget your terramancy charm." He reached back into his satchel.

Jen, still wearing the last bracelet, sat back down and earnestly waited for the unveiling.

Like a kid in a candy store, she thought.

Hephalon plucked out a small charm and placed it in her hand. It had the silver outline of a teardrop, but inside were the colors of the rainbow. He explained the colors as such: "Red and orange signify fire . . . yellow is for lightning . . . green for earth . . . blue, indigo, and violet for water . . . white for air . . . and silver to represent metal. All the elements of terramancy."

"Wow," Jen breathed. "Vic, you *have* to see this."

Victor walked over and gave his friend a look of gratitude after he saw the colorful charm. "You did well, Heph."

Hephalon self-deprecatingly waved his hand. "Ah, 'twas nothing."

"May I put it on?" Jen asked, looking to both Hephalon and Victor for approval.

Victor nodded while the metallurgist—who was already reaching for his stein—said, "Please, go ahead."

Jen clasped the charm onto her bracelet, feeling as if it were already a part of her. The teardrop design fit in well with that of the bracelet, giving her a sense of eagerness, but also a sense of responsibility to begin training as a tenderfoot.

"I look forward to awarding you the next charm when the time comes," Hephalon said, breaking through Jen's thoughts.

She winked. "You won't be able to get rid of me."

He bowed respectfully. "I wouldn't want to."

"Congratulations, Jen," Victor said. "Now that you have your totem and your first charm, you're one step closer to becoming a sorceress."

Joy filled Jen as she realized, in that moment, she wanted nothing more than to become a sorceress, despite the dangers involved. She felt as though she was closing the current chapter in her life, which included plans of becoming a doctor, and starting a new chapter that had more questions than answers. But Jen was fine with that realization, because, in that instant of pure bliss, she also realized that she was able to do what she had always wanted: to change the world and help out those in need along the way.

She got up and gave Victor a big hug.

One step closer to finding my parents and the Halostone.

"This calls for a drink!" suggested Hephalon, quite loudly.

"No!" Jen and Victor declared in unison, staring him down.

* * *

The night was still young, but, even though Hephalon invited them to stay the night after supper, Jen wanted to get back to Watercress to finally see if she could read the lost journal now that she had her own totem.

And so, with her sights set on Watercress Castle, Jen expressed her gratitude once more to Mystra Hephalon, who she knew would remain a good friend of hers, and waited for Victor to do the same. She could tell it was hard for him to leave his friend so soon—but not as difficult as it was convincing Skarmor to leave Pernissa.

At first, Skarmor pretended not to hear Jen or Victor, finally shaking his head after they repeated themselves five times. If it wasn't for Pernissa and her urging, Jen seriously thought that they'd have to walk back. To inflate Skarmor's spirits, Victor promised that he'd see Pernissa again soon.

With her newest piece of jewelry and a full stomach from Hephalon's famous wild boar roast, she hopped on Skarmor and, while holding on tight to Victor, took off into the midnight sky. Her gaze lingered on the diminishing form of Hephalon until he stopped waving and made his way back into his cottage.

As she turned back around, she marveled at the weight of the totem bracelet on her wrist. She hadn't worn a bracelet since her sophomore year of high school, so it felt slightly awkward yet still familiar. A smile crossed Jen's lips as she remembered the first bracelet her mother bought her; it was for her thirteenth birthday and had three translucent pink hearts on the front, with the middle heart being the biggest. She had cherished that piece of jewelry, never taking it off for a year—not even when she went to bed. Jen wondered where it could be now, but immediately remembered she had put it in her jewelry armoire, which was nestled safely in her childhood closet back home. At least she knew that bracelet was safe.

The full moon was high in the sky and very bright that night, projecting Skarmor's shadow onto the uneven ground as they flew westward. Jen began to feel relief wash over her now that she knew they were getting closer to Watercress Castle. Resting her head on Victor's back, she lazily followed Skarmor's graceful shadow on the ground when another shadow darted through his. Jen blinked twice and turned her head around just in time to see a shape fly in front of the moon, casting a silhouette of massive wings and a sharp tail.

"Uh, Vic?" Jen asked, apprehension seeping into her voice as she pointed at the silhouette. "What's that?"

Victor turned his head and followed her finger up toward the moon. Jen's left arm was still wrapped around his midriff for balance, so when she felt Vic flex, a sinking feeling developed in the pit of her stomach.

He swore then said, "Jen, whatever you do, don't let go." He leaned forward and pushed Skarmor into a dive.

"What's—"

A crackling fireball drowned her out as it zoomed past, narrowly missing Skarmor's right wing. She could feel the immense heat on her arm and shoulder, and checked to see if she was on fire. Luckily, she wasn't singed, but as another fireball shot past them, she didn't know how much longer she would stay that way. Trying to push her fear of fire from her mind, she found enough courage—probably due to her strong dose of adrenaline—to not faint and fall off of Skarmor.

A deep, guttural roar echoed over the mountainous terrain,

rattling Jen's bones. She had never heard an animal make that jarring sound before and prayed that she would never hear it again.

She tightened her grip on Victor as Skarmor tucked into a tight corkscrew roll, successfully evading two more blasts from the silhouette. Skarmor then quickly leveled out and started gaining altitude.

Jen shot a look over her shoulder and saw another fireball coming right at them.

The light from the last blast briefly illuminated the silhouette, showing a beast so hideous that it made Jen gasp in horror.

What she saw would haunt her dreams for years to come: a menacing, bloodred- and brimstone-gray-scaled wyvern dragon with enormous, venous wings and teeth that looked deadlier than the sharpest swords. Sickening bone spurs protruded out of the tops of its wings, slicing through the night air every time it flapped.

Even though Skarmor was flying at top speed, he wasn't shaking the dragon; in fact, he was losing ground. Victor knew it too, so he made a quick decision.

"Jen! Switch spots with me!" he yelled through the wind and between ear-splitting roars.

"Switch spots? Why?!" Jen yelled back. She couldn't move, even if she wanted to; her body was frozen with fear.

"I need to lay cover fire or Draconex will fry us!"

Jen couldn't believe it. "*Draconex* is on the back of that thing?!"

Victor didn't answer. Jen couldn't tell if he didn't hear her, or if he was just focused on switching spots with her. Jen let out a prolonged scream as Victor maneuvered around her and slid her up toward Skarmor's neck. Quickly after, he cast a volley of spells that exploded near the dragon, which was still hot in pursuit.

Jen grabbed ahold of Skarmor's neck, intertwining her fingers together so she wouldn't fall off amid his high-speed aerial maneuvers.

"Come on, boy," she whispered, fighting back tears.

Eyes squeezed shut, her world was consumed by ear-splitting

roars and buffeting explosions as Victor and the dragon exchanged shots. Just then, she felt a tingle on her wrist and opened one eye to see that her charm had started to vibrate and glow on her totem bracelet. A rush of energy swept through her, and out of nowhere a forceful gust of wind erupted from her hands, throwing her off of Skarmor and high up into the air.

Jen opened her mouth to scream, but nothing came out. Panic set in, making her temporarily mute as she flailed in the air, starting her descent to the rocky ground two hundred yards below. She was thrown forward and slightly to the right of Skarmor, so Victor, who was continuing to issue spells from his staff, didn't see Jen get knocked off.

She dropped past Skarmor's right side and hurtled toward the gray landscape. Shaking her bracelet, hoping it would do something, she began to see her life flash before her eyes—and a future life that she would possibly never experience.

The ground was getting closer and closer when Jen instinctively crossed her arms in front of her to try to break the fall—but she felt herself suddenly stop, as if a soft net had caught her.

Peering out of slitted eyelids and cautiously uncrossing her outstretched arms, she saw with disbelief that she was slowly floating down to the ground, which was now about three feet below her. Her charm was shining as it stood straight out from her bracelet, clearly channeling the power of her nexus.

Her knees were the first part of her body to touch the long, swaying grass, followed by the tips of her shoes, and finally the palms of her hands.

I must've done something to slow my fall, thought Jen. *But what?*

Without an ounce of strength left, she collapsed and rolled onto her back. As the grass blades pricked the nape of her neck, she opened her eyes—

To see the dragon's silhouette diving straight toward her.

Fear gripped her stomach, but her body was too weak from the fall to move more than a few inches. Helpless, all she could do was pray that the dragon would not slam into her.

Instead, Jen saw a dark figure leap from the dragon's back as the beast spread its enormous wings and swooped over Jen.

* * *

Skarmor's screech alerted Victor as he lanced a lightning bolt straight for the pursuing dragon. To his chagrin, it missed wide, but bought him enough time to quickly glance behind his shoulder. Fear washed over him when he couldn't find Jen anywhere. Forgetting about the immediate danger, he frantically looked in every direction, finally seeing her falling toward the ground, followed closely by the dragon.

In one fluid motion, he twisted back around to his proper riding position and commanded Skarmor to fall into a dive. Wind rushed over his face, making it hard to breathe, but he didn't care about that; all he cared about was saving Jen . . . he *had* to save her.

Skarmor was catching up to the dragon, but they were still too far away to make a difference. Their flight path was the same as that of the dragon, but between flaps of the its bony wings, Victor could see Jen lying on the ground. At first his heart stopped, but she seemed, somehow, miraculously unharmed. Relief faded into dread when he then saw Draconex leap from the back of the dragon and land near her prone figure.

He was about to jump off Skarmor when the dragon swooped around and shot back up toward them.

* * *

As the dragon rumbled past, whipping Jen's wavy locks over her eyes, Jen saw the figure of Draconex land with the grace of a cat not three yards away from her. In one smooth motion, the figure stood up and began to close the distance between them. Under the bright light of the full moon, Jen saw that he was lanky. His gait was smooth and purposeful, but carried a dishonest intention. She gasped when he pulled his hood back to reveal a stark, gaunt face that had a long scar splitting his left side from forehead to lip.

"Jennifer Lancaster. We meet at last." He sneered. "I am Lord Draconex. Big fan."

Jen didn't say anything back, but shot a glance up toward the sky. The dragon was blocking Skarmor and Victor from landing. More fireballs whizzed past Skarmor as he tried in vain to outmaneuver the dragon.

Victor would not make it to her in time.

Jen pushed herself up and tried to back away, but her feet felt like lead, so she quickly changed tactics. Holding up the bracelet on her wrist, she tried to will her totem to produce a spell of some kind that would shoot Draconex with a lightning bolt or sink him into the ground or . . . *something* . . . but instead it just jingled on her wrist like a common bracelet.

"I see you have a new totem. Is it broken?" Draconex feigned concern. "Well, I don't want that one anyway." He stepped closer. "I want your ring. The Ring of Lancaster."

Out of habit, Jen covered the area of her chest where it hung from her necklace, remembering too late that it was safe inside Watercress's Sacrarium.

"Oh, so it's on a necklace?" he asked, not waiting for a reply. "Show it to me!" Draconex lunged at Jen, grabbing the hair on the back of her head with one hand while pulling the necklace off with the other, only to contort his already hideous face into an expression of rage. "Where is it?!" He let the empty chain slide from his palm.

Somehow Jen found her voice and it came out braver than she was expecting. "Someplace where you'll never lay a finger on it."

Draconex laughed. "Don't be so sure, Lancaster. Everyone talks eventually, so until you disclose its location, you will be my personal guest aboard Feralot." He dragged her by the hair while he whistled a call to his dragon.

Immediately he was answered by a ground-shaking roar and Jen saw the dragon bank around and fly low for a strafing run toward Draconex and Jen. The dark sorcerer let go of her hair and jumped high into the air with the leg power of a kangaroo. Gracefully, he landed on the beast's back as Jen was snatched off the ground by the dragon's massive claws.

"Victor!" Jen screamed as she was lifted into the air.

* * *

Victor heard Jen scream his name. The desperation in her voice sent a chill down his spine, and he fought the urge to blast the dragon out of the sky. He couldn't risk it; he might hit Jen.

He was not about to give up, and neither was Skarmor, so they pursued Draconex until dawn broke over the mountainside and gave shadows to the cluttered trees in the forest below.

It was then that Victor noticed something strange. From this distance, Jen's body seemed stiff and hard, like a wax mold. Victor had Skarmor fly a little bit closer to the dragon and, with the aid of fresh sunlight, Victor understood why Jen had looked so strange: the dragon wasn't carrying the real Jennifer Lancaster, but an exoskeleton of her.

Victor, in all his years as a mystra, had only heard of the moltic spell; it was incredibly hard to master. Jen must have used animancy and channeled the ability to form an outer layer and shed it off like a reptile, meaning she had taken the plunge into the perilous Amaranthine Forest below, which spanned close to three hundred square miles.

A proud smile crossed his lips before he fiercely scanned the canopy below, realizing the new kind of danger Jen now faced, lost and alone in a forest that was known to confuse and swallow its wanderers. After telling Skarmor that Jen had fallen into the Amaranthine Forest, Victor had him peel off and start retracing their path for any sign of Jen.

We'll find you, Jen. We'll find you.

CHAPTER TWENTY-FIVE

WHOOSH ... WHOOSH ... WHOOSH ...

Volcanor flapped his large wings rhythmically, in a steady beat, pushing the air below him so he could keep his three-ton body aloft. Smoke was still wisping out from his crusty nostrils as Lord Draconex set his sights on Feralot, eager to update his army that he had captured the fugitive Lancaster.

He looked behind him and noticed that Skarmor was slowing down. With his eyes still trained on the receding form of Victor's griffin, he saw it turn around. A sense of complete victory flowed through his veins and he almost laughed aloud as he looked forward again. He never thought that Victor was the type to give up. Maybe those ten years living as a recluse had weakened his resolve. At any rate, his ambush could not have gone better; he humiliated his old friend and kidnapped the one person who had one of the keys to fulfilling his destiny . . . he'd worry about the lost journal of Merlin later. He glanced over the side of Volcanor to see a stiff arm of his prey.

Jennifer Lancaster had finally run out of luck.

Draconex never doubted that he would succeed in capturing her, but he had to admit to himself that he was surprised at how truly easy it had been; he didn't even break a sweat. Even harder to believe was the fact that Malcolm had failed so miserably twice, which led him to question the boy's level of intelligence.

No matter, he thought. *I got what I came for, and Lancaster should be easy to break. In no time, I will know the location of the Ring of Lancaster and have it in my grasp shortly thereafter.*

In a quick hour, he reached the gateway portal that would take him and his prize to Nyzanth, the fifth known realm. The portal was nestled between two large rock cliffs that seemed to stretch upward into the clouds. Nyzanth was a barren wasteland complete with deserts, volcanoes, extreme heat . . . and the current base for the ever-roaming Feralot.

Volcanor kept his speed as he broke the portal's dimensional plane, sending them into the ether, only to rocket out of another portal gate milliseconds later, this time on Nyzanth.

CHAPTER TWENTY-SIX

Jen awoke to something licking her face. Opening her eyes, she let out a surprised scream before realizing it was the same cat she had met on Hephalon's compound the night before. The feline wasn't startled, but shied away a few steps, dropping its head.

"Oh . . . I'm sorry. I didn't mean to scream at you," Jen consoled the little creature. "Thank you for waking me up." The cat lifted its head higher and moved closer to her as she spoke. "I'm gonna call you . . . Treeow."

Petting her new friend, Jen looked around and saw nothing familiar but trees, roots, and bushes. Bars of light filtered through openings in the dense canopy, letting her know that it was daytime. Morning or afternoon, she didn't know—but at least Draconex was nowhere to be seen.

Jen really couldn't remember how she had escaped that dragon's grip; it was like a vise. All she could remember before blacking out was feeling her body begin to . . . harden? . . . and then a sense of weightlessness as she lost consciousness. Shaking her head, Jen struggled to comprehend how she was even still alive. That fall should have killed her.

She seemed to have regained some movement in her limbs, so she cautiously stood up, shaking the soreness from her legs. She then reached upward to stretch her arms, but felt shooting pain erupt from both her shoulders. She winced as she slowly brought her arms down to her sides and saw that there were two diagonal gashes going up from her armpits to the tops of her shoulders—where the dragon had held her.

As her mind cleared, Jen thought of Victor and Skarmor. She hoped they had escaped the ambush unharmed—and if they did, she knew they would be searching for her. With that in mind, she needed to find her way out of this forest; the only problem was that she hadn't the slightest clue in which direction to start walking.

A rustling from behind started Jen, causing her to back away. Terrified, she watched as Treeow dropped low to the ground and slinked toward the noise, its shoulder blades rolling underneath its prickly fur as it prepared to pounce.

A low rumble shook the vegetation just before Treeow leapt into it, issuing a piercing growl that sent a shiver up Jen's spine. With a cold sweat, Jen held her breath as a painful yelp echoed off the trees and boulders before getting swallowed up by silence yet again.

Beginning to breathe once more, Jen fought every urge to run —run in any direction so she wouldn't be a sitting duck for whatever was behind that bush—but she stayed, waiting for Treeow to return.

As seconds turned into agonizing minutes, she dared not look away from that very patch of vegetation into which she saw the cat jump . . . until she heard something behind her. Feeling as if her heart had jumped out of her throat, Jen twirled around to see Treeow unscathed. It cocked its head to the side as Jen stumbled over a thick tree root and collapsed onto the soft, mossy ground. The pain in her shoulders was masked by the adrenaline still in her system.

Looking behind her at where the rustling had been, she sat up and said shakily, "How did you . . . ?" She let her question trail off as the cat pressed its body to her leg. "You were *protecting* me," Jen realized. "Thank you." She scratched behind its ears. "You probably can't understand me, but do you know the way out of here, Treeow?"

The cat looked at her for a moment, then walked in the direction to her left. After a moment's hesitation, she slowly got back up and followed it, hoping that it was leading her to the forest's edge.

The first hour was hard going. There was no clear path in the dense forest, so Jen found herself climbing over fallen trees, pricking her ankles in thorny bushes, or crawling under thickets just so she could keep up with her guide. Every so often she would hear the hooting of owls and the chittering of other woodland animals. Those noises didn't bother her; she was just thankful she wasn't hearing the fear-inducing roar of Draconex's nightmarish dragon.

The second hour was even harder. At one point, Jen thought that Treeow was taking her deeper and deeper into the forest, sealing her fate of dying hungry and cold. Fatigue was starting to take its toll as Jen huffed through cracked lips, trying desperately to keep Treeow in her sights, even though every part of her body screamed for her to stop.

I can't stop—not now. I'll die here if I do.

With thighs burning and shoulders stiffening from her injuries, Jen was looking around for a flashing sign that said VICTOR AND SKARMOR ARE THIS WAY when a crooked branch hooked onto her shirt. Whimpering from exhaustion, Jen tried to shake it off, but that only seemed to make it worse. Trapped, she felt her knees buckle as the will to go on left her drained and curled up in the dirt.

Letting her eyelids close, Jen felt Treeow nudge her chin with its head, as if it were trying to show her something. Squinting, she forced herself to look forward and noticed that the forest was clearing up ahead. Hope gave her a second wind as she felt the cat tear the branch from her shirt.

Jen looked at Treeow with thanks in her eyes before she pushed herself up off the ground and trudged to the forest's edge, fighting off the strong whisperings of exhaustion step by step.

Treeow, on the other hand, didn't even seem fatigued, spryly jumping over thick tree roots. Feeling herself smile, Jen pushed aside a pair of low-hanging branches to greet an open field that was filled with sunlight and a gentle breeze.

She had made it out. Jen fell to her knees and began to sob, letting out all her anxiety and exhaustion. The cat sat licking its paws as Jen wiped her eyes and found the strength to say:

"Thank you."

She knew that she was still lost and needed to find Victor, but at least she was out of that dreaded forest. Too exhausted to get up, she went to lay down, intent on resting for a minute before resuming her search; but she was fast asleep before her head hit the soft, warm grass.

CHAPTER TWENTY-SEVEN

Feralot had roamed a great distance since Lord Draconex had left to capture Jennifer Lancaster. It was nearly at the opposite side of the dwarf planet Nyzanth, so it took even more precious time—time that he did not have—to get there from the portal. Cracked, dry ground blurred into mottled brown as he coaxed Volcanor to fly faster.

He hadn't heard much commotion from his prisoner below. She must have given in to her fate; she was smarter than her parents. As they passed a small, steaming volcano that had just recently erupted, Draconex glanced down into its open maw, impressed with its natural power—enough to make the whole world quake. Draconex yearned to feel that kind of power coursing through his veins. Luckily for him, Lancaster would be the key to helping him obtain it.

The dark sorcerer scanned below a fierce midday sun as he made out Feralot's tracks in the dry, forsaken ground. Flying high above the moving city, Draconex took stock of his kingdom. Everything on it was his, of course, but that wasn't enough for him. Once he awakened Lord Ferox, he would be given a realm to rule, then before long he would add another realm to his dominion, and another, until they were all under his complete and utter control.

He licked his lips in anticipation. Soon . . . but right now, he merely ruled over Feralot. That would have to do.

His impregnable city had four towers in each corner, high walls connecting them. In its center was the tallest and most imposing structure, where at the top rested his den. Below that same tower was the mystical engine that propelled Feralot, housing the source of all dark magic: the ShadowCrystal.

As Volcanor came in for a landing near one of the guard towers, Draconex commanded his dragon to release Lancaster when they were three feet from the ground. He heard a satisfying thud as she struck Feralot's ever-moving surface. In seconds, Volcanor had retracted his wings and Draconex slid from his herculean beast, petting it on the nose for a job well done.

He was about to order Volcanor back to the dragon dungeon when he noticed that Lancaster was standing up. He pushed off the ground and sprinted toward her with his rings ready; but as he got closer, he slowed down, realizing that who he was looking at wasn't Lancaster or even a person at all, but instead merely a rudimentary *mold* of Lancaster.

Unable to comprehend how she knew the moltic spell, he picked up speed again and charged at the mold, screaming in his anger. He lowered his head and ran straight through it, channeling the bruteness of a rhinoceros and splintering it with ease. As pieces of the hard shell landed on the ground, Draconex unclenched his teeth, closed his trembling fists into balls, and lifted his chin to the sky, unleashing a deafening yell that frightened even Volcanor, the King of Dragons.

Draconex hoped Malcolm was well enough for a new lesson; he needed to take his anger out on someone.

CHAPTER TWENTY-EIGHT

Distorted sounds.

Muffled conversation.

Those were the sensations Jen felt when she woke up a second time.

Jen tried opening her eyes, but they felt so heavy that she could barely lift them open. She was still immensely tired, as if hit with a bad case of jet lag, but that didn't stop her from trying to say something.

"Vic . . . ?"

His name came out more like a moan, but it was loud enough to be heard. The far-off conversation stopped. She held her breath and listened as someone quickly walked over to her. Finding the strength to open one eye, Jen was able to pick out through her hazy vision a person standing over her. She blinked a couple of times to get her eyes to focus, and the fuzzy form in front of her sharpened into a man she had never seen before.

He was looking down at her with a concerned look on his face. Jen stared at this mystery man, intent on trying to remember if she had seen him before. He had short, dirty-blond hair that was blown up off his forehead; a straight, Romanesque nose; a chiseled jawline; and eyes so blue it was as if Jen were looking into a clear morning sky. He looked to be in his mid-twenties. He had a strong yet gentle grip as he checked Jen's pulse.

A marble-size pendant that held a miniature version of what Jen thought was the Milky Way galaxy swung on a chain around his neck as he looked back at the woman with whom he had been talking. "She's awake and stable. Send for Vic, please."

Soon it was just him and Jen in the space, which looked to be a small, circular hut. Two windows were cut from the stone walls, letting in natural light. There weren't many amenities to be seen: only the bed on which she lay, a nightstand on which her diary rested, and a chair propped up against the far wall.

"Vic?" Jen asked again, this time more articulate.

"Don't worry, he's coming," the young man reassured her.

With all of her strength, Jen pushed herself up so her back rested on the headboard of the bed. Feeling a chill, she wrapped her arms around her chest.

"Here," said the young man. He reached down and pulled out a fleece blanket from beneath the bed and draped it over her upper body. "I'm Gavin, by the way."

Jen immediately looked up and met his eyes. She wondered if he was the same Gavin that Victor had saved from the Pit. "Gavin," Jen repeated, smiling slightly. "Gavin Kingsland?"

The young man's head twitched back in surprise. "Yes . . . have we met before?"

Before Jen could respond, Victor walked in and declared, "Jenny, I'm so glad you're up!"

He propped his staff on the nearest wall before coming straight over to her. Gavin stood up and let Victor take his place on the side of the bed.

"We didn't know how long it would take for you to wake up."

He put a hand on her shoulder. Jen braced herself, but she was amazed to not feel shooting pain from the cuts from the dragon's claws. With renewed strength, she sloughed off the blanket and lifted her sleeves up to reveal scars instead of claw-like lacerations.

Remembering how Skarmor had healed Treeow back at

Hephalon's compound, Jen smiled and looked at Victor. "Did Skarmor heal me?"

He returned the smile and nodded. "When we saw you at the edge of the Amaranthine Forest, you were out cold and your shoulders looked pretty bad. It took them a few hours to heal, and since they were so deep they left some scarring. I'm sorry."

"Sorry? Don't be." Jen crossed her arms, touching both scars at the tops of her shoulders. "You both saved me—that's all I prayed for."

Where would I be without Vic and Skarmor? Jen asked herself, extremely thankful.

Then she remembered how she got out of the forest.

"Was Treeow there when you found me?"

Victor slightly furrowed his brow. "Tree . . . ow?"

Jen put a hand on her forehead. "Sorry, um, the cat that we saw at Heph's place? He led me out of the forest."

"No, you were all alone." Victor looked quizzically at Jen. "You named it?"

"Yeah, you like it? Treeow. Like 'meow,' since he's a cat, and 'tree,' since he came from the forest." Jen slid her fingers together, implying the fusion of the two words.

Victor looked at Gavin, who crossed his arms and shrugged, smiling. He then looked back at Jen with a serious gleam in his eyes. "The Amaranthine Forest goes on for miles and miles, and has the power to confuse whomever is unlucky enough to find themselves in it. The indigenous animals are nothing short of rabid. I'm so grateful that . . . *Treeow* found you first," Victor said, expressing relief. "No one who has entered has ever returned. Except for you. And Treeow, I suppose."

Jen blinked a few times, now realizing how dire her situation had truly been. "I'm seriously the only person who has made it out alive?"

Victor nodded, pursing his lips as he turned to look at Gavin.

The young man crossed his arms and dropped his gaze to the floor, dejected. "Years ago, one of my friends was dared to spend a night there . . ." Gavin recounted, his eyes beginning to mist. "He was never seen again." He grimaced as a lone tear trickled down his cheek.

Jen felt herself welling up, moved by what Gavin had said so much that she tossed the covers aside and stood up. "I'm so sorry. That's . . . horrible." She walked to Gavin and hugged him; her heart nearly skipped a beat when she felt his arms encircle her.

Gavin sniffed. "Thanks."

Closing her eyes, Jen squeezed him.

"And that's why I'm very thankful I didn't lose you, Jen," Victor said from behind her.

Jen went from hugging Gavin to hugging Victor. "I'm glad you were the one to find me. I'm still not sure how I even wound up in the Amarathon Forest."

"Amaranthine," Victor corrected with a tender wink.

"Amaranthine . . . right." Jen pulled away and touched her forehead with the palm of her hand, trying desperately to fill in the missing spaces between being taken by Draconex and waking up alone in the forest.

"I tailed Draconex for a while until I noticed you had escaped," Victor explained, bringing her back to the bed. "Volcanor, his dragon, was still holding you, only it wasn't you—it was a *mold* of you."

Jen lifted an eyebrow in mild confusion as she sat back down. "Okay, it's official: *this* is the weirdest thing that's happened since I've met you," Jen confessed. "A *mold* . . . of *me*?"

"That's right." Victor stood up and made his way to one of the small hut's windows, resting his elbows on the windowsill. "The result of a moltic spell." He turned around to face her. "You know how snakes and other reptiles shed skin as they grow or when they regenerate limbs? That is exactly what the moltic spell does, except the mold it creates is as protective as reinforced steel."

"I can't believe I *accidentally* did that," Jen breathed.

"It was no accident," Gavin chimed in, having regaining control of his emotions. "As an omnimancer, you have an inherently strong nexus—even if it might be undeveloped right now.

You must have instinctively tapped into it to save yourself." His eyes twinkled as he looked at Jen.

Jen blushed. Smiling, she broke eye contact. Feeling her forehead, she wondered aloud, "How did I survive the fall if my mold stayed with Draconex?"

Victor shrugged. "We'll never know. Maybe your nexus conjured another spell to cushion your fall."

"Yeah, maybe . . ." Jen stared through one of the windows at the blue sky.

A tense silence fell over the trio.

"Oh, I apologize," Victor said, adding a light chuckle in his realization. "Jenny, this is Gavin Kingsland."

Gavin laughed. "Your new tenderfoot is on top of her game. She guessed who I was right when she woke up."

"This is what I get for arriving late," Victor said, throwing his hands up in mock surrender.

"Well, I'm not *that* good," Jen admitted, perking up. "Vic already told me about how you two met."

"Then you'll know how much I mean it when I tell you that Victor is a great mentor and sorcerer." A tone of deep respect had entered Gavin's voice. "There's no one better to instruct you in terramancy. Made me wish I wasn't an astromancer."

Victor placed a hand on Gavin's shoulder. "Thank you, son, but I won't have her for long. *Omnimancers.*" Victor exaggerated that last word, sticking a thumb in Jen's direction. "They think they're so special since they can learn all of the Mancy planes."

"Hey," Jen said, sitting up straighter. "Don't hate the sorceress, hate the magic."

"Oh, that's good." Gavin snickered. He looked at Victor and was greeted with a deadpan expression.

"Don't encourage her," Victor said with a wink.

Jen lifted up her necklace chain and said to Gavin, "I like your necklace pendant."

Gavin looked down and held it between his index finger and thumb. "Thanks. It's my totem." He popped the marble out of its silver casing. Jen's jaw dropped when she saw it grow to the size of a softball.

"Correction: I *love* your totem," Jen said, seeing the Milky Way slowly spin inside his orb.

"So do I." Gavin smiled, shrinking it back to the size of a marble and replacing it in his necklace.

Victor looked at Jen, then at Gavin. "Sorry to interrupt, but do you mind if I talk with Jen in private?"

"Of course not!" Gavin left the hut, but not before saying, "It was nice meeting you, Jen."

"You too." Jen waved as he left. She glanced at Victor, who stood silent with a lifted eyebrow. "What?" she asked innocently.

Victor brushed off her question and dragged the only chair in the hut closer to the bed. "We may have to expedite your training. If Draconex has decided to go after you himself, we're running out of time."

"I can't believe he ambushed us." Jen was still reeling from her personal encounter with him. The way he spoke, smelled, dragged her by the hair . . .

"Draconex is starting to take matters into his own hands, I'm guessing since Malcolm hasn't been successful," Victor said.

Jen didn't say anything. Even though Malcolm had betrayed her and kidnapped her parents, Jen still felt a twinge of sadness. Sadness that Malcolm wasn't truly that great boyfriend he had portrayed for the first three months she had known him. Sadness that he was tricked by Draconex into converting to dark magic.

Victor changed the subject. "Well, before we start your instruction in terramancy, why don't I show you around?"

That was able to shake Jen out of her thoughts. "Yeah, where the heck am I?"

"Here." Victor extended a hand. "Let me show you."

Jen took it and was happy to find her strength had returned. Victor stepped to the door and pulled it open to reveal a community of similar small huts.

"Welcome to Camelore, the home base for the League of Light," Victor said as he stepped out into the sunlight.

Waiting for her eyes to adjust, Jen followed him outside.

* * *

Jen spent the next hour taking in the spectacular view of Camelore while Victor taught her of its origins. As they strolled around a shimmering lake and under beautiful Dogwood trees with white petals floating to the ground, making it seem as if it had freshly snowed, Victor explained that Camelore was the last remaining stronghold of the Sorcery Guild at the time of the Great Battle.

Not knowing if they could defeat Lord Ferox and his dark magic, the first Elder Synod combined their powers to lift Camelore from Earth, raising it to the sky where it would be eternally preserved, along with its traditions, culture, and school of sorcery. The twenty-four mystras charged with protecting Camelore and the last omnimancer, Philip Lancaster II, eventually became the last sorcerers in all the realms after the Great Battle.

"What about Genevieve's sister, Gwendolyn? Didn't she survive the battle?" Jen asked as they hiked an enormous bluff that showed its age by the different colors of sediment layers.

Victor's staff tapped the rocky ground as he ascended—*clink-clink-clink*.

"Unfortunately, Gwendolyn's injuries were far too great, and she passed on shortly after, but not before a few of the Camelore sorcerers arrived in response to Genevieve's beacon spell. They were too late to save both of the Lancaster sisters, but with Gwendolyn's dying breath, they were given the responsibility to guard the Halostone until Philip was old enough to take up the mantle and protect it." The emotion behind Victor's words conveyed sadness, but with a glimmer of hope. "They became known as the Camelore Twenty-Four and were responsible for rebuilding the Sorcery Guild here. After a century, the school had outgrown the small confines of this floating island, so they found an uninhabited realm to establish their new order." The sunlight glanced off of his staff, making it glisten as he reached the bluff's peak.

"Azumar," Jen realized, trying not to lose her balance on the rocks.

"Exactly. Now, Camelore is reserved for training new Light Seekers." Victor smiled and led her to the bluff's edge.

Stopping a few feet from the edge, Jen was given an almost complete view of Camelore. Sweeping her eyes over its verdant landscape, azure ponds, and community of stone huts, she rested her eyes on what looked to be the edge of the world. She remembered Victor telling her that Camelore had been lifted into the sky, but the realization that she was indeed on a floating landmass didn't strike her until she witnessed it with her own eyes. With awe, she saw the edges break off into the wispy, blue sky of the Earth's stratosphere. The cumulus clouds that swept by below gave her the illusion that Camelore was moving at breakneck speed when, in reality, it was motionless, miles above the Earth's crust.

"Pretty amazing, isn't it?" Victor marveled, looking down at everything.

A slight, warm breeze swayed Jen's curls. It felt nice. "I have yet to not be amazed at what you show me." Jen looked at Victor, and he met her eyes, his salt-and-pepper hair ruffling in the wind.

He grinned, then tapped his staff gently on the ground and pointed to the north. "You see that tree in the distance? That is the Arbor Sacré—the heart of Camelore."

Jen looked and saw the biggest and most beautiful tree she had ever seen. Its trunk was massive and its branches held the largest leaves, which were not only green, but every shade of the rainbow. Along the tree's border was the shape of a large pentagon.

"What's surrounding the tree?"

"That is the Pentarena—the original training ground for the Sorcery Guild, before it was moved to Azumar. It's predominantly used by Light Seekers and their tenderfeet now. It is split up into five sections, one for every Mancy plane."

Jen noticed the five sections that were divided equally to form a glass pentagon around the Arbor Sacré.

She looked at Victor eagerly. "Is that where I'll train with you?"

He looked at her and smiled. "Yes, my dear."

Jen smiled back, then returned her gaze over all of Camelore, taking in the enchanting view. To the east of the stone huts, Jen noticed something that she had overlooked when she first stepped outside of her recovery hut. The dwellings were placed in a large circle around a building that looked to be in the shape of a stout cylinder with no top. Instead of having a roof, it was open and had a metal arch that touched both sides of its rims.

"Hey, Vic." Jen pointed. "What's that building?"

"That, my dear, is the ceremonial chambers for the current Camelore Twenty-Four. Let me show you."

Victor waited until Jen was ready to leave, then began to descend the bluff.

The returning hike was quiet, giving Jen some time to think. She realized that the deeper she dug into her family's history, the more tragic it became: Genevieve sacrificed herself to stop Lord Ferox . . . Gwendolyn died from complications suffered during the Great Battle . . . Philip went mad after obsessing over the lost MystiCrystals . . . and her birth parents, murdered because they wouldn't reveal the Halostone's location.

Now it was Jen's turn to experience tragedy when her parents were taken from her.

Feeling a burden on her shoulders, she trudged down the side of the bluff behind Victor. They were almost at ground level when Jen saw something streak through the sky. Her worried expression dissolved into joy when she realized it was Skarmor. He was twirling, gliding, and playfully pecking with a flock of griffins in the late morning sun.

Looking up and covering her eyes from the intense glare, Jen wished she could be that carefree; able to drop all of her worries and doubts and blast off into the sky with no plan or purpose. For a moment, she fantasized about flying away from Camelore and letting the wind take her, until her conscience kicked in and berated her for even thinking of doing something so reckless.

Jen was never one to quit at anything. Growing up, her parents admired how she had focused and finished everything she undertook, no matter how difficult it might have been. Wishing that her parents were here so she could fill them in on everything that had happened to her, she was brought back to the present as she found herself walking up to the ceremonial chamber, which was even bigger than Jen had expected. With more determination than ever to face the unknown challenges that lay ahead, she crossed the chamber's threshold and followed Victor inside.

It was exactly midday when the two of them stepped into the ceremonial chamber, and what greeted Jen filled her with rapture: an enormous, wooden roundtable. It looked as if it had been hewn from the largest tree trunk Jen had ever seen; its petrified surface glistened with the smoothness of calm glass.

"This is the Table of Prophecy," said Victor distantly. Jen was so mesmerized by the table that she almost didn't hear him. "Taken from our very own Arbor Sacré, the tree that sustains all of the plants on this floating island."

Jen found herself inextricably drawn to the table. This breathtaking display of craftsmanship seated twenty-five, and on each chair rested a folded robe—except for one which was uncovered, the one facing the chamber entrance. The chairs looked to be carved from the same wood as the roundtable, which rested on a thick base wider than a manhole cover.

"How come that chair is empty?" Jen asked, pointing.

"That chair is reserved for the Light Bringer of Merlin's prophecy."

Jen was quiet for a moment. "I wish we could know who he or she is."

"If only it were that easy. Every sorcerer in the Guild has been tested," he reminded her.

Not me.

Jen pursed her lips in deep thought. "Well . . . what if the Light Bringer isn't a sorcerer?"

Victor crossed his arms and held his chin between his index

finger and thumb. After a few moments, he said, "The Light Bringer will be known when the time is right."

Hoping that Victor's faith wasn't misplaced, Jen conceded and set her gaze back on the table. The attention to detail was amazing, but Jen's breath was truly taken away once she saw what was on the tabletop. As the sunlight filtered through the shapes cut into the helioarch, a crisp artistic pattern began to form on the gleaming wooden table. As Jen walked closer, she got a better view of a mural that was solely made of light and shadow. In it, the profiles of two sorcerers seemed to be casting powerful spells at each other. She stopped inches short of the table and let her hands hover over the surface, not wanting to leave fingerprints.

"It's okay, you can touch it," Victor said with a wink. Jen relaxed a bit and gently placed her open palms on the table, still gazing in wonder at the sunlit mural. "This table was created by the first Elder Synod as a symbol of democracy for the original Camelore Twenty-Four. It's one of the last remaining artifacts of that time period, and a reminder of our history so we aren't doomed to repeat it."

"It's beautiful," Jen marveled. "Is that the Great Battle?" She pointed at the shadows on the table's surface.

"That's correct." Victor walked to the other side of the table to face her. "As the sun makes its journey through the sky, its rays filter through the helioarch"—he pointed at the metal arch above them, tracing it with a pointed finger—"giving a visual representation of Merlin's prophecy. In the morning, when the sun is at its lowest angle in the east, the first scene appears: the creation of the MystiCrystals in the Big Bang. As the sun rises, it moves to depict King Arthur pulling Excalibur from the anvil atop the stone, and reaches its zenith at the historic Great Battle, which is what we see now."

Looking down, Jen could tell the mural wasn't as clear as it was before—a sign that the sun was continuing its path in the sky.

"As the sun sets," Victor finished, "the shadows show events that have not yet occurred: the discovery of the Light Bringer and an enormous war."

Jen was confused. "But . . . we *win*, right?"

Victor let out a long breath before answering. "We don't know which side will be the victor . . . not even Merlin could say."

Jen's shoulders slumped. With effort, she picked up her chin and looked at Victor.

He noticed her dejected expression and quickly added, "The thing you need to know about Merlin was that he was human. But he had the rare gift of sensing energy, not only in the present, but also from the past and future. That's how he was able to explain the creation of the MystiCrystals, and prophesize the union of England under King Arthur, and the Great Battle, and the Light Bringer's arrival. But when his last prediction came, the energy was so strong that it overwhelmed him. He couldn't decipher anything apart from there being a war between two strong factions."

Victor made his way back toward Jen and gave her shoulder a reassuring squeeze. "With Merlin's final prediction as uncertain as a roll of dice, the only thing we can do is prepare for this inevitable battle so we have the best chance of winning."

Jen nodded once, trying to find her voice, but nothing came out.

"Jen, I know how you feel. I'm scared too. If this is too much for you, let me know and we will keep you safe on Camelore until this is all over."

After having seen—and felt—his memories, Jen knew that Victor meant every word. She remembered his feeling of heartbreak when he lost Malcolm to Draconex. With that, she knew that he would give his life before he lost another tenderfoot to this war.

The sun had moved farther west and, looking to her left, Jen noticed that the mural had elongated and turned into a person—the Light Bringer, she assumed. She couldn't identify the androgynous depiction as male or female, but Jen saw the being holding a book—probably the lost journal of Merlin—high above their head.

Until the Light Bringer was revealed, Jen owed it to all of her bloodline to be ready for whatever happened.

"No, Vic. I want—*need*—to help. The Light Seekers need every sorcerer they can get so that humanity can have at least a fighting chance in this war. This is my destiny as much as it is yours."

"You sound like a Lancaster," Victor commented, his voice ringing with pride.

Jen shrugged and with a resolute smile looked down at her totem bracelet, touching her terramancy charm. "So . . . when do we start training?"

CHAPTER TWENTY-NINE

When one sense goes, the others heighten.

That is what had happened to Richard and Beth Smith after five days in the pitch blackness of Feralot's prison bay. Their hands could feel everything around them so well that they didn't need sight to know every square inch of their small ten-by-ten-foot cell; their nostrils could smell the awful gruel that was their food even before it was given to the guards to hand out; their taste buds could pick up the individual ingredients of said gruel—and how their mouths would taste after long hours of dehydration; and their ears could hear the slightest rustle, raspy breath, or quietest whisper from the guards.

"Lord Draconex returned. Did you hear about it?" the tall guard asked. He was sitting down at the other end of the bay, but both Richard and Beth could hear him as if he were standing right in front of them.

"Nothing specific. Just that if you look at him the wrong way, he'll snap your neck quicker than usual." The short guard seemed to be sharpening something. It made a deafening *SHINK-SHINK-SHINK!*

"Well, I heard the reason he left Feralot was to capture that Lancaster girl himself," gossiped the tall guard.

Immediately after hearing his daughter's actual last name,

Richard felt his wife's grip tighten with surprise and fear. He continued holding her, gently rocking back and forth, dreading what would be said next.

"Really?" The short guard didn't seem convinced. "Ever since Draconex took over our army, he's hardly ever left his den. He orders his underlings to do his dirty work."

"You know the Shift C lead guard, Garrett? He told me that his buddy was manning the eastern tower when he overheard Draconex in a yelling match with his mistress."

"That Madame Diaema. She's smokin', isn't she?" The short guard whistled, stopping his sharpening. "I'd let her suck my blood any day."

"You bet," the tall guard agreed. "Anyway, he said Draconex almost beheaded her when she told him to calm down after he found out Lancaster had escaped."

Both Richard and Beth let out a barely audible breath of relief. Jen was still safe.

"What's with this girl? She must be pretty powerful to evade capture from two Dark Watchers *and* Lord Draconex."

The tall guard snickered. "She's just been lucky. It's a matter of time before we get her, but until then I'd advise keeping a low profile so you don't upset Draconex."

There was a pause as the short guard resumed the sharpening of his weapon, then he said, "Wait . . . does that mean I can't ask off tomorrow?"

"'Fraid not."

"For the love of . . ." The short guard's words trailed off as he threw something, making a loud clatter as it hit the ground. "I haven't had a day off in weeks."

"Better to be alive and working than dead," the first guard pointed out.

The second guard mumbled in frustration; that was when Richard stopped listening and hugged his wife, whispering, "Our Jenny Jasmine is safe."

"I don't know what I would do if they took her," Beth said, barely audible.

Richard held her, still rocking back and forth, as the guards left to do their rounds and their idle chatter faded into numbing silence, broken only by the slight rustling of uncomfortable inmates in their cells and an occasional wail.

Then, suddenly—

TINK . . . TINK . . . TINK . . .

Their friend, flicking one of the metal bars their cells shared. "Hey, are you two all right? You sound pretty tense."

Richard stroked his wife's cheek, which he noticed was wet with tears. "Those guards were talking about someone we know."

"You know Draconex?" His friend sounded surprised.

Richard inhaled deeply, mentally forcing himself to not get choked up. "No, we've, ah, actually never seen him. We know the girl he was after."

A shuffling sound, maybe from moving closer to the cell bars. "Lancaster?" There was a pause. "What's your relation to her?"

Richard felt his wife tightly hug him. "We raised her," he said.

There was a shuffling sound again, but it was fainter than before. Their friend was moving away from them.

"Friend?" Richard asked, growing more worried every passing second. He repeated it one more time, but there was dead silence. Regretting that he had ever mentioned his connection to Jennifer Lancaster, he prayed that his friend wouldn't inform the guards with this new information when they took him away.

Richard stopped waiting for a reply and tried to fall asleep, but his mind was too preoccupied to grant him that wish.

* * *

Malcolm felt as though he was turning a corner and feeling much better the day following his sudden-death battle with Draconex's anaconda, Quickfang. Breathing didn't hurt as much —unless he had to sneeze, which made him feel like he'd broken another rib. He was able to sit straight up on his cot, so he decided to kill the time by reading. He had spent hours trying to find a spell that would heal his broken ribs, collapsed lung, and, hopefully, his bruised ego; but each promising spell he came across needed certain ingredients that he didn't keep on hand.

No healing spell and no rings.

Malcolm was still bitter about Draconex destroying his Guild-sanctioned totem ring, but he was even more bitter about him keeping his *other* totem. He'd passed the most sadistic, suicidal test, and here he was being punished for it. He had killed Quickfang, unlocked the door with the key, and survived without using terramancy. What more did he need to do?

Instead Malcolm was confined to bed, stuck nursing a broken body back to health, and forced to be alone with his thoughts, which had only sunken to deeper depths of depression since.

Giving up in frustration, he slammed the book shut and threw it across the room. He had a bad sense of déja vu when the door opened just as the book flew into the wall next to the surprised visitor.

"You must be back to your old self—you're throwing books again," said Lord Draconex.

"Only my anger," Malcolm said dryly.

"Good," Draconex said mockingly. "I want you to channel that during your next lesson." He gave Malcolm back his totem, tossing it carelessly onto the boy's lap.

"I'm still recovering," Malcolm said, closing his eyes in both pain and relief.

Draconex glided over to Malcolm as though on wires, but seemed to restrain himself from choking the life out of the poor boy. "Do not give me excuses. I have been pushed to my limit already, so I suggest you take this"—he pulled out a vial of teal liquid from the folds of his cloak—"and cease your whining."

Without a second's hesitation, Malcolm took the vial, popped the cork, and drank it until the last drop was gone. He didn't even bother to ask what was in the vial, for fear that Draconex would make his threat come true.

After the liquid was swallowed, Draconex placed his fist on Malcolm's chest none too softly. The dragon ring on his middle finger glowed orange; a muted light poured out of his ring and onto Malcolm's chest.

"Reparer," Draconex said.

Malcolm was afraid to look at his chest, but he did once he felt a strange warmth radiate below his ribcage and inside his left lung as the orange light interacted with the liquid he had just ingested. He watched the light slowly fade away as his strength began to return.

"Now get up," Draconex said apathetically.

"What was that spell?" Malcolm pushed the sheets off and stood, feeling his ribs as he inhaled fully for the first time in days.

"I harnessed the healing properties of an Earth axolotl sala-mander to heal your external wounds. The libation you drank was a mixture of its secretions and a reactive agent that, when put in contact with my spell, regenerates organs and bones." Draconex put his hands on the sides of Malcolm's face. "I can teach you that —and much more—through dark magic."

Malcolm's eyes shined with wonder, his anger freshly bubbling inside.

"You're ready for your next lesson." It was more of a declara-tion than a question.

"Yes, master." Malcolm lowered his gaze as Draconex let go of his face.

"Do you still feel the anger swirling inside you?"

"Definitely," Malcolm said; a lopsided smirk curled his lips.

"Then put on your totem ring and don't disappoint." Draconex had already started walking toward the door.

Malcolm, letting his anger simmer like a pot on a stove, duti-fully followed. He didn't expect a conversation during the walk to Draconex's den; frankly, he wasn't in the mood to chat. After so many humiliating failures, Malcolm was ready to show how truly angry he was.

Angry at how he'd let Jen escape his grasp twice; angry at Victor for foiling what should have been such an easy kidnapping; angry at Draconex for making him spend forty-eight hours in sheer agony with broken ribs and a collapsed lung; angry at himself for letting it all happen. He was determined to either turn the tide and show Draconex that he was worthy of one more shot . . . or die trying.

* * *

Malcolm's lesson began the moment he stepped foot inside Draconex's den.

"Life and death . . . day and night . . . good and evil . . . yin and yang. There is true balance to everything in the universe, including sorcery," Draconex was saying. "When the MystiCrystals were forged at the advent of the universe, another crystal was created from their combined residual dark energy. This Shadow-Crystal possesses a wicked concoction of a more powerful, controlling, insatiable power than that of the MystiCrystals. A power that can even make its wielder read the heavily encoded lost journal of Merlin."

Malcolm's eyebrows shot up, but he didn't say what he was thinking. *Something only the Light Bringer can do . . .*

"And now, the fabled ShadowCrystal resides in the bowels of this fortress."

Malcolm found himself in a dark room with nothing but a pale light shining on his kneeling form. He could barely make out Draconex in the shadows, but was able to follow his glowing red eyes, which were slowly circling him.

"For ages, there have been sorcerers whose hunger for knowledge and power have led them to dabble in the forbidden art of dark magic. Lord Ferox felt it, *I* have felt it, and now it's your turn to feel it. But dark magic can only work if it is rooted in the strongest emotion known to man: anger. Through anger, you are uninhibited, focused, ruthless. You care about nothing else except fulfilling your purpose—which, in this case, is to resurrect Lord Ferox from his eternal slumber. And who has what we need?"

"Jennifer Lancaster," Malcolm said, letting the name slide through his barely-open lips, like a ventriloquist talking through his puppet.

"The girl whom you let escape . . . *twice,*" Draconex coldly reminded his pupil. "You should have been able to capture her with no effort at all, yet she has been able to evade you and evade you again. How humiliating, *boy.*"

Boy—there it was again. Malcolm simply hated being called that. "I had her, but Victor—"

"No excuses!" Draconex snapped, cutting Malcolm off. "Excuses are for the weak. Are you weak, boy?"

Again with that name. "No," Malcolm whispered, staring at the outer edge of the spotlight that was trained on him.

"Did you say something?"

"I said NO!" Malcolm screamed. His throat felt raw when he swallowed.

He watched as the red eyes stopped in front of him and stared into his soul. "Prove it." Draconex's words dripped with an appetite for a challenge. He licked his lips.

Malcolm's vision went red and he couldn't control himself as he flung his arms outward, throwing punches at an invisible target. Spell after spell shot forth from his hands as his only remaining ring glowed red with an intense fire that was mimicked in his eyes. He heard himself yell—but it was muffled, as though he were hearing someone else yell through a closed door—and felt the warm trickle of tears falling down his cheeks.

Draconex's red eyes jumped from one part of the room to the other, followed by spells that erupted from Malcolm's fists. Praying that one of his attacks would hit its mark, he saw the eyes blink out for a single moment. Unconvinced that he had struck Draconex, Malcolm kept shooting spells left and right, hoping he would hit his master with a blind shot. He punched the ground and roared at the glaring spotlight above him, shattering it; an eruption of sparks showered over his hunkered form.

Darkness swallowed the small amount of light in the room. Malcolm's heavy breathing was the only sound that was heard. He didn't know what would happen next. Malcolm waited in the silence for Draconex to do or say something . . . anything.

A sudden wave of exhaustion rolled over his body, but he

fought the urge to collapse to the ground. He could not afford to show any further weakness. Gritting his teeth, he stayed upright and strained his eyes so he could try to make out any kind of movement in the black void, but to no avail.

"Goooooooooooooood . . ." Draconex whispered, letting the word drag out until he ran out of breath. "You opened your soul to the ShadowCrystal. How did it feel?"

Light suddenly flooded the room, and Malcolm almost lost his balance when he brought his hands up to shield his unprepared eyes. He shut them, but an after-image of Draconex was burned into his retinas and stayed there for a few seconds before disappearing.

Malcolm slowly dropped his hands. "Invincible." His eyes were still clamped shut. "But it took all of my strength. I've never been this tired before."

"Open your eyes." Draconex's voice was right next to his ear.

Malcolm obeyed, but it took a while for his pupils to contract, so he squinted until he could see normally. In front of him on the ground were two fist-size craters that led into a deep fissure of cracked ground and rubble that zig-zagged to the wall. He looked up to see smoke still emanating from the floodlight he had shattered moments before in his fit of rage.

"I-I did this?" Malcolm asked incredulously.

"Yes, by surrendering to the powers of the ShadowCrystal." Draconex was becoming more animated as he spoke. "You let your anger swallow every other emotion. You tapped into all five Mancy planes."

Malcolm laughed weakly, amazed at what he had done and the praise awarded him by Lord Draconex.

"I can feel that you have no anger left inside. You've overextended yourself . . . and that's why you've failed," Draconex spat. Any semblance of approval he once had vanished like dew from morning grass.

It took several seconds for Malcolm to feel the sting of his master's words. He stopped swaying and stared into the distance, his eyebrows crinkling in surprise.

With his dark cloak rippling on the ground, Draconex glided over to the boy and pushed him over with a slight poke to the forehead. Malcolm's head felt slack as he pitched backward, and the sudden feeling of freefall caused him to black out. His eyes rolled into his skull and he remembered no more.

CHAPTER THIRTY

There was nothing stopping Jen from beginning her training—except Victor and his empty stomach. And so, her patience clearly being tested, Jen agreed to stop at the outdoor mess hall to grab a hot meal, which they hadn't had since their breakfast at Victor's cottage on Azumar. Jen was so focused on beginning her training that she sucked down the soup in front of her and waited for Victor to finish his meal.

With a bouncing leg, Jen sat there, anxious. She knew she had a long road ahead, but this was a step forward in becoming stronger, a step forward to not only stopping the Dark Watchers from finding the Halostone and releasing Lord Ferox, but also to rescuing her parents . . . wherever they were. Her throat tightened; she prayed they were both still alive and together.

"Well, that hit the spot," Victor said, bringing Jen out of her thoughts. "Now I can focus more on you and your instruction than my appetite. Thank you." He retrieved his staff from where it leaned on his side of the table.

Jen composed herself and looked up into the clear blue sky. "I've been noticing that, aside from the huts, every other building is roofless," Jen commented as she stood. "What if a storm hits?"

Victor paused, considering Jen's question, then stood as well. "Camelore is actually twenty-eight miles above the Earth's crust, safely in the stratosphere and above all weather activity. That's why you'll never see a single cloud above us. No storms, though about a hundred years ago we had to ascend a couple dozen miles to ensure Camelore wouldn't disrupt any air traffic patterns," he said with a wink.

"I didn't realize we were back on Earth," Jen said, trying to process it all.

"Yes, but don't worry, our location is privileged knowledge to only current Light Seekers," Victor reassured her as he waved her to follow. "Which reminds me—there's one more thing we need to do before we start your training."

Jen moaned and rolled her eyes. "What, are we getting dessert now?"

Victor perked up and said, "*That's* what I was forgetting!" He turned around and laughed, walking away and again beckoning for her to follow. "I'm just kidding, Jenny. I need to introduce you to some people first."

"Oh," Jen said with relief, catching up to Victor. She was glad that dessert wasn't on the menu this time. The only appetite she had now was for sorcery.

"Since I can only teach you terramancy, I've enlisted the help of other mystras to instruct you in the remaining four Mancy planes. Grand Mystra Cindergray wants to teach you chronomancy"—Jen's face lit up after hearing his name—"and you already know that Mystra Étoilier has reserved the right to teach you astromancy. You've met them, so I would like to introduce you first to your telemancy mystra." Victor veered toward the left side of the ceremonial chamber. "His name is Mystra Cornelius Blackfire, one of my closest friends. He'll help you grow stronger when there is no more I can teach you."

"I don't think I'll ever stop learning from you. You've done more than anyone else has been willing to do, and I doubt that'll stop anytime soon. I'm grateful." Jen slid an arm around his waist as she fell into step with him. They were now headed toward one of the small huts that helped comprise the outer circle around the ceremonial chambers.

"Thank you, sweetheart. But as much as I want to be there for you, I won't be around forever," Victor said solemnly.

"That's why you're giving me the greatest gift: being my terramancy mystra." Jen smiled with her eyes, still holding onto him.

"I haven't thought of it that way. I guess I am," Victor realized. "Thank you for lending me a new perspective."

"Anytime." She affectionately rested her head on the side of his shoulder as they walked up to one of the tallest huts in the community.

He knocked once and heard a masculine voice enthusiastically say, "Come on in!"

Victor flashed Jen a smile and turned the doorknob, pushing the door open. He entered, followed closely by Jen, and said, "I hope we're not interrupting you during meditation?"

"You're quite all right, old chap, I wouldn't have let you enter if I were. Salve!" said the man, getting up from his chair as they both grasped each other's forearms.

Jen silently tilted her head, expecting to see them shake hands.

Maybe it's a secret handshake they've done for years.

Blackfire was wearing leather-strapped sandals that went up to his knees, a long velvety cape that fell to just below his waist-line, and armor plating akin to an Ancient Roman centurion. "And you must be Jennifer Lancaster. Salve."

Jen shot Victor a puzzled look.

Holding in a chuckle, Victor whispered, " 'Salve' is Latin for 'Hello.' "

Oh, mouthed Jen as she looked back at Mystra Blackfire and said, "Salve."

"Mystra Cornelius Blackfire, resident master of telemancy, at your service." He bowed his head and lifted the ends of his cape up to shoulder height.

"Pleasure to meet you, sir." Jen bowed in return.

"I knew you were going to say that." Blackfire raised a finger, winked, and walked over to give her the same handshake that he had given Victor.

Jen laughed as she awkwardly took his forearm and felt the

cold steel of his wrist plate on her skin. "How long have you been studying telemancy, Mystra Blackfire?"

"Oh, a mere fifty years. A drop in the bucket, really!" His enthusiasm made his armor clink.

"In addition to his time as a general of the Light Seeker forces," Victor told Jen.

"This, coming from a far more decorated Light Seeker general," Blackfire mentioned, gesturing to Victor. "It's truly an honor. Every day we grow stronger." Blackfire walked over to a table and picked up a sword. He caught Jen admiring its craftsmanship, so he presented it to her on open palms. "This is a Roman gladius sword."

Jen gripped its hilt with her left hand and raised the tip up so the blade was vertical. She twisted her wrist and saw the smooth metal shimmer.

Blackfire continued, "Short and nimble, very durable, and one of the best weapons in close quarters combat. I know sorcerers lean on magic to do battle, but it never hurts to learn the art of combat and weaponry, I always say."

"What does it say here?" Jen pointed along the center of the blade. She squinted at the dead language, hoping that would make her understand it better.

" 'Sit deos libera celeri justitia,' " Blackfire read. "It's Latin for 'May the gods deliver swift justice.' Many ancient soldiers, especially the Romans, believed their actions on the battlefield were directed by their gods, so whenever there was a victory, they attributed it to them. I believe, in a way, that is true. In battle your senses are heightened, making you sharper, stronger, and quicker . . . fueling victory. To remind me of that, I had Mystra Hephalon engrave it onto this gladius."

"Heph!" Jen exclaimed with great surprise, then cleared her throat after remembering where she was. "Yes, Mystra Hephalon. Great metallurgist." She handed him back his sword.

Blackfire chuckled, sheathing his prized weapon in the scabbard on his belt. "I'm guessing you've already made his acquaintance—which means he's made you a totem! May I see it?"

Jen smiled and lifted her right arm, letting her totem bracelet dangle on her wrist.

"By Jupiter, this is marvelous!" Blackfire refrained from touching it, but held his hands out. "That rainbow charm is very alluring."

"Thank you—it's my terramancy charm, which is the first plane I'll learn," Jen said, glancing appreciatively at Victor. "And I'm planning to receive a new charm every time I begin a new plane."

"Very wise, Jennifer. A totem bracelet with charms is quite unique and will help you stay focused. Learning all five Mancy planes is a daunting task," Blackfire reminded her.

"Trust me, I'm up for the challenge," Jen said determinedly.

"I await the time when I instruct you in the art of telemancy," Blackfire said humbly, this time bowing a bit deeper.

"Thank you again for agreeing to help train Jen," Victor said gratefully.

"You don't have to thank me, Vic." Blackfire straightened himself out. "It is a veritable honor to train a Lancaster." He then asked Jen, "Have you met your other mystras?"

"All but one." Jen tucked a stray curl behind her ear.

"Ah . . . which one has yet to be graced with your presence?"

Jen shrugged, giving Victor a meaningful stare. "It's still a surprise to me."

"We are going to see Mystra Wingelius next," Victor said to Jen. Then, to Blackfire: "Do you happen to know where she is?"

"Yes, indeed! I believe she is finishing up a lesson with one of her tenderfeet in the Pentarena."

Victor clasped forearms with Blackfire once more. "Thank you for your time, Cornelius."

Blackfire gave his arm one pump. "My pleasure, dear friend."

After a tight smile, Victor turned and let Jen lead the way out of the hut. But first, Jen said, "It was nice meeting you, Mystra Blackfire."

"Likewise, Jennifer. I hope to see you soon. Valete, omnes!" He sent them off with a wave of his hand.

"Vale," Victor bid his friend goodbye as he ducked under the door frame, careful not to hit his head as he exited.

As they stepped out into the bright sunlight, Jen was reminded of how crystal-blue the sky was. Being in the stratosphere somehow made the sky even more radiant. She looked down and surveyed the verdant landscape around and behind the community of huts. "So our next stop is to see Mystra Wiggelus?"

"Wingelius," Victor corrected. "The first thing to know about her is that she doesn't like her name to be mispronounced."

"Right. Don't want to make a bad impression." Jen said the name five times in a row to help remember it. "What's her first name?"

"Choriandallalian Wingelius," Victor said without breaking a sweat.

"Choridi . . . churro . . . alien," Jen stammered as she scratched her head. Sheepishly laughing, she relented. "I'll just stick with Mystra Wingelius."

Victor laughed as he spun his staff around in a circle. "Good idea. She'll teach you animancy. Mystra Wingelius is very bold and comes off as a little rigid at first, but once you earn her respect, she'll be a life-long friend and ally."

Jen nodded. "I hope I'm worthy of it." She followed Victor to a fork in the path, near the shimmering lake with the succulent dogwood trees.

"I have no doubt you will, Jenny. You have a lot of your parents' qualities in you, and Mystra Wingelius was a dear friend to them both." Victor said. Instead of taking the left path that led back to the steep bluff, he turned right, toward the Arbor Sacré and the Pentarena. "Welcome to the Pentarena." He gestured toward the training center, holding his hands out before him.

As Jen took in the site from a new point of view, she noticed the closest section of the pentagon was occupied. She could see two sorceresses bobbing and weaving around each other, in what appeared to be some sort of elaborate dance.

"Would that be them?" Jen said, pointing.

"I believe so. It looks like we're catching the end of one of her lessons now."

As they walked through the Pentarena's open pathway, Jen watched in awe as Mystra Wingelius sped around the perimeter like a cheetah and clapped her hands, sending a wall of wind toward a girl who looked to be around Jen's age. The gust lifted the tenderfoot high into the air. She masterfully uncoiled a snakeskin whip that was clipped to her hip and spun it above her head like a helicopter, causing her to float in the air. The sound her whip made reminded Jen of a New Year's Eve party noisemaker.

Mystra Wingelius clapped her hands twice and said, "Well done, Mirabelle. That's it for our lesson today."

Mirabelle softly landed next to her mystra and, recoiling her whip, returned it to her belt. "Thank you, Mystra." She bowed her head in respect.

Wingelius bowed in return and then spotted the two visitors. "Mystra Huxley," she said, her posture as straight as a board. "What a pleasant surprise."

Victor placed his right hand on the glass-like wall in front of him, and a few seconds later, a soft green glow bordered his hand and a chime sounded, bidding them to enter.

"Come on," Victor whispered to Jen. He stepped into the animancy arena with Jen in close tow. To Wingelius, he said, "I'm glad to have caught you before you returned to Watercress, Mystra Wingelius."

He led the way toward the center while Jen followed closely behind, repeating the animancy mystra's name over and over in her head so she wouldn't mispronounce it.

Mystra Wingelius, graced in a robe made from bright peacock feathers, didn't move toward them, and neither did Mirabelle, who was smiling from ear to ear, seemingly happy to meet a new friend.

When Victor was close enough he said, "May I present Jennifer of the Lancaster Clan."

Jen was surprised at how he had worded her name. It did sound more official, she gave him that.

"There has been much talk about your unexpected return. I am Mystra Choriandallalian Wingelius." The woman took off her mirrored aviators and pretentiously bowed, making an L with her body.

Jen bowed in return, but finished hers too quickly. Noticing that Wingelius was still in the crest of her bow, Jen tried to bow again, but by that time Wingelius had begun to rise. Not sure what to do, Jen winced in embarrassment and froze halfway down, waiting until the animancer mystra completed her bow before standing up straight again herself.

Nervousness closed her throat and all she could do was flash a big smile and wave. Victor saw how flustered Jen had become, so he stepped in and said, "She is very excited to learn animancy from you."

"Oh, you're studying to become an animancer too?" Mirabelle jumped in. She stepped closer and stuck out her hand toward Jen. "Mirabelle Amian. My friends call me Mira, and you should too!"

Jen, still mute, nodded and shook her hand. Mira had shiny, jet-black hair woven into a thick braid that went all the way down to the small of her back. Her skin was a delightfully dark tan, and her high cheekbones made Jen think she was Native American. She was wearing a mustard-yellow halter top with form-fitting khaki cargo shorts and hiking boots. As she turned, the metal on her whip glistened as it caught the sunlight. The snakeskin was patterned in off-white and dark-gray scales, and its tip seemed to have thin, metal strands that swayed like tassels.

"Hi," Jen responded, finally finding her voice. She looked at Mystra Wingelius and said, "Thank you for your help, ma'am."

"It is my duty. If you're going to succeed as an animancer, you might as well learn from the best," Wingelius said matter-of-factly.

Jen's eyebrows twitched slightly in response to Wingelius's arrogance, but she remembered that Victor did warn her. "I'll try not to disappoint," she said politely.

"You have big shoes to fill. Your father was a gifted omnimancer, especially in the animancy plane." Wingelius didn't waver in her rigid posture.

"It's my goal to make him and my mother proud."

There was a pause. Wingelius's eyes closed to slits. "We'll see."

Jen didn't know how to respond, so she bounced her gaze from Wingelius to Mira, then to Victor, who finally said, "Jen's looking for a place to stay while she's here on Camelore. Mira, don't you have an open bunk in your hut?"

Mira's eyes lit up as she exclaimed, "I can definitely make room!" She looked at Jen for confirmation. "If you'd like?"

Jen was glad Victor had changed the subject. "Sure. Sounds fun!"

If it was possible, Mira's smile grew larger. "It's been so long since I've had a roomie!" She turned to her mystra and asked, "Would it be okay if I show Jennifer my hut?" Mira clasped her hands in front of her, trying to hold in her excitement.

After a few seconds of stoic pondering, Mystra Wingelius agreed. "You're free to do as you wish, since we're done with your lesson for today."

Mira squealed in delight and took Jen's arm. She spun her around and led Jen back toward the circle of huts. "It's not terribly big, but I think you'll find it cozy. And we need to start thinking about the decorating!"

Jen let herself be led by the exuberant girl, relieved to end her meeting with the intimidating Mystra Wingelius.

* * *

As Jen and Mira were sprinting off into the distance, Victor gave Wingelius a knowing look and said, "Go easy on her, Chanda. A week ago, she had no idea where she came from."

Wingelius didn't break her gaze from Jen's retreating form. "Draconex and his minions will not go easy on her, Victor. She hasn't the slightest clue what she's getting in to, and I intend to prepare her for the best chance of living to see another day." She looked at Victor squarely. "Survival of the fittest."

Jen swore her arm was going to pop out of its socket if Mira ran any faster. They were almost to the circle of huts, but as luck would have it, Mira's was of course the farthest one away.

"Mira, slow down!" Jen said.

Caught off guard, Mira decreased her speed and released Jen's wrist. Looking back at Jen, who was panting and rubbing her wrist, she turned red with embarrassment. "Oh, I'm really sorry, Jennifer . . . sometimes I forget about my powers when I'm excited." Mira flashed an apologetic smile as she put a hand on Jen's heaving back. "I have a condition."

"It's . . . all right," Jen said between gulps of air. Straightening up to feel a cramp still in her side, she added, "And you can call me Jen."

Mira turned from embarrassed to delighted. "Okay, *Jen*."

"You were using animancy before?" Jen asked, wiping sweat from her brow.

"Yep! I was channeling a cheetah, my favorite animal. Sorry again . . ."

Jen chuckled. "It's okay, really. Cheetah, huh? It must come easily to you."

"It's definitely second nature, but I've been told to be more aware of when I use it," Mira replied, looking back at her mystra, who was already far off in the distance.

Jen looked back too. "Is Mystra Wingelius always like that?"

Mira snorted. "Like what? Serious? Intense? Usually. But as you get to know her, you'll pick up on her sense of humor. Trust me, if you manage the impossible and get her to laugh, let alone *smile*, your day is made."

Jen laughed, quickly joined by Mira. "Have you ever gotten her to laugh?" Jen was curious.

"Only when I'm clumsy and do something silly during my lessons," Mira confessed, "but I don't care. I get her to laugh, so I know she's not all business all the time."

Jen liked that. She told herself to remember to look on the bright side if her training became too much.

Mira put her hands on her hips and looked in the direction where they were going. Pointing to the huts, she said, "Mine is on the opposite end."

Knew it: it's the farthest one. "Can we crawl there?" Jen asked, half joking.

"Ha! If we channel the power of a snail, maybe. But that's too slow, silly! We'll walk—come on!" Mira started up again, leaving Jen to catch up.

As they got closer, Jen noticed there was more activity around the huts. People were walking past them, some talking, some laughing, others carrying supplies. "Mira, what's going on here?"

"We're getting ready for the Sesquimillennial Jubilee next week! It's the anniversary of the Great Battle, when Genevieve Lancaster brought an end to the Dark Purge." Then, as if a bell had gone off in her head, Mira abruptly stopped before her hut's door and pointed at Jen with both of her hands. "Your last name is also Lancaster! I don't know why I didn't connect it until now. Great going, Mira."

"It's okay. Honestly, I'm still learning about my heritage."

Mira stepped on her hut's welcome mat and played with her hair braid. "I can't believe I'm going to be roomies with a *Lancaster*." She unlocked the door and let Jen step in first.

As she crossed the threshold, Jen said, "Trust me, I'm nothing special. I still don't have my powers under control."

"I have a feeling that you'll pick it up quickly," Mira said.

Like magic, the hut was suddenly filled with light as evenly placed, smokeless torches flamed to life around them. The first thing Jen noticed was a hammock off to the left, swaying from the breeze made by the door. Above it was a large dreamcatcher that had colorful gems and feathers. The stone ground was covered by a thick, furry rug that softened the room. Jen felt calmness wash over her as she slid off her shoes out of habit and stepped onto the rug. The fur hugged the curves of her feet and the spaces between her toes, making her feel as though she were walking on clouds.

After a few seconds of soaking in the atmosphere, Mira asked, "So . . . you like?"

"I *love*," Jen admitted, curling her toes deeper into the soft rug.

"Faux fur, of course." Mira skipped over to her hammock after taking off her boots. She unclasped her whip and put it on a stand next to her. "I'd be a pretty poor animancer if I didn't live in harmony with my fellow animals." She tapped her dreamcatcher, letting it spin around as she dropped into the hammock.

"Good point. Is that your totem?" She pointed at the whip, still swaying on its stand.

Mira sat up and dangled her feet off the hammock. "Yes! My pride and joy." She picked the whip back up and ran her hand over its smooth leather. "Imitation snakeskin, of course."

"Of course," Jen winked, smiling.

Mira patted the space next to her, inviting Jen to sit down on the hammock. After she sat down, Mira handed the whip to Jen and said, "Made it myself. I took inspiration from the construction of a snake whip, but added my own flair to it. Then I let Heph inlay my metal into the handle and poppers."

"You're very gifted, Mira." Jen noticed the handle was curved, able to bend like the whip itself. The metal in the handle had the same pattern as the dark-gray scales, which gave an added dimension to the overall design. Following the coil around, she came to the thin metal tassels on its tip. "This is beautiful."

"Thank you." Mira blushed. "To help me aim my spells, Heph also put metal strands on the tip, where the popper goes—that's what makes the snapping noise." Mira mimed herself snapping a whip and made the sound effect for good measure.

"I've never used a whip before. Is it easy?" Jen asked, curious.

"It takes a lot of practice." Mira pointed at a raised scar on her right shoulder. "I got this beaut during my first lesson at whip-cracking. It took me a while to get the hang of it, but now this whip is so comfortable, I feel like it's a part of me." She hung it back on the stand and gently bumped her shoulder with Jen's. "So, what's *your* totem?"

"Oh! A charm bracelet," Jen said, lifting up her right wrist.

Mira's surprise was evident as Jen unhooked her totem bracelet and handed it to her new friend. "Since I'll be learning all of the Mancy planes, I asked Heph to forge a bracelet so I can have a charm for each one."

Mira let the bracelet hang from her index and middle fingers as she marveled at its intricate design. "This is so *cute*, Jen!" Mira said gleefully. She pointed to the teardrop pendant. "Which plane is this charm for?"

"Terramancy," Jen answered. "I'll get a new charm forged every time I begin a new plane."

"So is animancy next on the list?" Mira winked and handed the bracelet back to Jen.

Jen chuckled as she put it back on her wrist. "I haven't thought that far ahead, actually. We'll see which plane Vic advises I go to next."

"Well, Mystra Huxley is the one to ask for those things," Mira agreed.

"How so?" Jen asked, confused.

Before Mira could answer, a knock came at the door, and she straightened her posture and quickly breathed in. "Speak of the devil. Come in, please!"

The door handle turned and Victor stepped into the hut. "I hope I'm not interrupting anything?"

"Not at all," Mira said honestly. She stood up, causing Jen to slide to the center of the hammock. "You're always welcome, Mystra Huxley."

"Why thank you, my dear." Victor turned to Jen. "I'm sorry I took so long with Mystra Wingelius."

"Oh, don't apologize," Jen said, deciding to stand as well. "It gave me more time to get to know Mira."

"Good." Victor smiled at both of them before saying, "Oh, before I forget." He reached into his cloak and pulled out Jen's diary. "Hopefully this'll make you feel more at home here."

Smiling appreciatively, Jen took her diary and placed it on her nightstand before hugging Victor. "You're the best, Vic."

Shrugging, he said, "I know." He chuckled. "Now that we're both free, how'd you like to start your training?"

The training!

"That would be great!" She turned to Mira while she slid her shoes back on. "Catch you later?"

Mira opened her arms and hugged Jen so quickly that she didn't see it coming. "Of course, roomie!" Mira pulled back and asked, "Would you like a hammock on your side of the room too?"

Jen tried to hide her surprised, rose-colored cheeks. "I'd like that, yes."

Mira clapped her hands so fast that they blurred like hummingbird wings. "Perfect! I'll start right on it."

"Oh, you don't have to make it for me . . ."

"No, I'd love to!" Mira insisted. "I enjoy making things, especially clothes and décor. I've sewn my own hammock"—she pointed at it, then gestured around—"and I've made nearly every item in this hut."

"Wow!"

"Fashion is my second passion—after animals," Mira admitted, flicking her braid behind her shoulders.

"If it's not too much trouble," Jen relented. "Thank you."

Victor still held the door open, expecting to have already left.

"It's the least I can do! Now, I don't want to keep you." Mira shooed both Victor and Jen out the door, but not before handing her a bag. "Here's some trail mix for the road."

Jen hugged Mira. "Thanks—this looks delicious."

They both exchanged goodbyes, then Victor and Jen were off toward the Pentarena.

"Looks like you made a new friend," Victor chuckled, spinning his staff idly.

"More like a soul mate," Jen joked, but part of her could tell that she and Mira would become close. Feeling happy, Jen switched her thoughts to her first training session as a sorceress.

CHAPTER THIRTY-ONE

Six days.

Six days of darkness, malnourishment, squalor, and imprisonment. The only thing that kept Richard and Beth Smith from falling into further depression was their frequent conversations with their friend who, for the past couple days, had been uncharacteristically silent.

Richard couldn't help but think his friend was bothered by what he had said the other day—or night—about how he and his wife had raised Jennifer Lancaster. He wasn't ashamed that he had told the truth; just confused. Richard had no clue as to why that information had changed his friend's demeanor so drastically. But there hadn't been any unscheduled visits by the guards, so he was certain that his friend had kept that information to himself —for now.

Deciding to try one more time, Richard said, "Hey, friend."

Cold silence was the only response.

Sighing in disappointment, he turned toward his wife, but his heart started to race when he heard familiar shuffling, then a single tap on a cell bar behind him. Richard didn't move—he just waited.

Finally, "Are you Lancasters?" His friend's voice was gravelly, having not been used in days.

Richard kissed his sleeping wife's cheek and slid closer to the prison bars. "No . . . we looked after Jen when her birth parents disappeared."

"Disappeared . . ." his friend repeated absentmindedly.

"We're the Smiths," Richard added. He heard a sharp intake of breath as if his friend had been burned. "Hey, are you all right?"

"I-I'm not sure," his friend admitted. "You must have told me your last name before, because I feel like I had already known that. I'm sorry . . . my mind gets worse every time I come out of Draconex's interrogations."

"Have you been doing the exercises I've taught you?" Richard asked, both as a friend and psychiatrist.

"Yes: let my body accept the trauma, relax, and breathe, then force it out like a bad dream."

"Good."

"You know, it's easier said than done," his friend pointed out. "But it gets easier every time. Thank you, friend."

"I'm sorry if what I said earlier upset you."

There was silence, then: "What do you mean?"

"After I told you my wife and I raised Jennifer Lancaster, you seemed to withdraw from speaking to us."

"My head started to throb. It wasn't you," his friend explained. "It's just that every time I'm brought to Draconex, I keep hearing about the Lancasters."

"How do you mean?" Richard was even more confused now.

His friend grunted, seeming to be waging a battle in his own mind. Finally, he said:

"He keeps insisting that I am . . . Charles Lancaster."

CHAPTER THIRTY-TWO

To kiss Jen was to fly, and right now Malcolm was flying.

He pulled away from her soft lips and tucked a few strands of curly hair behind her ear as he stared into her beautiful, deep violet eyes. They were sitting on a bench with a perfect view of the Washington Square Arch in Lower Manhattan, which was casting a long shadow as the sun set behind them. Malcolm put his arm around Jen and she rested her head on his shoulder as the fountain in front of them shot up water, shimmering like liquid gold.

No words were spoken; none were necessary. Malcolm was filled with happiness and wished for this moment to never end. He looked down at her and smiled. Jen met his eyes with hers. Slowly, they leaned in for another kiss. The world melted away as he hugged her close, smelling her vanilla-lavender perfume.

Jen kissed him harder as their embrace became more passionate. Suddenly, Malcolm couldn't breathe. Unable to pull himself away, Malcolm began to panic as his lungs screamed for air. He tried pushing Jen away, but he was powerless; he couldn't make a sound. He felt the life being sucked out of him with this kiss of death, and there was nothing he could do to stop it.

He was falling, falling . . .

Darkness enveloped his senses, and the next thing Malcolm

knew, he was in a pitch-black room, coughing from inhaling air too quickly. His eyes were stinging from sweat trickling down his forehead. He had been dreaming—or, more accurately, having a nightmare.

As his senses awoke, Malcolm remembered he was training with Lord Draconex, and his heart sank as cold reality came crashing back to him like a forceful tsunami. He was truly alone and wished he could hold Jen one last time. Malcolm hadn't realized it before, but he had somehow fallen for Jen during his time pretending to be her boyfriend.

"The mind is a truly amazing thing," Draconex's voice boomed from every direction. Malcolm's ears rang, and he felt as though he were recovering from the world's worst hangover. "But what continually fascinates me is what goes through the mind, especially when it can't get enough oxygen."

Even though Malcolm controlled his breathing, he still felt out of it. "You were suffocating me?" He couldn't believe the depths Draconex was willing to reach.

Ignoring Malcolm's question, Draconex continued, "From what I've encountered, the brain begins to shut down when it's starved for oxygen. It discards everything trivial, inconsequential, and unimportant, and focuses on what matters most to the person." He flew over and pinned Malcolm to the floor beneath a heavy boot. "So imagine my surprise when I reached into your mind to discover that you have feelings for Jennifer Lancaster." His tone was filled with equal parts disappointment and accusation. "*Strong* feelings."

Malcolm's throat clenched shut. He shook his head.

"Don't try to deny it, boy. The brain never lies. If I had known you were this weak and impressionable, I wouldn't have chosen you for the mission—but this is good." He released Malcolm from his boot. "We can cauterize it from your soul now that I have pinpointed the root of your problem."

Malcolm felt his chest to make sure his ribs weren't broken again. With all of his resolve, he fought the urge to yell. Instead, he said, "I'm sorry, My Lord."

Draconex let the side of his mouth twitch—his version of a spiteful grin. "That was the first time you haven't talked back to me. You must be learning."

"I've learned that I have unresolved feelings for Jen. Help me," Malcolm admitted. He stood up and faced Draconex with a tired but determined gaze.

The leader of the Dark Watchers grinned insidiously. "You're ready for your next lesson. But first I have some pressing business to which I must attend. Wait for me in my antechamber. Madame Diaema is expecting you." Draconex spun, pulling his cape around his body, and deftly walked out of the chamber.

Malcolm, still shaking off the daze he woke up in, shook his head and trudged like a zombie toward Draconex's antechamber, hoping that he would revert back to normal while he waited for his master to beckon him once again.

* * *

It was a good thing Richard Smith wasn't standing, because he would have crumbled to the ground after he heard his friend say that he was Charles Lancaster.

Charles Lancaster.

The man who had visited Richard and Beth two decades ago at their home in Arizona. The man who had saved his life from a home invader who'd turned out to be a Dark Watcher. The man who trusted him and his wife enough to raise their only daughter, Jennifer.

Thoughts and questions swirled around in his head too quickly to comprehend. He took a deep breath and said as calmly as possible, "You're Charles Lancaster?"

His friend—Charles—rubbed his knuckles on one of the bars that separated them. "Or so I'm told. I don't remember much before waking up here in this hole."

Richard slid closer to the bars and found Charles's hand. At first, he felt his friend's hand tighten around the bar, but his grip relaxed. "You're Jen's biological father!" he whispered. "You asked my wife and me twenty years ago to raise your infant daughter. You don't even remember *that*?"

"I'm sorry, friend. I've only known life here on Feralot." Charles withdrew his hand from Richard's.

Disheartened, but unwilling to give up, Richard promised, "My wife and I will help you remember. You saved my life years ago and gave me a precious girl to raise. It's the least I can do for you."

"Thank you, but don't expect much. Draconex has tried to make me remember in every inhumanly way possible—and a few utterly inhuman ways—and has only failed in all these years."

"Maybe he hasn't been taking the right approach." Richard's voice held hope for the first time in days since he'd arrived in the steely darkness of the Lair of Despair.

Then, a chill ran down his spine when he heard the sound that had begun to bring him anguish ever since he woke up in Feralot: metal keys.

Richard opened his eyes—again for the first time in days. "Stay strong, Charles," he said, tightening his grip on the other's hand. "We'll get through this."

Charles didn't say anything as the guards stopped at his cell and unlocked his door. Richard heard shuffling as the intruders tried to drag his old friend out of his cell, but he held firmly onto the metal bar. The guards grunted, trying to break his hold, but Charles's strength surprised them—and Richard. Finally, one of the guards had had enough of this game of tug-of-war and blasted Charles with a spell that knocked him unconscious. It was so bright that it left an after image on Richard's retinas: Charles stoically staring at him, as if he knew exactly where to look, even though it was pitch-black.

Richard felt Charles's grip go slack, and the guards forcefully dragged him away, down the cold corridor, to an unknown room where Draconex was waiting.

CHAPTER THIRTY-THREE

With budding excitement, Jen was on Victor's heels as she stepped into the terramancy section of Camelore's Pentarena, ready for her training to finally begin. Separated by glass-like walls from the animancy section on their right and the telemancy section on their left, they were given an abundant space to train without putting other sorcerers in harm's way of stray spells.

Looking around her, Jen was reminded of the Chimera Course back at Watercress. She saw a man-made pond the size of an Olympic diving well; an outgrowth of craggy rocks; a translucent tunnel with a vertical chimney stack, which looked like an enormous, upside-down letter T; and a large, charred patch of lava-cracked earth and coals, which held a tiled platform in its center, holding a basin that crackled with dancing flames. Lingering on the last spectacle, Jen noticed the heat rising from the superheated ground, causing the air to waver.

"What you see around you are representations of the four basic elements: water, earth, air, and fire," Victor began. Jen noticed a shift in his demeanor. His soothing, gentle tone of a friend was replaced by the firm, determined tone of an instructor. "These four elements create harmony and balance on every life-based planet, but there are sub-elements such as lightning, metal, blood, and chemistry. Mystra terramancers can conjure these sub-elements on command, making them extensions of their mind and body." He raised a finger, pausing. "But that comes with practice as your nexus grows stronger, and knowledge of how each element compliments and contrasts with one another. Having said that, it is easier for tenderfeet to learn by first controlling the basic elements."

Jen nodded, taking it all in.

Victor continued, waving Jen over to the clear tunnel. "We'll start with the element that is the most abundant and easiest to control: air." He placed a hand on its curved outer wall and motioned Jen to enter.

"Inside? How far would you like me to go?" Jen asked, unsure about how this was going to play out.

"To the other side. I want you to get a feel of the space before we start anything else," Victor answered, peeking into the tunnel.

"Got it." The tunnel's opening was a little over three yards in diameter, so Jen had no problem fitting inside, but she felt claustrophobia begin to tug at her throat and twist her stomach into knots as she started toward the other end, which was fifty yards away.

Jen's steps echoed as she walked the entirety of the tunnel, glancing up into the chimney stack as she passed it. Once she got to the other side, Jen let out a breath she didn't realize she had been holding in. Feeling more at ease, she turned around and looked at Victor's miniature form at the other end of the tunnel.

"How did it feel?" Victor's voice rushed toward her, sounding as if he were right in front of her instead of fifty yards away.

"Tight," Jen replied, then added, "and echoey." She smiled when she heard Victor's disarming chuckle.

"Okay, now we are going to make this tunnel sing like a train whistle."

"How?" Jen asked, squinting into the tunnel.

"That chimney pipe will produce a high-pitched sound if air rises through it, and the only way to make that happen is if you and I shoot air into this tunnel at the same time," Victor explained.

Jen tapped her teeth together as she thought. "Seems simple enough." She remembered how she'd whipped up a strong breeze in the Chimera Course.

"Just focus and you'll be fine," Victor reassured her. He held his staff firmly in both hands and pointed its tip inside the tunnel. "On my mark. Three . . ."

Jen took a deep breath, filling her lungs with fresh air.

". . . two . . ."

She moved into a walking stance, with her left foot forward and right foot back.

". . . one . . ."

She wiggled her fingers in anticipation.

"Now!"

WHOOSHHHHH!

Victor sent a wall of air into the tunnel at thirty miles per hour, hoping that it would be met with an equal gust by Jen.

Jen cupped her hands and thrust them in Victor's direction, expecting a sensation of swirling wind on her fingertips, but nothing happened. She tried again, but to no avail. Disappointed, she looked at her open palms just as she was buffeted by a strong wind, almost taking her feet out from under her. Jen's hair stuck straight back and her loose blouse whipped behind her as she staggered back a few paces, trying desperately to remain upright.

Victor lowered his staff once he noticed that Jen was fighting against his spell. The gust turned into a breeze, which faded into nothing. Jen put her hands on her knees, her labored breathing carrying through the tunnel.

"Did you feel mine?" Jen asked, with a hint of jest.

"A little," Victor joked back. "Did you feel my gust?"

"No," Jen said unconvincingly. "Barely a breath." She waited a few seconds, then said, "Okay, you got me . . . I couldn't make any wind."

"Did you focus?" Victor asked.

"Yes! I don't get it, Vic. It was so easy for me to whip up a breeze in the Chimera Course. Now I feel like I'm powerless."

"You're everything but powerless, Jenny," Victor consoled.

"You're still getting used to channeling your nexus through your totem bracelet instead of the Ring of Lancaster, which you've had a chance to connect with over the twenty years you've worn it. And remember—you drank the elixir before starting the Chimera Course, which temporarily heightened your powers. For now, focus on your new totem, and let your will flow through it." He tapped the end of his staff on the ground twice, getting ready for another attempt. "On my mark again."

Jen slid into a walking stance once more, holding her hands up and keeping them open. She glanced at her totem bracelet and focused on its only charm.

"Come on . . ." Jen said to herself.

Suddenly, she felt a slight electrical pulse travel through her body as she heard Victor count down. She was still looking at her totem and saw her teardrop charm start to glow and lift away from the bracelet. Her palms felt cold as an invisible force put pressure on her hands, causing her to push back. Wind brushed into her, but it wasn't as forceful as before, letting her know that she was shooting air back into the tunnel. Her arms started to ache from the pressure and she grew more tired. Jen eventually let her arms drop—

And Victor's spell rammed into her, knocking her over. She remained on her back, trying to catch her breath and wait for the wind to cease.

Victor ran across the tunnel and stopped at Jen's side. "Are you okay?"

"Yeah, just resting." Jen tried to keep the disappointment from her voice, but her mentor picked up on it.

"That was much better than your first attempt. You're getting the hang of it," Victor said.

Jen couldn't look Victor in the eye. "I couldn't hang on to it, though."

"But you will. That's why we practice." He held out a hand. Jen finally nodded and took his hand, standing up. She brushed dirt from her blouse and jeans as Victor said, "I noticed that you used your totem this time. Now try to focus on the molecules in the air. We take the oxygen in the air to breathe, but it's also made up of copious amounts of nitrogen, argon, carbon dioxide, and methane. Try to control all of them. We'll go on your mark this time."

In a blink of an eye, Victor was back at the other end of the tunnel, waiting. Jen centered herself and closed her eyes. Feeling her nexus awaken, she reached out all around her and took a deep breath. As air filled her lungs, she could pick out all the types of gas molecules around her as easily as though they were wearing name tags. There were too many to count, but she felt them respond to her touch, one by one. Jen smirked and opened her eyes, imbued with the rich powers of her nexus.

"Three . . ." Jen started the countdown. She lifted her arms and willed the charm on her totem bracelet to glow. ". . . two . . . one . . . NOW!"

The young omnimancer felt a blast of wind shoot from her palms and into the tunnel. She dug her feet into the ground for added balance and waited for Victor's gust to slam into her—but it never came. Continuing to let the power of her nexus flow through her single charm, Jen squinted across the tunnel to see Victor stumble backward a couple steps, his cloak flapping straight behind him.

I'm doing it! I think . . .

Jen suddenly flinched as a high-pitched whine drowned out her inner thoughts. Before her concentration could break, she realized it was from the air passing through the chimney. Beaming with pride, Jen felt a drop in air pressure and assumed Victor was finished with the exercise, so she also decreased her spell until the whistling stopped.

She looked silently at Victor with a big smile plastered on her face. Amazingly, she felt completely rejuvenated, unlike a few minutes ago when she had been on the ground, exhausted and with deflated spirits.

"You did it!" Victor yelled through the tunnel.

Jen squealed, raising her arms and jumping up and down in delight. She had never felt such control before. Disregarding her claustrophobia, she sprinted through the tunnel to embrace Victor at the other end.

"What a rush!" Jen exclaimed.

"I knew you had it in you," Victor said proudly. "We'll work on tighter control as we progress—like your hug."

Jen laughed, releasing him. "Sorry, Vic," she said as she mock-punched his shoulder. "So, what's next?"

He jokingly rubbed the spot where she'd hit him, mouthing the word "Ouch," then said, "Well, if you're up for it, we'll see how you do with the element that is the opposite of air: earth."

"I'm always game," Jen said, feeling energized.

He led Jen to the rocky outgrowth near the back wall. As she stepped onto the rocky plateau, she was reminded of her family trip to the Grand Canyon. Of course, what she stood on was minuscule compared to one of the US's natural wonders, but the colors and shapes of its rocks were very similar.

"Where air is fluid and transitional, earth is solid and durable," Victor explained, then smiled, adding, "but only to the untrained."

He walked over to a large boulder and put a palm on its side. Focusing on his hand, he applied pressure. Jen's jaw dropped as his whole hand disappeared into the boulder like quicksand. Victor smiled at Jen and took his hand out of the solid boulder just as easily as he had put it in.

"That's—that's . . ."

"Magic?" Victor laughed. "Some say it is. Terramancers say that it's an understanding of the properties of the mineral and developing a symbiosis with it."

"That's what you did the night of my birthday!" Pieces were falling into place for Jen. "When you walked through my locked door."

"Exactly," Victor said. "Now you try."

Jen stepped closer and put a hand on the boulder. It felt surprisingly smooth, but very dense. Decidedly solid. Hesitation dampened her confidence, but she persevered and tried to identify the boulder's properties. Unlike the air molecules, which floated all around her, the boulder's molecules were stacked in tight rows and columns, much like a lattice fence. She tried separating them, but they wouldn't budge. Jen pushed the boulder, willing her hand to sift through, but all she did was make her palm hurt from the pressure.

"Jen." Victor lifted her hand from the rock. "You're trying to control the boulder like you did the air. This is an entirely different element, so you must change your approach. Instead of trying to move the boulder's molecules, move *your own*." Victor tapped the boulder and its surface cracked like sugar glass.

Jen followed the cracks to where Victor tapped his finger, now showing a small hole. "What did you do *that* time?"

"I made my finger more dense than the boulder," Victor explained. "Most people think that earth is immovable and they are not, when in reality it's the opposite. Learn to adapt your molecules to fit your needs."

Jen tilted her head and put her hand back on the boulder.

"Adapt," she told herself.

She felt the structured molecules again, but instead of forcing them to move, she focused on her hand. A slight tingle shot through her fingertips and traveled over her knuckles and palm. Jen opened her eyes in surprise to see the charm on her totem bracelet come to life and glow. Her hand began to feel squishy and she watched it meld into the boulder; before long the only thing showing was her arm, up to her wrist. Jen let out a breath of amazement.

"Now slowly retract it," Victor instructed. "Don't lose your focus."

Nodding, Jen did as she was instructed; concentrating on keeping her hand porous, she slowly brought it out of the boulder.

Victor was visibly relieved. "Well done. Once you understand the earth and its minerals, it lets you in and becomes a part of you."

"Okay, that felt really weird." Jen wiggled her fingers as feeling rushed back into them.

"Now try and crack the boulder."

Without saying a word, Jen focused on the tip of her left index finger, feeling it warm up as she tapped into her nexus. When she was ready, she touched the boulder and pushed.

CRACKKKKK!

Stone crumbled underneath her fingertip. "Whoa," Jen said, impressed at the result. She took her finger away and clenched her fist, focusing on her knuckles. With determination, Jen hit the boulder with a strong jab. It splintered like balsa wood as she drove her fist deep into the massive rock.

Convinced that the impromptu rain of rock shards had stopped, Victor lowered his arms from his face to reveal a look of disbelief. "You're even stronger than I thought."

"Ditto," Jen agreed, amazed. She pulled her fist out and inspected her knuckles. "Not even a scratch," she pointed out.

"When you become denser than earth, you will not break," Victor said as he looked into the crater his tenderfoot had made.

Jen laughed. "You sound like a fortune cookie."

Victor leaned on what was left of the boulder and added, "And your lucky numbers are: six, fourteen, twenty-eight, and forty." They both laughed at that, enjoying a moment of respite.

When the laughter died down, he said, "The last ability is to match your strength with that of the earth's. Think of Sir Isaac Newton's third law of motion: for every action there is an equal and opposite reaction."

He walked to a slightly bigger boulder, waving Jen over. She followed and watched as he slid into a deep walking stance. In one fluid motion, Victor brought his hands down to the right side of his hips and thrust them out at the boulder. When his open palms made contact, the massive boulder, which had to have weighed close to four tons, immediately slid ten yards across the rocky plateau before coming to a halt.

"I enacted the same amount of density that the boulder has, causing it to react by sliding away, much like how pool balls interact during a game of billiards."

Jen followed the trench made by the enormous boulder to

where it now rested. "That's amazing!" She looked at Victor and eagerly asked, "My turn?"

"You read my mind." He smiled tightly, waving for her to begin.

Jen made her way to the other side of the boulder and said, "I'll try to push it back to its original spot."

"Sounds good." Victor crossed his arms and stepped out of the way.

Copying what Victor had done, Jen placed her feet into a walking stance and focused, touching the boulder first to pick up its exact level of density. After she was satisfied with what she felt, Jen took her hands off the boulder and brought them down to her right hip, as though she were holding a large softball. She opened her eyes, fully primed, and drove her palms into the hulking mass in front of her.

At first, Jen thought she missed the boulder, but then it flew away from her. Like a rocket, it sped across the open space with such force that it tumbled over. End over end it rolled, creating deeper depressions in the ground. With no intention of stopping, it zoomed past its initial resting place and clear off the rocky plateau, digging up large chunks of sod. It stopped when it finally careened into the Pentarena's back wall, transferring the kinetic energy to the barrier, which sent waves of prismatic light rolling away from the point of impact.

Jen remained in her stance, too shocked to move.

Victor blinked a few times before slowly turning around to face Jen.

"I think it's time for a break," he declared.

CHAPTER THIRTY-FOUR

Malcolm knelt in front of the Throne of Dragons, meditating. Breathing in, breathing out. Trying to focus . . . trying to push Jen from his thoughts.

But he could not.

He couldn't help but remember all of the fond memories they had shared, even when he knew that it was a means to an end. He shouldn't have let her affect him so, but he'd let it happen anyway, foolishly thinking he could forget about her as easily as tearing off an old bandage.

Now he was stuck paying the price, and it was affecting his performance and mission. He didn't know how many more chances he had left.

The soft beating wings of Madame Diaema sounded as she fluttered around him, finally swooping across the room to hang on her branch next to Draconex's throne. He took in a deep breath, letting his lungs fill to capacity, and held it for a count of five seconds, then released it slowly as he focused on his calm heartbeat.

"Obediently waiting for your master to return, Mal?" the sing-song voice of Diaema cut through his focus.

Several seconds passed as Malcolm tried to regain focus, ignoring her loaded question.

"You must be uncomfortable down there," Diaema teased.

Malcolm could smell her perfume now, which meant that she must have already changed into her human form. Realizing that his meditation was over, he finally said, "It's not that bad." He opened his eyes to see the wickedly elegant Madame Diaema sitting on the throne's right armrest.

"If you're only waiting for a few more minutes . . . but what if Draconex doesn't return for another hour?" She crossed her long legs and let them dangle.

"I don't mind waiting," Malcolm said indifferently.

"But you should. Your time is just as important as his," Diaema pointed out. "Especially with what's at stake."

Malcolm searched for the angle she was playing. "Lord Draconex knows how sensitive our quest is. He wouldn't waste valuable time if he didn't deem it worthy."

"True . . . but what if he doesn't think you're worthy enough to include you in everything he does in your little 'quest'?"

Malcolm's eyes widened in surprise and flashed with annoyance. "He *does* find me worthy, because he's training me. What's more, he's even shared with me every step in his plan to retrieve the Halostone."

"Maybe . . ." Diaema inspected her long nails. "Maybe not." She looked straight at Malcolm.

He swallowed, feeling doubt creep into his mind.

"He's told you about your late friend Archie Blake and his demise at the hands of the Grand Mystra Cindergray?"

Malcolm looked to his knees, feeling mixed emotions. Even though he had been furious to find out that Draconex had sent another Dark Watcher to kidnap Jen, Blake was a good friend and loyal to the cause. Malcolm was beside himself when he'd heard Blake had died.

"Yes."

"Of course. What a shame." Diaema shook her head, letting her silky blond hair brush across her shoulders and back. "Surely, then, he filled you in after he returned from his own attempt to capture the Lancaster girl, right?" She waited, not moving a muscle.

Malcolm blinked, making sure he'd heard her correctly. *"He went after Jen? Draconex did?"*

Diaema put on an injured expression and pouted. "I was hoping he told you, though I'm not surprised he didn't when he returned without his prize."

Malcolm felt his face flush red with anger and betrayal. "What happened?" he demanded.

"Draconex took Volcanor to ambush her when she was alone, but she had company."

"Victor," Malcolm seethed.

Diaema didn't say anything to that, only snickered. "After separating Lancaster from her *company*, he had Volcanor grab her . . . or so he thought."

Malcolm's annoyance grew—not at how Diaema was dragging the story on, but at how Draconex had kept it a secret from him.

Diaema sighed dramatically. "Turns out, Jennifer used the moltic spell on herself to escape. Draconex flew all the way back here with a cheap imitation mold."

His anger now boiling, Malcolm scoffed, too angry to appreciate the well-deserved irony. Draconex had been mercilessly scolding him for constantly failing to capture Jen, but now, not even he, Draconex, the great Dark Watcher commander, could succeed in the same endeavor. That double-standard fanned his anger into rage and he jumped out of his kneeling position and yelled at the top of his lungs.

Diaema smirked as she looked at him out of the corner of her eye. "Are you beginning to see how he plays people? Even the ones closest to him?"

Malcolm felt that she was speaking from experience.

Watching Malcolm pant, she hissed, "Want to get back at him?"

Malcolm coughed in surprise. After struggling to regain his composure, he silently stared at the ghoulishly gorgeous vampire, afraid to ask but also curious to hear what she had in mind. "How?"

Diaema's smirk stretched into a full smile. "First, sit next to me." She rubbed the Throne of Dragons' cushion next to her.

A chill shot through Malcolm's spine. His rage melted away and was replaced by dread.

I couldn't do that . . . could I?

"What if he finds out?" Malcolm asked, trying and failing to hide his fear.

"He'll never know." Madame Diaema mimed zipping her voluptuous lips and throwing away the invisible key.

Warily looking behind his shoulder, Malcolm walked slowly toward the Throne of Dragons.

"You're almost there," Diaema urged him on. She softly patted the cushion now.

Fearing that Draconex would walk in and catch him at any moment, Malcolm shot a look over his shoulder every five seconds until he was standing in front of the throne.

Diaema placed her hands on her lap and winked.

Malcolm shut off his hesitation and sat down, surprised at how comfortable it felt. For some unknown reason, he felt more confident, sitting high on the Throne of Dragons.

"Isn't it intoxicating?" Diamea asked, breaking Malcolm out of his daydream. "That feeling of power?"

"Yeah—" Malcolm cleared this throat. "Yes."

Still sitting on the armrest, Diamea giggled. "Oh, honey, you're sitting on *the* Throne of Dragons. Act the part."

She slid off the armrest and stood in front of Malcolm. Slowly, she leaned over and gently grabbed both of his wrists, then paused with her face inches away from Malcolm's. His heart began to pound as strands of Diaema's hair fell from her shoulders and dangled just above his thighs, sending wisps of her perfume in his direction. Without blinking, she picked up his arms and placed them on the throne's armrests. Once she felt confident that he wouldn't immediately remove them, she let go and took a few steps back.

Malcolm looked down at the new placement of his hands. The more time he spent on the throne, the more he noticed that his body language and demeanor began to transform. As he clenched the cold, hard dragon heads at the end of each armrest, he relaxed his shoulders, moved his feet farther apart, sat up straighter, and even puffed out his chest. The familiar sense of crippling fear was quickly replaced by one of powerful confidence as he envisioned himself doling out punishments to his genuflecting underlings begging for his forgiveness.

Diaema crossed her arms and smiled. "And that's why Draconex never allows anyone to sit on his throne—if they feel its ancient power, they develop a desire to possess it."

Malcolm shook his head, finding it hard to believe that seconds ago he was scared of Draconex, like a mouse to a cat; now, he felt like the lion. "I've heard stories about the power of this throne. I've never thought it to be true."

"That's the hidden power of the Throne of Dragons. It holds powerful traces of every dark sorcerer who has sat where you sit now," Diaema said, then added, "including Lord Ferox."

That caught Malcolm's attention. "Why are you telling me this?"

Diaema looked away as if silently replaying a painful memory, then returned her gaze to his and said, "To make you realize that Draconex isn't this all-powerful sorcerer you make him out to be. He's just like you, except he has limitless ambition."

Her comment stung Malcolm, but he held his tongue because he knew it was true.

After sensing he was not going to respond, she continued. "See, you expect to be given everything instead of earning it through patience, hard work, and the shrewd ability to play politics. How do you think Draconex became the high commander of the Dark Watchers? He played the game and waited until the time was ripe to usurp the throne and begin his reign."

"If I'm lacking ambition to succeed, then why are you helping me?" Malcolm questioned, his spirits sinking as a ship with a massive hole in its hull.

She strutted toward Malcolm and lifted his chin with a pale index finger. "Because I've seen the way he treats you, and you don't deserve it. Hopefully, by giving you a taste of what you can become with the Throne of Dragons, you'll find enough ambition to play *his* game until you are ready to claim your own destiny, Malcolm."

Malcolm . . . she called me Malcolm. Not "boy."

Diaema leaned in and kissed his forehead before resuming her place on the armrest.

Malcolm tapped his foot, thinking.

Draconex was just like me . . . and I can be what he is now. But first, I need to earn my place and play his game until I'm ready.

He let a smile form on his lips as he began plotting.

CHAPTER THIRTY-FIVE

After the impromptu rockslide, Victor and Jen took a quick break in the Pentarena's central courtyard, underneath the shade of one of the Arbor Sacré's towering branches, giving them full viewing access to each of the five training sections.

"See those veins in the Arbor Sacré's trunk?" Victor pointed out. "Magic is taken from reserves deep within its trunk and sent throughout Camelore. It's what keeps this haven of ours aloft."

"Wow," Jen marveled as she munched on some of Mira's trail mix. "How much magic does it store?"

"Limitless, as long as the Arbor Sacré remains alive," Victor explained, placing a hand on the tree's ancient bark.

Jen looked up and followed the shimmering veins as the ancient magic coursed from its prismatic leaves and strong branches down to its trunk. There, partially behind the Arbor Sacré, she noticed movement in the astromancy section. She stopped in mid-chew when she realized that it was Gavin, doing some drills with his totem orb.

Victor, seemingly reading her mind, said, "Hey, let's go say hi to Gavin!"

Jen choked, nearly coughing up some half-chewed pretzels and nuts.

"You okay there, Jenny?" Victor asked, holding out her water bottle and back a chuckle.

"Yeah," Jen said, taking the water. "Something went down the wrong pipe, is all." Handing it back, she wiped tears from her eyes and cleared her throat. She set the trail mix bag down and said rather unconvincingly, "Oh, is that who it is?" Jen squinted and slightly leaned forward for extra measure, feigning disinterest. "Nah, he looks busy. We shouldn't interrupt his training."

To her embarrassment, right as Jen finished making the excuse, she saw Gavin put his orb back into his necklace casing, pick up his things, and walk toward the exit.

"Looks like he's all finished," Victor pointed out, clearly enjoying watching Jen squirm. He got up from the bench, but she stayed seated, looking at him with reluctant eyes. Victor laughed and said, "Come on. He'll appreciate it."

Jen pushed herself up and followed Victor, absentmindedly playing with her hair.

As they made their way to Gavin, Jen noticed he had his shirt in his hand and a towel hung around his neck. His toned shoulders and arms glistened in the sunlight as he let the scanner read his handprint to exit the astromancy section. He looked up and smiled brightly at Victor and Jen.

"Hey, what a surprise!" He shook Victor's hand, then waved at Jen.

She felt her cheeks warm up, but didn't look away. "Good to see you, Gavin."

"Likewise," he said, then asked Victor, "What brings you guys here?"

"Jen's first official training session." He smiled proudly at her. "We're taking a break after she caught on a little too quickly."

Gavin raised his eyebrows in mild surprise. "Is that so?" He set down his shirt and pack and grabbed the ends of his towel with both hands.

Jen brushed a strand of curly hair behind one ear, not missing the way his muscles slightly bulged with his movement. "I sorta slammed a boulder into the back barrier." Out of habit, she reached to fiddle with the ring on her necklace, but when she only felt the thin necklace, she remembered it was in Watercress's Sacrarium.

He smiled again and Jen felt a jolt of electricity shoot through her chest as she then started to fidget with her charm bracelet. "On your first day, too? Very Impressive."

She smiled back at him, desperately trying to think of something to say back. "Hopefully we're not interrupting you or anything?"

"Oh, not at all. I just finished up a little training as well. Gotta keep the mind and body strong." He tapped his temple with one finger and pointed up at the sky.

"Totally," Jen agreed, nodding.

"Do you have an astromancer teacher yet?" Gavin asked.

"Mystra Étoilier," Jen responded, still playing with her charm.

"He personally asked for Jen's permission," Victor added.

Gavin was clearly impressed. "He's the strongest astromancer I know. Not many tenderfeet get his approval. You must've shown significant promise when you met him."

"I guess so."

Yep, I'm definitely blushing, thought Jen.

"Well, we don't want to keep you. Jen just wanted to say hi," Victor said.

Jen shot him a quick look before Gavin said, "I'm glad you did." He smiled again at Jen and held her gaze before breaking off toward the exit pathway, waving goodbye. "Time to hit the showers!"

"Bye!" Jen waved, then quickly turned around and said, "Can we get back to training now, Vic?"

"Totally," Victor said, his eyes twinkling.

"Oh, stop it!" She rolled her eyes and lightly slapped Victor on his arm as she made her way back toward their section.

Victor picked up his and Jen's water bottles that were left by the bench, then caught up with her just as she scanned herself into the arena.

She looked at him. "Not another word."

"Okay," was all Victor said, putting a finger up to his lips.

"Thank you."

Jen was surprised that she was having feelings for Gavin—feelings that only seemed to amplify whenever she ran into him—especially after her dysfunctional relationship with Malcolm. She honestly thought that she'd need more time to heal after his utter and complete betrayal; but deep down Jen realized that what she truly needed was someone to fill that void in her heart, someone she could love unconditionally—and who could love her back equally.

Promising herself that she'd sort out her feelings later, Jen reverted back into training mode. "So . . . what's next?"

Victor nodded and walked through the semicircle opening in the barrier, shaking Jen's water bottle then handing it to her.

Jen took the bottle and before she started sipping, she said, "Let me guess: water?"

"Precisely." Victor was once again Mystra Huxley, her terramancy instructor. "Water is the key to life." He led her to the man-made pond off to the left side of the arena. He knelt down and swished the placid water around with two fingers, sending ripples in every direction. "It is constant and dynamic, never still . . . fluid and responsive, always adapting. Terramancers strive to emulate these qualities themselves."

Jen finished her water, not realizing how thirsty she had been, and placed the bottle down on a flat rock next to the pond. "All hydrated!"

Victor nodded. "Let's begin with a simple exercise that'll help you sense the presence of the water." He told Jen to stay where she was while he walked around to the other side of the pond, then called to her, "We'll start with a slow, swaying motion. I'll demonstrate, and when you're ready, fall into rhythm with me."

Victor stuck his staff into the soft grass and swirled his hand above it; its orb glowed a light blue. In one fluid motion, he swung his arms forward like he was unrolling a tablecloth, then retracted them while curling his fingers into his palms. He fell into a rhythm, repeating that motion over and over again as a wave formed in the center of the pond, matching his movements exactly. "Push and pull. Push and pull. You see what I'm doing, Jen?"

Jen acknowledged that she did, noticing how Victor commanded the wave to roll forward then backward. She then copied his stance and waited for the right moment to join into Victor's dance with the wave.

"Remember to focus on the individual hydrogen and oxygen molecules that make up the water. You can control them like you did with the air molecules." Victor nodded, implying that he was ready for her to join him.

Jen closed her eyes and slowly breathed out as she pinpointed the individual molecules in the wave and noticed how smoothly they were moving under Victor's influence. She reached out and felt them respond to her touch as a slight tickling sensation danced across her fingertips. With her eyes still shut, she could feel her nexus reawaken. Opening her hyper-focused eyes, she saw her charm illuminate with the same color. Feeling confident that she had control of the molecules now, she swayed in rhythm with Victor, feeling like an interpretive dancer, as she watched the wave grow a few inches in height.

Jen was completely focused. All she could sense was the water in the deep pond and her nexus's power flowing through her charm. Curious to see if Victor was willing to take it to the next level, she brought her hands well above her head, watching in glee as the wave defied gravity and rose as a shimmering wall right before her eyes. Then, she made a circular motion with her index fingers and the wall of water effortlessly changed into two twirling cyclones, between which she could see Victor.

Jen noticed he had stopped his spell and she was the only one controlling the water. That sudden realization caused her to lose focus. Her eyes stopped glowing as she let the long watery spires crash toward the surface, sending forth a large wave in every direction. Not wanting to drench herself and Victor, she panicked and opened her hands toward the miniature tidal waves.

A weird crackling noise accompanied a waft of cold air that

raised goosebumps on her arms. A large wall of clear ice loomed over her, frozen in place.

Jen heard a muted sound on the other side, and dread shot through her heart.

"Vic? *Vic?!*"

She bolted around the ice sculpture she had unintentionally made to check on her mentor's safety, and was relieved to see him unharmed and laughing. With her hand on her chest, she sighed and walked toward Victor.

"What's so funny?"

Victor leaned on his staff, wiping tears of laughter from his eyes. "You just skipped ahead five lessons. You completely froze every square millimeter of this pond!" Victor slowly clapped his hands, shaking his head in disbelief.

Jen laughed with him, then scratched her head. "I don't know how I even did it."

"You let your instincts take over. That's an important lesson to learn, no matter what kind of sorcerer you are." Victor removed his staff from the ground and finished with, "Always trust your instincts."

Jen mulled over what Victor had said, then conceded, "I don't think my instincts can thaw out the ice, though."

"That's fine. You'll melt it during your last lesson for today." Victor pointed the tip of his staff at the last element Jen had yet to control: fire.

Jen reluctantly looked at the flickering fire as that traumatic childhood memory flashed before her eyes—just as it did in the Chimera Course. She absentmindedly tucked her right arm to her chest, remembering how terrifying it was.

"I-I think the pond can melt on its own. It's pretty warm in here," Jen stammered as she reluctantly followed Victor toward the fire section. She shuddered, finally stopping a few feet short of the charred ground that was strewn with hot coals.

He scrunched his eyebrows and looked at the frozen, curling wave behind him. "It'll take *days* to fully melt. Besides, this'll be a perfect target on which to test your fire spells." He paused, seeing

Jen's uneasy expression, and put a hand on her shoulder. "Hey . . . you can do this, Jen. Just like how you overcame the Chimera Course."

Jen was quiet for a moment. Seeing the burning coals—feeling their heat—transported Jen back to that night. The night she was burned. She bit her lip and looked at the ground.

"I haven't told anybody this, but . . . I was burned once. Badly," she confessed softly.

Victor turned his body so he was looking straight at her, but didn't say anything.

"It's just . . ." She trailed off, then forged ahead. "When I was a little girl, a neighbor of ours was hosting a party one night. They had a nice telescope set up in the backyard to view the stars and full moon, and liters of warm apple cider." Jen grimaced. "I wanted to roast marshmallows, so my parents took me out to the firepit. Right as I stepped up to the fire, a gust of wind blew the flames right into me." Jen rubbed one of the spots that had been burned. "It was pretty bad. Third-degree burns along my right arm and all the way up to the right side of my face." She shivered, reliving the experience. "I went into shock, and my parents sped me to the hospital. Once there, they learned that I had been so badly burned that I needed to have skin grafts. It was too painful to move, let alone breathe, so I stayed the night. I remember waking up the following morning to a room full of doctors and nurses staring at me. They showed me to a mirror and, to my surprise, it looked as if I hadn't been burned at all. I was completely healed."

She looked up at Victor and placed her hand over his, which was still resting on her shoulder.

"They called it a medical miracle. No one could explain how I was able to heal so quickly. I couldn't understand it, either . . . but now it's clear to me that the Ring of Lancaster healed me while I was asleep. I can still remember the pain, though. So intense . . ."

Victor enveloped her in a hug and said, "That's horrible, Jenny. I'm so sorry that happened to you." He gently pulled away, holding her at arm's length and looking into her eyes. "We can focus on fire another day, if you'd like."

Jen drew in a long breath, then quickly let it out. "No. We have to speed up my training so I'm ready for whatever Draconex and his Dark Watchers have in store for us. What do I need to do?"

Victor looked ahead at the fire section. "We're going to make our way to the central basin . . . barefoot." He removed his long cloak as he spoke.

"Barefoot?" Jen shook her head after scanning the large area between her and the basin, which was densely packed with glowing pieces of hot coal. "Why can't I cast an air spell and float over to the tiles right next to the fire?"

Victor finished unlacing his boots and looked up at her. "That would defeat the purpose of learning to control fire, but you are on the right track." He slid his boots off and stood up. "And you have nothing to worry about. I'll be by your side every step of the way." Victor surveyed the hot pathway. "It's more of a mental block than a physical one. That's why non-magical people have been known to calmly walk across hot coals and not get burned."

"Those people are crazy," Jen declared adamantly, feeling like her heart could not race any faster.

"They might be, but you have your nexus protecting you. Come on, take my hand." He extended his hand and waited.

Rolling her eyes, Jen slid off her shoes and grabbed his outstretched hand. "Don't let go."

"You know I won't," Victor reassured her. "Make a straight line to the basin and focus your attention on the coals. Fire is comprised of carbon, hydrogen, oxygen, sulfur, and nitrogen, and its molecules can stay burning for years thanks to the chemical reaction known as combustion. What I need you to do is to negate its combustion effect by adding more oxygen molecules into and around the coals so the temperature drops within a safe range to walk on."

Focusing, Jen visualized her path toward the basin and pinpointed the oxygen molecules above the glowing bed of coals.

"Ready?" Victor asked, gently squeezing her hand.

Jen nervously curled her toes around the grass blades at the edge of the fire section and repeated, "Ready."

Both took an exaggerated step forward, and Jen immediately felt the heat from the ground, causing her adrenaline to spike and her nexus to shut down. She lost her balance and leaned on Victor for support, all the while keeping her foot safely off the bed of coals.

"I can't, I can't, I can't," Jen repeated, shaking her head vigorously as she placed her foot back on the green grass. She was squeezing Victor's arm so tightly she thought his radius and ulna bones would snap, but for the life of her, she could not ease up.

"You can do this, Jenny," Victor said evenly, barely grimacing at Jen's grip. "Control the fire—don't let it control you."

He might as well have been speaking in a different language, because his encouragements were not getting through to Jen. She tried making her breathing less erratic. Finally, she opened her eyes and stared at the coals in front of her. Holding her breath, she held her bare foot over the coals, this time even closer than before, but she could not bring herself to touch the embers.

"I just . . . *can't*," Jen breathed.

Looking toward the Arbor Sacré, Victor said, "You know what? You've done a great job today. Let's call it and try again tomorrow." He put a hand on hers for both physical and emotional support.

All Jen could do was nod. She knew how important it was to not waste any time, but she needed to first overcome this debilitating fear of fire that had been following her around for her whole life. Sighing, she stepped backward, away from the blisteringly hot coals.

"Take your time," she heard Victor say before he asked, "Would you like me to walk you to your hut?"

Jen shook her head. "Thanks, but no. I'll be fine." She glanced back at him and put on her best *I'm okay, don't worry about me* smile.

"I'll be with Skarmor at the griffin stables if you need me.

You've made so much progress today." He rubbed her shoulder before making his way out of the Pentarena.

Quickly, Jen became the only person in the Pentarena, feeling small and weak.

Alone, she stared intently at the basin that held the mystical eternal flame—her training objective. As the sun started to dip in the sky behind her, Jen wondered if she would ever get over her fear and master the element of fire.

CHAPTER THIRTY-SIX

Draconex waited in the interrogation room, his patience getting extremely thin.

How much longer would he put up with Charles Lancaster?

Ever since Draconex took control of the Dark Watchers, he'd purposefully increased the frequency of visits with Charles, hoping to learn the Halostone's location quicker. Unfortunately, he underestimated the trauma Charles had incurred during the explosion and hadn't received an iota's worth of actionable information. Instead, he was forced to go after his long-lost daughter and the Ring of Lancaster, which he came to discover she no longer had. The aggravation that his meticulous plans had been subverted made the scar on his face throb.

To calm himself, Draconex pulled a vial of dark blood from the folds of his cloak and swallowed it with an intense appetite. He shuddered in delight as the smooth, coppery taste washed over his taste buds, down his throat, and into his stomach, quenching his thirst and honing his senses.

His pointed ears twitched as he heard the sound of unlocking latches.

The heavy door opened on rusty hinges to reveal two guards dragging a shackled Charles Lancaster into the interrogation chamber. The years since his capture had not been the least bit kind to the omnimancer. Charles was easily forty pounds underweight, with long, shaggy jet-black hair and a beard belonging to a man who hadn't shaved or showered in years. His clothes were torn to shreds and his feet bore thick calluses that had formed from lack of footwear. Draconex's scar flushed deeper when he set eyes on his emaciated prisoner, unexpectedly unconscious.

"What have you done to him?" the dark sorcerer demanded.

"He was being uncooperative, sir," the tall guard breathed.

Draconex was losing his patience. "Do you know when he will wake?"

The guards exchanged dumbfounded glances before one stammered, "M-my best guess?"

"Rouse him!" Draconex shouted, towering over both guards, then became eerily quiet. "Now."

The guards clamped their mouths shut and nodded their heads incessantly before clumsily plopping the limp prisoner on a chair and charging their rings with their respective nexus. Draconex could have easily woken up Charles, but he liked pulling rank and instilling fear in his peons. He watched as the short guard rubbed his ring fingers together before placing one on each side of Charles's sternum. Taking a deep breath, the guard willed his totem rings to illuminate and expel an electrical charge. Like a defibrillator, the jolt shocked Charles awake.

A smile curled Draconex's lips, reveling in the pain inflicted to the shell of Charles Lancaster. It was hard to believe that he had once been friends with this shadow of a person, back when they were both tenderfeet.

Children make mistakes, Draconex thought.

After Charles's eyes fluttered open, he locked his gaze on Draconex, who cocked his head to the side in mild surprise, sensing a change within the amnesiac omnimancer. Draconex slithered and stopped right in front of Charles's face, trying to intimidate him. Charles didn't even blink.

The guards noticed it too. "He could still be recovering from the shock, sir," said the first guard.

Draconex sneered at the one who talked, baring his sharp teeth. He looked again at Charles. "Welcome back."

Charles stared through Draconex, acting as though he didn't hear him. The dark sorcerer stood to his full height and clasped his hands behind his back. "I think we're making progress. Pray that I'm not wrong."

If he didn't move his chest up and down to breathe, Charles could've been mistaken for a statue. Draconex audibly exhaled all of the air from his lungs, feeling his blood begin to boil.

"What . . . is . . . your . . . name?" he slowly asked.

Charles pursed his lips and several seconds passed.

"Name!" Draconex demanded, this time louder.

"Prisoner 51493," Charles stated.

With the speed of a coiled-up snake, Draconex pulled out a butterfly knife and, masterfully flicking it open, sunk it deep into Charles's left thigh. He felt the knife blade nick his prisoner's femur bone, sending a jolt of insatiable pleasure through his body. Charles flinched as he stared down at his leg. Draconex was hoping he would scream out in pain, but was disappointed when he saw Charles stay silent and close his eyes.

"Name," Draconex whispered menacingly. He twisted the knife, tearing more muscles in the process.

A single tear, followed by a shuddering breath. "*You* say that I'm Charles Lancaster."

Draconex scoffed in frustration. "That's because you *are* him, the last mystra omnimancer in all of the realms."

"You're mistaken. How can I be this Charles Lancaster if I can't remember who I am?" Charles retorted, a look of utter indignance upon his face.

Draconex turned away and rubbed his temples with bony fingers, not bothering to pull out his knife from Charles's thigh. "You sustained a severe head trauma when you and your wife were caught in an explosion on Ocuul twenty years ago. You survived by casting a protection spell, but the blast left you in a coma and your wife dead," he said, turning to stare intently at Charles's face.

Charles's eyebrows raised but a millimeter—enough to be noticed by Draconex. A surge of excitement flowed through him. There it was, a flicker of recognition in those steel-blue eyes of his former friend.

The first real result in years. This changes everything, thought Draconex.

Switching tactics, he said aloud, "You don't even remember your beloved wife? That's probably a good thing, considering how she died."

The Dark Watcher leader never took his eyes off Charles, who was visibly flushed and continued to stare at the ground. Draconex began to pace.

"The explosion was too much for her meager powers, so much so that it ripped her apart, but only enough for the real Charles Lancaster to hold her as she died in his arms."

Draconex stopped right in front of his cuffed prisoner, pausing for effect.

"You can't imagine the dread I felt when I heard of that tragic event . . . after all, I courted her when we were younger."

That caused Charles to shoot a malicious look at Draconex, who let the side of his mouth twitch.

He's beginning to remember.

"We were perfect for each other." Draconex bit his lower lip and looked away, feigning sorrow. "But she ended up choosing an entitled, conceited, weak *imp*."

Hoping for a reaction, Draconex turned back around once he heard the metal legs of the chair scrape the stone floor to see Charles seizing, fighting against his restraints.

Finally . . .

Charles's long, scraggily hair and unkempt beard masked the majority of his face, but the open skin around his nose and cheeks turned a bright red due to the effort. Veins protruded from the side of his neck. His eyes rolled into his head as he began to convulse wildly, causing his chair to rock from side to side.

"Mintaka," he said through clenched teeth.

Suddenly he slipped into unconsciousness, going limp in his restraints.

Convinced that Charles had fully regained his memory, Draconex took this opportunity to read his prisoner's mind. He licked his lips in anticipation of finally unearthing the location of the Halostone, but tensed up when he felt a powerful warding spell block his dark magic. Exasperated, Draconex ground his sharp teeth together, biting his tongue and the inside of his cheeks as he worked his lower jaw in a circular motion, but he didn't care. As the taste of his own warm, coppery blood filled his mouth, he berated himself for not expecting an impregnable warding spell from Charles as a last resort.

Again, just another obstacle in his path.

His scar turned the deepest red it had ever been.

The two guards stood at attention in the corner of the chamber and flinched when Draconex let out an ear-splitting yell that was accompanied by a breath of searing flames.

"He stays here until I say so. I'm not finished with him," he said to the petrified guards.

Draconex pulled his bloodied butterfly knife out of Charles and kicked his chair over. It tipped on its side, sending Charles crashing to the ground in a heap as Draconex stormed out.

Shaking from frayed nerves after witnessing Draconex breathe fire, the guards waited for their commander to clear the chamber before they bolted out, leaving Charles to bleed out on the ground.

* * *

Malcolm's eyes flicked open. He could sense a wall of furious aggravation headed his way.

"Draconex is coming," he said aloud.

Madame Diaema tensed up in fear, then slid off the armrest and tugged at Malcolm's arm. "All right, time's up—off of his throne."

Malcolm mulled it over. "I'm sort of curious to see how he'd react if he saw me sitting here." He rubbed the dragon-headed armrests.

"*I* can tell you how he'd react," she snapped at him. "He'd kill you because you're *on his throne*, then me because I let you *sit* on his throne."

Malcolm calmly stared at Diaema, watching her wiggle in fear. Finally, he stood up and resumed his place on his knees in front of the throne.

"Remember: not a word to Lord Draconex," she reminded Malcolm before morphing into an albino bat and latching onto a branch, gently swaying upside down.

Malcolm smirked and closed his eyes, just as Draconex flung the door of his den wide open, nearly knocking several flaming torches from the walls. His ears picked up the quickened gait of his master; his nostrils detected a hint of burnt fabric.

Stomping past Malcolm, who was pretending to meditate, Draconex paused before the Throne of Dragons and sniffed the air. Malcolm opened his eyes just in time to see Diaema's beady little eyes fill with terror. He would have felt the same, if it wasn't for the boost of courage from his time sitting on the Throne of Dragons.

What—or who—got him so angry? thought Malcolm.

As if Draconex had heard his inner thoughts, he spun around and snapped his fingers at the boy. "Get off your ass and follow me. I've given you enough time to be ready for your next lesson." He walked so close that his cape, fluttering out behind him, brushed over Malcolm's face.

"You have no idea," Malcolm whispered back, slowly getting up off of his knees and following the dark sorcerer with a wicked grin.

CHAPTER THIRTY-SEVEN

Jen was torn.

With every fiber of her being, she wanted nothing more than to never be around fire again, but she needed to continue her training so she could rescue her parents and have a fighting chance in this war against the Dark Watchers.

So, with that mentality, Jen found herself back in the Pentarena the next day with Victor—barefoot—staring dreadfully down at the simmering, hot coals, trying to keep herself from unraveling with grief. Knowing full well that she had to walk on those coals to get to her objective, the basin with the floating flame—much like the Eternal Flame—Jen rocked from side to side, anxiously cracking her knuckles.

Victor was by her side, patiently letting her announce when to start.

"I'm sorry," Jen said softly.

Victor furrowed his brow, looking at her. "About what?"

"For disappointing you yesterday."

Grimacing, he looked squarely at her. "Jen, look at me. I'm not disappointed in you. On the contrary—I'm quite proud."

Now it was Jen's turn to be confused. "What do you mean?"

"You came back here to face your fear." He gestured to the fire section of the arena. "Not many people do that. You're not giving up, and that makes me proud."

Jen looked away, letting a few seconds pass before asking, "How do you do it? Not get scared?"

"Jenny . . . I *am* scared. Terrified. This situation we're in . . . it's a lot to ask of anyone. But what I've learned during my time fighting Dark Watchers is that my fears will never go away. The key is to not let those fears get the best of me, no matter how scared I am. What you're doing here is the first step in making sure you use your fears to your advantage—*that* is how you are going to rescue your parents and help us find the Halostone before the Dark Watchers do."

Jen found the strength to look Victor in the eye. "You really think I'm strong enough?"

"You are the strongest person I've ever met. I believe in you."

Feeling the warmth of tears forming in her eyes, she hugged Victor and started crying.

"Let it out." Victor wrapped his arms around her, making Jen feel protected and safe.

For an instant she forgot about the fire and focused on how much Victor cared about her. Every step of this journey, he had been by her side with endless support. It was time for her to show Victor that she was as capable as he thought she was.

Wiping away her tears, she said, "You have no idea how much that means to me."

"I believe in you. Now it's your turn to believe in yourself." He winked.

Jen let go of Victor and felt compelled to walk closer to the coal-infested ground. "I can do this . . . I *need* to." Saying it more to herself than Victor.

Filling her lungs with fresh air, she closed her eyes and reached deep into her nexus, this time taking her traumatic memory and nightmares with her. Surprisingly, she felt her fears ignite a chain reaction within her nexus, sending unprecedented energy to every nerve throughout her body.

What Jen felt next could only be classified as an out-of-body experience.

Jen saw herself standing at the edge of the lava-cracked ground, slightly glowing. She wondered if she could still control her body, so she tried to step onto the coals. Almost immediately, she saw her eyes flash open, glowing a brilliant light purple, and her left leg step onto several glowing coal pieces. The coals felt comfortably warm, as if she were stepping on sun-kissed stones near the shore of a lake.

She watched Victor start toward her but immediately stop when he saw Jen touch the sizzling ground. Jen was amazed that she could see all around her and still have control over her body.

She felt more confident than ever before, so with every step she took, she sent oxygen down upon the coals that were in her path. Before she knew it, she had made it onto the tile platform that held the central basin—she had made it all by herself.

As Jen felt her nexus draw her spirit back into her body, she saw Victor lightly pad toward her, kicking up embers as he flew across the coals.

"Whoa . . ." Jen exclaimed as her vision returned to her body's perspective.

"That was simply amazing! I knew you had it in you," Victor said, clapping.

"You were the one who helped me find my peace, Vic," Jen said, smiling. "I feel . . . renewed."

"You look it," he said. "You ready for this next part?"

"One thing: do my eyes glow when I use my powers?"

Victor chuckled. "They do. Another sign that you are an omnimancer. You know the saying 'Eyes are the windows to the soul'?"

Jen nodded.

"Well, they're also the windows to the nexus."

"Cool . . ." Jen flicked her hair behind her shoulders with a hand.

"A trait that I wish I had, believe me," Victor added as he brought his hand into the basin, scooping up a portion of the fire. The remaining flames grew back to their original size, unfazed.

"Now, like I said before, adept sorcerers can conjure fire out of thin air. But for our training, we will practice with some that has already been created."

He held out the ball of flame in his cupped hands. Jen was amazed at how it floated an inch above Victor's palms, making a bright yellow-orange bowl that extended upward into flickering fingers of flame.

"Fire sets itself apart from the other elements because of its unpredictable, volatile, and destructive nature. That is why it's our final stop for today. Unlike the other elements, fire cannot be controlled, only contained."

He kept his left hand underneath the flame and brought his right one above it, then lowered his hand, turning the bowl of fire into a cube, then a pyramid. With a quick flick of his hands, the fire disappeared, sending out a hot breeze.

He continued, "Like all matter, fire can be converted into many shapes and forms, like superheated air."

Victor clasped his hands tightly together. Suddenly, Jen could see light trying to break through the spaces between his fingers. Then he slowly opened his hands to reveal a single flame that grew larger before her eyes.

"Magical," she breathed.

"Sorcery *is* magic, but it is truly rooted in science and chemistry. You just have to know where to look."

Victor held the flame out to Jen, who froze—for just a second. Steeling herself, she let her fears flow through her nexus and focused on the fire's molecules. Once she felt confident that she had locked onto them, she quickly scooped it into her hands, willing the flame to levitate safely above her bare palms. Jen watched as the fire swayed to the rocking motion of her hands, as if she were putting a newborn baby to sleep.

"There you go," Victor said encouragingly. "Now grow the flame by getting the oxygen, nitrogen, and carbon dioxide molecules to the ignition point of your flame."

Jen slitted her eyes as she focused on sending her nexus's power to the molecules that surrounded the flame she held.

Almost immediately, the flame doubled in size, then quadrupled.

"Good," Victor said calmly, careful to not disrupt Jen's focus. "You remember how I converted my flame into superheated air?"

Jen nodded, still staring at her enlarging fireball.

"I used fission to split the molecules. I want you to do the same thing over the ice." He pointed to the other end of the arena at the frozen pond.

Jen took her eyes off of the flames to glance at the frozen wave of water. "Okay . . . but I'm afraid if I move, the flames will go out."

"That's fine. You can float it over the center of the pond from here, but once you do, spread out the fire until it covers the area above the pond."

Jen took a deep breath and willed the fire to be carried on a blanket of air molecules. Like a hot air balloon, it rose and glided silently away from her until it was squarely above the icy pond. Jen spread her hands apart, flattening the fire so it hovered a foot above the ice.

Satisfied with Jen's placing, Victor said, "Good. Now use fission to split all the molecules in the fire. This'll superheat the air, causing the ice to melt."

Jen, still reaching out toward the fire, locked onto every molecule with her mind and, using her nexus, rapidly tore through each and every one. Almost immediately, the orange glow above the pond vanished, leaving behind a swath of blazing-hot air.

"Now contain it," Victor said, "and fully encapsulate the ice."

Jen blocked the hot air from escaping then lowered her arms, causing it to descend over and around the chilled pond. Steam became noticeable as the ice started to splinter and crack from the abrupt change in temperature, causing huge chunks to break off and slam onto the ground, where they then melted. Before long, the pond was completely shrouded in a dense blanket of steam which quickly pervaded the entire terramancy section. Feeling as though she was in a sauna, Jen waited several seconds before she saw that the pond had completely melted, the only noticeable difference being its lower water level.

"Well done! You couldn't have done that better," Victor said as he spun his staff off to the side.

Jen's eyes focused once more and she said, "Thank you . . . but I couldn't have done it without your help, per usual."

Victor made his way off the coal bed and Jen followed. "You did all the heavy lifting—plus, you showed extreme control over all of the basic elements today." He paused, then added, "But thank you." He winked and leaned his shoulder into Jen's.

Jen nudged him back as they set foot onto the green, grassy sod.

As they were putting their shoes back on, Victor said, "Well, you definitely deserve the rest of the day off. Would you like to see what Skarmor is up to?"

"Would I ever!" Jen said enthusiastically. She had so much she wanted to tell Skarmor as he took her on a nice, relaxing flight around Camelore. "I've missed him so much!"

"Oh, he misses you too," Victor mentioned as they made their way out of the Pentarena. "The past couple of times I've visited him, he keeps checking behind me to see if you're there."

Jen placed her hands over her heart. "Aw, Skar . . ."

* * *

Outside of the griffin stable's entrance, Jen was waving to her favorite griffin when she doubled over in immense pain, a migraine suddenly blossoming in her head. Victor reached out to steady her as Skarmor screeched in concern and landed by her side. Her ears rang with a crippling intensity and her skin felt numb to the touch.

"Jenny—Jen, what's wrong?"

Jen barely heard Victor as another wave of nauseating pain shot through her. She sharply inhaled through gritted teeth, unable to put what she was feeling into words. Jen dropped to her knees as she pinched her eyelids shut and rubbed the sides of her temples, willing the massive migraine to go away. For a millisecond, an image flashed in her mind's eye, one so strong that it felt as though it had burned itself into the insides of her eyelids. Focusing on the image, she was able to pick out Lord Draconex, who was shoving a sharp knife in her thigh—but, she realized, it wasn't *her* thigh. She could feel a dull pain where the knife had struck, but when she opened her eyes to check, her leg was completely unscathed. Then, without warning, more images rushed through her mind, like flipping through a photo album at blinding speed. The images were moving at such a high velocity that it became impossible for Jen to distinguish between them, eventually fading into white light. As if a light bulb inside her mind had exploded, everything went dark. Jen cautiously opened her eyes to see Victor and Mira looking down at her, wearing worried expressions.

"Mira?" Jen was surprised to see her.

"What happened, Jen?" Mira repeated the question Victor had asked, and together, they helped Jen sit up.

Jen labored as she drew in a few quick breaths, feeling the pain slowly subside and her strength return. "I don't know." Her mouth had gone bone-dry. Victor noticed and gave her his water bottle. She took it with both hands and shakily put the nozzle to her lips. Relief washed over her as the lukewarm water splashed over her tongue and gums. She swallowed; water had never tasted so good before.

"Thank you," she said, setting down the bottle and preparing to answer both Victor and Mira's question. "I had another vision . . . I saw Draconex stab me in the thigh." Jen put a hand on her left leg where the knife had protruded. "But it wasn't *my* thigh . . . it was someone else's."

Victor pursed his lips and furrowed his brow. "Do you know whose it was?"

Jen shook her head. "No, but I sensed that it was a man's, like I was looking through his eyes."

Skarmor bent down and brushed his head on hers.

270

"Before anything else happens, we'd better get you inside," Victor advised. "Mira, do you have her hammock ready?"

"I just finished it before coming to the stables," Mira said.

"Good. Jen, can you make it back to the hut?"

Jen used Victor's arms for balance as she stood up, but immediately grew lightheaded. Her legs buckled, and Victor steadied her before she fell down again.

"Skarmor," he called. "Sedere." On command, his trusty griffin sat down. Victor laid Jen on his back, interlocking her arms around his feathered neck. "Skarmor will take you to the hut. Just hang on. We'll be right behind you," Victor assured her.

"Thank you." Jen closed her eyes and let Skarmor take her into the air.

* * *

By the time they arrived at the hut, Skarmor was already safely on the ground and Jen was sitting upright, waiting for them. "I'm feeling much better," she said to them.

"You should still rest." Victor took Jen's hand as she slid off of Skarmor.

"Thanks, boy." Jen patted Skarmor on his neck. He cooed in gratitude as he stretched his mighty wings.

Victor made Jen hold onto his arm as he took her inside the hut.

"I hope the hammock is to your liking," Mira said as she held the door open for them. "If you need it firmer, I can always tighten the cords."

Jen found two identical hammocks across from each other, hers with a purple throw folded on it. "This looks beautiful," Jen said as she laid down, "and feels so comfy."

"Phew!" Mira pretended to wipe sweat from her forehead. "Is there anything else you need? Oh, I'll get you some more water!" Answering her own question, Mira left the hut for the communal well.

Jen put a hand on her forehead and asked, "Do you know what happened to me, Vic?"

"I have no clue . . . but I believe your telemancy powers are starting to awaken. My guess is that you picked up on the distress of a fellow telemancer." Victor crossed his arms and shook his head. "It doesn't make any sense, though. Why would Draconex be torturing a telemancer?" He looked at Jen again. "Is there anything else that you can remember from your vision?"

Jen closed her eyes and began retracing her steps. "I saw Draconex in front of me, then felt a sharp knife in my left thigh . . ." Jen grimaced as she tried to remember more. "Then I heard someone—I'm assuming the telemancer—say . . . 'Mintaka'?"

A clatter sounded, so she opened her eyes to see that Victor had dropped his staff.

"Vic, is everything okay?"

Victor was speechless, frozen in shock.

Before he could speak, Mira came in with a gallon of water. "This should keep you hydrated for a while." Sloshing the liquid back and forth, she walked to the opposite end of the hut to pour Jen a glass.

"Vic?" Jen asked again.

"Yes," Victor said distantly. He went to the side of her hammock and took her hand. "Are you certain you heard that word? 'Mintaka'?"

"Completely." Jen cocked her head to the side in question. "Vic, you're scaring me."

Victor put on a soft smile and squeezed her hand. "There's nothing to worry about, Jenny. Right now, the most important thing for you is to rest. I need to return to Watercress. I'll be gone for a few hours. You'll be fine while I'm gone?"

"Yeah, of course." Jen squinted, suspicious. "Is there something else you're not telling me?"

Mira was patiently waiting in the wings with a glass of water as Victor hesitated. "All in good time." Victor smiled again and said, "Mira will take care of you while I'm gone. I shouldn't be long." He let go of Jen's hand so she could take the glass from Mira. He made his way toward the door. "I'll see you soon."

"No. I'm coming with you," she insisted, making a move to get out of the hammock.

"Jen," Victor said, rather sternly, then reverted back to a sympathetic tone. "You've just been through a harsh episode of a mind meld. You need to rest."

Jen searched his eyes, hoping to glean the secret she knew he was keeping.

"I'll fill you in when I return," he conceded. "Trust me."

"You know where to find me."

Jen crossed her arms, feeling a twinge of frustration and sadness as she watched him leave the hut. This was the first time Victor had voluntarily left her side since he had shown up on her birthday. Taking a sip of water, she couldn't believe that had been only a week ago; it felt like years.

"You do look a lot better," Mira said, jerking Jen from her thoughts.

"Thanks." Jen rubbed the glass with both of her thumbs as she sat back down on her hammock, thinking. "I've had visions before, but this one was the most intense. I'm glad it's over with." Jen took another sip of water.

"I can only imagine how it felt." Mira took a seat on her hammock, rocking herself with her feet.

Jen swung her legs off the side of her hammock so she was facing Mira. "I'm glad you were there to help me, though." She smiled, raising her glass to her friend. "Were you also there to go riding?"

"I actually work as a stable-hand," Mira said. "I help care for the griffins when I'm not training. It's like my second home."

"Oh, that's awesome! I'm not surprised, given your love of animals," Jen pointed out.

"Very true." Mira laughed. "I'm hoping that Mystra Wingelius will let me adopt one when I make Paladin."

"Why can't you adopt one now?"

"Tenderfeet aren't allowed to care for any creatures during

training," Mira said disappointedly. "Having one is said to distract us from our 'development.' " She made air quotations with her fingers around the word *development*.

Jen laughed. "How close are you to finishing your training?"

"I'm on my last year!" Mira said excitedly. "I can't *wait* to begin the Sorcery Trials . . . but I'll miss seeing Mystra Wingelius every day. I've studied under her for eight years."

"Eight *years*?" Jen repeated, astonished. She didn't think she had close to that amount of time to learn terramancy, let alone the other four Mancy planes.

"Yep, since I was ten years old!"

Just then, Jen realized that she had become too hard on herself. Learning sorcery took time, and she shouldn't have expected to pick up each Mancy plane with sudden ease.

"I'm sure it'll be quite an adjustment," Jen said, nodding, "but you seem more than ready."

"I hope so." Mira played with her single braid as she rocked back and forth in her hammock .

Fatigue hit Jen unexpectedly, so she finished the glass of water and said, "Thanks for the water, Mira." She set it down on the floor beneath her hammock. "I'm still a little bit out of it, so I think I'm going to take a quick nap." She tucked her legs back into the hammock and unfolded the throw cover over her body.

"Good idea. We need you to get back to full strength." Mira got up from her hammock and put Jen's glass on the small counter next to the sink. "I'll be tidying up the stables if you need me." She smiled and left, closing the door behind her.

As if the lights were reading Jen's thoughts—*Maybe they are!* she thought—they dimmed down enough so she could fall asleep. Getting comfortable, she nestled in her hammock while her mind kept replaying her vision.

Who was Draconex torturing . . . and why did she see—and feel—it?

And why did Victor react that way when he heard the word "Mintaka"?

With those questions plaguing her mind, she fell into a troubled sleep.

* * *

Malcolm couldn't wait to surprise Draconex with his boosted power; couldn't wait to see the shock on his face; couldn't wait to finally pass one of his demented tests. But it was he who was surprised when Draconex led him back to his chambers.

Draconex stopped and half-turned so Malcolm could see him cross his arms in impatience. "Well, aren't you going to let me in?"

"Yes, Master." He cautiously walked past Draconex and slid the face of his totem ring into the matching indentation on the handle, opening the door. His chamber almost immediately self-illuminated, torches springing to life on every wall. Keeping the door open, Malcolm gestured inside. "Would you like to come in?"

Draconex silently walked past him, the only sound the flutter of his thick cape. He glided to the center of the room and turned around to face his apprentice. "From the state of disrepair you left my chamber in after our last lesson, you've shown me that you can tap into dark magic well enough. But once you did, you let *it* control *you*. That was your first mistake. It's important to know that dark magic is not only an independent entity, but also one that can be tamed. It has a nasty habit of deceiving a sorcerer into believing that he has all the control, when in reality, it's the complete opposite. If you're not careful enough, dark magic makes you its conduit for destruction and anarchy.

"The true mark of a worthy sorcerer," Draconex continued, glaring at Malcolm, "a rank I'm skeptical that you can attain—is when he becomes dominant over dark magic and uses its power to augment his deepest desires and lower his restricting inhibitions."

Without saying a word, Malcolm reached deep within himself and let his emotions rise. He became angry for constantly being thought of as weak and stupid; envious of Draconex's power and ambition; hateful of everyone who had ever scorned him; arrogant that he deserved to be the first to find the Halostone. He let all of these emotions stir as Draconex continued with his pompous lecture.

"Now that we're in your chambers," Draconex said, clasping his hands in front of his dragon-enameled belt, "feel free to break *your* belongings when the dark magic again proves too challenging for you."

Almost immediately after he finished speaking, Draconex was taken clear across the room and slammed into Malcolm's bookshelf by a ball of condensed air, rattling several books loose. They clattered to the floor as Draconex gasped for air, his diaphragm spasming from the unexpected spell.

"Try . . . that again . . . *boy*. You won't . . . be so . . . lucky."

WHOOOOOOOOSHHHHH!

A quick breeze picked up and extinguished all the lit torches until darkness reigned. Draconex adapted by channeling the night vision of a bengal tiger just in time to see Malcolm rush toward him. Using the agility of a patas monkey, Draconex leapt up and dodged Malcolm's body slam, twirling away just as the boy rammed into the bookshelf, knocking more books loose. Malcolm cried out in frustration as he illuminated the torches once more and turned around, flinging the discarded books at Draconex on pockets of air.

"You're going to have to use more than just terramancy to beat me, boy," Draconex said as he batted away the books like harmless houseflies, "or can you not command any dark magic to help you channel the other mystical planes?"

His rhetorical question was met with more books until the floor and shelves were empty.

Without saying anything else, Draconex summoned dark magic to invoke astromancy. As his eyes turned fully black, he raised his hands, lifting Malcolm off the ground with a zero-gravity spell.

Malcolm, expecting this, snickered, his eyes also turning black.

He immediately countered by increasing the gravity of the chamber tenfold. He gracefully regained his footing while his master was crushed to the ground, wheezing from the immense pressure.

"Is this what you wanted, *Master*?" Malcolm retorted as he stood over Draconex, who was still immobilized and couldn't move his hands to protect himself or conjure any counter spells. Increasing the crushing weight on the dark sorcerer, Malcolm let the dark magic flow through his nexus and gain access to the astromancy plane.

"I see that you've tamed the nexus within you." Draconex barely had enough air left in his lungs to speak. He knew Malcolm had bested him, but the lesson wasn't over yet. "Though I doubt that would make any difference if you saw the Lancaster girl again."

Malcolm clenched his jaw. "She doesn't stand a chance."

"You've said that before, and yet she's still out there. Either you're not as powerful as her, or . . ." His lungs were quickly losing air.

"That's not true," Malcolm whispered, fighting the urge to murder Draconex.

"You . . . *love* . . . her," Draconex said just as he ran out of air.

"*That's not true!*" Malcolm yelled as his eyes returned to their normal color and he lost focus, releasing his hold on the gravity spell.

* * *

Capitalizing on the boy's moment of weakness, Draconex knocked Malcolm to the ground with a quick leg sweep. Looking behind him, he noticed a full beaker resting on a table. Using terramancy, Draconex drew the liquid from the container and froze it just as he shot it into Malcolm's nostrils. Stunned from the cold and the inability to breathe out of his nose, Malcolm's strength abandoned him. Draconex placed a leathery hand over his mouth, fully cutting off his supply of fresh air.

"I'll admit, you had me for a second . . . but you made the mistake of letting me get inside your head."

Draconex poked Malcolm's forehead with a filed fingernail several times, drawing blood. Malcolm clawed for air, but Draconex's hand remained immovable over the boy's mouth as he channeled the strength of an African bush elephant. Licking the blood from his fingertip, he pushed harder on the boy's mouth and heard a muffled scream.

"You're so pathetic. Love only makes you weak and undeserving of power. You leave me no choice now."

With dead eyes, Draconex watched his apprentice start to convulse as his lungs fought for air. Malcolm was getting weaker with every passing second, until his eyes rolled to the back of his head, deprived of oxygen—and passing yet another test.

* * *

A dull headache brought Charles back from unconsciousness, letting forgotten memories rush back into his mind. He was overjoyed to remember his wife, Jocelyn, but that feeling was momentary as he also remembered that she had died in the same explosion that gave him amnesia. The same emotional turmoil came when he thought of his baby girl, Jennifer; he didn't even know what she looked like now. Determined more than ever to see her again, he tried moving his arms and legs, only to find that they were still bound together. With effort, he opened his eyes to see not darkness, but the world on its side, which meant that he was still in the lighted interrogation room.

Draconex wasn't done with him.

Moving his sore neck muscles, Charles slowly craned his head around to check if anyone was nearby. After he was certain he was alone, he shimmied off the chair and rolled to the nearest wall to prop himself up. He didn't know how long he'd been out, but he guessed several hours because the blood from his thigh wound had dried on his tattered pants. Since his ankles and wrists were still bound, he couldn't fight his way out of Feralot . . . not yet.

Thinking about the Ring of Lancaster, he instinctively rubbed his right ring finger with his thumb and was caught off guard when he felt only bare skin. His chest sank in defeat when he realized that he had asked Richard and Beth Smith to protect the ring, along with Jennifer.

Richard! Charles remembered.

He tried reaching into his nexus to tap into telemancy so he could communicate with his old friend, but it was extremely difficult, nearly impossible, like walking on legs that have atrophied from years of disuse. In his desperation, he didn't give up. With each attempt at telemancy, he grew stronger, repeating his friend's name until he felt a channel open up.

Richard . . . Richard!

* * *

Charles hadn't been returned to his cell, which was making both Richard and Beth worried. Usually the guards brought him back a few hours after his interrogation, depending on the level of torture that he underwent. By now the guards had tossed in two daily rations, indicating to Richard that it was closing in on twenty-four hours—one full day—since Charles was taken away from the Smiths.

And just when they'd discovered his true identity.

It wasn't fair.

Beth had been awakened by the conflict that had ensued when Charles refused to leave his cell, so Richard had explained to her his unbelievable realization. Beth had broken down in tears—both happy and sad. Happy to hear that their dear friend was still alive, but sad that he had lost his memory and languished in the Lair of Despair for nearly twenty years while they raised his daughter.

They had anxiously awaited Charles's return so they could help him remember more and possibly ask him further questions. Now, their spirits were fading as another hour ticked away into the ever-hungry darkness, still with no sound of Charles.

"Does he know where Jocelyn is?" Richard asked her husband after a good period of silence.

"I didn't get a chance to ask him. His memory was starting to come back in fragments when the guards took him." Richard paused. "Beth . . . I saw Charles's face. The guards knocked him out with some kind of spell, but it gave off a flash of light. He looked so gaunt."

Beth slid over and gave him a hug. "Maybe now that you've helped him remember who he is, he'll find it in himself to get stronger."

"I hope you're right, honey." Richard rubbed his wife's back, praying that he would be able to see Charles once again—when, all of a sudden, he heard a distant voice.

Richard . . . Richard . . .

At first, Richard thought someone in the cell bay was trying to get his attention. But Beth would have heard it too. Instead, she gave no indication she'd heard a thing. He shook his head, scared that he was beginning to show signs of dementia from being in this hellhole of a prison for too long. But the voice kept saying his name; the voice sounded eerily familiar.

Richard . . . can you hear me?

Who is this? Richard thought.

It's me, Charles.

Charles?! How are you doing this? Richard was more relieved that his friend was still alive than concerned that he might be developing schizophrenia.

Thanks to you, I now fully remember who I am and the powers I possess. One of them is telemancy, which gives me telepathic abilities, Charles explained.

I'm so thankful you're alive! Richard thought. *Beth and I thought we lost you for good this time.*

Don't count your blessings just yet. Draconex isn't done with me now that he knows I've regained my memory.

Beth, having noticed that Richard was distracted, put a soft hand on his cheek. "Honey, are you okay?"

Richard didn't respond, not breaking his concentration.

What does he want from you? he sent to Charles.

Richard felt Charles put up a mental wall before he said, *Something that I don't want you to have the burden of knowing. I couldn't bear to live with myself if Draconex found out that I had told you.*

I understand, Richard thought to Charles. *I probably wouldn't be much help anyway.*

Richard, you cared about me even before you knew who I really was. You've helped more than you can imagine, and I'm even more indebted to you than ever before.

Richard smiled for the first time since he was imprisoned. *Help me and Beth escape and we're even,* he said, adding levity to their deep conversation.

There was the hint of a chuckle in Charles's voice. *Trust me, I'm not leaving this place without you.*

Richard then felt a spike in alertness from his friend. *Charles?*

Draconex is on his way back. I have to go. Charles was curt, understandably so. *Richard, no one can find out that we're telepathically linked, or they'll hurt you and Beth. I'll reach out when I can. Stay strong.* Charles quickly cut his link with Richard.

"Rick? Is everything okay?"

"Yeah, everything's fine . . ." Richard held onto her tighter, fighting the urge to tell his wife about his conversation with Charles.

CHAPTER THIRTY-EIGHT

As Skarmor touched down on the Elder courtyard lawn, Victor was already off, making his way with a barely contained eagerness to see Grand Mystra Cindergray.

Victor reminded himself not to get his hopes up, but the more he thought about it, the more he wanted—*needed*—it to be true. If he was correct, the balance of the war would shift; in whose favor, though, was still unclear.

With a confident push, he opened the doors into the Elder Synod's council chamber and strode up to the Well of Mystras. Victor chose Cindergray's dye and squeezed a droplet into the well, watching the colored liquid plume out and illuminate. Reminding himself that he was in the hallowed Elder Synod chamber, Victor calmed himself and patiently waited as a bright light emanated from the central chair up on the dais. Before long, the light coalesced into the sitting form of Grand Mystra Cindergray, who smiled at his visitor.

"Victor. It's good to see you."

"Grand Mystra." Victor bowed for a count of three seconds.

"What brings this unexpected but most welcome visit?" Cindergray asked.

"I saw the white buffalo grazing in the fields of Elysium." Victor held his breath as he saw Cindergray recognize the code.

"Let's hope we don't scare it away," he replied with the prescribed response and waved Victor toward him.

The terramancer ascended the steps to Cindergray's chair and was enveloped in white light as he was transported to the Grand Mystra's private office.

* * *

In the shadows, hidden behind a pillar, a dark figure slinked away.

* * *

As Victor felt his physical body manifest in the sanctity of Cindergray's office, he felt more at ease. Cindergray let go of his arm and walked over to his desk.

"I'm glad Jennifer is safe on Camelore," Cindergray said, interpreting Victor's coded message. He sat down slowly, as if in pain.

"It was a close call, but yes. Draconex ambushed us after Jen received her totem from Mystra Hephalon." Victor saw Cindergray tense up. "His dragon took her away, but she managed to escape."

Cindergray was surprised. "How did she accomplish that?"

"On instinct," Victor said, still impressed by Jen's maneuver. "She used the moltic spell, letting the dragon carry away a mold while she landed in the cover of the Amaranthine Forest."

"Merlin's beard!" Cindergray exclaimed, standing up. Victor had never seen Cindergray so animated. He leaned over the desk on his knuckles. "Her nexus is more powerful than I had realized."

"She amazes me every day," Victor said with a proud smile.

"Even so, Draconex must be getting desperate if he showed his face. This worries me," Cindergray said with a stone expression, sitting back down.

"I agree, and that's why I'm accelerating Jen's training."

"Good, then I shall leave for Camelore to instruct her sooner than expected." Cindergray played with his tasseled beard as he thought.

Victor swallowed hard. "There's one more thing, Grand Mystra."

Cindergray looked up from his desk. "Yes?"

A lump formed in Victor's throat. "I have reason to believe Charles and Jocelyn Lancaster are alive." His voice wavered as he said the names.

Cindergray froze in place; his skin turned almost as white as his beard. "That's impossible." His voice was barely a whisper. "You yourself witnessed their deaths in that horrific explosion on Ocuul."

"Yes, but now I question what my eyes saw. Jen was sent a vivid vision earlier today from a telemancer who was being tortured by Draconex." Victor walked closer to Cindergray's desk. "She felt his pain and heard him say 'Mintaka.' "

"Mintaka?" Cindergray still hadn't moved since Victor voiced his unbelievable hunch. "One of the stars in the Orion constellation?"

"Yes—but more specifically, one of the three stars in Orion's Belt." Victor paused for a brief moment, locking eyes with Cindergray. "And also Jen's middle name."

Cindergray sat up straighter in his chair. "How do you know this?"

"They announced it during Jen's private baptism." Victor's eyes welled up as he remembered the ceremony. "When Jen was born, Charles told Jocelyn that their baby girl was their Mintaka . . . their shining star. Ever the astrologer, Charles said that he and Jocelyn were the stars Alnitak and Alnilam, and together their little family completed Orion's Belt, which symbolizes the divine aspects of Will, Love, and Intelligence. Jocelyn was so touched by what Charles had said that they decided to give Jen the full name of Jennifer Mintaka Lancaster."

"The timing of this is too strong to be a coincidence," Cindergray agreed. "Who else was at Jennifer's baptism and knows her middle name?"

"Both Charles's and Jocelyn's parents, who have all since passed . . . Simone Chen, who was Jocelyn's maid of honor . . . and myself, Charles's best man."

Cindergray seemed to relax a bit. "Then Draconex will have thought nothing of that name's significance. But it is unwise to assume."

"Right. We mustn't waste any more time. If there's the slightest chance that they're still alive, we need to find them. We owe them that much."

"It will prove challenging and treacherous," Cindergray pointed out. "It seems that Draconex has them, and we've no inkling as to where."

Victor stood at attention. "Grand Mystra, I volunteer to lead the search."

"What about Jennifer? Haven't you just begun her training?"

"Yes, but Draconex is forcing our hands, so I regret to say that we don't have sufficient time to put Jen through our orthodox training schedule. But she is grasping terramancy quicker than I had initially thought. Jen should be ready to begin the next plane within the week."

"Desperate times . . ." Cindergray began.

"Desperate measures," Victor finished. "I'll tell the League, select my team, and report back to you."

Cindergray stood and extended his hand to Victor. "Tell only those with whom you trust your life. Good luck, Mystra Huxley."

"I will. Thank you, Grand Mystra." Victor shook his hand, which still felt firm and strong. Twirling his staff, he left Cindergray's office to recruit the first member of his team.

As Victor descended a tall spiral staircase, he prayed more fervently than ever that Charles and Jocelyn were still alive.

Who else could have sent Jen that vision? No other telemancer has been reported missing.

He walked the halls in a trance, more focused on his thoughts than where he was actually going. From pure memory alone, he made it to the mystras' narthex of the castle. Digging deep into his memory bank, he went to the last office on the left. He hesitantly knocked on its large, mahogany door. There was a moment or two of silence. He lifted his hand to knock again when the door opened to reveal the mystra for whom he was searching.

"Simone," Victor said warmly.

"To what do I owe this immense honor?"

The sarcasm in her voice made Victor second-guess his decision, but he needed someone of Simone's caliber to make his mission a success.

"May I come in?" Victor asked as he absentmindedly rubbed his silver staff with his thumb.

Simone sighed and opened the door wide enough to let him in. She didn't say anything, just nodded.

"Thank you." Victor walked in and was astounded to see Simone's office look exactly as it had before he was banished. "This place—"

"I don't like change. You of all people should know that." She brushed past him and went over to a window overlooking the east courtyard.

"Is that why you won't forgive me? Because my status changed and you couldn't bear it?"

"You were banished, Victor, because you broke one of the highest rules of the Sorcery Guild," Simone retorted coldly. "There was a time when I thought you respected the Guild. *You* were the one who changed, and it broke my heart."

"Even though I saved Gavin—and probably everyone else down in the Pit—from Draconex?" He walked up behind her, afraid she would recoil if he put a hand on her shoulder. "Even if the right thing meant breaking that certain rule?"

Simone abruptly marched away from the window. "It's much more than that, and you know it."

Victor hung his head, knowing that he could not reason with her. "I didn't come here to fight, Simone. I came here to ask for your help."

"You've already used up my favor of goodwill." Simone pointed at the door, alluding to Jen's audience with the Elder Synod. "You may leave."

Victor slammed his staff on the ground in irritation, blurting out, "Jocelyn and Charles are alive!"

Simone quietly withdrew her hand and put it to her mouth. "They're . . . what?"

"Alive, and I need your help in finding them." Victor stepped closer to her, but stopped when she held out a hand.

Simone sat down in her chair.

"Look, I know how close you and Jocelyn were and how badly you took it when she disappeared. I fell into depression too." Victor took another step closer. "But we have another chance to save them."

" 'Save'?" Simone finally said. "Where are they?"

"Draconex still has them." Victor shook his head. "But I don't know where."

Simone looked dazed. "What evidence do you have that they are alive?"

Victor knelt down in front of her and said, "Jen was sent a vision by a telemancer who was being tortured by Draconex. Before the link was cut off, she heard him say 'Mintaka.' Jen doesn't know this, but that's her—"

"Middle name," Simone finished.

Victor nodded, so overcome with emotion he began to shake. "Please, we need to find them before we lose them for good."

Simone stood up and walked back to the window. "In light of this unforeseen development, I will overlook our differences and help you," she said. Victor picked his head up, widening his eyes in both surprise and relief. He made to thank Simone when she firmly denoted, "I'm not doing this for you, Victor. This is for Jocelyn and Charles."

"That's all I ask. In the meantime, keep this between us. If any Dark Watcher sleeper agent gets wind of this, our search will be for naught."

"Finally something we can agree on."

Victor let that verbal jab slide. "I'll be back for the Sesquimillennial Jubilee. By then, I'll have assembled the rest of our team." He walked to the door to let himself out.

"You know where I'll be," Simone said as a goodbye.

"Thank you, Simone."

Victor closed the door behind him, setting his sights on Camelore.

CHAPTER THIRTY-NINE

Jen woke up from her nap and was unable to fall back asleep, so with a lot on her mind, she decided to get some air and walk around Camelore. The sun was at a steep angle as she emerged from her hut, turning the sky into a lovely royal blue. Lights were shining through a few of the surrounding huts: a sign that nighttime was approaching. As a brisk wind tousled her hair, she decided to visit Mira at the stables, stretching out her tight arms as she walked. Before long, she could hear the faint chirping of crickets and, as she got closer to Camelore's only lake, the croaky calls of frogs and something rhythmic that she couldn't quite distinguish.

Ta-ta-ta-ta-ta. Ta-ta-ta-ta-ta.

With a chuckle, Jen realized the sound was from rocks skipping across the lake. She traced the ripples back to the shore and stopped dead in her tracks when she discovered that Gavin was the one responsible for the rock skipping. Stuck in a mental tug-of-war between seeing Mira at the stables or returning to her hut, she was frozen like a deer in headlights. With the latter winning out, Jen turned to briskly walk back to her hut when she heard her name.

"Jen? Hey, Jen!"

Gavin had spotted her. Jen's body tensed up as she mentally

palmed her forehead, feeling embarrassed that she had been seen. She debated if she should pretend that she didn't hear him, but her feet turned her around and her hand began to awkwardly wave.

"Howdy!"

Howdy?! Really, Jen . . .

"Want to skip some rocks? I found some really nice flat ones along the shore." Gavin held up his finds like long-lost treasure.

"I don't know. It's getting dark and . . ." Jen motioned toward her hut, but her legs kept taking her closer to Gavin.

"Oh, come on! We still have more than enough light. Plus, you can't get smoother water than this." He leaned to the side and flicked a stone out over the lake. *Ta-ta-ta-ta!* It spun so fast that it skimmed on the water fifteen times before finally submerging.

"Okay, fine." Jen laughed, coming to a stop by Gavin. Her heart raced faster the closer she got to him.

"Here you go." He handed a few rocks over to her. "So what brings you over this way?"

Jen looked down at the stones, turning them over. "Just needed to clear my mind."

Gavin flicked another rock across the lake. "Hopefully your training isn't giving you second thoughts?"

"Oh no." Jen wasn't expecting to hear that and found herself flustered. "I'm enjoying it and learning lots. Vic's a great instructor."

Gavin nodded, turning toward her. "I trust him with my life."

She felt her cheeks blush. "I do too." She cleared her throat and threw a rock at the water's surface. It skipped once before making a splash.

Gavin eyed her and smirked. "I'm gonna take a wild guess and say you haven't skipped a lot of rocks in your lifetime."

Jen giggled, then quickly composed herself. "What do you mean? That's my championship-winning throw!" She mimicked the motion again before raising her arms in triumph. "It's a trade secret."

"I'm sure it is," Gavin played along. He then showed her how he held the rocks. "Try it this way once. Put your thumb in the center, curve your index finger around the edge, and flick it away from you." He let the rock go, watching as it skipped halfway across the lake.

"Okay." Sticking her tongue out in concentration, Jen grasped the rock like how Gavin showed her and let it rip. It hit the surface at an angle, sending out a larger splash than her first throw, not even skipping once.

"Here." Gavin stood behind Jen and bent down to her eye level, taking her arm. "You held it perfectly. You just have to make a few adjustments to your stance."

When Gavin pressed his chest up to her back, Jen felt a strong jolt run up and down her spine. She could feel him breathing: steady and sure. She didn't want him to let go.

Gavin continued, "Lean on the side of your dominant eye and pull back your throwing arm like you're an archer pulling back a compound bow."

Jen could feel his warm breath on the back of her neck.

He gently pulled her arm back with his. "And flick it in front of you like a frisbee."

His strong hand felt like it was one with hers as he flicked her wrist, sending the rock spinning across the lake's surface. It skipped several times before being swallowed by the water.

"How did that feel?"

Jen swallowed. "Perfect." She turned to look at Gavin. The distance between them was inches, but she wanted there to be none.

After a sweet smile, Gavin finally let go of her wrist and went to the shore to look for more rocks.

Jen was shaking with adrenaline, kicking herself for not kissing Gavin just then. After letting out a quick breath, she found a large, polished stone next to him to stand on. "So, what brings *you* over this way?"

"This is my favorite spot on Camelore to think." Gavin picked up a smooth stone. "And it's near the stables." He pointed off to his right.

"Do you like watching the griffins fly?" Jen asked. Maybe he knew Skarmor.

"I wait here for Mira to get off her shift, but the view doesn't hurt either." Gavin winked at Jen after finding an acceptable rock.

"Oh, you know Mira?" Jen uncomfortably shifted her weight to her other leg.

"Yeah, we're dating."

Jen felt as if she'd been sucker-punched in the stomach.

"How do you know her?" Gavin asked, starting the motion of throwing his rock when Jen let out an unexpected noise that caught him off guard. The rock flew out of his hand and rocketed straight into the water as he looked to see what was wrong.

Jen's breath caught in her throat, causing her to cough, which made her lose her balance on the large stone she was standing on and slip down the steep shoreline toward the water.

"Jen!" Gavin reached out and grabbed her wrist, but instead of stopping her fall, her momentum pulled him down with her. Both of them plunged into the placid water, sending out an enormous splash that startled the geese and frogs nearby.

Sitting in two feet of water, with her hair matted to her face, Jen felt like dying.

"Well, we definitely didn't skip, I'll tell ya that." Gavin peeled his soaked shirt from his chest and flicked his fingers, sending drops of water everywhere.

Jen looked at him through bands of wet hair. Without saying anything, she splashed him.

Gavin brought this arms up to block some of the spray. "Too soon?" he asked with a smile.

Before Jen could respond, she heard someone approach.

"Gavin?" Mira stood at the top of the hill, shocked. "Jen?!"

"I fell," Jen said unenthusiastically, "and Gavin tried catching me."

"You can see how well *that* worked out."

Gavin was met with another splash to the face.

CHAPTER FORTY

Stay strong . . .

That was the last thing Charles had sent to Richard just after he had sensed the imminent return of Lord Draconex. Trying desperately to not arouse any suspicion, Charles scrambled back to his tipped chair and returned to the position in which he had woken up before Draconex entered the interrogation chamber, with his bound hands behind the chair's backrest. If he had waited another second, it would have been too late, for right as Charles returned, he heard the door handle turn behind him. Feigning unconsciousness, he closed his eyes and hoped he had made it in time.

Charles' ears picked up the heavy footfalls of Draconex, knocking into the ground like deliberate swings of a hammer. They stopped in front of him, giving way to a rustle of fabric as Draconex bent down.

"Been working up a sweat while dreaming, Charlie?"

Fighting the urge to open his eyes and look at his old class-mate, Charles controlled his breathing and swirled his eyes around underneath his eyelids to give the impression that he was still asleep, dreaming. The only thing that broke the silence that followed was Draconex's sporadic, painful coughs.

"Difficult work keeping a warding spell active around your

mind, perhaps?" he said after his coughing had stopped, but Charles did not reply.

A few more seconds passed before Draconex kicked one of the chair's legs, sending a jolt of surprise throughout Charles's body. The Dark Watcher commander was clearly getting irritated. He grabbed the back of Charles's chair and slammed him upright. That was when Charles decided to open his eyes.

"Oh, sorry, did I wake you?" Draconex asked sarcastically.

Again, no answer. Charles could see Draconex's scar deepen in color.

"To my surprise, I received word that Victor Huxley thinks you're alive." The scar pulsed; Draconex was clearly trying to keep his anger in check.

Charles's ears perked up at Victor's name.

"Now he's assembling a team to rescue you, wherever you are," Draconex scoffed, then ran up to Charles in an attempt to scare him. "How did you manage to communicate with him? He's a terramancer!"

Charles could smell brimstone on Draconex's breath; close to spitting fire, perhaps.

Draconex straightened, cleared his throat, and said, "No matter. You'll give me what I want well before they come close to finding you . . . one way or another."

Charles blinked once, never taking his eyes off of Draconex's faintly throbbing scar. With slight satisfaction, he remembered the day he'd given it to him.

Draconex dug his fingernails into Charles's shoulders, his sharp nails slicing through muscle sinew like hot knives through butter. As warm pain erupted in his deltoids, Charles did everything he could to not scream; the only sign of anguish he showed was a slight twitch of an eyebrow.

"You've always been so righteous . . . but your silence will cost you."

Sliding his bloody nails out of his prisoner's shoulders, Draconex paced around the chair, smearing the blood over his hands and face. Charles noted that the color of his blood matched Draconex's scar almost perfectly.

"Sesquimillennial. Do you know what that means?" The question was rhetorical. "It's the anniversary of fifteen hundred years, and believe it or not, we're coming up on one. Do you know what it's for?"

Charles knew, but didn't dignify Draconex with a response.

"The premature end of the Dark Purge—or, as you deluded sorcerers like to call it, the Great Battle." Draconex wiggled his fingers in the air, feigning amazement. "Where your ancestor supposedly brought peace to the eleven realms by locking away the evil Lord Ferox." He laughed. "How backward!" Draconex yelled, making the light fixtures rattle in their wall sconces. He stopped pacing and launched into a coughing fit, doubling over. He smacked himself in the chest until he stopped, then bored into Charles's soul with his dead eyes. "Lord Ferox was on the brink of bringing true peace and order, and he was betrayed by his so-called brethren!"

Charles knew it would get him nowhere to argue, so he let Draconex continue to rant.

"There's even going to be a celebration at Watercress Castle, and it's looking to be a sold-out event," Draconex said matter-of-factly. "Do you remember that place? We had a lot of good times there. That's where you met Jocelyn, right?"

Charles clenched his teeth, but still said nothing.

Draconex added, "Right before you stole her from me, of course."

Charles balled his hands into fists and fought with his restraints, rocking his chair from side to side.

"Did I strike a nerve there?" Draconex asked coyly.

Charles was getting more uneasy by the second. He didn't like where this was headed. He watched helplessly as Draconex patted him on the head and laid a hand on his shoulder in mock reassurance.

"*Someone* is clearly living in the past." Draconex brushed some dirt off Charles's shoulder. "I don't blame you. I bet it's hard to forget the fact that you simply weren't powerful enough to save your own wife." Draconex shook his head in farcical tragedy, relishing in the joy he found in tormenting Charles. "Such a travesty."

Since Charles regained his memory only hours before, the death of his wife felt as fresh as if it had happened yesterday. Emotionally vulnerable, Charles dropped his chin to his chest as tears streamed down his cheeks. If he had known Jocelyn wouldn't have survived the blast, he would have gladly sacrificed himself to save her . . . but some part of him was at peace knowing that she was in a better place than by his side being tortured endlessly for two decades.

"But now you have the power to save every other sorcerer. All you have to do is tell me where the Halostone is, or I'll be forced to take the lost journal of Merlin and your Ring of Lancaster in order to find it myself." Draconex pulled on Charles's ratted hair so that he could look long and hard into his eyes. "This is your last chance. How many lives is the Halostone truly worth?"

"Mine," Charles said, looking through tear-blurred eyes.

Draconex let go of his hair and spun around, laughing. "He speaks! But, unfortunately, with the wrong answer." He turned back, now deadly serious. "Since you and your daughter will not cooperate, and Victor now knows that you're alive, my hands are tied." He pulled out his butterfly knife and brought its tip to Charles's throat. "Trust me, you'll die . . . but only after witnessing the horrors that will come next."

He pulled the knife back and flicked it upward into the light, throwing the interrogation room into darkness after a shower of sparks fizzled out.

* * *

Richard. Richard, can you hear me?

Charles's voice floated into Richard's head, waking him up from a dreamless sleep.

Loud and clear. I'm so relieved that you're okay, Richard

responded. He didn't move, even though he was awake, mostly because he didn't want to stir his wife from her sleep.

Thank you, old friend. I'm glad you're holding in there too. Charles's voice seemed tense and worried.

What happened? Richard asked, feeling a knot form in his stomach.

There were a few beats of silence before: *Draconex is at the end of his rope. We need to escape sooner rather than later.*

Please. I'm not sure how much more Beth or I can take.

Listen closely. This will take patience on both our ends . . .

Charles began to unveil his plan, and Richard did indeed listen closely.

CHAPTER FORTY-ONE

"Thanks for lending me some dry clothes," Jen said to Mira as she wrung lake water from her hair with a towel. Wearing a purple halter top, dark gray cargo shorts, and a thin black belt, Jen looked like Mira's twin as her clothes dried outside.

"Anytime, girl. I keep extra clothes on hand at all times." Mira took off her griffin whistle from around her neck. After hanging it onto one of the wall hooks, she took a seat on her hammock and lightly swayed. "I'm just glad I didn't fall in, too! Those rocks are slippery."

"*Tell* me about it," Jen said, not wanting to relive that experience. She expertly wrapped the towel around the top of her head and plopped down in her own hammock, letting out a tired sigh.

Mira looked at her as she continued to sway back and forth. "So, you met Gavin . . ." Clearly she was fishing for some girl talk.

Jen reluctantly took the bait. "Oh . . . uh, yeah!" Jen pretended to be upbeat, even though she was still reeling from finding out that Gavin was dating her new friend. "He's really good at rock skipping."

"You can blame that on me," Mira said, raising her hand. "I'm usually late, so he has to pass the time somehow."

"Athletic and patient. What a guy," Jen commented, trying to keep positive.

A taken guy, she reminded herself.

"He is," Mira said dreamily. She flipped her legs up and fell back into the cross-hatched hammock. "We've only been casually dating for a couple weeks—and I don't wanna get ahead of myself—but I'm excited to see where this might lead, ya know?"

Jen wanted to be happy for Mira, but she had developed feelings of her own for Gavin. It was like pulling teeth, but she looked at Mira and mustered, "I'm glad he makes you happy."

Mira propped herself up on an elbow. "Thank you! Plus, he's a *great* kisser."

She was interrupted by a knock on the door.

"Come in!" Jen said quickly, hoping to change the subject. The last thing she needed was to hear about just how great a kisser Gavin Kingsland was. As Jen's eyes flitted to the open door, she thought, *Speak of the devil.*

There he was. In dry clothes this time.

"Hey, Gav! We were just talking about you," Mira said as she gazed at the astromancer.

Gavin stayed by the door, leaning on it as the night air blew in. "Hopefully I arrived before you told Jen about my action figure collection." Gavin winked at Jen, then said, "You look nice."

"Thanks, I'm wearing Mira"—Jen gestured to her outfit, then pointed at her head-wrap—"and Bed, Bath & Beyond."

Both Mira and Gavin laughed at her joke, which made Jen feel better about the situation in which she found herself.

"It works." Gavin closed one eye and looked through a pretend lens made by his thumbs and index fingers. "Anyway, would you mind if I steal Mira for dinner?" He patted his stomach and smiled at his date.

"Oh, sure! You don't have to ask me. *I'm* the klutz who threw a wrench into your evening plans."

"It was . . . unexpected," Gavin said with a smile, "but fun."

"I gotta tell you, I was *not* expecting to find you both sitting in knee-deep water after I finished my shift." Mira got up and walked toward Gavin. "It gave us another chance to bond, Jen, but I am starving!"

"I second that," Gavin agreed. "Would you like to join us, Jen?"

Jen didn't expect an invite, but she declined. "Thanks, but I'll pass. I'm not that hungry right now."

"You're always welcome!" Mira said as she left the hut.

"Have a good night," Gavin said, closing the door.

Jen blew out a stifled breath as she dropped her head back onto her hammock. Not five seconds passed before another knock resounded on her door.

"Door's open," she said, not quite sure who to expect.

"Hey, little lady," Victor said, reminding Jen of when she woke up in his cottage for the first time.

"Vic!" Jen pounced out of the hammock and hugged him tightly. "I missed you."

Just then, she realized it was hard to think about her life before her twenty-first birthday as anything other than a dream. Even though she had grown up thinking sorcery was pure fantasy, it seemed more real than ever. And now, only a week later, Jen was pleased at how far she had come: she was getting more in tune with her nexus, and learning who she really was and where she truly came from.

"How was your trip?" Jen was still suspicious, but she was happier to see him.

"It went well, but everyone's busy with getting ready for the Sesquimillennial Jubilee next week." He looked quizzically at her. "What's that on your head?"

Jen let out a single laugh. "It's a towel to dry my wet hair so it doesn't drip on my clothes." She unrolled it from her head, letting her dark curls fall over her shoulders.

"Did you just come from a shower?" Victor asked.

"No, I—" Jen thought better and didn't get into it. "Never mind."

"Okay, good, because I was wondering if you'd be up for some nighttime training."

Glad that Victor had offered that, Jen said, "Definitely! But first can we grab a bite to eat? I'm starving."

Victor laughed. "Now look who's the one holding up training."

* * *

Three hours later, Jen opened the door to her hut and tiptoed in so she wouldn't wake Mira, who was already fast asleep. The full moon cast enough light through the skylight to allow her to see where she was walking, so she didn't need to use the hut's torch-lights as she took off her shoes and totem bracelet. Before heading straight to bed, Jen decided to start chronicling her new life in her diary.

As she opened up its stiff binding and smelled the woody scent of the paper, Jen brushed the moonlit pages with her hand, wishing her parents and Tyler were safe on Camelore with her. Sighing, she finally put pen to paper, letting her innermost thoughts flood out.

* * *

For Jen, the days leading up to the Sesquimillennial Jubilee became a blur of training, which included very little down time, lots of soreness, and a neglect of her hammock. Victor ran a tough schedule for her, but she rose up to each challenge and proved not only to her instructor, but also to herself, that she was rapidly improving.

As the sun set on the day before the Jubilee, Jen was beaming after being told by Victor that she was ready to begin a new Mancy plane. She remained set on learning animancy next, so she could not wait to see what kind of charm Hephalon would make for her this time.

She finished her most recent diary entry on a high note and placed it by her totem bracelet on her nightstand as she blew out her bedside candle. Staring up through the skylight at the waxing gibbous moon, she peacefully dozed off into a relaxing sleep, looking forward to the following day's agenda.

CHAPTER FORTY-TWO

Let us help you. You need us.

Let us heal you. You're sick.

Let us feed you. You're stronger with us.

Let us be you . . .

Malcolm awoke with an uncomfortable numbness in his legs, as though he had slept for hours in an unnatural position. Groggily, he opened his heavy eyelids to see a black, jagged crystal levitating in the middle of a dark chamber he had never set foot in before. Purple bolts of lightning silently played across the surface of the crystal, ever so often shooting outward, illuminating the room with an eerily soothing light.

Could that be . . . the . . . the ShadowCrystal?

He felt weaker and more insecure than ever before, and he realized the power of the Throne of Dragons had left him. Wanting to scream, Malcolm tried moving his jaw, but instead groaned as waves of nauseating pain rippled through his mouth and up his cheekbones, causing him to pitch forward and knock his head on the cold ground. Fighting back tears, he knew then that Draconex had dislocated his jaw just before he blacked out.

Steeling himself for the pain that he was about to endure, Malcolm twisted his wrists upward, put his thumbs in his mouth on his back molars, and wrapped his fingers on the outside of his chin. Rocking his jaw back and forth a few times, he quickly pushed up and out as he felt and heard the wet, sucking *pop!* as both ends of his jaw found their sockets. Stabbing pain almost caused the beleaguered Dark Watcher to faint, but he forced himself to remain alert when he heard a devilish cackle echo from the far corner of the chamber, eerily shrouded in shadow.

Fear kicked in, sending Malcolm into fight-or-flight mode. Choosing flight, he tried standing up to escape the hellhole in which he woke up, but quickly fell to his knees, his legs still uselessly asleep, just beginning to feel the prickling sensation of a thousand sharp, invisible pins. He reached down to rub them, but gasped when he found cuffs strapped to his ankles, connected to thick chains that led into the wall behind him.

"Good . . . you're awake."

Malcolm recognized the voice of Lord Draconex. At first he couldn't see him, but then the dark sorcerer stepped out from the shadows behind the floating crystal. Ironically, Malcolm felt himself become calmer, just because there was a familiar face in this unfamiliar place. Malcolm opened his stiff jaw to speak, but his throat was so dry that he ended up hacking and coughing.

"You must be wondering why you're here." Draconex paced around the crystal.

"W-why am I chained up?" Malcolm's voice was so raw and his jaw so sore that he sounded like a different person.

"That's more for your protection. Madro!" Draconex called.

Silently, a small, pale humanoid limped out of the corner—the same corner from which Malcolm had heard the blood-chilling cackle. Madro slinked over to Draconex's side and stayed there, awaiting his next command.

Patting the being on his head, Draconex continued. "Madro here is the guardian of the ShadowCrystal"—he gestured to the twirling object in the center of the room—"but he's also a cannibal with a unique ability to control beings while they sleep. Your shackles keep you behind this warded line that Madro cannot cross." The lord brushed the tip of his boot along a wide, brownish-red line painted on the floor. "Thank you for the paint, by the way."

As Madro cackled once more, Malcolm looked down in horror to see a line of crusted blood running up the insides of both his exposed forearms. A chill ran down Malcolm's spine as he looked up to see the unsightly being staring deep into his soul.

"You're down here because you've failed yet another lesson." Draconex slid the hood off his head, showing his chiseled yet bony features. "Your love for Jennifer Lancaster makes you weak and unfocused."

Malcolm tried to ignore Madro and opened his mouth to contradict Draconex, but he was quickly interrupted.

"Do *not* try to deny it! I can see it in your eyes, your mind"—Draconex pointed first at his eyes, then his forehead—"and I'm determined to rid you of that weakness. Only then can you fulfill your full potential . . . even if it is well below mine."

Malcolm breathed hard through his nostrils, trying to contain the anger he felt from being verbally harassed yet again.

"For this reason, you've given me no choice but to stick you down here." He gestured to the room around them. "You need to absorb dark magic in its crudest form to suppress your foolish notions of love." He walked past the warded line and stared down at his apprentice. "You've been down here for nearly a week. Your body's cells have been feeding off of the crystal's radiation and slowly getting accustomed to its effects. By now, you should have a better communion with the ShadowCrystal and its magic."

Let us help you . . . you need us . . .

There was that voice again! The one that had invaded Malcolm's mind before he had awakened. He knew by now that it was coming from the ShadowCrystal.

Let us free you . . .

Malcolm put his hands around the rusty cuff on his left ankle.

Love is your shackle. Break it off!

Malcolm pulled at the restraint as the voice repeated itself more aggressively.

Love is your shackle! Break it off! NOW!

Malcolm's eyes turned black as he let the dark magic flow freely through his veins, and with the effort akin to snapping a toothpick, he broke the cuff off his ankle. The voice let out a distant hiss of approval. Malcolm smiled and reached for the cuff on his other ankle, which clattered to the ground with the same satisfying *crack*.

* * *

Draconex felt the first flicker of pride as he watched Malcolm break his restraints like they were nothing and stand up, glaring at him with eyes black as coal.

He's ready.

CHAPTER FORTY-THREE

Jen woke up as the sun was breaking across the Earth's surface, eager to get a new charm for her totem bracelet and to see Mystra Hephalon. She turned in her hammock to see Mira at her desk, quietly making touch-ups to her Jubilee dress.

"Good morning!" Mira greeted her roommate when she heard movement behind her. Without looking up, she continued to thread her needle through a side seam.

"Morning." Jen rubbed her eyes. "Looks like you're wide awake."

"Oh yeah. I need to finish preparing my outfit for tonight."

"I thought everything was set?"

"I thought so too, but then this part started bugging me." She lifted her dress, indicating the seam that annoyed her so. "It has to be perfect. A Sesquimillennial Jubilee doesn't happen every day, you know."

Jen laughed. "Very true. Thanks again for helping with my gown. If it wasn't for you, I'd probably be going in a shirt and capris."

Mira put down her dress and smiled at Jen. "Think nothing of it. That's what BFFs are for!"

"Well, either way, I owe you." Jen slid on her shoes. "I'm gonna grab some breakfast at the mess hall. Want anything?"

Mira didn't look up from sewing. "No, thank you. I've already eaten."

"Okay. Hey, I probably won't make it back here before the Jubilee, so I'll need to take my dress with me. Mind if I borrow your shoulder bag?" Jen asked, seeing the bag in Mira's closet.

"Sure! It's in my closet," Mira directed, flattening her dress out on the table.

"I'm sorry, add it to my tab—I promise to bring back some of my own belongings after the Jubilee so I don't keep stealing your things." Jen blushed as she took the bag off its hanger.

"Don't sweat it, girl." Mira broke her gaze from her dress to look at Jen. "I'm not using it. What's mine is yours."

"Ditto," Jen agreed, "once I actually have things to share, that is."

Both girls laughed as Jen folded her dress.

"Thanks again. Bye!" Jen shouldered the bag and walked into the crisp morning air.

After a light breakfast of fruit and yogurt, she made her way to the stables. Victor must have had the same idea, for he was already busy preparing Skarmor for their flight.

"Hey, Vic! How was your sleep?" Jen said as she petted Skarmor.

"I could have used more, but once I'm up, I'm up." Victor bent over and rolled Skarmor's feeding plate to the wall. Wiping his hands, he looked at Jen with a glint in his eye. "I can't believe you're on your way to begin another plane."

"Me neither!" Jen laughed, scratching her head. "It's all happening so fast . . . I'm excited *and* nervous." Jen pretended to shake the nerves off.

"You have nothing to worry about, Jen." Victor put a hand on her shoulder. "You're more than ready."

"Thanks, Vic." Jen hugged him. Skarmor tried to fit his beak between their arms, causing both of them to laugh. "Thank you *too*, Skarmor." Jen wrapped her arms around his neck.

In his most regal tone, Victor suggested, "Shall we disembark to the metallurgy?"

Jen raised her chin to the sky. "Quite." She slid her arm through his and they walked out of the stables side by side, closely followed by Skarmor. Looking out over the lake, Jen hopped on Skarmor in her usual place and waited for Victor to join her.

"Why don't you sit up front?" Victor said, smiling.

Jen grinned from ear to ear. "Really?!" She scooched into the rider's spot, setting her sights ahead as Victor sat behind her, holding onto her waist.

"On your call," Victor said, giving Jen full control.

"To Azumar!" Jen announced, and off Skarmor went, galloping across the grassy field. The griffin extended his mighty wings as he pushed off the lip of the hill, soaring high above the azure lake and away from Camelore. With the wind blowing through her hair, Jen knew she would never get used to the wonderful feeling of flying.

As Camelore shrunk behind them, Jen saw that there was a dense dome of clouds miles below. That didn't seem to faze Skarmor—he tucked his wings in and dove headlong into a swirling bank of clouds. Jen couldn't see anything in front of her for a few heart-racing seconds, until Skarmor broke out of the band of clouds. Her vision returned to see only a mottled gray landscape below.

"Where are we?" Jen yelled over the wind.

"The Atlantic Ocean, just off the eastern seaboard of the United States!" Victor responded. He pointed due west at a coast-line, and sure enough, they were flying high above the Statue of Liberty.

Jen looked down at the Lady Liberty and smiled, bittersweetly remembering when she and her family visited it for the first time. Back then, the only thing that worried her was if Wes Stanley from homeroom liked her back.

My, how times have changed . . .

Jen's stroll down memory lane led her to start daydreaming about the design of her animancy charm, followed by a dance shared between her and Gavin, slowly turning into a kiss . . .

Jen, stop it! Mira *is Gavin's girlfriend, not* you!

Clamping her eyelids shut to push out her shameful fantasy, Jen felt her stomach lift as Skarmor dropped in for a landing deep within Chestnut Ridge Park. Once Skarmor had touched down, Jen slid down Skarmor's wing and waited for Victor to dismount before she entered the Eternal Flame Falls cave.

Drip . . . drip . . . plonk!

The water droplets falling from stalactites all around created a sound symphony as the trio made their way to the floating flame deep inside the cave. Jen put her hand out and said the two words that would take her to a different realm: "Ad Azumar."

Everything turned white as she was brought to Azumar's version of the cave. Seconds later, Jen saw balls of colored light spring forth from the flame, which formed into Victor and Skarmor.

As they walked out of the cave's mouth, Jen took a deep breath and said, "I've missed this place."

"Me too," Victor agreed along with Skarmor, who trilled his approval.

"Oh!" Jen snapped her fingers as she remembered, letting Victor and Skarmor walk a few paces in front of her. "When we go back to Earth, remind me to stop by my apartment so I can bring some of my things back to Camelore."

"Consider it done."

"And I'm also thinking of not renewing my lease at the end of this month."

Victor raised his eyebrows, reading between the lines.

"I want to stay with you on Camelore full-time so nothing can get in the way of my training."

Skarmor cawed in delight and stood on his tawny lion hind legs.

"Well, I think Skarmor feels exactly the way I do," Victor said. "Ecstatic." He extended a hand to Jen after he hopped onto his griffin.

She took it with gratitude and, after getting situated,

commanded Skarmor to take them to Hephalon's metallurgy, which took surprisingly less time than she remembered.

In the distance, Jen saw the burly terramancer chopping firewood outside, just like he had been when she had first met him. Hearing Skarmor's call, he stuck his axe in a wood stump and turned around, waving his hands high above his head.

"Good tidings, my friends!" he shouted at the top of his lungs.

"Heph!" Jen shouted back. She ran into his muscular arms after Skarmor had landed.

"Great to see you again, my dear," Hephalon said as he returned the hug. "I hear that you are already in need of another charm for your bracelet?"

"Yes! An animancy charm, please," Jen mentioned after she finished her hug.

"So you've chosen animancy next. Splendid!" Hephalon said as he opened his arms to greet Victor. "Come here, you old sorcerer! I hope you haven't been going easy on your new tenderfoot here."

"Oh, no. She's been able to take everything I've dished out," Victor finally said after being released from Hephalon's tight bear hug.

"Good." His grin made his beard fan out, making his face look even wider. "If you don't mind carrying in some wood, I'll make a nice fire for this chilly morning."

Jen and Victor picked up a few chopped logs and followed Hephalon into his cottage. After setting them on the pile by the fireplace, they politely declined a serving of Hephalon's Azumarian ale.

"Suit yourself," he said as he threw his head back and downed a full stein.

In minutes, a dazzling fire was crackling in the fireplace, wrapping Jen in a blanket of warmth as she put her shoulder bag by the door and sat on his bear-skinned rug.

Hephalon briefly went into his metallurgy, and when he returned, a small leather pouch was in his hand. Sitting down next to Jen, he started, "After you left with your terramancy charm, I was overcome by an outburst of creativity and took the liberty of forging the rest of your charms. I hope that was all right."

"Of course, Heph!" Jen said, crossing her legs and staring at what might be in the pouch.

"I hope that you find my design worthy." Hephalon reached in and daintily pulled out a silver charm about the same size as her terramancy one. A very intricately sculpted dragon was the clear inspiration for this charm's design. It looked to be coming in for a landing, its wings spread and its tail curled beneath its taloned feet. "The dragon is in honor of your family crest," Hephalon noted.

Jen's mouth inadvertently opened in wonder as she took the charm. "Heph, this is *beautiful*." She looked at the charm from all sides, watching the firelight dance across the treated silver. "I had no idea my family had a crest."

Victor was sitting on a rocking chair on the other end of the fireplace. He said, "The Ring of Lancaster also has your crest on it."

Finally understanding, Jen said, "I've always wondered about that." She looked back down at her new charm and closed her hands over it. "Thank you, Heph." She leaned in for a hug.

He embraced her, then picked up a poker to tend the fire. "It is my pleasure, milady. I'm glad you approve. Will I see you at the Jubilee this afternoon?"

As Jen put her animancy charm onto her totem bracelet, Victor responded, "Yes, of course! We're actually going to Watercress in a little bit. Jen wants to get ready there, and I need to meet with the Grand Mystra."

Jen had been so focused on training this past week that she had forgotten to follow up with Victor on his last meeting with Cindergray. "Oh, that reminds me: What meaning does 'Mintaka' have to you?" Jen asked. She twisted her wrist, letting her bracelet and two charms spin around and softly jingle as she waited for him to respond.

Victor leaned forward and pursed his lips, suddenly very serious. "Before I tell you, I need you to know that I was protecting you. Do you understand?"

Jen laughed out of confusion. "Okay, I understand. It can't be *that* bad."

Victor cast a glance at Hephalon, who got the hint and went to pour himself another drink in his kitchen. "Jen, there's no easy way to say this: I believe that your birth parents are still alive and being held hostage by Draconex."

Jen immediately forgot about her bracelet and shot up off of the rug, trying to contain her surprise. "Wait . . . what?!"

Victor put a hand out in front of him as he used his staff to ease out of the chair. "Mintaka . . . is your middle name."

Jen felt the air leave her lungs in one fell swoop. She couldn't believe what she was hearing. "Y-you kept this from me?" Her eyes shone with betrayal.

"Only because I knew you'd want to postpone your training to help me search for them." Victor stood up straighter. "I wouldn't allow that."

Jen closed the distance between them and pointed a finger at Victor's face. "You had no right to keep that from me!"

Victor didn't bat an eye. "I was waiting until I had conclusive evidence that they were still alive before I brought it to you, because what if I was wrong? I would've gotten your hopes up just to dash them. I made a judgment call," Victor said calmly, tapping his staff on the ground for emphasis.

Jen put her hands on her hips and stood by the fire.

Hephalon, from the kitchen, could be heard awkwardly slurping down more ale.

After wiping the tears from her eyes with a sleeve, she said, "I know you meant no harm, Vic, but it still hurts." She turned around. "I mean, even if it's not a sure thing, it's still something. What if Draconex is holding my parents in the same place?"

Victor blinked, clearly having not considered this.

Jen rested her head in her hands. "If it concerns me, I would like to know from now on, please."

Victor sighed. "You're right." He walked up to Jen and said, "I should've told you from the start and trusted that you would've made the right decision. You're an adult, not a child."

In an even tone, Jen said, "As much as I want to drop everything and find my parents—both sets of them—I'll continue to train . . . on one condition."

"Let's hear it." Victor patiently waited.

"That you let me help you search for them after I've gone through all five Mancy planes," Jen requested, not backing down.

Victor grinned. "Deal."

"Deal." Jen sniffled, then looked into the kitchen and said, "Heph, I think I'll take some ale now."

"Coming right up, milady," Hephalon said as he took a clean stein from the cabinet behind him.

She walked over to him as he filled the foamy ale from his oversized keg to the stein's brim. Victor, however, didn't move, and Jen got the impression that he still felt regret for not telling her about her parents right away. Taking the stein, she vowed to herself that she wouldn't let this make her lose her focus, and that she would always keep her priorities in line.

"Cheers," Jen repeated after she clinked steins with Hephalon. Even though she only had a few sips of the sour ale, sharing a drink with him helped settle her nerves. Jen still felt the initial stab of betrayal, but it died once she realized Victor had noble intentions; she knew he would not purposely hurt her in any way. She also felt hope rise in her heart that she could actually meet her birth parents after all.

* * *

The sun had hit its peak when Jen decided it was time to head to Watercress Castle and get ready for the Sesquimillennial Jubilee. "Thank you again for the beautiful charm, Heph." Outside, a gust of wind brushed strands of hair into her eyes. She tucked them behind one ear and repositioned her bag's strap on her shoulder.

"'Twas an honor, milady!" Hephalon bowed his head in respect. "I'll see you later this afternoon!"

"Can't wait." Jen hugged him once more before getting on Skarmor.

"See you at Watercress," Victor said as he took his position behind Jen.

"Where it all started." Hephalon waved as Skarmor flapped his wings and steadily rose into the sky.

"Watercress Castle, boy," Jen told Skarmor.

With a piercing call, the mighty griffin flew westward.

A few minutes passed before Victor broke the silence.

"Jen, I'm sorry I—"

"No need to apologize . . . again." Jen looked back and winked at him in reassurance. "I've had a chance to calm down. I was just so caught off guard at first. I'm sorry for raising my voice."

"It's in the past. Let's just focus on having a great time at the Jubilee."

"That's the best idea you've had today," Jen joked, facing forward as Skarmor glided over Azumar's breathtaking landscape.

They flew for twenty more minutes until they could see a squadron of Shepherds guarding the skies above Watercress Castle. Below was Lac Cravath, deep blue with wisps of white as the wind churned up surface waves.

"Mystra Huxley." It was the Shepherd who brought them into Watercress during their first visit. "Tenderfoot Lancaster. Good to see you both."

"Good to see you again as well," Victor said over Jen's shoulder. "We're here for the Jubilee."

"Right this way." The Shepherd pulled at the reins and turned his black pegasus around, bidding them to follow. Instead of bringing them to the east courtyard, this time he led them to a circular enclosure near a promenade that led toward the main gate of the castle.

As the Shepherd resumed his post in the sky, Victor pointed to an open spot near a line of trees near the edge of the enclosure. "Right down there, Skar." Skarmor spread his talons out, landing softly on the neatly-trimmed grass.

The first to dismount, Jen noticed movement by the tree line and made her way over to check it out as Victor stayed with Skarmor, explaining to the griffin that he had to stay in the enclosure. A few seconds passed before the familiar face of Treeow poked out.

"Hey," she said with a smile, "what are *you* doing here?" Jen reached out to pet the cat, but it jumped back into the bushes as Victor approached.

"Jen, you ready?" He said behind her.

"Right." Jen got up slowly, wondering why the cat showed up.

"Our flight didn't get you sick, did it?" Victor asked, concerned at Jen's change in mood.

Jen shook her head. "No, I just . . . Treeow's here." She pointed at the bushes.

Victor pondered this. "Watercress is a long way from its home. It probably smells the food being prepared inside and wants the leftovers," he joked.

"Maybe," Jen responded, too preoccupied to pick up Victor's attempt at humor. She remained thinking about it as they made their way along the open promenade toward Watercress Castle. There were bouquets of carnations and banners that said Sesquimillennial Jubilee adorning the pathway as they walked by.

"So you'll be fine while I meet with the Grand Mystra?" Victor asked.

"Trust me"—Jen patted the bag containing her dress and makeup—"I have work to do."

Victor laughed. "I'm sure you do."

They walked across a stone-cobbled bridge to a drawbridge that overlooked one of Lac Cravath's spring rivers. Jen stared down and around in splendor as she tried to keep up with Victor.

"Is there anything this castle doesn't have?" Jen asked, half-rhetorically.

"Air conditioning," Victor said to her, looking out the corner of his eye.

"You're kidding." She snapped her fingers after discovering

Victor was indeed not kidding. "Darn. I hope we don't get over-heated tonight."

"You don't need air conditioning when you have terramancers who can cool this place down with one spell." Victor twirled his staff lavishly.

"Good point," Jen said as she walked under the retracted spikes of the main gate.

"The main bathrooms are past the first hallway on the left." Victor pointed ahead. "And I'll see you in the ballroom later."

"Sounds good," Jen said, already beginning to unzip her shoulder bag to check if she remembered to pack her eyeliner. She did.

"I'll let you know how the meeting goes," Victor said in all seriousness.

"Thank you." She touched his arm, then broke off before she missed the hallway that led to the bathroom.

Victor continued on to the Elder Synod council chamber, where the rest of his search team was waiting for him.

CHAPTER FORTY-FOUR

Beth Smith was nestled comfortably in her husband's embrace as she lay awake. Even though she was scared, being in the Lair of Despair as she was, her fear was greatly suppressed whenever she was next to her Richard. Feeling somewhat safe and calm, she hugged his arm close and felt his chest rise and fall. Before long, she had synced her breathing to his: in and out . . . in and out . . . in and—

Beth inhaled, but didn't feel Richard's chest move at all. Her eyes shot wide open in fear. Beth turned around and put her ear to her husband's chest. She waited and waited for her worry to be a false alarm, but with every passing second, it instead turned into shock.

"Rick . . . ?" she whispered. She found one of his wrists and took a pulse.

Nothing.

"Honey, wake up."

She caressed his face, feeling a lack of warmth that only meant one thing.

"Richard!" she screamed, not caring about her volume. All she wanted was for her husband to wake up and tell her that every-thing would be okay; that he loved her.

Instead she was met with silence and a limp grip.

"Richard!" Beth screamed again, feeling all her strength leave her. She let her head fall to Richard's lifeless chest as her sobs echoed in the darkness, joining the mournful calls of the destitute and forgotten.

Beth's commotion must have caught the attention of one of the guards, for amidst her weeping, she faintly heard the jangling of keys as her rusty cell door swung open.

"No!" She desperately hugged Richard, refusing to give him up. Softly kissing her husband's lips, she whispered, "I love you, Rick. I love you so much." She lashed out when she felt a hand grab her shoulder. "Get away from us! You're not taking my husband away from me!"

The guard tapped her with a finger and she went limp as the sleep spell took effect, sending her into darker unconsciousness than ever before.

* * *

Beth stirred. Richard was nowhere near her. Still keeping her eyes shut, she frantically patted around her, praying that she would feel him, but the ground felt . . . different. She knew the texture of every inch of her cell, and she wasn't in it any longer.

"You can open your eyes," a muffled voice said.

Beth tried her hardest, but she could barely open her eyelids a sliver against the harsh light in the room . . . whatever room she was now in. Having kept her eyes closed for almost two weeks in the dark prison bay, her eyes hurt from the sudden blast of light. Bringing her hands up to shield her eyes, she demanded, "W-where am I? Where's my husband?"

Blinking through tears, she made out a dark figure wearing a visored helmet and, immediately to his left, the prone form of Richard.

"Rick!" she exclaimed, crawling over and sweeping him into a hug. Her elation quickly faded into sorrow as she felt him limply sway in her arms.

It hadn't been a dream. Her husband was dead.

"You're in a containment chamber just outside the prison bay," the masked guard said.

Too shocked to respond, she stared at Richard's face for the first time in two weeks. He had a full beard, which masked his sunken cheeks, and looked to have lost twenty pounds. Beth guessed she didn't look any healthier.

"What are you planning to do with him?" She brushed a tuft of graying hair behind Richard's ear, not wanting to take her eyes off her husband.

The guard took off his helmet and said, "We're going to wait for him to wake up and then make our escape."

Beth whipped her head around to look at the guard. Her jaw dropped when she recognized the man staring back at her. Granted, he looked twenty years older and considerably thinner than she remembered, but she could never forget his face.

"Charles!" she gasped.

"It's all right, Beth." Now fully shaven, he smiled solemnly, placing his guard helmet on the floor and kneeling down next to her.

"Is Richard really gone?" Tears streamed from her eyes.

"It only *looks* that way. Richard is completely fine. I used a tele-mancy spell to slow his heart rate to make him seem dead."

Beth looked back at Richard, whose skin had regained some color. With elation, she could feel a murmur of a heartbeat.

"Richard and I agreed that this was the only way to get you out of your cells. I hope you can forgive us." Charles put a hand on her forearm.

"Richard knew?" Beth could not believe what she was hearing. She wanted to be furious, but all she could feel was relief.

Suddenly, Richard twitched and lurched upward, gasping for air. Charles stood up, smiling tightly as he let Beth calm her husband down.

"Hey, it's okay, it's okay." Beth rubbed Richard's chest with her hand.

Richard squinted from the light as his eyes adjusted. "Beth?" he said between shallow breaths.

Beth kissed him long and hard, and everything else melted away.

Beth pointed at Richard, sniffling as tears rolled down her cheeks. "Don't you ever do that again."

"I'm sorry I didn't tell you," Richard whispered, closing his eyes to give them a break from the light.

"All that matters is that you're alive," Beth replied. She propped Richard up and turned to Charles. "Thank you."

"No thanks necessary," Charles said, tipping his head forward.

"Where's Jocelyn?" Beth asked.

Charles pursed his lips and looked at the ground. "She died twenty years ago in an explosion."

Beth and Richard stared, shocked. "I'm so sorry, Charles," Beth said.

Charles exhaled. "Me too."

"How did you escape?"

Charles cleared his throat and picked up his helmet. "I'll fill you in later. We have to keep moving." He went to stand next to the chamber's door. "I apologize for my curtness, but Draconex should be coming back soon. Do you feel like you can walk, Richard?"

Richard swallowed. "Yes." He leaned on Beth as he stood up—a little wobbly at first, but he quickly balanced.

"Good, but let me know if you need to rest." Charles walked toward the door.

"What's over there?" Beth pointed at a sleek, black cylinder jutting out of the far wall.

"That is where burial pods are prepared for deceased inmates." Charles slid on his guard helmet and peered outside.

"We're escaping in burial pods?" Beth asked, her voice incredulous.

"No, it's nothing like that," Richard reassured her, rubbing her arms.

Charles stepped back inside the chamber and lifted his visor. "No . . . we're not *that* crazy. Those pods are blasted out the bottom of Feralot and burrowed deep below the planet's crust.

320

We'd be signing our own death warrants." He peeked outside again.

"We're going to walk out of here," Richard explained.

"We'd be spotted almost immediately, though." Beth plucked at her dingy inmate garb to make her point.

"We've got company!" Charles put a finger to his mouth and dropped his visor back over his face.

Both Beth and Richard hid behind the burial pods and held their breaths, hoping they wouldn't be caught.

Beth remembered how their guards would often joke about the penalty for trying to escape, and she came to the conclusion that she would rather die than be slowly eaten by zombie leeches—or whatever they were . . . she didn't intend to find out. She reached out and took her husband's hand as her heart raced in her chest. It slowed slightly after Richard affectionately squeezed her hand and looked her in the eye, giving her a look that told her that everything would be all right.

Motionless, they both peeked through an opening between two of the pods to see Charles quickly step out into the corridor.

"Hey, burial pod 1620 is jammed. Can you give me a hand?"

Beth didn't hear a response, but she saw Charles step aside to let two guards enter. Behind the guard mask, one was stocky and tall. His friend, who looked to be no older than a teenager, was a few inches shorter—and a healthy amount of pounds lighter.

For a second, Beth's heart caught in her throat when she thought she locked eyes with the bald guard, but she started breathing again once she saw his eyes continue their sweep over each burial pod.

"The red malfunction light isn't on for any of the pods," the stocky guard pointed out as the younger guard crossed his arms. "Who did you say you were again?"

He never got an answer. Just as he turned around, Charles struck his solar plexus with a well-timed roundhouse kick, sending the stocky guard pinwheeling back on his heels, sputtering. Before the younger guard could call for help, Charles quickly dropped him to the ground with a leg sweep, knocking him unconscious. The stocky guard was still trying to find his breath as Charles quickly walked over and introduced him to Mr. Sandman.

With a single wave of his hand, Charles motioned to the Smiths that the coast was clear. "Your regulation prison guard uniforms." Charles tossed a helmet to Richard once he came out from behind the burial pods.

"Which are fitted perfectly," Beth mentioned in surprise. She held the shorter guard's uniform out in front of her as she looked at her husband.

"Charles knows how to pick 'em," Richard said as he and his wife donned their disguises.

A few minutes later, Charles, Richard, and Beth walked out of the chamber wearing matching uniforms and leaving two Dark Watchers tied together in tattered prison clothes.

In silence and amidst tears of relief, Beth and Richard followed Charles out of the prison bay.

Fighting every urge to pick up and run away from the Lair of Despair as fast as she could, Beth anxiously marched non-nonchalantly behind her husband and Charles. She did not look back, for she knew that would only bring horrible, scarred memories of her imprisonment, which would surely and relentlessly assault her— and she knew that Richard felt the same. She didn't know how long they had languished in their dark cell, but it felt like decades. The only thought that kept her relatively calm was making it out alive so she could see her children again.

Her erratic breathing sounded amplified in the enclosed guard's helmet, and Beth prayed that she didn't look as distraught on the outside as she felt on the inside. The silence painfully dragged on as she and Richard followed Charles, trusting that he knew where he was going. Dark Watcher after Dark Watcher passed the trio, not paying any attention to them.

Is this actually working?

As the corridor opened up into an immense hangar, Beth saw that the ground dropped off ahead into a chasm that was so deep that light could not reach its true depths. Not slowing down,

Charles kept making his way toward the chasm and Beth almost said something—until she realized that there was a wide bridge that connected both sides of the hangar.

Their guard boots clanged on the hollow metal bridge as Beth began to hear strange noises echoing all around her. At first they sounded like the groaning of rusted metal, but as she walked off the bridge toward a winding staircase that led to Feralot's dungeon, she found the noises becoming more organic, but just as terrifying.

What is that . . . ?

Their boots resonated on the metal stairs like the mournful calls of ghosts as they descended deeper and deeper into Feralot. The groans became louder and more frequent, sounding more like angry roars than metalwork. One particular roar was so ear-splitting that it shook the entire spiral staircase, making it feel as if it would buckle at any second.

Unable to contain herself any longer, Beth grabbed Richard's hand and asked, "What's making that horrible noise?"

Her husband shrugged, having never heard that kind of noise before, but Charles answered.

"Dragons."

Richard squeezed his wife's hand reassuringly. Naturally, neither of the Smiths had seen a dragon before—let alone believed them to be real—but now, as they followed Charles to the bottom of the staircase and could see cages filled with creatures that could only be dragons, there were no doubts left in their minds that those mythical creatures were real.

A stale smell of burnt flesh wafted to their noses, causing them to stop in their tracks. "Your helmets have air purifiers. Press the button by your right ear," Charles explained as he turned on his purifier. They followed suit as cool, fresh air filtered in, nullifying the putrid stench.

Still holding her husband's hand, Beth followed Charles down a row of caged dragons.

All were enormous hulks of scales and horns, each creature having its own menacingly distinct look. There were dragons that looked malnourished while others had bulging muscles as they paced in their cages, hungrily eyeing the trio as they slowly walked by. A few were sleeping, wrapped up in their wings in the back corners of their cages. A couple of the dragons that noticed the three walking by either rammed their scaly tails or spewed white-hot flame into their cage's electric barriers, making both Beth and Richard flinch. The barriers held the onslaught as the dragons fumed, frustrated that they could not get out.

In some way, Beth sympathized with them. Not that long ago, she, her husband, and Charles were the ones stuck in a godforsaken prison.

"Why are we down here?" Beth whispered to her husband once she found her voice.

"We're going to fly out of here on Charles's dragon," Richard said.

"He has a dragon?!" If events weren't happening as fast as they were, Beth would have surely fainted. "How does he know if it's even here? It's been twenty years! Do they even live that long?"

"Jocelyn and I were captured on my dragon. Draconex brought us through that tunnel"—he jutted a thumb to his right to a dark path—"and tossed Silvress in here as a souvenir. He collects them for sport," Charles said with contempt.

Finally, Charles halted in front of one of the last cages. Letting his helmet drop to the ground, he stared longingly into the cage.

"Silvress."

The Smiths came up behind Charles to see a slate-gray female dragon sleeping in the center of her cage. Her tail curled around her body and her wings spread over her back like a blanket as she slept.

Looking back at the Smiths, Charles said, "Do you trust me?"

Both of them nodded.

"In a few seconds I'm going to open Silvress's cage and have you get on her back."

Underneath their visors, Richard and Beth were scared to death. Unable to offer a better plan, they stayed silent and watched as Charles willed terramancy through his makeshift totem ring—a tight band of torn cloth from his old prison uniform—to block the energy current to the cage's electric barrier.

ZZZZZZZZZZ—

The noise made by the power block awakened Silvress. She shook her massive head and stood on her haunches, bearing sharp teeth. Stepping inside, Charles put a hand out and said, "Easy, girl. Remember me?"

Silvress swiped a large claw at Charles, who evaded the attack by rolling out of the way. "It's me! Charles!" He put two fingers to his temple and sent out a familiar telepathic message to the dragon.

Almost immediately, Silvress backed away and growled. Her eyes were searching the intruder cautiously until her irises dilated in recognition. Issuing a rumble deep in her throat, the dragon stepped forward and bowed her head.

Charles smiled. "Hey, it's good to see you, too, girl." He patted Silvress's nose, then turned to the Smiths. "It's safe now. Hop on."

Richard and Beth hesitated, paralyzed with the thought of getting near a massive dragon.

"Hey! You two!" a voice shouted from down the corridor.

The Smiths turned to look at where the voice came from, but said nothing.

"I wasn't notified there'd be any prison guards down here!"

Charles repeated, this time louder, "Hop on—now!"

Choosing the dragon over the Dark Watcher guard, they side-stepped over to Charles.

"You're going to need those helmets" Charles picked up his. "The wind feels like glass shards when dragons fly at top speed."

Nodding, they slid on their helmets.

"You go first," Richard said to his wife, helping her walk up the dragon's leathery wing.

After Beth and Richard were straddling Silvress's bony spine, they made room for Charles.

"Okay, now hold on." He slid his helmet's visor over his face and patted Silvress, and she took off out of the cage and into the corridor, roaring in freedom.

The guard backpedaled and fell to the ground as he saw the dragon stretch its wings and lift off into the air. Before he could call for backup, Charles shot him with a knockout spell and proceeded to open every other cage in the dungeon.

Beth fought to hold on to Richard, who in turn was doing the same to Charles, as Silvress swooped high then low, gliding the length of the dungeon past every cage. Different colored lights spewed from Charles's fingertips as he shorted out each and every electric barrier, instantly creating mass chaos in the dungeon.

Craning her neck this way and that, Beth saw two smaller dragons slice the air straight above her head, belching fire in triumph as they found themselves free after countless years in their cages. A huge dragon came lumbering out of its cage, shaking the dungeon as its enormous clawed hands and feet struck the stone floor, creating small craters wherever it went.

Beth caught movement on the stairwell and looked to see several Dark Watchers file down into the dungeon in a foolhardy attempt to help the outnumbered dungeon guards establish some semblance of order. After an unlucky few were either charred alive by dragons' breaths or trampled underfoot, the rest retreated back up the stairs.

As the last of the barriers deactivated, Charles took no time in waiting to see what would unfold; instead he directed Silvress down into the exit tunnel. Before their vision was cut off, Beth and Richard saw the metal spiral staircase tear free from its housing and crumble, adding to the debris on the dungeon floor.

"We're almost out of here! There's an opening straight ahead where Draconex brings in every dragon he captures!" Charles had to scream so he could be heard over the terrified screams of the guards who were trapped after the staircase collapsed, desperately trying to hide from the hungry, roaring dragons.

Beth looked over Richard's shoulder to see natural light at the end of the long tunnel.

"Does Draconex have his own dragon?" Richard asked as he fought to stay on Silvress.

"Yes—he calls it Volcanor! I didn't see him in the dungeon, though!"

"Uh, Charles?!" Richard asked, fear in his voice. Beth saw him point toward the opening ahead, which seemed to be not as bright as it was only moments before. "What's that?!"

* * *

Charles looked forward again and saw two red dots above the tunnel's exit, followed by a silhouette that formed into the unmistakable shape of a wyvern dragon.

"Volcanor!" Charles cursed.

As Silvress flew closer, he noticed that Draconex wasn't riding the beast, so he decided to capitalize on that opportunity. Commanding his dragon to speed up, he watched what the wyvern dragon would do. Charles saw Volcanor drop low, preparing to fly up into Silvress and skewer her with his massive horns.

"What are you doing?!" Richard frantically asked.

"Close your eyes! And duck!" Charles ordered both of them. He clicked his tongue and Silvress ascended a few dozen feet before belching out a dense cloud of smoke that overtook every inch of the tunnel. Without slowing, Silvress flew into it, blinding her three riders.

As Volcanor roared in confusion, Silvress shot out of the tunnel and into the dry air of Nyzanth, barely missing Volcanor's deadly horns. Finally free after two decades, Charles silently wept before nudging his passengers.

"You can open your eyes now. We made it out."

CHAPTER FORTY-FIVE

Anger. Hate. Lust. That is all we feel.

Dominance. Control. Power. That is all we crave.

Use our power that now flows through you . . .

Malcolm was no longer Malcolm, even though his appearance hadn't changed—except for his coal-black eyes that bore through Lord Draconex as he stood to his full height.

Madro started bouncing on the balls of his clawed feet, licking his lips as he eagerly stared up at Draconex, like a dog that was expecting to be fed.

Draconex ignored the primitive creature's grunts and snorts, not breaking his gaze from Malcolm's. Silently, he stepped forward and dragged a metal heel through the line of blood that stained the ground, breaking the warding spell. Now nothing was preventing Madro, the Keeper of the ShadowCrystal, from falling upon Malcolm.

But that was exactly what the young Dark Watcher *wanted* to happen.

Like a rabid animal, Madro lunged at Malcolm as Draconex nodded to his apprentice and retreated into the shadows, keen on watching the melee unfold.

Malcolm hardly had any space to play with, so he dropped into a low crouch and raised his arm in front of his face just as

Madro clamped his drooling maw on his forearm. He didn't feel anything, since he'd used terramancy to turn his entire arm into diamond, the hardest mineral in the known universe.

Madro whimpered but did not release his bite, despite the clattering of chipped teeth on the stone floor. With a quick swing, Malcolm flung the cannibal into the ShadowCrystal at the center of the chamber, sending purple-white sparks in every direction and electrifying Madro.

Smoking, Madro dropped to his haunches and set his bulging eyes once more upon Malcolm, who looked back just as furiously. Grabbing one of his busted chains, he tugged at the end, feeling that it was still attached to the wall. As he waited for Madro's next move, Malcolm let the ShadowCrystal's sentient dark magic invade his thoughts once again.

We need more.

Fighting is poor sport.

Give us death to feed on.

Malcolm watched as Madro silently slinked into the shadows, producing the same bone-rattling cackle as when Malcolm had awakened . . . but this time he was excited, not scared.

Malcolm's body tingled as he felt the dark magic penetrate his nexus, granting him the powers of animancy. Wanting to see his opponent in the deep shadows, Malcolm blinked twice, channeling a pit snake's infrared vision. As his irises slitted to those of a reptile, his world turned into neon colors. As if the lights has suddenly flicked on, Malcolm could clearly see Madro off to his right, slowly crawling like a crab.

And there was Draconex, standing in the corner with crossed arms on the other side of the room. Smirking out of the side of his mouth, Malcolm was glad Draconex was watching; he wanted him to see this.

Malcolm looked back at Madro, and once their eyes locked, the creature launched at the Dark Watcher like a bat out of hell. Reestablishing his grip, Malcolm yanked the chain free from the wall, bringing with it a clump of concrete. He swung it with such force that when it hit Madro in the chest, it shattered, showering

Malcolm with debris and cutting off the cannibal's devilish scream.

CRACK!

Madro hit the wall so hard that his skull split open and started oozing brain fluid before his body crumpled to the floor.

Letting go of the chain, Malcolm stood up and looked straight at Draconex, saying more with his actions than he could ever say with his words. White noise rang through the enclosed chamber, save for the erratic crackling of purple-white sparks from the ShadowCrystal.

Behind you—!

A powerful hand gripped his ankle, tearing into his skin with its claws. Madro was still alive, intent on at least tasting the blood of his combatant before he died.

The dark magic swallowed Malcolm's scream, and before Madro's broken, unhinged jaw could reach his ankle, he struck Madro's neck with a knife strike, severing the head from the body as his rigid hand cut through muscle, vertebrae, and vocal cords.

Normally, a chop like that should have only bruised the neck, but since Malcolm used chronomancy to speed up his attack, it was as though his hand were as sharp as a samurai's katana blade. As Madro's head rolled into the shadows, leaving behind an opaque blue trail of brain fluid and blood, Malcolm stared at his hand, slowly wiping it on his cloak.

* * *

Klaxons blared throughout Feralot, alerting Lord Draconex that there was an emergency. "Come with me," he said to Malcolm, who was still standing over the headless—and finally lifeless—body of Madro.

Malcolm looked up at Draconex through blackened eyes. "Right behind you." He tossed the cannibal's body to the side and fell behind his master, who was sprinting like a cheetah toward the lift that would take them to the main level.

Draconex couldn't help but think that Charles Lancaster had

something to do with this unexpected development. When the lift came to a stop, a frazzled guard nearly rammed into Draconex. Grabbing hold of the Dark Watcher, he calmly asked, "What is going on?"

The guard pointed toward the dungeon. "Three prisoners have escaped and let all the dragons out! They're destroying everything!"

"Lancaster," Draconex seethed. He pushed the guard away and sped toward the dungeon staircase, which was now nothing more than a heap of twisted, melted metal, leaving a gaping hole in the floor. A large dragon soared high above, rattling the walls with its booming cry as others emerged from the opening.

Forgetting about the loose dragons on the main level, he and Malcolm dropped down to the dungeon floor below. Their twenty-meter fall was softened by a quick blast of air as they looked around to see a score of dead Dark Watchers lying around pockets of growing flame. Draconex's eyes burned with the same intensity of flames as he sped toward Silvress's cage.

"They've escaped," Draconex growled.

An explosion shook all of Feralot as metal girders crashed to the ground.

"Who has, Master?" Malcolm asked, watching behind them for signs of any dragons.

"Charles Lancaster." Draconex's burned from the rage he felt inside. "And I'm willing to bet your girlfriend's foster parents too."

As Draconex was reevaluating, Malcolm powered his ring with dark magic when he saw a hungry dragon spot them. Right before he cast a killing spell, a larger dragon intercepted the smaller one, snapping its neck between its enormous jaws.

Draconex turned around to see Volcanor swallow the decapitated head while the headless body of its prey twitched on the burning ground. He walked past Malcolm and decided to change his plans.

"We have a party to crash," he said, sneering.

CHAPTER FORTY-SIX

After putting Mira's shoulder bag in one of the open cubbies in the bathroom, Jen stepped into the hallway looking like a princess. Wearing an evening gown that blended modern fashion with medieval, Jen couldn't remember a time she had looked more formal. Thankful that her gown covered the scars on her shoulders, she turned the corner and fell into step with the crowd of other well-dressed sorcerers and sorceresses as they made their way to the ballroom, which had a breathtaking view of Lac Cravath through its storied windows, which glimmered golden as the sun started its daily descent below the horizon.

Above the archway leading into the ballroom, Jen noticed that SALVE was etched into the stone. Chuckling to herself, she remembered that was how Mystra Blackfire first greeted her back on Camelore.

Salve indeed.

The ballroom's hardwood floors were polished to a shine, and had different stains to accentuate the different kinds of wood that were used. Looking up from the floor, Jen was amazed to see how high up the ceiling was—easily three stories—and hanging from it were several glistening chandeliers that flared with colorful art-deco designs, classily offsetting the painted ceilings that reminded Jen of the Vatican in Rome.

Straightening her filigree headpiece that had shifted on her head as she looked up, Jen focused on trying to find Mira and Gavin, scanning the mass of bobbing heads.

Every sorcerer must be here tonight!

Just before she gave up, Jen perked up when she spotted them across the ballroom, standing in front of a column as tall as King Kong. Mira looked stunning in her two-piece gold-and-black gown, while Gavin seemed slightly stiff in his white-gold swallowtail jacket, but it was nearly impossible for him to not look handsome.

Jen walked up to the couple. "Hey, strangers!"

"Jen!" Mira hugged her joyfully. "You look amazing!"

"All thanks to you—you practically *made* this gown."

"You are too cute! I only cut the fabric. The rest was all you, girl." Mira held Gavin's arm, smiling.

"You look good too, Gavin," Jen said, trying to play down how gorgeous he was.

Gavin smiled. "I'm not used to being this formal," he said uncomfortably, trying to loosen his collar, "but thanks. The purple really suits you."

Jen blushed and glanced down at her velvet gown, tucking a curl behind an ear. The way he downplayed his looks made her find Gavin that much more attractive. Some part of her wanted to be his Jubilee date and dance the night away in his embrace, but guilt quickly set in after her conscience reminded her that Mira was that girl, not her.

"Well, if you don't mind," Gavin added, "I would like to ask Mira for a dance." He looked at his date.

"I'd love to!" Mira smiled at Jen. "See you later?"

"Definitely. Have fun!" Jen watched as the couple left for the center of the dance floor, swaying to the orchestra. All alone, Jen played with her totem bracelet while she walked to the wall of windows that overlooked Lac Cravath, taking in the beautiful sunset.

How can there be evil when something so beautiful exists?

Jen caught herself silently swaying to the music. She turned around to notice another familiar face by the buffet table. Jen strode up to Hephalon, who was busy filling two plates with food. "They have any Azumarian ale here?"

"Jen!" He almost dropped several bacon-wrapped water chestnuts. "Merlin's beard, you gave me a fright." He laughed as he set down his plates to give her a hug. "And as for the ale—they have but a cheap imitation." He slyly pulled a flask out of his leather vest.

Jen laughed, leaning in to whisper, "You came prepared, I see."

"I always do," he whispered back. Seeing someone was approaching, Hephalon slid his flask back into his vest and picked up his plates. "Victor, you've got to try the mutton!"

Jen turned around to see Victor, who was wearing an olive-green brocade doublet jacket. "I'll wait until they bring out more. You seem to have it all on your plates." Victor pointedly eyed the food Hephalon had stockpiled.

Shrugging, the metallurgist said dismissively, "He speaks the truth!"

Victor took Jen's hand and lightly kissed it. "You look radiant, my dear."

Flattered, Jen curtsied. "Thank you. You clean up nicely too."

"Yes, well, even an old sorcerer like myself has nice clothes."

"It's stylin'! How did your meeting go?"

Victor glanced at Hephalon, then responded. "As expected. My team and I will begin the search tomorrow with some solid leads."

"If your parents are out there, we will find them, milady," Hephalon said between bites.

Jen blinked in surprise. "You're helping Vic out too?"

"I wouldn't let him go without me." Hephalon raised a turkey drumstick in Victor's direction.

Jen's heart wanted to go with both of them, but her brain told her that if she wanted to help, she needed to finish her training. "Thank you both. So, so much."

The lights dimmed and the orchestra stopped playing as Grand Mystra Cindergray stepped up to the podium at the far end of the ballroom. A lone spotlight pointed to him, and he began, "Welcome, everyone, to the Sesquimillennial Jubilee. Tonight, we honor all who perished in the Great Battle fifteen hundred years ago, and the sorceress responsible for bringing peace back to the eleven realms, Genevieve Lancaster." Cindergray waited for the applause to die down before continuing. "Tonight is doubly special, for we also happen to have her only living descendent here in attendance, Jennifer Lancaster."

A second spotlight positioned itself on Jen, who couldn't decide if she was more surprised or blinded.

"Would you do us the honor, my dear?" Cindergray asked as thousands of eyes turned to look at Jen.

As murmurs of surprise and awe came from the crowd, Jen instinctively shied away from the unwanted attention—but something inside smothered her fear, making her stand up a little straighter and face the onlookers with confidence.

On this hallowed night of the Sesquimillennial Jubilee, Jennifer Lancaster publicly accepted her destiny and wore it on her heart as a badge of honor.

Now that every sorcerer knew that the rumors of the return of a Lancaster heir were true, Jen wanted nothing more than to share this moment with Victor—her instructor, her guardian, her friend. Calmly surveying the crowd, she waited until her eyes fell upon the one she was looking for.

Without missing a beat, Victor smoothed out his doublet and walked her to the podium, all while the spotlight followed their every move. "I am so proud of you, Jenny," he whispered before handing her off to Cindergray.

Smiling sweetly, Jen kissed Victor on the cheek before taking the Grand Mystra's hand. Picking up her gown and ascending the stairs, she heard warm applause blossoming throughout the grand ballroom as Cindergray brought her beside the podium. She could barely see the audience in front of her, but she easily spotted Mira, who was frantically waving near the back. Being able to see her friend helped keep her nerves stable and, with a shining smile, Jen waved at the crowd as the applause died down.

"I know these past years have been trying for us all, but just as a flower blooms at the beginning of every spring, hope is just around the corner." Another round of applause rippled through the ballroom as Cindergray leaned over to Jen. "Would you like to say something?"

"Um . . . sure," Jen said, even though inside she immediately regretted it.

What am I gonna say?!

Jen walked up to the microphone, but before she could speak, loud footsteps echoed throughout the main level. Soon after, a Shepherd by the main gate boomed a warning:

"Everybody at arms! A Dark Watcher has infiltrated Watercress!"

Every sorcerer in attendance turned around, brandishing their totems and preparing for action, as someone sprinted into the room and slid to a halt when he saw a crowd of sorcerers at the ready. Out of breath, he yelled, "You're all in danger!" Before he could say anything else, two Shepherds tackled him from behind, knocking him to the ground.

The crowd murmured until Cindergray shouted, "Quiet!" He no longer needed the microphone to be heard. He took two steps to the edge of the stage and asked, "Who are you and what is your purpose here?"

By that time, the Shepherds had restrained the intruder and picked him back up on his feet. Still trying to catch his breath, he said, "My name is Charles Lancaster and I'm here to warn you that the Dark Watchers are coming!"

Jen couldn't believe what she was hearing. Her birth father was *here*? Multiple gasps echoed around the ballroom as she saw Victor push his way through the crowd and stand in front of the man claiming to be Charles Lancaster. Every sorcerer still had their totems drawn and glowing, but when Victor hugged the man, they relaxed and dropped their guards.

"Jennifer, please come," Cindergray said as he left the stage to see for himself.

Jen was right behind the Grand Mystra as a path parted for

them. Shaking from nervousness, Jen passed Mira and Gavin, who had their hands over their mouths in complete shock. Training her eyes on what lay ahead, she held her breath as she walked up to Victor, who was still embracing Charles.

Cindergray waited for Victor to step away and when his face was revealed, Cindergray said, "It really is you, then."

Jen couldn't believe it, but she ducked behind Cindergray, scared to let her birth father see her. She had spent so much time focusing on how to find him that she never once thought about how she would act if they met.

"Jennifer?" Charles asked.

He had the same voice as the one she'd heard say "Mintaka" in her most recent vision. Jen closed her eyes and let out her breath before she stepped out from behind Cindergray. When their eyes met, she nearly broke down in tears. Even though he wore the slate-gray uniform of a Dark Watcher, it did not hide his thin frame. She saw the resemblance from his curly, silver-streaked hair to his hazel eyes, which had an inner ring of brown that transitioned to an outer ring of violet. His freshly shaven face was gaunt, leading Jen to only speculate how tough his imprisonment had been over the past two decades; but when he smiled at her, she knew in her heart that they were related. She reached out and time stood still as they hugged.

"You look just like your mother," Charles said as tears streaked lines down his dirt-covered face.

"Where is she?" Jen asked, not caring that her makeup was getting ruined.

Charles cleared his throat and his voice wavered. "She died twenty years ago"—he looked at Victor—"at the hands of the same madman who is on his way to attack this castle and steal the lost journal of Merlin and find the Ring of Lancaster."

"Jocelyn is . . . dead?" Victor said, turning white.

Charles put a hand on Victor's shoulder. "I'm so sorry, Vic. She didn't make it out of the explosion."

Victor dropped his head to his chest, clutching his staff with both hands. "When I found out you were alive, I prayed that my sister was too."

Jen was taken aback, but made sure she heard Victor correctly. "Wait, my mother was your sister?" She swallowed hard. "You're my . . . my uncle?"

Victor smiled weakly at her. "Yes, Jen."

Tears of joy mingled with tears of sadness. Her birth mother was dead, and Victor was family.

"We're all that's left of the Lancasters, Jen," Charles said, "and Draconex is not going to let us get in his way. He's coming for blood, and for the journal." He looked around at the people in front of him.

Cindergray was the next to speak. He pointed at the two Shepherds behind Charles. "Go and warn the other Shepherds. I want you to set up a perimeter around Watercress. You're our first line of defense." The two guards saluted and briskly ran to the main gate to hop back on their pegasuses. Then, without missing a beat, Cindergray spun around on his heels and faced the crowd of sorcerers. "Everybody, if you are able to fight, man your designated battle stations! A Dark Watcher invasion is imminent!"

The crowd dispersed as Cindergray said to the small group around him, which consisted of Charles, Victor, and Jen, "This is an all-hands-on-deck situation."

Mira and Gavin approach. "We're here to help you, Grand Mystra," Gavin said.

"Thank you. Two of you help maintain control at the front gate. The other three, guard the other vulnerable areas of entry on this level. The Sacrarium is built for situations like this, so the journal should be safe as long as we prevent them from invading this castle. I will warn the rest of the Elders. The nexus will protect you." Cindergray reached to the sky, turning into a white beam of energy that shot off toward the Elder council chamber.

Immediately, everyone looked at Victor, who started delegating positions. "Mira and Gavin, hightail it to the front gate—you'll help hold our forces there. We need to expect that Draconex will look for a weaker spot to exploit, so Charles and I will guard the east and west wings." Victor clapped and Gavin and Mira took off toward the front gate, where two lines of sorcerers had already begun to form.

"Wait—what about me?" Jen demanded.

"You're coming with me," Victor said.

Before she ran to the west wing with Victor, Jen grabbed Charles's arm. "Charles—Father—did you hear anything about a Richard and Beth Smith?"

"They escaped with me. They're safe on Camelore until this blows over." Charles smiled reassuringly, putting his hand over hers.

"Thank you." Relief washed over Jen as she hugged her long-lost father.

Charles clearly wanted to hold her longer, but he broke away and said, "I have so many questions for you, but now we need to focus on—"

A massive explosion shook Watercress as the ballroom's glass window detonated, revealing Draconex atop Volcanor, his monster dragon, in the retreating sunset. The blast sent a wall of razor-sharp shards inward, headed straight for Jen, Victor, and Charles.

Quickly, Charles opened his hands and created a gravity field around them, turning the projectiles into dust. Jen watched in horror as a few sorcerers outside of his protection spell fell to the ground after being flayed by a barrage of glass shards.

Behind her at the front gate, Jen could hear commands being issued as her fellow sorcerers fought back a battalion of Dark Watchers.

"No matter what, stay behind us, Jen!" Victor ordered as he held his staff out in a fighting stance.

Spells were ricocheting around them as Draconex flipped off of Volcanor and landed on a bed of broken glass. He slowly walked toward them with his hands behind his back. "Is this how you greet a former classmate on this historic day?"

He deftly dodged a spell from Charles. Victor still hadn't moved from his fighting position.

"We know what you want and you'll never get it." Victor said. He lifted his staff high above his head and with two hands brought the head of his staff to the ground. Energy rolled through the tiles, lifting them up as it sped toward Draconex.

With a flick of his hand, the Dark Watcher commander diverted its course, sending the earth spell around him, not slowing down. "There are few things I cannot obtain. Exhibit A and B." He pointed at Charles, then Jen. "I don't intend on being denied a third."

Draconex closed his fists, choking Victor and Charles and throwing them across the ballroom with a telemancy spell.

"My, my, *you* look gorgeous tonight, Jennifer. Would you like to dance?" Draconex taunted.

With her eyes shining purple, Jen tapped into her nexus and cast a fire spell. A flame wheel spiraled out of her palms toward Draconex, but right before it hit his chest, he clapped his hands together, sending out a pressurized burst of wind, extinguishing her attack and leaving her frozen in fear.

Still five yards out, he chuckled. "I need you alive, so I can't kill you—but I can get you within an inch of your life." Draconex's hands sparked with red lightning as he brought them to his chest, containing the energy. Like a loaded spring, he thrust his hands out, sending tendrils of electricity toward Jen.

Unable to escape, she waited to feel the searing jolts course through her body, when all of sudden a man jumped in front of her, taking the brunt of the spell. The lightning strike was so blinding that she couldn't tell if it was Victor or Charles, but either way she was saved.

After he fell to the ground in a heap, Jen slid over to see Charles. He was seizing from the lightning strike. "Charles!" She cradled his head.

"If you wanted to go first, Charles, you could have just asked!" Draconex laughed. He lifted his fingers to unleash another round of lightning, but it never came. A sideways pillar carried Draconex off of his feet and trapped him to a wall, pinning his arms.

Jen looked over to see her savior, Victor, lower his staff and rush over. "We need to get him out of here!" he said as he knelt down, sliding one of Charles's arms over his shoulders.

"Leave me. I'll only slow you down," Charles rasped, wincing from his injuries.

"Never," Jen said, picking up his other arm. She looked at Victor for support, but his eyes were glued to where Draconex hung, trapped.

"Simone, watch out!" Victor warned, watching as she walked in front of Draconex.

Simone acted as if she didn't hear him. Instead, she turned toward the pillar and punched it with her glowing rings, shattering the marble into dust and freeing the dark sorcerer.

"What are you doing, Simone?!" Victor yelled, unable to comprehend what he was seeing.

She sneered. "You wouldn't understand."

"Thank you, my dear," Draconex said appreciatively, dusting off debris from his spiked shoulders. "It's true . . . you *wouldn't* understand, Victor."

"Jen," Victor said quietly, not taking his eyes off the enemy in front of him, "you have to run." Before Jen could refuse, he continued, "I know what you're going to say, and don't. I'll be fine. Take Skarmor and get to Camelore. Now!"

As sorcerers were dueling to the death all around her, Jen tried to think. Blasts shook the open space of the ballroom, amplifying their noise to almost deafening, giving Jen an urgency to heed Victor's request or stay.

Still kneeling in front of her, Jen looked, conflicted, at Victor, her uncle: the man who risked everything—and everyone—in his life so that he could protect her. Between them lay an injured Charles, her birth father: the only other living omnimancer, who did the impossible and escaped Feralot's prison with her parents and took it upon himself to warn the entire Sorcerer's Guild about Draconex and his surprise attack.

Jen could not physically leave them—especially when she had no guarantee that she would ever see them again. Deep down, though, she knew that Victor was only asking her because he knew it to be the safest option for her. Also, if she stayed, he would be more worried about making sure she was protected than defeating Draconex and whomever would attempt to hurt her.

With heart-wrenching reluctance, Jen said, "I'll come back for you," and pushed off of the cracked ground, not looking back.

As Jen's feet took her farther away from Draconex and into the main hallway, she saw Mira, Gavin, and the other sorcerers hold the front gate as Dark Watcher after Dark Watcher either fell into the steaming river below or dropped dead on the drawbridge.

How am I going to get to Skarmor? Jen thought, frantically looking for another way out.

Her thoughts were interrupted by Malcolm, who dropped down from one of the second-story balconies, blocking her exit path.

"Miss me?" Malcolm laughed as he cracked his knuckles, preparing to fight.

Explosions boomed on all sides, causing Jen's ears to ring. With her nexus already powered up, she extended her hand and shot out a condensed ball of air toward Malcolm. It connected with his shoulder, but he only slightly flinched.

Surprised that her spell barely affected Malcolm, Jen felt a different energy exuding from him. His voice seemed altered, and when he stepped further into the light, his eyes were as black as Draconex's.

"Is that all you've got? I forgot to mention that I've grown stronger since we last met." Clenching his fists, he rose into the air, levitating three feet off the ground.

Realizing that she was not going to make it to the front gate, she banked to her left and ran down the east wing. As Jen checked each locked door, panic began to set in until she was at the end of the hallway, backed up against a large window and running out of escape options.

As Malcolm flew toward her, she looked out the window to

see a steep drop-off into the river. A jump like that could kill a person.

But Jen was no ordinary person.

She was a sorceress who knew animancy.

"Looks like your luck has run out, Jenny," Malcolm said as he hit the ground running.

Jen didn't respond; instead, she took a few quick breaths to steel herself before she made the jump. Seconds before she opened a window pane and Malcolm reached her, something shot through the window. Jen crouched to protect herself from flying glass and Malcolm skidded to a halt as Grand Mystra Cindergray burst in, riding a gray pegasus and wielding a sword.

"No!" Malcolm yelled as he shot spell after spell at Cindergray and his winged pegasus.

Cindergray deflected all of the attacks as though swatting away flies, and with a cut of his sword sent out a white energy arc that struck Malcolm so hard that he crashed through a locked door and into a darkened room.

"Jen, there's no time." Cindergray slid off his Sacrarium signet ring. "The lost journal! The ChronoCrystal! The Ring of Lancaster! Protect them all!" He tossed it to Jen, who caught it in her hands. "Do whatever you must to keep them safe." He fired a few cover spells at the broken door, sealing Malcolm inside. "Go! I can only hold him for so long!"

Jen slid the signet ring onto her thumb and made her way toward the Sacrarium, but first stopped to pick up Mira's shoulder bag from the bathroom in which to carry the journal. Returning into the hallway, she noticed that the drawbridge had been successfully pulled up and the sorcerers stationed there were leaving to assist in other areas.

"Mira! Gavin!" Jen called as she saw them running toward the ballroom. "I need your help!"

CHAPTER FORTY-SEVEN

Camelore was deserted. Everyone was at the Sesquimillennial Jubilee—everyone except Richard and Beth Smith. Charles had asked them to wait in the ceremonial chamber until he returned with Jen.

Sitting quietly underneath the helioarch of the ceremonial chamber, Richard looked at the shadow on the table and tapped Beth. The sun was at the perfect angle to depict an individual raising an open book toward the sky.

"Who do you suppose that could be . . . ?"

CHAPTER FORTY-EIGHT

"Having Jen run was a bad move, Victor," Draconex said, slowly circling Victor and Charles, trying to find a weak spot. "If you had just given her to us, I'd have let you two live as a gift."

"Somehow, I don't believe you," Victor said, keeping Charles by his side while he watched Draconex and Simone, who had them surrounded.

"No matter. I'll make quick work of you, then capture her myself." Draconex took another step on the littered battleground.

Victor was right in the middle of both Draconex and Simone. Thinking on his feet, he said, "What would you do with Jen? Mold her into a Dark Watcher while promising ultimate power?"

Draconex laughed. "Don't play coy, Victor. You know as much as I do that the only way to break the Halostone's spell is with the Ring of Lancaster and the blood of the sorcerer who cast it!" He took another step, and so did Simone. "Or any relative for that matter. Since Genevieve died fifteen hundred years ago and Charles will croak any minute, that leaves Jen."

Victor's breathing was controlled, almost trance-like. "If you haven't been able to capture her now, you never will." He glanced behind him. "Unlike you, Simone, easily tricked into betraying the Guild."

"I wasn't tricked into anything," Simone spat from behind him.

Victor's emotions were raw. Charles, his brother-in-law, was miraculously alive; Jocelyn, his sister, was truly dead; and Simone, the love of his life, was a traitor who had turned her back on everyone who cared for her. Now, more desperately than ever, Victor prayed that Jen had made it to Skarmor.

"She understands that a cleansing needs to happen, and the only sorcerer who can start it is Lord Ferox," Draconex said.

"I don't believe it." Victor's heart ached at the thought of Simone being so corruptible.

"Believe it, old friend. She proved her allegiance after she helped me track down and capture Charles and Jocelyn twenty years ago."

Cold chills ran up and down Victor's body, leaving him sick to his stomach. "What?" he breathed. *Simone was responsible for their capture?!*

"And I'd do it again in a heartbeat," Simone said without a trace of remorse.

Victor was speechless. How could someone he loved as much as Simone betray him in such a way? Fighting the urge to give up, he looked down at Charles and was given strength. Suddenly, he felt subtle vibrations in the ground, telling him that both Draconex and Simone were about to unleash spells of their own. With the timing of a mystra, he waited for them to fully commit to their attacks before he jumped high into the air with Charles, channeling the air around him to make him jump higher.

Below, Victor saw the spells collide where he used to be, but only for a split second. Their combined powers released an explosion that struck both Simone and Draconex head-on, sending the former into a wall and the latter farther toward the center of the ballroom.

As the dark sorcerer came to a stop twenty yards away and Simone lay unconscious, Victor dropped to the ground unharmed.

CHAPTER FORTY-NINE

The Sacrarium was only accessible through Grand Mystra Cindergray's office, which was on the opposite end of Watercress Castle. Jen was lucky that she had Mira and Gavin by her side to hold off several Dark Watchers who had either attempted to cut them off or follow them.

Mira cracked her snakewhip, sending tendrils of toxic needles at their pursuers, while Jen unlocked Cindergray's office door with the signet ring. "Got it!" Opening up the door wide enough, she slipped in, followed by Gavin and Mira.

Slamming the door shut, Gavin reinforced the locks with a protection spell—but he wasn't relying on it for long. "This won't hold them forever."

Out of breath, Jen said, "We only need a few seconds." She closed her eyes and thought back to when Cindergray led her to the Sacrarium. She remembered he turned one of his desk knobs two times to open up a secret stairway.

Jen ran to Cindergray's desk and turned the handle he had turned, and behind her, the floor fell into a staircase. "Come on!" Jen waved as she started down the stairs. Mira quickly re-coiled her whip and took Gavin's hand, following Jen. Once they were down the stairs, it disappeared, reverting back into a flat floor.

Even though Jen had put another barrier between her and the

Dark Watchers, she refused to slow down. The more time that she spent away from Victor and Charles, the more she began to worry. She didn't know if Charles would make it for much longer. Praying that she could return in time to help them escape before it was too late, Jen picked up the pace even more.

She hoped that Cindergray was keeping Malcolm at bay, who seemed like a completely different person, one filled with evil of its purest form. Any glimmer of him as her loving boyfriend had been snuffed out, twisting her heart in sorrow. Pulling herself from her thoughts, Jen focused on the current objective as she led her friends down a staircase.

Just two more turns and down one more staircase . . .

It felt like it was taking them forever to get to the Sacrarium. Making sure Mira and Gavin were still close behind her, Jen's heart jumped in joy when she saw the brick wall that would grant them passage into the Sacrarium.

"Jen, *please* tell me you didn't forget the way." Concern filled Mira's voice.

"No, we're right where we're supposed to be." Jen reached out like she was warming her hands over an invisible fire and a stand emerged from the wall.

"Whoa," Gavin breathed. He watched as Jen put the signet ring into the center of the stand's wheel.

"Hold on to me." As her friends both grabbed an arm, she recited, "Counter-clockwise, never clockwise." The ground they were standing on rotated them into the wall, but they went through it like a mirage. Before they knew it, they were staring at the floor of the Sacrarium.

"Follow my lead," Jen said.

After a count of three, they all re-oriented themselves to their new surroundings.

"Okay, *that* was trippy," Mira admitted, hanging onto Gavin for support until her balance came back.

"Every time," Jen remembered, holding Mira's hand. "It wears off." She looked across the room and saw first the Ring of Lancaster, untouched in the same cylindrical display case. Right next to it was the glass room that housed the lost journal of Merlin and the ChronoCrystal. Running up to its entrance, Jen's breath caught in her throat with anticipation as she slowly pushed open the glass door and approached the journal.

Will I be able to read it? Am I the Light Bringer? she thought at she stepped closer.

Gavin and Mira followed Jen inside, making sure to give her enough space.

"It looks exactly as I had imagined it," Gavin said, a smile etched across his face.

Ready to reveal her destiny, Jen glanced at both her friends before she opened it up to the first page.

CHAPTER FIFTY

Malcolm's attacks were strong, but Cindergray had years of practice over the young Dark Watcher so that they only had weakened his spell shield by only a fraction. Praying that Jen was able to reach the Sacrarium unharmed, Cindergray noticed that his shield wasn't repelling any more attacks.

Commanding his pegasus to land, he walked up to the busted door and peered through to see no one in the room. Deactivating his spell, he stepped over the splintered door and stood over a large whole. Malcolm had escaped.

Cursing, Cindergray jumped back on his pegasus and flew out into the main hall. Attempting to cut off Malcolm before he got to the Sacrarium, he took a shortcut through the ballroom, but noticed that Victor was in dire straits and needed help.

* * *

Victor's arms and legs quickly began to stiffen from over-exhaustion. Still clutching Charles, he was about to make his final stand when a payload of spells came raining down upon Draconex. The first one struck the dark sorcerer in the forehead, causing him to stumble to the ground, angrier than before.

Victor glanced upward at Grand Mystra Cindergray, who was

laying down cover fire for him. Grateful, he smiled weakly as he watched Draconex try to evade or block each and every spell, some managing to hit their mark.

Draconex, having enough of this one-sided affair, jumped out of the way of Cindergray's limitless spells and reacted almost instantly with a quick succession of his own. Cindergray's pegasus was able to evade a few of the larger ones as Victor carried Charles farther away to safety, but one lucky shot clipped one of its wings.

The pegasus called out in pain as it dipped downward, and Victor caught it with an air spell, taking all that was left of his nexus's strength to place it gently on the ground. Resuming his original task of carrying Charles to safety, he caught a glimpse of Cindergray, who was still casting spells at Draconex.

He yelled, "Enough, Orin!"

"Don't call me that, *old man*," Draconex yelled back amidst spells of his own. His back was toward Victor, indicating that he had taken Cindergray's bait so that Victor could get Charles to safety.

It was a battle of two great sorcerers as spells were cast, parried, blocked, and redirected.

* * *

Now safely out of range, Charles was going in and out of consciousness when he tapped Victor on the shoulder. "Brother, stop."

Victor didn't falter. "No," he said as he carried his brother-in-law toward a protected alcove.

"I'm responsible for this," Charles admitted, trying to pry himself from Victor's grasp.

"No, you're not. You gave us a chance by warning us."

Victor was almost there. The farther Charles got from the battle, the more energy it would take him to end this . . . if he had enough strength left inside him, that was.

"The only reason Draconex attacked tonight was because I

wouldn't disclose the Halostone's location." Charles got his feet under him.

"You didn't have any choice!" Victor yelled, but before he could say anything else, Charles surprised him with an elbow strike to the solar plexus. Wheezing, Victor fell down, inches away from the alcove.

"Yes, I did. I'm sorry, Vic." Charles pushed Victor into the alcove. Turning around, he set his sights back on Draconex after making sure Simone was still out cold. "Tell Jen that I love her." It felt like blades were stabbing his chest every time he breathed, but he limped closer to the duel.

Charles reached into his nexus and found the strength to block out the pain. As his eyes turned bright purple, he began to walk normally—even run. Purpose flared in his eyes as he charged headfirst into Draconex, picking him up and slamming him onto the littered ground like a linebacker sacking a quarterback.

Draconex let Charles punch him in the face, smiling all the while. He dropped his hands to the ground as he absorbed hit after hit.

"Charles!" he heard Victor say distantly.

"I won't let you hurt anybody else," Charles said as he summoned astromancy, conjuring a dagger out of compressed and pressurized carbon.

Draconex formed his bloodied, split lips into a grin as Charles began to bring down his weapon for a final blow. An instant later, Charles found himself slammed up against a wall and his dagger shattered next to him.

Volcanor roared, vibrating the entire frame of Watercress Castle. Whipping its tail on the floor, it stretched its mighty wings outward, claiming victory after saving its master from a deserved death.

Draconex got up and spat out blood. "I told you. Everyone you care about . . . will die." He tensed up, charging both of his hands with deadly, crackling energy.

At that moment, as Charles propped himself up against the

wall, he realized that it would be impossible to save both Victor and Cindergray.

He summoned the full power of his nexus, preparing himself.

It's the only way . . .

CHAPTER FIFTY-ONE

Jen couldn't believe it.

She couldn't read the lost journal.

Not one single word.

Trawling through the pages, her heart sank.

I'm not the Light Bringer . . .

"Jen." Mira's voice intruded into her thoughts. "Jen, we have a problem." Mira pointed at the stand that brought them into the Sacrarium. It was slowly sinking into the ground; that meant one thing.

"They've discovered the Sacrarium," Jen said, doubly disappointed now.

"What does it say?" Gavin asked, getting closer and looking over her shoulder.

"I can't read it." Jen flipped the pages, stopping at the first page.

"You're not going to believe this," Gavin started, sounding completely caught off guard, "but *I* can."

"What?!" Jen and Mira asked in unison.

"I can read it," Gavin repeated. He pointed at the first sentence and read it aloud: " 'I, Grand Mystra Merlin, hereby dedicate these pages to catalog the search for the six MystiCrystals that will lead us to the Halostone.' "

"*You're* the Light Bringer!" Mira exclaimed.

To the side, Jen blinked, awestruck. "But how?"

Gavin didn't take his eyes off of the journal as he explained: "I missed my class's viewing of this journal when a couple of bullies dragged me to the Pit." He looked between Jen and Mira. "That was the night that Victor saved me, but not before I fell into a coma. After I woke up, I forgot about the journal and searched for Victor so I could thank him." Gavin lightly ran his hand across the millennia-old page. "I guess I got caught up with the League of Light so much that I never thought about my missed chance at reading the lost journal."

Just as Gavin finished, a loud explosion shook the ground. Looking behind him, he saw a smoldering hole where the secret entrance used to be.

"We need to get out of here," Jen said, closing the book and sliding it into her shoulder bag.

"How? Dark Watchers are coming through the only entrance," Mira pointed out, fingering her snakewhip's handle.

"We'll take the back way. Follow me!"

Jen reached over the empty podium and took the Chrono-Crystal from its resting place. Surprisingly, the gem was warm to the touch, like a living entity. Its dancing colors of blue, green, and orange mesmerized Jen—but only for a second—before she tucked it in beside the journal.

As the first wave of Dark Watchers crawled into the Sacrarium, Jen led her friends through the side door behind the Ring of Lancaster's display case, which was now also empty.

* * *

Feeling whole again as she slipped the Ring of Lancaster on her necklace, Jen took up the rear as they ran into the tunnel, which quickly narrowed to an opening barely wide enough for Jen's shoulders to fit through. She could only imagine how much tighter it was for Gavin.

At first, when Cindergray had told her of the Sacrarium's

auxiliary tunnel, Jen had wondered under what kind of circumstance would anyone need to use it, but as she was being chased by a horde of Dark Watchers through the underbelly of Watercress Castle, she finally understood.

The tunnel looked like it hadn't been used in the past century, though: it was filled with cobwebs and mold, and had no air circulation or light. Gavin, who was in the lead, illuminated his totem orb so they could see where they were going. Mira was behind him with Jen taking up the rear.

"Do we know where this tunnel goes?" Mira asked, claustrophobically nudged between Gavin and Jen.

"Grand Mystra Cindergray said it leads to an access hatch by Lac Cravath," Jen said as she used terramancy to collapse the tunnel behind her, hoping cave-ins would slow down their pursuers.

"I wonder if he ever had to use this tunnel," Gavin thought aloud as he lit the way ahead.

"Probably only to see where it went," Jen replied, bringing down more rocks.

No one said anything else, which led to an unsettling silence that was broken occasionally by the clatter of falling rocks, until Gavin slowed down. Tentatively shining the light upward, he looked at the girls and commented, "Time to climb."

The sound of their shoes on the metal rungs reverberated off the walls as they ascended toward a closed hatch. With one hand, Gavin tried turning the latch, but to no avail.

"It's rusted in place. Jen, can you unlock the latch with terramancy?"

A rumble of rocks made its way to the trio on the ladder, signaling that Dark Watchers were hot on their heels.

"I can give it a shot," Jen said. Before she received her animancy charm, Jen had to master the hybrid forms of terramancy: steel, lightning, and blood. With those skills unlocked, Jen calmed her mind and reached out to the metal hatch. Years without maintenance had corroded the metal lock components together, but as she opened up her nexus and focused harder, the mechanism began to unlock.

CREEEEEEAAAAKKKKK!

The latch moved on its own. Gavin slammed his palm into the hatch, and it flew open, letting fresh night air swirl over them. After they were all out, Jen immediately welded the hatch shut by dousing it with white flames.

"I hope Skarmor's all right," Jen said as she heard waves crash along Lac Cravath's shoreline in the background.

"Here, I'll call him," Mira offered, pulling out her griffin whistle. Pressing her lips together, she blew into the whistle. To the human ears of Jen and Gavin, they could only faintly hear air escaping from its small holes; but to a griffin, it was like a ship's horn.

Everyone looked skyward when Skarmor's piercing call split through the night.

"And Mystra Wingelius thought I was wasting time at the griffin stables," Mira said, jumping and waving to catch Skarmor's attention. She whistled once more, directing Skarmor to land near them.

Jen felt the wind pick up and fought to stay upright. "We need to get Victor and Charles, then we'll be out of here!" She hopped onto Skarmor. Mira and Gavin sat behind her.

"Jen—" Gavin began to say when the tunnel's hatch rocketed high into the air.

They all froze as Malcolm floated up from the tunnel. With blood trickling down his left nostril and eyes as black as soot, he shot both fists outward, unleashing a devastating energy blast so fast that it was impossible to evade.

Jen winced as she hugged Skarmor with all her might, expecting to be immediately vaporized, but it never came. Something intercepted the blast at the last second . . . something very large and humanoid in form. Flying backward from the full force of the blast, it shrunk into a familiar friend.

"Treeow?!" Jen said as she caught the cat.

"A leshy saved us?!" Mira exclaimed as she looked at the cat.

"A leshy?" Jen asked, confused.

Gavin didn't take his eyes off Malcolm and yelled, "Skarmor, get us outta here!"

Skarmor must have been thinking the same thing; with a few quick flaps of his wings, he was already gaining altitude.

Jen looked up to see that they were headed straight for Malcolm. She screamed, "Watch out!"

Skarmor cried out and sliced Malcolm's face with a sharp talon as he flew by.

As Malcolm plummeted to the ground, screaming in pain, he managed to spin around and fire several spells, which harmlessly sailed off into the night.

Jen heard another chilling yell as she set her sights on Watercress.

"Jen!" Gavin said. "What are you doing?!"

"Victor and Charles!" was all she yelled back, still cradling Treeow.

"You don't even know if they're still inside! Jen, we need to go! The Grand Mystra entrusted us with keeping the lost journal and ChronoCrystal safe, and that's what we need to do!" Gavin yelled, this time more forcefully.

"Jen, listen to Gavin! Please!" Mira pleaded.

Jen ignored her friends as tears rolled sideways into her hair. She would not leave them behind. "I can't lose you," she whispered, thinking of Victor.

As Skarmor sped back toward Watercress, it became unsettlingly quiet—just before a blinding explosion rocked the steep bluff overlooking Lac Cravath, sending out a shock wave that crumbled the entire middle section of the castle. Not believing her eyes, Jen yelled, but her voice was lost over the resulting cacophony from the demolishment of the once-regal Sorcery Guild headquarters. The shock wave quickly overtook Skarmor, buffeting his flight.

As the world spun around her, Jen fought to stay on. "Get us to Camelore, Skar!" Saying the words hurt Jen more than she could have ever imagined.

The mighty griffin acknowledged her with a mournful call, stabilizing before flying off into the night's full moon. Looking behind her, Jen found it difficult to tear her eyes away from the smoldering wreckage that was once Watercress Castle. Mira put a consoling hand on Jen's shoulder, saying more than any words could.

Not knowing if she and her friends were the only surviving sorcerers left, Jen prayed that more would make it back to Camelore. As the wind dried her tears, she clutched the shoulder bag which held the keys to finding the Halostone, while the other held the curled-up form of Treeow. In that moment, Jen had never felt more alone and overwhelmed.

That was when, on the fifteen hundredth anniversary of the Great Battle, Jennifer Lancaster's new life teetered on the brink of collapse and she had no idea what to do next.

ABOUT THE AUTHOR

Gregory Heal is the first one to admit that he has an over-active imagination. Everything from writing to painting, he is constantly finding outlets to express himself.

He is a frequent guest of Walt Disney World, and you'll find him with his family in the Wisconsin outdoors either on a lake or a ski hill, depending on the season.